REVENGE

BLOOD AND HONOR
BOOK 1

*Happy Reading!
Dana Delamar*

DANA DELAMAR

ACKNOWLEDGMENTS

Many people contributed to the creation of this book. No writer goes it alone, and I am certainly no exception.

First and foremost, I'd like to thank my wonderful critique partner, Kristine Cayne, who read every word of this book multiple times and poured her time and attention into the shaping of it, down to individual word choices. Kristine, I couldn't have done this without you. You are the best!

Ann Charles and Wendy Delaney came to the rescue when I was floundering about and needed help replotting this book. Thank you, thank you, thank you for giving up part of a weekend to help me.

The amazingly generous Delilah Marvelle also helped me with plot pointers and an early critique that was instrumental to reshaping some characters and scenes. Thank you, sweetie!

I'd also like to thank my beta readers, Kim Schmeller and Ninia Ingram, for their insights, comments, and catches. You suffered so others don't have to.

Getting started on this journey was tough; without the help and support of Romance Writers of America® and specifically my hometown RWA® chapters, Eastside RWA and Greater Seattle RWA, I would have struggled for many more years toward my dreams. These organizations provided inspiration, support, guidance, friendship, real-world craft advice, and industry contacts and knowledge that proved invaluable. Thank you all.

Last but not least, I'd like to thank my family, my friends (especially David Shank for giving me the push to get the hell out of software and start my second career), and most of all my real-life hero, James Davis, for bearing with me during the madness and putting together an awesome home office for me. You will always be my honey bunny.

CAST OF CHARACTERS

Enrico Lucchesi (loo KAY zee) – *capo* (head) of the Lucchesi *cosca* (crime family)

Kate Andretti – wife of Vincenzo (Vince) Andretti

Domenico (Dom) Lucchesi – first cousin to Enrico Lucchesi and *capo di società* (second in command) of the Lucchesi *cosca*

Carlo Andretti – *capo* of the Andretti *cosca* (Milan branch)

Vincenzo (vin CHEN zoh) **(Vince) Andretti** – nephew of Carlo Andretti

Antonio Legato – bodyguard to Enrico Lucchesi

Ruggero (rooj JAIR oh) **Vela** – bodyguard to Enrico Lucchesi

Rinaldo Lucchesi – Enrico Lucchesi's father; former *capo*

Dario Andretti – son of Carlo Andretti and *capo di società* of the Andretti *cosca*

Vittorio Battista – godfather to Enrico and Dom Lucchesi; second in command of La Provincia (quasi-ruling commission of the 'Ndrangheta, the Calabrian mafia)

Silvio Fuente – officer of the *carabinieri*

Benedetto Andretti – brother of Carlo Andretti; *capo di società* of the Andretti *cosca* (Calabrian branch); head of La Provincia

GLOSSARY OF TERMS

arrivederci (ah ree vah DAIRT chee) – goodbye (formal)

basta (BAS tah) – enough (as in "I've had enough!")

bella, bellissima (BAY lah, bay LEE see mah) – beautiful

bene (BEN ay) – good

buona sera (BWOH nah SAIR ah) – good evening

capisci (KAH pee shee) – you see, you understand

capo (KAH poh) – head (don) of a crime family (*cosca*); plural *capi* (KAH pee)

capo di società (KAH poh dee so chay TAH) – second in command of a *cosca*

cara (CAR ah), *caro* (CAR oh) – dear, sweetheart

carabinieri (car ah bin YAIR ee) – Italy's national police force; a single member of this force is a *carabinere* (car ah bin YAIR ay)

ciao (CHOW) – informal hello and goodbye

come stai (COH may sty) – how are you

comparaggio (cohm pah RAH joe) – the Southern Italian institution of co-parenthood, whereby the person making this vow swears to be as a parent to the child. A co-father is referred to as *compare*; the "parent" and "child" are *compari*. The vow is thought of as indissoluble and incorruptible. Within the Mafia, *compari* will not betray each other.

contabile (cone TAH bee lay) – accountant; treasurer for a *cosca*

cosca (KOHS kah) – a crime family; plural is *cosche* (KOHS kay)

Cristo (KREES toe) – Christ

Dio mio (DEE oh MEE oh) – my God

dottore (dote TOR ay) – doctor; the "e" is dropped when used with a last name

faida (FEYE dah) – blood feud

figlio (FEEL yoh) – son

grazie (GRAHTZ yeh) – thanks. *Mille* (MEE lay) *grazie* means "Many thanks."

Madonna (ma DOEN nah) – the Virgin Mary; Mother of God

malavita (mah lah VEE tah) – the criminal underworld, the criminal life

GLOSSARY OF TERMS (cont.)

Maresciallo Capo (mar ess SHAH loh KAH poh) – Chief Marshal

merda (MARE dah) – shit

molto (MOLE toe) – very, a great deal, a lot

'Ndrangheta (en DRAHNG eh tah) – the Calabrian Mafia, or "The Honored Society." Members are *'Ndranghetisti* (en DRAHNG eh tees tee), or "men of honor."

nonna (NOHN nah) – grandmother

padrino (pah DREE noh) – godfather

papà (pah PAH) – dad

per favore (pair fah VOR ay) – please

perfetto (pair FEHT toe) – perfect

polizia (poh leet TZEE ah) – Italian police

prego (PRAY go) – welcome

puttana (poot TAH nah) – whore, prostitute

salute (sah LOO tay) – to your health; cheers!

scusa (SKOOZ ah) – excuse me

sì (cee) – yes

signore, signora, signorina (seen YOR ay, seen YOR ah, seen yor REEN ah) – sir, madam, miss; the "e" is dropped from *signore* when used with a last name

Sottotenente (soh toh teh NEN tay) – Second Lieutenant

strega (STRAY gah) – witch

ti amo (tee AH moe) – I love you

troia (TROY ah) – slut

vaffanculo (vahf fahn COO loh) – go fuck yourself

zio (ZEE oh) – uncle

PROLOGUE

Twenty-eight years ago
Cernobbio, Lake Como, Italy

As his assassins set the trap, Carlo Andretti leaned forward, his nose nearly touching the window. *Vengeance is mine. Just like the Lord above.* His pulse quickened, his mouth went dry, his body itched to be in on the action. To aim a gun. To pull a trigger.

The Lucchesi family's driver and their bodyguard waited outside the restaurant in a large black Mercedes, smoke from their cigarettes floating out the open windows. *Idiots. Anyone could get the drop on them.* These *were the men Lucchesi trusted with his family?*

Bruno, the man Carlo used for all his dirty work, snuck up behind the car, followed by one of his assistants. The two men dispatched the guard and driver without effort, slitting their throats in tandem, the strike perfectly timed.

Sipping an espresso in a room across the street, Carlo watched his men melt back into the dark. It wouldn't be long now until they attacked their true prey. He savored the hot bitter brew he swallowed. Rinaldo Lucchesi, the *capo* of the Lucchesi family, had interfered in Carlo's business for the last time. He thought he could come up north, into Carlo's territory, and impose his principles and his will.

Rinaldo and his ridiculous, short-sighted philosophy would be the ruin of the 'Ndrangheta. Carlo was not going to let Lucchesi expose their bellies to the sharp teeth of Cosa Nostra or the Russians. Lucchesi might be suicidal, but Carlo most assuredly was not. He had a family to look out for, a child he adored. He couldn't let Lucchesi destroy her future, and he couldn't let him destroy the future of all 'Ndrangheta.

1

Taking Carlo's son hostage to force him to capitulate was where Lucchesi had miscalculated. He'd taken the wrong child. In a contest between Dario and Antonella, Toni won every time. Had Lucchesi taken Toni…. Carlo's gut quivered. Everyone would know his weakness then. He'd make any sacrifice for his tigress, his cunning little she-wolf. The child of his heart. The child who *was* his heart.

If Toni knew he was risking her twin brother's life this way, she'd be appalled. But if his plan worked, he'd have the boy, his vengeance, and the way clear in the north. Milan and the lake would be his alone. And once their riches were his, nothing could stop him from pushing his father and his brother off their perch, high at the top of the 'Ndrangheta. They'd censured him once, they'd exiled him up north, thinking that would keep him weak, that their lapdog Lucchesi would be able to muzzle him. They were about to learn otherwise.

The front door to the restaurant swung open, its glass catching the light of a streetlamp, and the Lucchesi woman and two of her children strolled out, the boys flanking her on either side. Rinaldo and their middle boy, Enrico, were not with them. Unease wormed through Carlo's belly. *Where are they?* He glanced around and saw nothing out of the ordinary, but the nighttime shadows could be both friend and foe.

The woman and her boys had almost reached the Mercedes when they stopped short, the woman placing a restraining hand on the shoulder of her youngest child. The eldest son, Primo, nearly a man now, the one who was supposed to be *capo* someday, pulled his gun and looked in the passenger side front window. No doubt he saw the bodies, because he shouted, "Go back!"

It was too late.

Bruno and his four men charged toward the family, opening fire. Primo whirled around to meet them, but bullets slammed into his chest before he could get off a shot.

Carlo felt an odd sort of admiration as the boy fell, blood blanketing his once-white shirt. Primo had tried to defend his family like a good man of honor. But the boy was ruined, his mind tainted by his father's notions.

None of Rinaldo's line would survive the night. It was fitting that Lucchesi's heir died first.

The woman and the youngest boy, Mario, sought cover by the car. Apparently they crawled inside, since Bruno whipped his arm overhead, signaling the men to surround the Mercedes. The hit men didn't hesitate, spraying the car with bullets. The percussive blasts of gunfire beat a joyful staccato in Carlo's chest. How well he remembered the wild buck of a gun in his hands, the acrid smell of gunpowder, the coppery tang of blood in the air, the ringing in his ears in the wake of a kill. But he was *capo* now, and he had to be protected for the good of the family. Still, he missed the old days when he had administered justice firsthand.

Mario attempted to flee through the far door onto the street. One of the shooters fired into him, not stopping until the boy's body grew still, his head and shoulders hanging out the back door. It was a shame about this boy as well; he was a fighter.

After slapping in a fresh clip, Bruno leaned in the car and fired a final bullet, presumably finishing off the woman. Then he walked over to Primo and shot him in the head.

Three down. Just two more to go, and his vengeance would be complete.

Except no one charged out of the restaurant. No more guards. And no more Lucchesis.

Where the hell are they? This was supposed to be a rout, a decisive victory. A definitive end to the feud. And Carlo was supposed to be the victor.

Setting his cup on the sill, he rose, peering out the window, looking up and down the street as he pushed the curtains wide. With a deafening roar in his ears, the horrible truth sprang upon him, sending his stomach plunging to the floor, the espresso threatening to come back up. *Rinaldo and Enrico weren't there and never had been.* No self-respecting man of honor could stand by while his family was slaughtered.

Carlo watched, fists curled, as Bruno and his men left the scene. They'd reconvene at the house, where it was safe to talk. Already, sirens keened in the distance, though no one had interfered during the shooting. That didn't mean there weren't witnesses, but he wasn't concerned. Only someone exceedingly foolhardy would testify against the 'Ndrangheta.

ℴℙ

Waiting for Bruno in his study, Carlo clipped the end off a cigar and lit it, inhaling in sharp, short puffs. *Who had fucked up?*

Bruno knocked on the door, then entered. Bruno's suit strained across his shoulders, but somehow there was a new smallness to him, a hunched quality that made Carlo's face go hot. Along with gunpowder and fine cologne, Bruno smelled of guilt.

"Why should I let you live?"

The man looked at the floor, his hands jammed in his jacket pockets, his dark hair, usually carefully slicked back, now half falling in his face, hiding his eyes. "Our informant told us the entire family would be there. It was the youngest boy's birthday."

"Where are Rinaldo and Enrico?"

"At home, I assume." Bruno glanced up. "Trying to eliminate them there would be suicide."

Carlo wanted to rage at the man, but a fuckup, even a monumental one, shouldn't rattle him. He was *capo*; he was in charge. The men looked to him in a crisis, and if he faltered, he would be lost. *They* would be lost. "Hands on the desk."

3

Fear flashed through Bruno's eyes. "Both hands?"

"When did you become deaf?" Bruno probably thought he was going to take a few fingers, maybe one of the hands. Maybe he even feared that Carlo would take both. Smiling, Carlo picked up the cigar cutter.

Bruno swallowed, but he didn't beg. Good for Bruno.

On the other hand, he'd fucked up. Bad for Bruno.

Carlo couldn't suffer such incompetence unchecked; it was bad for business, it was bad for discipline, and it was bad for morale. A little fear liberally applied kept the men content.

But worst of all, Bruno had cost him probably the only opportunity he'd ever have to get rid of the Lucchesis with minimal bloodshed. Now the long bloody war between the families would continue. Carlo would lose many more men. Someone had to pay for that mistake.

The man's eyes followed the cigar cutter as Carlo returned it to his jacket pocket. Bruno let out a short quivering breath when the tiny guillotine disappeared. Carlo gave him a smile, a distraction. Before the man could react, Carlo pulled a gun from the same pocket and shot him in the face. Blood and brain matter and bits of bone sprayed out the back of the man's head, then he slumped to the floor. Seeing the pool of blood spreading from the body, Carlo let out a sigh. He should have taken Bruno outside. He'd liked that carpet.

Hell, he'd liked Bruno too, but there was no place for sentiment in this business. A *capo* had to hold his love close; the fewer vulnerabilities he had, the better. Loving Toni the way he did was all the risk he could afford.

Placing the gun on the desk, he sat down and picked up the cigar, taking a long drag. He let the aromatic smoke fill his lungs, let it bring him calm. After a while, he smiled.

It is so much sweeter this way. He picked up the phone, punching in a number he knew well. Rinaldo answered after a few rings. "There's something I must tell you," Carlo said.

"Carlo? Are you ready to be reasonable now and end this trouble between us?"

Laughter bubbled up from his gut. "Oh, I'm ending this, but not how you think."

"What do you mean?"

"Tell me, Rinaldo, did you hear the sirens earlier?"

Lucchesi's voice shook with urgency. "What did you do?"

"I've taken what you love most in this world. Your wife and sons. Shot down in the street outside Marinucci's. Only one boy left. It'd be a pity to lose him too."

The howl of rage, of anguish, that came down the line stirred something greedy in the pit of his belly. When the howling stopped and the cursing started, Carlo broke in. "I will not be trifled with, Lucchesi. And I will never

4

be reasonable." He hung up, and when the phone rang, he pulled the cord from the back to silence it.

Picking up the cigar, he took another drag. Sometimes life was very, very good.

There was no need to send other men after Lucchesi. He'd made his point, and every other boss who thought about crossing him would think twice and repent such scheming.

He'd sent a clear, unambiguous message: Carlo Andretti would bow to no one.

Even if he had to leave his own boy to Rinaldo Lucchesi's doubtful mercy.

CHAPTER 1

Present day
Rome, Italy

This time, the end of Enrico Lucchesi's world arrived in a beautifully wrapped box. The package, covered in a fine, silvery foil paper with a crisp white satin bow, arrived early that morning at Enrico's hotel suite in Rome. There was no card, no return address. Enrico's pulse rate kicked upward. In his line of work, nothing good ever came from an anonymous delivery.

Ruggero, his senior bodyguard, eyed the package on the wooden writing desk as if it were ticking. When Enrico touched the box, Ruggero nudged his hand away. "Let me, Don Lucchesi." Enrico bowed his head and stepped back, watching his guard slice into the wrapping. Ruggero's hand was steady, his cuts deliberate.

Inside was an ornately carved wooden box that looked oddly familiar. Enrico had seen it somewhere, but he couldn't place it. Ruggero put his hand on the latch, then looked up at him. "Perhaps you should stand farther away." Never an order from his guard, always a suggestion. But one he'd be a fool to ignore.

Enrico stepped over to the far wall by the sofa and crossed his arms. How incongruous. He and his men were dealing with a possible bomb while the vacationers and business people in the suites surrounding them enjoyed a full five stars of luxury. What was it like to almost never know fear, to live every day with the comforting certainty that another one was coming? The only certainty he'd ever had was that any day could be his last.

His heart jumped in his chest. How was it that this situation never became routine? The sick expectation, the sense he'd finally meet his death today, his skin going clammy, his stomach twisting, his mouth dry, his skin practically twitching from anticipation of a fatal stab from a knife or the punch of a bullet. Or in this case, the tearing of shrapnel from an explosion.

He frowned when Antonio, his newest bodyguard, stepped in front to shield him from a potential blast. He never should have endangered the boy this way. A familiar litany filled Enrico's head: *Will he be just one more dead body you walk away from? Just one more unfortunate mistake? Just one more eventually forgotten casualty in your quest to outlive Carlo Andretti?*

Ruggero eased open the latch, then edged the lid up, its metal hinges creaking. The stern lines of his face deepened as he stared at the contents. He ran a hand through his dark curly hair.

Enrico uncrossed his arms and took a step forward. "What is it?"

The guard let the lid fall completely open, then stepped away from the box, shaking his head. "You'd best see for yourself, *signore*."

Enrico crossed the room and looked into the box. As he registered the contents, his stomach flipped like a dying fish. Nestled within white tissue paper, a falcon stared up at him, its gray and white feathers limp, its round dark eye filmed over. A black cord cut into its neck, strangling the bird. The raptor's open beak suggested it was giving a last angry cry at the injustice of its death.

He looked up at Ruggero, their eyes locking. A falcon was featured on the Lucchesi coat of arms. The message was obvious.

As he lowered the lid, Enrico's fingers lingered over the etched surface. A pattern of vines and flowers danced around the edge, and a boar-hunting scene occupied the center. Where had he seen this box before?

And then it came to him. It was the box Carlo Andretti stored his cigars in, the one he'd offered to Enrico on several occasions when he'd been in Carlo's study. And if he had any doubt about who was sending this message, the timing of it couldn't be ignored.

"It's from Andretti," he said to Ruggero. He drew in then let out a deep breath, seeking calm. Andretti wanted him dead. That was nothing new.

"You aren't surprised."

"Do you remember what day it is? What happened exactly a year ago?" Enrico fought to keep his voice steady, yet still he detected a catch.

Ruggero thought for a moment, then understanding dawned on his face. "Your wife. I'm sorry, I forgot."

"Carlo didn't forget. He still blames me."

"He thinks you can cure cancer?"

"I don't know what he thinks. Only that I didn't do enough." *And maybe I didn't.*

Ruggero motioned to the box. "What do we do about this?"

"For now, nothing."

The guard's brow creased. "You are virtually undefended with only me and Antonio. We should call in more men before leaving the city."

"We leave today, as planned. Just us three." He'd be damned if he'd let Carlo pick the tune he danced to. He'd seen what fear had done to his father, what mistakes it had caused him to make. What a bleak future it led to.

"Don Lucchesi, that's suicide," Antonio said.

A muscle in Ruggero's jaw jumped and he pinned the boy with his eyes, not looking back to Enrico until Antonio lowered his eyes and mumbled, "Forgive me, *signore*."

Ruggero took a breath then said, "With respect, *capo*, Andretti knows where you are. He could have men waiting for us outside."

Enrico shook his head. "Carlo likes to play with his food before he eats it."

"So, you are the mouse?" Ruggero asked.

Enrico scrubbed a hand through his hair. "He thinks he'll see me cower and run. But I am no mouse."

"At least let me call in reinforcements for when we arrive in Milan."

Enrico nodded. "There's no sense being completely foolish." As he watched his guard make the call, he rubbed his stomach, a queasy feeling growing, like he'd just eaten a pound of pancetta. He hoped he wasn't leading them into a trap. A giant, man-sized mousetrap.

❧☙

"Carlo is a dead man," Enrico muttered to himself as he strode through the crowd in the hotel lobby hours later, his empty stomach knotted, drawn up tight under his chest. His eyes swept the area, noting the details of his surroundings, the placement of people and weapons—at least those he knew about. His guards were good; in fact, Ruggero was one of the best. But no one was perfect.

"What did you say, Don Lucchesi?" Antonio asked as he matched Enrico's pace.

"Andretti is dead."

"So you've decided then?" asked Ruggero, on his right.

Enrico heard the anticipation in Ruggero's voice and wondered again if there wasn't a touch of the sociopath to him. Enrico hated killing, though it was sometimes necessary. But Ruggero seemed perfectly suited to his line of work.

"Don't get excited yet. I decided the moment I saw what was in the box. Now all that remains is the when."

"Soon, I hope," Ruggero said.

Enrico gave him a tight smile. "Soon enough." If only Antonella hadn't made him promise not to harm her father, he'd have given the order long ago. He owed his mother and Primo and Mario justice. But he'd promised his wife that he'd keep the peace between their families, that he'd honor the truce that had been sealed by their marriage. Those twenty-six years of peace were over now—undone by her death. At least Andretti seemed to think so.

Perhaps Enrico had been naïve to think that Carlo would honor his daughter's memory by keeping the peace she'd helped broker. He should have known better. A vulture would never be anything but a vulture. Andretti had never had a scrap of honor and never would. The man was a bottom feeder, a scum, a leech on society—

Enrico's attention was caught by a large, heavyset man in a sharply tailored suit standing to the left of the lobby doors. Massimo Veltroni, Carlo's man. Veltroni's black eyes snapped to his, the intent in them clear. A chill ran through Enrico, that sick anticipation rising again, his skin prickling with awareness. Damn it—he'd been stupid, stupid, stupid. And now it was going to cost them dearly. *Per favore, Dio, spare Antonio. He's too young.*

He tapped both guards on the shoulders and they followed his gaze, closing ranks in front of Enrico, automatically shielding their *capo* from danger.

Enrico's hand fell down to grip the Glock 9mm in his jacket pocket. As *capo*, he rarely carried a weapon, but Ruggero had insisted after seeing the dead falcon. Now he appreciated his guard's caution.

He couldn't tear his eyes off Veltroni. The image of a cobra looking to strike came to Enrico's mind. The man reached into his suit jacket, a tight smile on his face.

Enrico tensed, and Antonio and Ruggero pulled their weapons, Ruggero's movements so fluid and practiced they made Antonio look like a clumsy amateur. Which he almost was. Antonio had his gun out and ready mere seconds after Ruggero did. But seconds counted. Seconds meant the difference between alive and dead. Enrico heard women shriek at the sight of the guns, and then the scuffle of feet as people scrambled to get away from them. But he didn't look behind him; eyes on the threat, always. That was the rule. Distractions meant death.

When Veltroni saw the guns, he broke into laughter, a genuinely mirthful smile creasing his features this time. Enrico was puzzled. There was nothing funny about the situation. Not in the slightest.

Veltroni slowly withdrew his empty hand from his coat, his fingers in the shape of a gun. He pointed at Enrico and pretended to take a shot, even blowing off smoke from the end of his thick forefinger. Reaching up, he tipped the brim of his fedora to Enrico. Then he turned and ambled out the door.

"Fuck," Antonio said, his voice hushed.

Fuck was right. They'd almost walked into a trap, and Enrico's pride had led them there.

Antonio and Ruggero put up their guns and Enrico released his grip on the Glock. Glancing around them, they hurried outside to the car waiting to take them to the private airstrip.

This day had started off bad, and it was quickly going straight to hell.

ଛୠଓ

Kate Andretti snuck out of bed, careful not to disturb her sleeping husband. She looked down at him, his wavy, sandy brown hair scrunched up by the pillow, his tanned face slack and innocent as he snored. She hated sneaking off to take her birth control pills, but Vince couldn't understand why she didn't want to get pregnant now. There was no sense bringing a child into a marriage that was less than stable.

But she had hope. Three months ago, Vince had told her about a job at the Lucchesi Home for Children. Even though the work was glorified data entry, she'd taken it. She was happy computerizing the orphanage's records and helping out with the kids.

And she was happy that Vince had actually listened to her when she'd said she needed to work, that she needed to make friends. Maybe he'd finally understood—at least in part—her reasons for waiting. But still she hid the pills from him. Just in case.

Easing the bathroom door shut behind her, Kate crouched down and pulled a box of tampons out from under the sink. Vince would never think to look in that box. For a big tough guy from New Jersey, he was bizarrely squeamish about her "woman things." Fishing around the bottom of the box, her fingers connected with the packet of pills.

Every day, she pulled that box out. Every day she hated the necessity of doing so. Vince was under a lot of stress—he'd been working long days and sometimes nights in his uncle's business—but that didn't give him a free pass to yell at her. He'd always begged forgiveness later, so she'd let it go. To a degree. But something told her to stay cautious. To wait.

She stared at the pill packet in her hand. How had she'd gotten to this point? Lying to her husband. Lying to herself. Hiding things and hoping their marriage would survive somehow.

This sucks. It just does. I want to trust him, I want him to trust me.

But what about the spots on his jacket last night, the reek of gunpowder all over him?

Maybe he'd just splashed wine or something on the jacket. And he often went target shooting; she'd gone with him many times and had proven herself an excellent shot. The first time she'd pumped a full clip into the two kill zones on a target, Vince had looked at her with more than a little admiration.

But what if it wasn't wine? What if it was… blood?

Dread coiled in her belly. Something wasn't right. She'd known it ever since she'd met Vince's uncle, Carlo Andretti. Her immediate impression had been favorable; Carlo was relatively handsome for a man in his sixties, with thick silvery hair swept back from his hawk-like nose and dark eyes brimming with intelligence. He'd kept himself trim, his waist showing only the slightest paunch, despite his love of cigars and fine Scotch. His grasp of English was nearly impeccable, though his accent was a war between British and Italian inflections.

Carlo had seemed charming enough until they were actually introduced. His keen eyes had flicked over her in a lightning-quick inventory that had made her think he wanted to see her wearing much less. She'd told herself she was imagining things, but when Carlo took her hand, his index finger had snaked across the back of hers, not once, but three times. Then he'd smiled at her, and she'd barely suppressed a shudder, feeling like a small and tender animal who'd been sighted, and the wolf was licking its chops.

That was when she started wondering about Carlo. Who he really was, what his business really was. Why he thought he owned her. Why he thought he owned Vince. Why everyone around him jumped when he spoke.

Supposedly Vince was acting as a liaison with Carlo's import/export operations in the United States. More or less the same job he'd had in New York, except that now he was handling matters from the Italian side. He'd told Kate it was a promotion of sorts, a tryout to see if he could handle additional responsibilities in the organization.

Was any of that true? Something about Carlo screamed "Mafia." Was it his swagger, the way he seemed to view everything around him as his property? Or was it just her dislike of the man that was coloring her viewpoint?

Vince couldn't be Mafia too, could he?

The day they'd met, at her cousin Terri's party in Jersey, Vince had played airplane and ball with Terri's kids for hours. Her heart had melted at the sheer joy on his face, and then it had turned to absolute mush when he'd asked her out, after saying that he'd cleared it with Terri, because he thought it important that her family approve of him.

Could a Mafioso be that tender?

Kate shook the memory away and pushed a pill through the foil backing on the packet. Taking a swig of water, she swallowed it. She loved him, her tough guy with the soft heart. But something had happened to him in Italy, something that had changed him.

The bathroom door swung open. Vince blinked, scrubbing a hand through his rumpled hair, his handsome face creased from the pillow. Then he squinted at her hand. "What's that?"

Kate flushed, her heart hammering, and closed her hand around the packet. "Nothing, honey."

"Give it." He held out his hand.

She cursed under her breath. *Why hadn't she put the packet away first?* "It's just some pills."

"I'm not gonna ask again."

That tone, too familiar of late, raised her hackles. "Fine." She slapped the packet into his open palm. He held it up to the lights above the mirror so he could read it. After a moment, his face went dark.

"Birth control? You're on fucking *birth control?*" His anger seemed to expand in the small space, echoing off the marble tiles on the walls and floor.

Kate forced herself not to cringe. "Look, I told you. We've only been here six months. It's just too soon."

"So you fucking *lie?* You told me you'd stopped these." He tossed the packet in the toilet and flushed it. "I've been fucking you for *nothing.*"

Kate's jaw dropped open. It was time to whip out her NYC-girl attitude. Never mind that she'd been raised upstate. "Piss. Off. What do you mean you've been fucking me for *nothing?* Supposedly you love me, right?"

"I been trying to make a baby with you. And you been lying to me."

She snorted. "I'm not the only one of us who's lying."

His hazel eyes bore into hers. "What're you saying?"

"You reeked of guns when you came home last night. And what was all over your jacket?"

He hesitated, just the barest millisecond, but she caught it. "I went shooting with the boys. And I dropped my fork in some sauce at dinner, got it all over my jacket."

Funny how when he said it, it sounded like the lie it was. She was about to call him on it when he grabbed her by the shoulders and shook her, his eyes darkening. "*You're* the fucking liar. Who is he?"

What the...? Oh, he was back to the pills. "Calm down, Vince. I just wanted to wait."

He stared at her, disbelief on his face. "Fuck!" His fingers dug into her arms. "I *knew* it. You been acting weird for months. You never want to go to my uncle's. And now I know why. You're fucking him."

Kate choked. "I'd rather slit my wrists than fuck your uncle."

"Then what the fuck is it?"

If he says "fuck" one more time, I'm going to kill him. If I say "fuck" one more time, I'm going to take a vow of silence. She had a Masters in social work, from Columbia no less, for Christ's sake. Why was she letting him drag her down to his level? She took a breath, deliberately lowering her voice. "All you do is yell at me these days. It's not like when we were first married. I'm worried about us."

"What does that have to do with my uncle?"

She couldn't meet his eyes. "I don't like him. That's all."

"Why the fuck not? He puts food on our table. You damn well better like him."

She looked at him this time. "Unlike you, I don't *have* to like him."

He flushed red. "You're not answering the question. You fucking my uncle?"

"For the last time, no!" She blew out fiercely, striving for control. She wanted to scream at him, to slap him until he saw sense.

He shook his head, his eyes turning mean. "You're lying; I can see it. I'm gonna kill him. And then I'm gonna kill you."

His hand came out of nowhere, backhanding her across the right cheek. The blow made her stagger, her hip striking the sink, her eyes instantly welling up with tears. She touched the spot where he'd hit her, the skin flaming hot and prickling beneath her fingers. Her stomach ached and she thought she was going to vomit up that damn pill.

She had one crazy idiotic thought: *Karma's a bitch. Serves me right for thinking of slapping him.*

No. That was Vince talking, telling her she deserved his lack of control, his anger.

With that slap, he'd just crossed her personal Rubicon. Now it was war. "What kind of limp-dicked loser hits his wife?"

Vince stared at her, his breathing ragged. "Who you calling a limp dick?"

"You, you pathetic, wife-beating, *loser.*"

She saw him shudder, knew he was furious, knew more slaps were coming. Knew she wouldn't back down, no matter the consequences. "Ever since we got here, Vince, you've changed. You've become someone I don't want to know anymore. You've turned into a big bully, just like your damn uncle. *That's* why I hate him. *That's* why I'm taking the pills."

He threw his hands up and she flinched. When he saw her recoil, guilt flashed across his face, his features softening. His voice fell to a whisper. "I'm sorry. You know I got a temper."

That old excuse. Anger roared up, making her stomach roil and her skin go hot, the pain draining away. "Face it. You're a wife beater. The lowest of the low. The weakest of the weak." She hissed her accusation, punctuating each word with the punch of her index finger into his bare chest.

"I'm not! Jesus!" He turned away for a second, then took a deep breath. "I won't ever do it again."

She narrowed her gaze. "You're damn right you won't."

He met her eyes. "What's that supposed to mean?"

Kate put her hands on her hips, her cheek throbbing. "Nobody hits me. *Ever.*"

"Come on. It was a mistake. I got carried away." He reached for her arms, trying to pull her close.

She pushed him away. "Leave me alone."

He looked at her for a moment, his eyes wounded. "I'm sorry. How many times do I got to say it?"

"I can't forgive this."

"Damn it, Katie. You're my wife. We're married. That *means* something to me. Don't it mean *anything* to you?"

Some part of her wanted to say that it did. But if she gave in now, he'd just do it again. *I'm gonna kill you.* She'd never forget him saying that. She looked down at the marble tiles on the bathroom floor, her eyes idly tracing the honey-colored veins that ran through the creamy stone. Anything to keep from looking at him. Anything to keep him from seeing the truth in her eyes.

"Let me think about it," she mumbled. She needed him gone, ASAP, and if she had to lie, she would.

"Okay. But we got to talk about this later."

She nodded. She'd have to call her parents and ask them for money to get home. She could hear her mother now. "But Katherine, what did you expect? He's from *Jersey*."

"Katie, look at me." When she met his eyes, he said, "Look, I'm just a dumb fuck. I'm not thinking straight. I love you. I would never hurt you."

"But you just *did*."

He shrugged, his eyes sliding away. "I don't know what came over me."

She looked at him for a long time. The words she spoke were thick and shaky, not the cool tone she'd intended. Her marriage was over. And it did mean something to her. "You are *not* the man I married. *That* man would never hit me. *That* man loved me."

His chin came up and he met her gaze again. "Don't say that." His voice held a pleading note she'd heard too much of recently.

"Just leave."

He took a deep breath and looked like he wanted to say something else, but she pointed to the door. "I don't want to hear it."

Anger and sadness warred on his face. He took a step toward her, but when she moved back, his shoulders slumped and he put up his hands in surrender. "You're pissed. I can see that. You got to cool off, so I'm leaving—for now. But we got to talk this through."

"We will," she lied. She waited until he closed the door behind him, then she sagged against the sink, her arms trembling. Tears blurred her vision, and she stifled a sob, her throat aching, her eyes burning. She listened intently to the sounds of him moving around in the other room, waiting for him to leave. Finally she heard the outer door to their apartment close. He was gone.

She was alone. Again.

Kate rubbed her throbbing cheek and let the tears fall. How had their marriage degenerated so quickly? The first three months had been great, but the last six… and now this. She walked into the bedroom, her eyes going to the chair where the jacket had been.

It was gone.

A chill ran through her, instantly stifling her tears. It *had* been blood on the jacket.

If Vince was in the Mafia, if he'd killed someone, what reason would he have to let her go?

What was to stop him from hunting her down?

What was to stop him from killing her?

Not a damn thing.

ℰᎧᏣᎡ

Carlo Andretti rooted for Giotto as he tore into his brother Giorgio. The two Rottweilers growled and snapped at each other, their teeth and coal-black coats gleaming in the sun as they fought over the ball Carlo had tossed in their midst. Giorgio lost his hold on the ball, and the dogs raced across the lawn after it, their huge paws ripping the turf. Carlo smiled at their antics. The dogs were the best children he could ever hope for. Smart, loyal, and unquestioning. Vicious when so ordered. And convinced the sun rose and set on Carlo.

He corrected himself. Giotto and Giorgio were the best children he could ever have, aside from his dead Toni, God rest her soul. Her surviving twin, Dario, had all the initiative and thought process of a clam.

Twins. He could have had two clever, cunning children. But God had given him only one. And that one was dead.

Dario would inherit everything Carlo had worked for. Fucking shit-for-brains Dario. *He'll just let everything dribble through his fingers like piss.*

Unless of course Vincenzo proved himself. His nephew seemed to have the brains and the balls to be *capo*. He certainly had the ambition. He'd asked Carlo for the opportunity to take out Enrico Lucchesi, and Carlo had agreed to give him the chance. So far, Vincenzo had planted his pretty wife near Lucchesi, to give himself an excuse to get close to Lucchesi when he was under little guard. It was a decent plan, but it was moving far too slowly. So he'd nudged things along by sending Enrico the box. Vincenzo wouldn't like it, but he'd have to cope.

Waiting out the entire year of mourning after Toni's death had been agony enough. When Lucchesi had taken up with Franco Trucco's red-haired daughter just six months after Toni's death, Carlo had almost broken his mourning vow and avenged Toni's honor. But then Lucchesi had crashed his car and the red-haired *puttana* had died. So Carlo had held back his anger for the moment, even though the affair proved, despite Lucchesi's protestations of love for Toni, that he'd been a liar all along.

Carlo never should have agreed to the wedding. But Toni had desperately wanted Dario back, worthless shit that he was. And he was Carlo's only son. Agreeing to the wedding, ending the feud, getting Dario back, had seemed like the right thing to do at the time. But letting Rinaldo and Enrico Lucchesi live had been a mistake.

A mistake he didn't intend to continue, now that his Toni was dead and her death properly mourned. At least he had the satisfaction of knowing he'd respected his daughter's memory, even if Lucchesi hadn't. Toni couldn't fault him for what came next.

"Don Andretti." Carlo heard Massimo's gruff voice behind him. He took his eyes off the tussling dogs and turned to watch his man approach. Massimo was a large man, but well-dressed as always, his dark double-breasted suit

15

hiding some of his bulk. A true Mafioso, Massimo's fine clothes added to his swagger. The smirk on Massimo's face only enhanced the impression of a man who thought he owned the world. Carlo forgave him his arrogance; it was well-earned. Massimo never let him down, never failed his assignments. Unlike Dario.

"How did it go?" Carlo asked.

Massimo chuckled. "Lucchesi and his guards about shit their pants. You should have seen it. I thought the young one was going to shoot himself in the balls."

Carlo laughed. "*Bene*, Massimo, *molto bene*." He clapped Massimo on the back. He was glad he'd waited for this particular day to send his message, glad he'd let Lucchesi get complacent, comfortable. He'd be easier to kill that way. But first, Carlo wanted to have some fun. Death by a thousand cuts was far preferable to something quick. Lucchesi might disagree, but fuck him. He and his father had thwarted Carlo at every turn; in some ways, the son had been worse than the father.

But now it was Carlo's turn to make the Lucchesis suffer. To make them feel what they'd done to him, to all of them. To make them see they were leading the 'Ndrangheta down the path toward oblivion.

And he'd never forgive Enrico for not taking better care of Toni. He hated Rinaldo, but that was business. His hatred of Enrico, that was personal.

It was the dream that had decided him, in the end. The dream where he opened a box and found Toni's delicate little hand inside, severed neatly at the wrist. He'd had that dream only twice since Dario's kidnapping. Once the night before Toni's wedding. And then again early this morning, on the anniversary of her death.

He'd warned Enrico when he married her. He'd warned him what would happen. And now it was time to make good on that promise.

CHAPTER 2

No one spoke. When Enrico and the guards boarded the private jet, he took a seat at a table by a window, and Antonio and Ruggero sat across the aisle. They'd learned by now it was best to say nothing when he was angry, to not speak until spoken to.

Crossing his arms, Enrico stared out the window as they taxied down the runway. He kicked the table leg in front of him and swore. Of course it didn't give. The table was bolted down. Curling his toes experimentally, he was fairly certain none were broken.

Antonio looked at him questioningly, maybe hoping to be sent to the galley for some ice. Enrico looked away from him, dismissing his silent entreaty. If he was suffering, so would they.

The plane picked up speed as they lifted off. Soon they were soaring above the chaos that was Rome. The Eternal City teemed with the beautiful and the ugly at the same time. Making a slow circle above the dense jumble of buildings below, the plane eventually headed north, to Milan.

Foolish. So damned foolish. His father would never forgive him for being so reckless. And he couldn't forgive himself. He was not the sort of man who believed a Mafioso had to prove himself every minute of the day. All he had to do was prove himself prudent. Prudent would keep him safe. Prudent wouldn't get him or his men killed.

Enrico noticed Antonio peering at something in the back. Following the direction of his gaze, Enrico's eyes lit upon the pretty flight attendant. Of course it was a woman.

He opened his mouth to chide Antonio, then closed it. The attendant had dyed her hair a deep auburn, and now she reminded him of someone *he* couldn't ignore.

Kate Andretti. The married woman he couldn't get out of his mind. The

17

woman he'd be seeing later today. The woman he could not have, could not allow himself to have, even if she were agreeable. And yet she'd plagued his thoughts since their first meeting.

Enrico had been upset when the director of the Lucchesi Home for Children, Dottor Laurio, had hired an Andretti three months ago. But short of informing the director that he'd inadvertently hired the wife of an enemy, there was nothing Enrico could do. He'd carefully maintained the fiction with Laurio that he was just a businessman, and he wasn't about to tell the man otherwise.

But once Enrico met Kate, his concerns evaporated. Her exotic looks—auburn hair, striking green eyes, alabaster skin—piqued his interest, but her manner was the thing that bowled him over. Competent, intelligent, kind: all qualities that reminded him very much of Antonella.

He'd spoken to Kate a half-dozen times, making several unscheduled trips to the orphanage to do so. Not that that was far out of the ordinary. Providing handsomely for the children made him feel, at least in some small way, that he was balancing the scales with God, with the universe. Bringing some measure of happiness to the world instead of more misery.

But today's trip to the orphanage, though regularly scheduled, wasn't about the children. He hoped to see Kate. And after Carlo's threat, seeing her seemed more important than ever. He wanted to stop wasting the days of his life. To stop quietly longing after Kate and to do something about it. But it was impossible, this desire. Simply impossible.

He almost hated that she'd invaded his thoughts. He should be focused on Toni, should be mourning her loss, on this day of all days. But he couldn't. Not without reopening the raw aching hole that had been in his chest since her death. He'd tamped down his grief, but still it lingered, dark and murky, waiting to suck him under. Thinking about Toni was dangerous; he might break down in front of his men.

The time for tears is over. Toni had told him he had to remarry. But how could he just forget twenty-six years with the woman he loved?

He scrubbed his hands over his cheeks and chin and summoned up Kate's face in his mind, needing the distraction. He had no idea what Kate thought of him. He had to assume she loved her husband and the Andretti family. Just because she was newly arrived from America, just because she seemed to enjoy his company, that didn't make her any different from the rest of the Andretti clan.

He studied his reflection in the plane window, in the voids between clouds. He looked tired. His hair was tousled, his beard starting to shadow his cheeks and chin already, even though he'd shaved just a few hours ago. He adjusted his tie and smoothed down his dark blue suit jacket, pulling at his white shirt cuffs. In just a few hours, he'd be seeing Kate. He swallowed against the adrenaline that jolted through him. He finger-combed his hair, then stopped. He was a grown man, not a nervous schoolboy. And she couldn't be his anyway. *Or could she? What if she could be?*

The crotch of his trousers tightened in a most embarrassing way. He shifted in his seat. *Cristo,* he was a pig. He was still Antonella's husband. Hers. Even though their vows had ended with her death, he still felt the weight of her presence, still wore his wedding ring.

"*Signore?*" Enrico turned toward Antonio. Seeing that he had his boss's attention, Antonio continued. "Shall I call Don Domenico?"

Enrico shook his head. "I'll call him myself." Antonio looked like he had something more to say. He'd punished them enough with silence. "What is it?"

Antonio colored and hung his head. "I beg your forgiveness, Don Lucchesi, for not seeing Veltroni in the lobby. I was closest. I should've spotted him." He looked up at Enrico, meeting his gaze. "If you wish to demote me, I won't argue."

Ruggero cut in. "If anyone should be punished, it should be me."

"Perhaps both of you are right. But it was my decision to leave without backup. It was my foolishness that nearly got us killed. Not your inattentiveness."

"But—" Ruggero started.

Enrico cut him off with an angry wave of his hand. "Enough. Just do your jobs. And I'll do mine."

"I have failed you, *signore.*"

He met Ruggero's intense gaze. "Agreed." When the guard didn't flinch, Enrico continued. "We'll discuss this when we return home."

Ruggero nodded, saying nothing.

"I've failed you too," Antonio said.

"You're learning. Ruggero is responsible for you."

Antonio reddened again, his fair cheeks becoming mottled. "He can't take the blame for my mistakes."

"He can and he will." Enrico studied Antonio for a moment. "You will not make this mistake again, yes?"

"Of course, Don Lucchesi."

"Then you have learned an important lesson at no cost to you." When Antonio opened his mouth again, Enrico waved him off. "Ruggero will take your punishment. Think on that."

Silence descended on the cabin. A silence big enough to think in. But a silence that gave him no peace. He had to call Dom. And he had to figure out some solution to this mess with Andretti. But there was no dissuading a man of honor bent on a *faida*—a blood feud.

Enrico picked up the satellite phone kept on board and punched in Dom's number. He answered on the second ring. "*Ciao,* Rico, to what do I owe the pleasure?"

19

Enrico took a deep breath before answering. "Carlo sent me a present today. A dead falcon."

"At your hotel room?" Dom's voice was tinged with alarm. "How did he know where you were?"

"Either he has someone watching me, or there's a traitor in our midst."

Dom said nothing for a moment, then he ventured, "If there's a traitor, it's the boy."

Enrico snorted. "You're not serious."

"Aside from Ruggero and me, he's the only one who knows where you are at all times." Dom let that sink in, then he added, "And he is an outsider. I told you not to take him into the family."

"I remember." Enrico risked a glance at Antonio, the boy's straight blond hair, blue eyes, and pale skin clearly marking him as *other*. Not one of them, not Calabrian. But he just couldn't picture it. Of all his people, Antonio was the one whose loyalty he was most sure of. The boy loved him. He would stake his life on it. He *was* staking his life on it. He'd sooner suspect Ruggero, but he had no reason to doubt him either; the Velas had long been tied to the Lucchesis. And when it came to Dom, there was no question. Dom was his first cousin and his best friend. He took a breath. "It's someone else."

"I'd still keep an eye on him. He came to you looking for a job, remember?"

They'd had this argument before. Such caution was a good quality in a *capo di società*, a second in command, but it was wearing at times. And unwarranted in this case. "Let it go." Dom sighed, but said nothing. "There's something else," Enrico said. "I've been thinking."

"That's never good," Dom teased.

Enrico smiled, then sobered. Dom wasn't going to like what he had to say. "We have to stop doing business with the Andrettis. And the other families who don't abide by the code."

Silence, then he heard Dom clearing his throat. "You don't know what you're saying."

"I do. We're not men of honor if we don't live by the code."

"The fucking code!" Enrico could practically see Dom's eyes rolling. "The code is antiquated. How do you expect us to compete with the Sicilians and the Russians if we don't change our ways?" Dom was careful not to mention the drugs or prostitution forbidden by the code, in case the phones weren't secure. One never knew.

"There are plenty of other ways for the families to make money. Look at ours."

"Hmm. Yes, every family has an investment banker at the top."

"I'm hardly an investment banker."

"You're far too modest. You're a banker *and* an excellent shot."

Enrico laughed. "If you say so."

20

"You and I both know most of the families haven't the brains to do what we do. Hell, *I* don't have the brains to do what you do. I know that. That's why you run the banks and take care of the wash." The wash was their code for money laundering. Most of the families used the Lucchesis to clean their money—by running it through legitimate businesses or through a byzantine series of dummy corporations—and to manage it.

He heard Dom exhale before he continued. "You can't really mean to cut ties with Andretti. If you think he wants to kill you now, just wait. And we can't cut off the others. It'll be suicide."

"I do mean to cut Carlo off. At least him. Preferably all of them. I know it'll hurt our profits, but I can't stomach it anymore."

"You and your father. Such men of principle. Principles are the excuse people use when they don't want to be practical."

"I *am* practical."

"Of the two of us, when have you ever been described as the practical one?"

Enrico heard a hint of humor in Dom's voice. But what he said was true. "You're right. As usual. My head's in the clouds looking at lofty goals, not at the situation on the ground."

"So will you listen to me? We already charge Carlo and the others more to deal with their dirt. We cannot cut off all the families. If we're to deal with Carlo, we'll need all the friends we can get—or at least no more enemies." Dom paused for a second. "You do agree, yes?" When Enrico gave his assent, Dom continued. "You ought to be smoothing things over with Carlo. I've been thinking about it, and since your marriage to Antonella kept the peace for so long, what about marrying Delfina?"

A bolt of surprise hit Enrico in the chest. "Dario's Delfina? She's far too young. And she's my niece."

"She'll be twenty-two next month. And she's blossomed this last year. I saw her recently, and it's been on my mind ever since to propose the match."

Enrico turned the idea over. Kate was an impossibility. And, if Carlo would agree to it, marrying his granddaughter would solve Enrico's problems—it would end Carlo's threats to his life and his business, and it would provide him with the heir he needed. What was there not to like?

Nothing. Except that Delfina wasn't Kate.

"Rico, are you there?"

"I'm thinking."

"So it's not an automatic no?"

Enrico didn't miss Dom's hopeful tone. "It's not a yes, either."

"Fine. But in the meantime, let's not upset Carlo further. Or any of the other families. We have enough trouble as it is."

"All right, all right. I'm listening to you. As usual."

"As you should. I didn't get to be your right hand based solely on my

CHAPTER 3

At the sight of the dark purple bruise on her cheek, a lump formed in Kate's throat. She was *such* an idiot. Tears rolled down her face, and she turned away from the bathroom mirror.

Wiping her eyes, she sucked in a lungful of air. She *wasn't* an idiot. She'd just been too quick to trust. Too impulsive for her own good. The next man she thought about marrying would have to prove himself to her—in spades—before he ever put a ring on her finger. She wasn't going to make the same mistake twice.

If she ever decided to marry again.

Swallowing down the tightness in her throat, Kate grabbed an overnight bag and filled it with clothes, toiletries, a few photos, and some keepsakes she didn't want to leave behind. Nothing Vince would miss in case he came home early. Her passport went in her purse.

Then it struck her: just where exactly was she going? She couldn't go to her parents. Or Terri. Vince knew where they lived. And he knew her friends in New York. Not that she felt close enough to any of them to ask for help.

Fuck! What was she going to do?

The exact opposite of what he would expect. Vince would automatically go to New York looking for her. He wouldn't think she'd stay in Italy. All she needed to decide was where.

The next big problem was money. She needed cash he couldn't trace. All her credit cards were in his name; her own credit was atrocious. If only she'd known back then what her poor choices were going to cost her now. But what was done was done.

Damn it. She had to call her parents. Kate picked up her cell phone, then put it back down. She'd better get out of the apartment first. That call was bound to be a long one, and it would be just like Vince to march back in and demand to talk to her. And if he saw the bag, he wouldn't let her leave.

Not if he was in the Mafia.

She rubbed her aching cheek again, then her eyes flew open. What was she thinking? She couldn't go out in public with a big bruise on her face. Jesus, her mind was careening all over, like she'd turned into a kid with a monster case of attention deficit disorder. Kate took a deep breath. She needed to get a grip.

In the bathroom, she rummaged through her makeup kit, applying concealer and powder to little effect. She was just too damn fair; every little freckle stood out, much less a bruise. Kate cursed her genes. Why couldn't she have nice olive skin like everyone else here?

After repacking her makeup, Kate picked up her bag and gave the little apartment one last sweeping look. It wasn't much, but she'd had a lot of hope for the future when she and Vince had moved in.

So much for that.

Breathing in deep, Kate tried to shove down the emotions that threatened to overwhelm her. Vince had been the guy she'd hoped for—a man's man who wanted a family, who loved and cherished her, who wanted a long and happy future with her, not just a night or a weekend in the Hamptons. He wasn't like all the rich, slick men she'd dated before him; Vince wanted to settle down. He wasn't afraid of commitment.

On their second date, he'd told her that one day they'd marry, that he, Vince Andretti, would be her husband. She'd known him just two months when he'd proposed, and she'd thought it the happiest day of her life.

But he'd just proven that their courtship, their marriage, was all illusion, a fairytale. Her prince was a villain in disguise. If she'd learned anything useful from her mother, it was that you never forgave a man who hit you. Constance had been quite vehement on that point. She'd never explained why, and Kate hadn't asked. She'd just trusted the look in her mother's eyes when she'd said it.

It was the only advice she'd ever taken from her mother. Maybe she should have taken more.

Well, it wasn't too late for that. But first she had to get out of harm's way.

Kate hurried out of the apartment and hopped on the nearest autobus that headed toward the orphanage. Dottor Laurio owed her a month's pay.

She just hoped the director didn't ask too many questions about Vince's handiwork. Kate smirked as she thought about the word. Handiwork—pun fully intended. At least she could still laugh.

As the tiny bus lumbered through Cernobbio and then up into the hills above the town, she thought about where to go. What about Florence? She hadn't seen it yet, and it was big enough that she wouldn't stand out. She'd be just another tourist.

A little bubble of hope warmed her chest. She could manage this. All she had to do was get her check and get out of the Lake District without running into Vince.

ꕥ

If I'm lucky, he won't pry, Kate thought as she headed straight for Dottor Laurio's office. Hopefully he'd be in early—never a certainty with Italians—and could cut her a check right away.

She knocked on his door, her heart fluttering. No answer. Time to try his secretary. She knocked on the door next to the director's. A throaty voice bid her to enter.

Gina, a fading beauty in her late fifties, gave Kate a soft smile when she walked in. That smile immediately turned to concern. "Caterina, *la tua faccia*!" she said, gesturing to Kate's face.

Kate's hand flew up to cover the mark and she flushed. "It's nothing. I ran into a door, that's all."

The secretary clucked her tongue. Cocking her head to the side, she studied Kate. "Caterina, that is not what happened to you."

She took a deep breath. "Do you mind if we don't talk about it?"

Gina pursed her lips and sat back in her chair. "If you insist. How can I help you?"

"I need to see Dottor Laurio. Do you know when he'll be in?"

"He is ill. He will not be here today."

Damn. Now what? "I need my paycheck."

Gina glanced at Kate's cheek again. "*Sì.* If you can wait, Signor Lucchesi will be here this afternoon. He can issue your check."

Kate nodded. The wait was risky; then again, it would be that much less money she'd have to ask her parents for.

Hopefully Enrico wouldn't inquire about the bruise, although he seemed like the kind of man who would. Even if she'd spoken to him only a handful of times, he felt like a friend. He'd definitely tried to make her feel welcome and to help her fit in. He'd even advised her to teach the children English in order to learn Italian, and it had worked. She still had a lot to learn before she'd be fluent, but her Italian was much improved.

She said goodbye to Gina and headed to her office. Nothing to do now but wait. And write a letter of resignation to Dottor Laurio.

Kate sat at her desk and looked around her cramped little office. It wasn't much, but it was hers. She'd personally gone through at least a quarter of the papers in the still overflowing metal file cabinets behind her, had read the histories of the children as she'd converted their information to the new electronic system.

Oh God. She'd have to say goodbye to the children. Tears filled her eyes again—could she do nothing today but cry?

At least she had one thing to thank Vince for; he'd inadvertently led her to her calling. After she'd gotten her degree in social work, she'd worked with homeless people, trying to find them permanent housing, but her days had filled her with hopelessness. Even when she'd succeeded in securing all-too-scarce low-income housing for her clients, many had ended up back on the street due to substance abuse or mental health issues.

She'd been frustrated, adrift, when she met Vince. Maybe that was why she'd been so attracted to him—he was so sure of himself, so confident. And he had a future mapped out for them right away. A future that had brought her here to the orphanage, to a place where she finally felt she could make a difference.

Maybe she could find work at another orphanage—no, that would be the first place Vince would look for her. Damn it, how could she work anywhere or rent an apartment with a false name?

Jesus. This plan was getting more and more complicated. But she'd figure it out. Vince was not going to get the best of her.

Kate Andretti was no man's punching bag.

ॐൠ

How should he respond to Carlo's threat?

Enrico sat on the sofa in his study, while Ruggero stood by the window, waiting for his boss to speak. Various strategies tumbled through Enrico's mind, as they had during the entire forty-five minute drive from Milan to his home on Lake Como. Should he strike out at Andretti's holdings, put him off-guard? Should he respond at all? Dom urged him to make peace, but Carlo might see that as weakness. And that could be fatal.

In the meantime, he'd have Dom organize thorough yet discreet surveillance of Carlo and his men. They needed to know everything about the Andrettis, every base of operation, every safe house, every official who was on the Andretti payroll. If he had to strike at Andretti, Enrico wanted to be able to hit him hard. Perhaps if he could make Carlo feel enough pain upfront, he'd be able to stop more bloodshed later.

Perhaps.

Carlo had killed Enrico's mother and brothers, despite the risk to Dario, who'd been a Lucchesi hostage at the time. If the man didn't care about his own son, what would he care if he lost some men?

Money. That was the key. Cut off the money, and Carlo would howl.

His thoughts were interrupted by Antonio coming into the room. He was carrying the carved box, now empty. "What should I do with this, *signore*?"

"Put it behind my desk." He pointed to the shelves built into the far wall, which were filled floor to ceiling with books and pieces of art placed here and there by Antonella to break up the monotony. He'd give Carlo a cigar out of that box. Right before he pulled the trigger and ended Carlo's life.

He'd have vengeance for his family at last.

But like so many things he wanted to do, it wasn't possible. Sighing, he rubbed a hand across his eyes. He'd promised Toni.

Carlo had to make the first irrevocable move. And most likely, it would be Ruggero pulling the trigger, not Enrico himself. Revenge, as they said, was a dish best served cold. *And best not served by the chef.*

Enrico watched Antonio leave the room, then looked over at Ruggero, who as always, was watching him intently. There were few men he counted on as much as his guard. Ruggero's lapse in the hotel lobby this morning was puzzling. And more than a little worrisome. Was it possible, as Dom had suggested, that there was a traitor close to him?

Ruggero waited, hands clasped behind his back, his dark eyes expectant. Waiting for Enrico to say something. Perhaps waiting for the order to kill Carlo. Such a task would be difficult, possibly even suicidal, and yet Ruggero would accept it. Perhaps he'd even relish the idea. The man was ruthless, amoral, and cold to the bone. Could Ruggero have any genuine honor, any real loyalty? Could he truly be trusted?

Enrico cleared his throat. He fingered a handsomely bound book lying on the coffee table in front of him. Niccolò Machiavelli's *The Prince*. It was a gift from his godfather, and his bible for navigating the underworld he found himself in. But it didn't necessarily have the answers to this situation.

He looked up at Ruggero. "As you know, this will be a difficult time. I will call upon you at some point." He held the man's eyes with his. "You will not fail me." Ruggero nodded. "However, you are to do nothing now but keep your eyes open." He paused, trying to read the bodyguard's face, but as usual, the man gave him nothing. If Ruggero was surprised, it didn't show. "Do you have any questions?"

"You have your reasons for waiting. I don't need to know them."

Enrico rose, walked over to his desk, and picked up the phone.

"Shall I go?" Ruggero asked.

"No, I'm having Pino bring the car around." He started to dial, then looked up at Ruggero. "I want you with me today." On a routine local trip, like the one he was about to take, Antonio was usually the only accompaniment. At Ruggero's look, he added, "Both of you. I'm adding Claudio and Santino as well."

Ruggero nodded. Although taking four guards was highly unusual, Ruggero didn't comment further, perhaps thinking the circumstances warranted the extra manpower. But that wasn't the full reason for Enrico's caution.

Enrico set the receiver back in the cradle without completing the call. He should have told Ruggero about Kate some time ago, but it had seemed of little importance before. That was all changed now. "One of the employees at the orphanage, Kate Andretti, is married to Vincenzo Andretti, Carlo's nephew."

Ruggero absorbed that information without blinking. "Do you think they've planned something?"

"I don't believe she's involved. But I can't take any more chances." He picked up the phone again and punched in the number for his driver. He asked Pino to bring the car around and told him to have Santino and Claudio travel ahead and report on whether Vincenzo Andretti was at the orphanage. If Carlo heard about the four guards, he'd laugh with glee. But better to live with his pride wounded than die with his bravado intact. Carlo had already called his bluff once today. The next time might be for real.

He hung up the phone. "One more thing. I'm a businessman to Kate. Do you understand me?"

Ruggero nodded. "I'll make sure the others are aware as well."

"*Va bene.* You may go."

Ruggero hesitated. "What is it?" Enrico asked.

"My punishment."

Enrico sat back in the chair and looked up at Ruggero. "There is nothing I can do that will hurt you as much as the knowledge that you've failed me." He allowed a small smile to touch his lips. "But don't tell Antonio that."

"I would feel better if you punished me."

"That is why I won't." Enrico caressed the wood top of his desk. "Just make sure Antonio learns from this."

Ruggero nodded, then left.

The paramount lesson Enrico had absorbed from *The Prince,* the one upon which his very life hung, was this: it was best to be both loved and feared. Walking that line often proved a struggle, however. Too much leniency, and he risked mutiny. Too little, and he risked being hated.

He turned to the window that looked out from his study over the broad expanse of lawn and gardens leading down to the lake. Enrico smiled involuntarily at the deep blue water glittering with sunlight, the lush green of the gardens, the gentle sway of the trees in the wind. He loved living in Cernobbio, near the tip of the southwest leg of Lake Como. Enrico had been born here, had grown up here. He loved many parts of Italy, but he couldn't imagine making his home anywhere else.

But the villa had felt empty since Toni's death. Even though they'd never had children, the house had been more alive when she was in it. Her laughter, her singing, her humming, the way she talked to herself, the cheerful chatter of her voice, the huskiness that entered it when they were alone—he was haunted by her voice, and the absence of it whenever he returned home still struck him at odd times. Today most of all.

He'd been fortunate in falling in love with his wife. True, her nose was too aquiline for anyone to call her beautiful, but Toni had large kind eyes, glossy black hair, and a grace that surprised him during their obligatory first dance at the wedding. Enrico remembered Carlo openly weeping when he'd embraced his daughter after the wedding ceremony. And then Carlo turning to him with naked menace on his face, his voice a low hiss as he said, "If you ever hurt my Toni or let harm come to her, I will make you suffer. And then I will strangle you until the light leaves your eyes."

Was that why Carlo blamed him now? He'd made it clear Enrico wasn't good enough for his daughter. Never mind that Enrico had treated Toni like a rare and precious gift, even when she couldn't give him the family he wanted, the family he needed.

Carlo thought he'd stayed with her because he didn't want to reopen the feud between their families. But he would have endured any hardship for Toni. She'd been worth any sacrifice.

He twisted the wedding band around his finger. It was the last connection he had left to her. His throat closed up, and a piercing ache rose in his chest. He'd never thought he'd outlive his wife, had never imagined a future without the woman he'd given his heart.

She'd told him she wanted him to remarry, that it was the best thing for him, even though he hadn't wanted to hear it. But when hadn't Toni been right?

Still, it seemed an impossible thing to do.

Delfina was the right choice. The choice he had to make.

If I can't have Kate. He shook his head.

Delfina it was. Delfina it had to be. What he wanted didn't matter. He'd sworn it: the 'Ndrangheta, first and last.

She had to speak to Enrico privately, and it was going to take more than a few minutes. More time than Vince would spare her. And there was the little matter of the overnight bag. Vince had taken it; it was sitting at his feet right now.

Except for the photos, she could replace everything. If he thought taking the bag would stop her from leaving, he was dead wrong.

All he'd done was make her more determined. But first she had to get rid of him. *Fake an illness.* She let out a little cough and rubbed her arms again.

Enrico touched her forearm. "Are you unwell?"

While she was nodding at Enrico, Vince stepped down, pulling her to him, his body curving around hers. "Maybe I should take you home."

No! "You were right earlier. I'm not feeling that great." She pressed a hand against her stomach. "I think I'm going to be sick."

"Come on, I'll take you home then."

She shook her head. "What about the Ferrari? The road is so twisty, I might throw up."

"I don't care about the car."

Ooh, that was a lie. But of course he'd say that. He knew she wasn't sick. "I'd like to stay put for a while and see if this passes."

"Come on." His eyes cut into her. No doubt he was thinking of the overnight bag.

"I can take her home when I leave," Enrico offered.

Vince stared at him. "I can take care of my wife."

"I did not imply otherwise. It is clear she would like to stay here for a time. Since I have business here, I can accommodate her. And you."

"I don't need no accommodating from you, *signore.* Just mind your own business. This is between a husband and wife."

Enrico looked at her cheek, then he said dryly, "I can see that."

Kate flushed and jerked away from Vince's hold. "Signor Lucchesi can bring me home."

"Fine," Vince said, though his tone indicated the situation was anything but. He kissed her on the cheek. "Call if you want me to come get you." She nodded, and he leaned in close, whispering in her ear. "Come home to me, Katie." The pleading note in his voice tightened her throat.

"I will," she lied, then watched Vince head to his car after picking up her bag and giving a curt nod to Enrico. Part of her still didn't want to believe that he'd hit her.

Part of her still didn't want to believe it was blood on his jacket.

But maybe she'd get some answers about that. If Enrico had been Carlo's son-in-law, he knew the family well. He would know who they really were. And she would find out how much trouble she was in.

Then again... Guards surrounded them. *Maybe Enrico has a secret of his own.* He looked down at her, concern evident in his gaze. Could she trust him?

35

Some instinct said yes.

She took a deep breath to calm her nerves. "May we speak?" She looked around at the guards. "Without your entourage?"

Coloring slightly, Enrico studied his shoes and nodded. He followed her inside and down the hallway, their steps echoing on the marble floor. As always, Kate thought the place was quite ritzy for an orphanage. Enrico spared no expense when it came to the children. They had new clothes, sparkling furnishings, an extensive library, excellent teachers. He even sponsored private university educations for the children with top marks. A man like that, a man who really cared—that was a man worth trusting, right?

When they reached the door to her office, Enrico's hand brushed the small of her back as he leaned around her, pushing the door open for her. He'd never touched her in such a possessive way before. The heat of his hand branded her through the thin blouse. He was a great deal taller than she was; in fact, he positively loomed over her. Perhaps she should have felt intimidated, but his height served only to highlight the contrast between his masculinity and her femininity.

Her attraction to him had always lurked in the background, but she'd done her best to ignore it, to keep Enrico firmly in the friend category, despite that easy smile, those deep brown eyes, that wavy black hair—she'd wondered more than once what it would feel like, running through her fingers. That strong, straight nose, that firm chin, that square jaw that all conspired to make him fashion model handsome. That deep voice with its upper-crust British accent and the liquid lilt of Italian as an undercurrent running through it. But now, after what had happened this morning, some traitorous part of her was thinking otherwise....

Cool it, Kate. She was not in the market for a new husband. Rather, she was in the market for a divorce.

She marched into the room and sat down behind the desk, wanting the expanse of wood between them. *There, that was better. Much better.*

He closed the door, then took the chair across from her. "You are not actually ill, yes?"

It was her turn to blush. "No. I needed to speak to you. Alone."

He leaned forward and gestured toward her cheek. "May I ask what happened?"

So polite, this man. It brought tears to her eyes. He was nothing like Vince. "I'd rather not talk about it."

"Kate, *per favore*, allow me to be frank. There is trouble between you and your husband, yes?"

She kept her eyes glued to the pathetic little plant on the corner of her desk. Her one attempt at making the cluttered office more homey. She opened her mouth to speak and found a lump in her throat that threatened to strangle her. Trying to speak around it, she managed a hoarse whisper.

"*Signore*, I beg you not to mention it again."

He sat back. "At least call me Enrico when you dismiss me." He put enough lightness in his tone to tell her he wasn't offended. "If you did not wish to talk about your husband, why did you want to see me?"

"Dottor Laurio is ill. And I need my paycheck for the month."

"Ah." He reached inside his jacket pocket and withdrew a fine leather wallet. "I assume cash will be preferable?"

"If you have that much on you."

He smiled. "How much do I owe you?" She named the amount and watched as he counted out the bills and handed them to her. A thick stack of euros remained in his wallet. Who the hell carried that much cash around?

"Is there anything else I can do for you?" he asked.

Kate hesitated. How did she go about asking whether her husband was in the Mafia? Could she just come out with it, or should she hint at the subject? It was difficult to tell with Italians sometimes. They could be so oblique.

Clasping her hands together on the desk, she decided to go with the indirect approach. But first she'd put him in the hot seat. "Why do you have all the guards with you? Usually it's just you and your driver. Antonio, isn't it?"

"Actually, Antonio is my personal bodyguard. I have two. Ruggero is the other."

Kate raised an eyebrow. "You have two bodyguards?"

"Well, four today, but Claudio and Santino aren't always with me."

"Okay, but why are they here *now*?"

When he rubbed his chin, she heard the faint scrape of stubble against his fingertips. "Unfortunately, Italy is not as civilized as you might think. The Mafia has a bad habit of kidnapping well-to-do businessmen. I received information today that suggests I am in imminent danger. Therefore, I must have protection. More than usual." He let out a brief chuckle. "My insurer would lock me up without it. It is a bit of a nuisance, really. But there is a cost to having money."

"But four guards? Really?"

"The 'Ndrangheta has infiltrated all aspects of society here in recent years. It is worst around Milan, but they are here at the lake now too."

"N-drang-ayta? What's that?" Kate asked, her stomach tightening. *Is this what Vince had gotten himself mixed up in?*

"The 'Ndrangheta is the Calabrian Mafia. The name means 'The Honored Society.'"

"So they're not part of the Sicilian Mafia? That's the only one I've ever heard of."

"Yes, the 'Ndranghetisti are separate from Cosa Nostra. And they are much trickier for the law to stop."

"Why?"

"Because the 'Ndrangheta is organized along family lines—blood family. Any man who is caught will not easily turn on his father, his brothers, his cousins."

Interesting. Vince worked for his uncle. It fit the profile. "How many 'Ndrangheta families are there?"

"About one hundred and fifty. And each family has a boss who has no boss."

Kate whistled. "A hundred and fifty bosses?"

"So you see the problem."

"These are the men you have to watch out for?"

"Yes." Apparently seeing the alarm on her face, he hastened to add, "Do not worry. You are probably not in any danger. They typically kidnap only the very wealthy. And they usually do not kill the people they kidnap. There is no money in that. They are, fortunately, a practical people."

"Then why all the guards? It doesn't sound so bad."

"Their victims often do not go home in one piece." He wiggled his fingers.

Kate felt faint. *Oh God.* "They cut off fingers?" *What if Vince had done that?*

"Proof of life. Or a threat of its opposite. It tends to motivate payment."

"But wouldn't they get paid anyway?"

"If the family can afford it. The ransom demands are often... exorbitant." He smiled ruefully. "Millions of euros, usually."

"I had no idea it was so lawless here."

"Lawless? No. But certainly this is not America." He paused and looked at her closely for a moment. "You did not ask me here to talk about my troubles."

"It's interesting though." Kate wanted to keep him talking; she wasn't quite ready to ask her question. "I want to learn more about Italy, and certainly the Mafia is a big part of this country."

"Yes and no. The Mafia organizations are more pervasive in the south. In some towns in Calabria, every man is a member of the 'Ndrangheta. That is hardly true here in the north. Still, they do have influence."

"Only to the extent that criminals everywhere have influence."

"That is where you are wrong. The Mafia controls much of the Italian state as well, from the Prime Minister down to the local chief of police." He paused. "Even now, the Italian government is rewriting laws to avoid having to prosecute our Prime Minister, Italo Baldassare, on various Mafia-related charges."

"Why don't the people fight it? Why don't they try to stop the Mafia?"

"The situation is complicated. Cosa Nostra and the 'Ndrangheta date back over a hundred years. Originally, they protected villagers from bandits, and later they helped defeat the French. The Bourbons did not care about the Italian people. They just saw us as a source of revenue." His smile was wry.

"The Mafia had noble origins, noble intentions. And they still do in some cases. They help people who cannot find justice any other way. And they do help the less fortunate."

Kate snorted. "You make it sound rather romantic. They kill people, Enrico. They would kidnap you and cut off your fingers if they could."

"I do not disagree. But one cannot be Italian and not understand why they exist, what purpose they serve."

"You can't be noble and terrorize people at the same time."

"You do not understand Italians, do you?" Enrico smiled at her.

"They're just like other people."

Shaking his head, he leaned forward. "Every Italian male thinks he is a prince. One must be a bigger, badder prince to get him to obey. Intimidation is all most Italian men understand."

Kate smiled with her lips pursed. "You're kidding me."

"I am not." He shook his head again, laughing.

"So what did you do to impress the men who work for you? What did you do to stop your competitors?"

Enrico's smile faded and he sat up straight. "I did what I had to do. I put on a big, swaggering show. I dressed better, I thought better, and I was ruthless in my business dealings. I crushed some other companies. It was necessary."

"Did you ever have business with the 'Ndrangheta? Did they do your dirty work?"

He held her eyes. "Why are you asking me this?"

Her heartbeat accelerated. "That's a yes, then."

"Answer my question, and I will answer yours."

She broke their eye contact and cleared her throat. "I suspect...." She stopped and started over. "You were married to Carlo's daughter. So you know him well."

"I do."

"Is he...." Her voice failed her. "Is Carlo, is my husband, are they...." She looked up at him, hoping he'd finish her question. He didn't. *Shit.* She was going to have to say it. "Are they part of the 'Ndrangheta?" Her voice had fallen to a whisper.

He held her eyes for a second. "Yes."

She froze, a chill hand sliding its fingers down her spine. Her chest squeezed by bands of iron, she could scarcely draw a breath. Vince was a mobster. *What the hell am I going to do?*

"Are you all right?"

She looked up at Enrico. She'd forgotten about him for a moment. *Jesus.* He could be a mobster too! Jumping to her feet, she backed away from her desk. She couldn't leave the room without walking past him. What if he tried to stop her?

Enrico gave her a puzzled look. "Kate, please sit down. Please *calm* down. You are looking at me like I am a Mafioso too."

"Aren't you?"

ಬಿಂದ

Enrico laughed, perhaps a bit too loudly, and shook his head, trying not to betray his alarm. *Dio mio, this woman.* He sighed, scrubbing a hand over his face. "No, of course not." When he saw she wasn't laughing, he motioned for her to sit down, and she slowly took her chair. He drew in a deep breath. He hated lying to her, but what alternative was there?

"I made a bad decision many years ago, and it has haunted me ever since." He shifted in his seat. "Shortly after I married his daughter, Antonella, Carlo approached me about a business deal. I said yes, even though I knew it was not entirely legal." He took another breath, noting her rapt attention. "I was young and greedy. I did not think I needed to consult my father." He let a faint smile cross his face. "I was foolish."

When he paused and didn't immediately continue, Kate asked, "What was the deal?"

"I would own a series of legitimate businesses and allow Andretti to funnel some of his money through them."

"Money laundering, you mean."

He nodded. "After a time, I realized I was taking a substantial risk for only a small profit. So I tried to back out. Of course, Carlo told me that was impossible." He smiled again, picturing what Carlo would have actually said in such a case. "So I thought I would force his hand. I started to skim off the top. When he caught me, I said that since he could not trust me, he ought to drop me as a partner."

Kate looked at him, her mouth open. "Weren't you afraid he'd have you killed?"

"I was nineteen. And naïve. I thought he would never harm me because I was his son-in-law. He loved Antonella more than anything. And she loved me. He would never devastate her by killing me."

"So what happened?"

"He obviously did not kill me."

"But?"

Should he tell her what Carlo had done to his family? No; it was too horrific. "He tried to have my father killed. He was badly wounded; he almost did not survive."

Kate's jaw dropped. "My God."

Enrico nodded, letting his bitterness toward Carlo show. "So I gave up my foolish notions about getting him to leave me alone." He paused. "As you have probably heard, Antonella died. Since then, I have been trying to extricate myself. Carlo, of course, is not pleased with my efforts."

She stared at the papers on her desk. "Not pleased," she murmured, then she looked up at him. "That's why Vince hates you?"

"Carlo wants my head. To set an example." He watched her, waiting for her to say more, wondering what he'd just done. *Dio.* He was in it now. Even if she didn't take up with him, if she left her husband because of what he'd said…. *Madonna.* He was screwed either way.

She stared at him, her pale skin even whiter, the bruise on her cheek standing out even more. Her voice rose in panic, and the sound made him want to comfort her. "I'm leaving Vince, but how can I ever keep myself safe from him?"

Enrico leaned forward, the words leaving his mouth before he could stop them. "You could stay with me for a while. I could help you get out of the country." A thrill ran through him, and his heart sped up. *This was it. The declaration of war.* This was madness, suicide. But he couldn't turn his back on Kate, not when he was the only person who could help her.

She held his gaze for a moment, then shook her head. "I can't do that." Her eyes left his. "I barely know you."

"You can trust me. I can keep you safe."

"With a price on your head? No thanks. I'd be safer on my own."

"Do you actually think a man like Vincenzo Andretti would let you walk away from him?" He looked at her cheek, then into her eyes. "That bruise is but a hint of his true nature."

"You could be as much a bully as he is."

"I would never hit a woman." He paused, watching her closely. "Please trust me."

Kate laughed, but it was bitter. "'Trust me' is what men always say right before they fuck you over."

The balls on this woman! He almost laughed.

She sighed and rubbed her forehead. "Please forgive my language. I'm not myself right now."

"If ever an occasion called for cursing, this is it." He waited for her to respond, then he said, "Let me help you."

Despair settled over her features. "I can't."

Pushing her wouldn't work. Perhaps if she had time to reconsider. "As you wish." He reached inside his jacket, retrieved a business card, and wrote on the back. "This is my private mobile number. Call me if you need help." He set the card on her desk, then walked out.

Merda! That didn't go well. That didn't go well at all. He couldn't leave her here, but he couldn't force her to go with him either.

How the hell was he going to fix this?

He walked down the hall. Antonio and Ruggero should have been waiting for him outside her office. Why were they out front? He stopped. *Dio mio. Two lapses from Ruggero in one day? Unheard of. Damn it all to hell.* Now he had to replace Ruggero as well. *Would this day never improve?* Having to replace Ruggero was at least an improvement over getting a death threat. A smile crossed his face; the day was looking up after all.

He stalked out front and found his guards standing in a loose group, talking and smoking on the front stairs. He confronted Ruggero. "Why are you still out here?"

Ruggero gave him a bland look, then motioned Enrico a few steps away from the others. "I thought you wanted privacy."

"Why?"

"The woman. You want her. She said she didn't want us around. I thought...." He let a shrug speak for him.

It was that obvious. Had her husband seen it too? "You thought wrong."

"If you say so." Ruggero shrugged again, his hands clasped behind his back.

Now Ruggero was openly disagreeing with him? "I do say so."

A slight smile appeared on Ruggero's lips. "You're a man without a woman. She's beautiful. I can't help but think that like the Lady Macbeth, you protest too much."

Enrico stared at him open-mouthed. Ruggero read Shakespeare? He was full of surprises today. "When you're right, you're right." He paused. "However, that is no excuse for laxness. When I want privacy, *I* will let you know."

Ruggero bowed his head. "I beg your forgiveness, *signore*."

Cristo. He'd just taken out his frustration on the wrong person. "I need to think. I'll be over there." He pointed to a bench under a large tree.

He took a seat in the shade. How could he convince her to let him help? He ran through and discarded several ideas. Damn it, there was nothing he hadn't already said. Maybe he just needed to say it again. Rising, he headed for the front stairs.

☙ⷍℭ

Walking back to his car, Kate's overnight bag in hand, Vince shook his head, cursing. He'd been feeling bad for nothing. He *had* been right to hit her. She was cheating on him, just not with his uncle. Fucking Lucchesi. There was no doubt about the way Lucchesi had looked at her, the lust in his eyes. And Katie—God, *Katie*—she'd responded to him. Vince saw the way she'd touched her hair as she'd walked toward Lucchesi, the extra lightness in her step, the extra sway in her walk.

He'd barely been able to keep it together during the meet and greet on the steps. Now he knew why she'd wanted him out of her office so fast. It wasn't just the overnight bag she didn't want him to see. She'd probably been planning on fucking Lucchesi on her desk. God only knew how long that had been going on, right under his nose. He never should've encouraged her to

42

take that damn job—

But that was all part of the plan to get close to Lucchesi, to find a way to take him out. If he got rid of Lucchesi, Uncle Carlo would reward him. Very, very well. He'd even hinted that someday Vince might be in charge of the Andretti *cosca*. There was no love lost between Carlo and Dario, that was for damn sure. Oil and vinegar, those two.

Dario rubbed him the wrong way too. At least he always knew where he stood with Carlo. With Dario, it was anybody's guess. If Carlo had been his pop, he might have done what Dario did—kept his big mouth shut in self-defense. But that wasn't a major problem for Vince; he and Carlo got each other. They both wanted to be top dog, and he was willing to put in the work to get there. He was learning a lot from Carlo; the old guy was a nasty SOB, but he was smart. And he knew how to inspire cooperation. Nobody dared cross him.

Except of course, for Lucchesi. And now the fucker wanted Katie too.

They weren't going to get away with it. Not Katie and certainly not Lucchesi.

He parked the red Ferrari a short distance down the road, out of sight behind some trees, and circled back on foot.

Maybe he was wrong about her and Lucchesi. He loved Katie—she was beautiful and smart, and she'd make a great mom for his kids. Yeah, she had some flaws—she asked too many damn questions for one. If Carlo knew she was an outsider, he'd kill them both. Maybe he should have told her, but he wanted her to have a baby first. Once she had a kid, once she was settled in, once she saw the money from his promotion and how they could live, she'd be on board then. He knew it.

But now—God, if she was fucking around on him…. Could his Katie really be a cheating slut? She was pushing thirty when they met, and there had to be a good reason why a beauty like her wasn't taken. Something he'd missed that other guys hadn't. But those days were over. He was getting to the bottom of this. Today.

He snuck back to the orphanage and entered through a side door, then crept down the hall to Kate's office.

Lucchesi was with her, and their voices were low and intense. Vince's heart dropped to his toes. It stank of secrets in there.

He waited, listening, but he couldn't make out what they were saying until her voice rose, high and all panicky, and she said, "I'm leaving Vince, but how can I ever keep myself safe from him?"

A scalding hot burn filled his chest. He'd been pissed before, but now he knew what rage felt like. He stalked away to wait for Lucchesi to leave. The bastard was going to pay for this.

And so was his wife. No woman would cheat on him and live to laugh about it.

CHAPTER 5

After Enrico left his card on her desk, Kate laid her head down in the circle of her arms. She wanted to weep. Or scream. Vince was a killer. A cold-blooded killer. And if she didn't play this right, she could be his next victim.

But losing her head wouldn't help. She took a deep breath. At least she knew where she stood. She had enough cash to see her through a few weeks. Once she knew where she was staying, her parents could wire her some more.

Enrico's offer seemed sincere; she was more than a little tempted to take it. But he'd been married to a mobster's daughter; he'd participated in Carlo's business. Enrico could be as dirty as the Andrettis, only with a finer veneer on top.

A shoe scuffed the floor, making her start. Kate looked up as Vince stepped into her office. His cheeks reddened and his eyes narrowed as anger crawled over his face. Her pulse skittered like a frightened mouse. "What are you doing here?" she asked.

"I waited until he left." He paused, breathing fast. "What do you think, I'm fucking stupid?"

"What are you talking about?"

"Lucchesi." Vince leaned across the desk. "How many times have you opened your legs for him?"

Kate's skin heated at the accusation. He might be a Mafioso, but she didn't have to put up with this. "You have a lot of nerve."

"No. *You* have a lot of nerve. I saw the two of you. No man like Lucchesi just *looks* at a woman he wants. And you acted like a perfect little *puttana* too, playing that game so I'd have to leave. So you could be with him."

"You're calling me a whore?" For some reason, the word hurt.

"It fits." Vince's fingers opened and closed on her desk, his knuckles turning white when his hands clenched into fists.

44

Seeing his near loss of control, she rose, her body trembling, a chill racing up her spine. She struggled to keep her voice even. "It's *over*, Vince. I don't have to take this from you."

He lunged, grabbing her by the hair, and yanked her halfway across the desk, sending her papers and laptop flying. She heard the computer hit the floor and break. He mashed her cheek flat against the wood, then pulled her head up, forcing her to look at him. "You're *my* wife, and I'll call you whatever I want. You're a whore. A dirty, fucking, *whore*." He spat the words at her, his voice low and menacing. For the second time that day, he backhanded her, sending her sprawling into the chair.

Kate's eyes flooded from the pain in her lip and jaw. Her face throbbed and stung from the slap, her scalp burned as if he'd pulled out a fistful of hair. She tried to gulp down air, but her throat felt too tight. *Get up, run, damn it!* Her muscles shook, her heart thrashed in her chest, but she couldn't move, couldn't speak. Couldn't run.

Vince stalked around the desk. Finally she regained control of her body and launched herself out of the chair, but he slammed her back into it, trapping her. "I'll see you dead before I see you with a Lucchesi."

℘℃ℜ

Enrico had nearly reached Kate's office when the sound of her husband's raised voice turned his blood to ice. He threw the door open, heard the click of Andretti opening a switchblade. The man bent over Kate, the knife gleaming.

As Andretti's head turned toward him, Enrico sprang for his knife hand. Capturing the man's wrist, he crushed the bones, grinding them together. Andretti grunted with pain and lost his grip on the blade, the stiletto clattering to the tiles between them. Throwing his body into Enrico's, Andretti sent them sprawling to the floor.

Andretti landed on top. The impact jarred through Enrico and he struggled for air. Andretti's meaty fist hurtled toward his face. He eluded the blow and grabbed Andretti's left forearm, digging his fingers into hard cords of muscle. They were well-matched, but Enrico had the advantage when it came to weight and height. Straining hard, he finally flipped Andretti onto his back and held him flat, both of them panting with exertion. His voice came out rough when he spoke to Kate. "Get the knife."

"Don't you fucking help him!"

Kate picked up the shining blade, then clicked it shut and closed her fist around the knife's pearl handle, her body shaking. She looked at Enrico with wide eyes.

"Now call my guard, Ruggero."

"Fucking cunt!"

Kate stepped into the hall. While she was calling Ruggero's name, Enrico looked down at Andretti. "You will *never* speak to her or touch her again."

"You make me fucking sick. Sniffing around another guy's wife."

Enrico's cheeks burned. It was true. But it didn't excuse Andretti's behavior. "Take your anger out on me, not her."

"With pleasure, buddy." Andretti bucked against Enrico and tried to wrench his arms free. "Let me the fuck up."

Enrico stared at Andretti until the man looked away. Then he slowly let him go and stood, watching him. Andretti rose from the floor smoothly, appearing little affected by their struggle. He straightened his jacket and dusted off his trousers. Then he stepped close, his face darkening. "I ain't forgetting this, Lucchesi." He spat at Enrico's face. Enrico dodged, but some of the spittle found its mark and ran down his cheek. He wiped it off with the back of his hand.

Antonio and Ruggero burst in and trained their guns on Andretti. Ruggero's face grew stern as he sighted along the barrel. Enrico's heart seized. Ruggero was about to pull the trigger. Killing Andretti in front of Kate would ruin everything. "No!" Enrico held up his hand for emphasis and stepped into Ruggero's line of sight. "No," he repeated. Ruggero looked at him questioningly. "This is a misunderstanding."

Andretti snorted. "I didn't misunderstand you wanting to fuck my wife." He took a step in Kate's direction, and she jumped away from him, her back hitting the wall.

"Stay away from her." Enrico made his voice a low commanding rumble, the tone he'd use with a snarling dog.

Andretti whipped back to look at him. "Fine. She's your fucking *puttana* now. I don't want her no more." Then he turned to Kate again, his eyes blazing. "This ain't over, bitch," he said, then left the room.

"Make sure he's gone this time," Enrico said to Ruggero, putting his anger into it.

Ruggero followed Andretti, and Antonio stepped out into the hall, taking a position to the left of the doorway.

Enrico turned to Kate. She was shivering and hugging herself. When he moved toward her, she flinched. "Kate," he said, his voice as soft as he could make it. "Are you injured?"

She took a breath that sounded more like a sob. He eased toward her, even though she shook her head, backing up along the wall away from him until she reached the file cabinet in the left corner. Stopping there, she sank to the floor, her arms still crossed over her torso. He stopped a foot or so away and crouched down. He refrained from touching her, trying to use his voice to calm her. "He is gone. Ruggero will make sure."

She continued shaking her head, and he inched closer. "Everything is okay."

"How is my husband almost killing me *okay*?" she cried, her voice thick.

Enrico took a deep breath and reached out for her, putting his hands on her shoulders. "I will keep you safe. I promise."

Kate burst into tears, and he pulled her into his arms. She sobbed against him, her body racked with one great shudder after another. Her safety had been ripped away, and by the one person who should have been protecting her. Her husband. Anger welled up in Enrico anew, a molten bolt of iron in his chest. The man was a prick of the first order. He swallowed hard. *Dio mio,* what Andretti might have done if Enrico had arrived only a few seconds later.

And it was all his fault.

He waited for Kate's sobs to subside before letting her go. She walked to her desk, groping for the tissue box on the edge, the only thing still on it. Her plant was lying on the floor, the pot smashed, the dirt scattered. She stared at the mess, her lower lip quivering. Then she inhaled deeply and straightened her shoulders. Drying her eyes, she surveyed the wreckage of her office for a few moments before she started gathering her papers.

Enrico picked up her laptop. The case was cracked and so was the screen. "I will make sure this is replaced straight away."

She looked up at him from where she was kneeling. "Do you really think I'll be able to come back to work here?"

He frowned. "Probably not. At least not for a while." He set the damaged laptop on her desk and then leaned against it, crossing his arms. "You should stay with me until this matter is settled."

She paused in her work, her arms full of file folders and papers. "I'm not sure how long it's going to take me to settle things with him."

Enrico blew out a breath. "We both have an enemy in the Andretti family. I may be able to negotiate a truce with Carlo, one that covers you as well." He paused. "What is the alternative for you? A life of running from place to place, looking over your shoulder, hoping Vincenzo has not found you?"

She looked away, shaking her head. "Maybe he'll eventually forget about me."

"He thinks you have put the horns on him. He will not forget that."

"What does that mean?" she asked.

He made the gesture for her, folding down all his fingers but the index and the pinky. "He thinks you have made him a cuckold."

"But I haven't done anything! Can't he see that?"

"He is past reason. Giving a man the horns is the worst possible insult to his honor."

"Then he shouldn't mind giving me a divorce."

She truly did not understand. "Kate, you cannot divorce the Mafia."

She blanched. "I have to try. I'll hate myself if I don't."

"I cannot let you do that, and I cannot leave you alone."

"I refuse to let other people fight my battles."

"What you want is irrelevant. All that matters is what you need, and that is protection. Protection that I can provide." *Dio,* he sounded like the worst sort of pushy bastard. But he had to get through to her somehow.

She stared at him, irritation riding high on her face. "What are you going to do? Kidnap me?"

"If I have to." He took a breath and softened his tone. "I am not speaking in jest. Your life is in danger. And I will not stand by and see you killed." He met her eyes. "I will not allow it."

"And I will not be ordered around."

He sighed, unhappy about what he had to do. "Do you have a mirror?"

"In my purse. Why?"

"Give it to me, please." She got her purse and gave him a compact. He opened it and held it up to her face, reflecting the bruises, the swollen lip, back at her. "Take a look, Kate. Do you think the man who did this to you will ever see reason?"

Her eyes glittered with tears. She took the mirror from his hand.

"I am only concerned with your safety." He paused, as she stared blankly at her reflection. "You *must* come with me."

She took a hitching breath, then blew it out. "You certainly don't give a girl a lot of options."

She'd finally heard him. A smile twitched across his lips. "What is that saying you Americans have? It is my way or the highway?"

She laughed, a little too loud, and stood, clutching papers to her chest. "I'm telling you now, Enrico, that it's *my* way or the highway, not yours."

It was his turn to chuckle. "I never had any doubt."

She set the pile on her desk, starting to sort the papers into neat stacks. He put a hand on her forearm. "That can wait. Or you can take it with you. I can get you a new laptop so you can work from my home, if you want."

"I'd like that. I'm going to need something to occupy my mind."

"So you will come with me then?" *Grazie a Dio.*

"You made your point. I'm stubborn, but I'm not a fool."

"That makes two of us." Though in his case, he wasn't sure about the fool part.

ଛୠଔ

As they were getting in the car, Ruggero caught Enrico's eye. He leaned close and murmured, "I've never known a Lucchesi who didn't get what he wanted."

"I assure you, this isn't how I wanted to get it." When Ruggero turned to leave, Enrico caught his sleeve. "We need to talk later."

Ruggero nodded. "I expect my punishment to be severe."

"It will be," Enrico said, though he wasn't sure of his course. Losing Ruggero, when he needed him most of all? Unacceptable. Though neither could he accept such a serious lapse.

They settled themselves in the car, Ruggero up front with Pino. Antonio rode in the other car with Claudio and Santino. Kate huddled against the door, cradling the plastic bag that held her plant in her lap. When Enrico reached for her hand, she allowed him to hold it only briefly.

"Are you all right?" he asked.

"I hate this. I really hate this."

"By 'this' you mean?"

She gestured around them. "The guards. The need for them. The fact that I can't go home to my husband or my parents. The fact that my husband is trying to hunt me down, that I'm relying on the kindness of a relative stranger." She took a breath. "Sorry, I'm ranting."

Enrico nodded. "You are upset. I would be too, in your position."

"You *are* in my position."

"Carlo Andretti has wanted me dead for most of my life. I suppose I have grown used to the idea."

"You're awfully blasé about it."

"I assure you, I am anything but blasé when it comes to Carlo. At the same time, I cannot let him rattle me."

"So you think I'm overreacting?"

Madonna. She was touchy. "No, I think you are reacting exactly how one would expect." He stroked her hand. "There is nothing wrong with being frightened."

She made a small sound. Would she start crying again? But she swallowed it down and hastily wiped her eyes, looking out the window. "So I'm finally going to see the famed Lucchesi estate."

"I do not know how famous it is. But I think you will like staying there."

"Whenever I tell anyone where I work, they always ask if I've seen your place."

"When my father moved the family here, he wanted to establish a worthy home for generations of Lucchesis. He gave the villa to me as a wedding gift."

"Where did your family come from?"

Merda. "Calabria."

She raised an eyebrow. "And you told me you weren't part of the 'Ndrangheta."

"Not all Calabrians belong to the 'Ndrangheta."

"Just most of them?"

He nodded, wanting to change the subject. "How did you meet your husband?"

"At a party in New Jersey. He knew my cousins. They thought he was a good guy." She snorted. "So did I."

"I am sure he has some good qualities. He must care for you a great deal to be this upset."

"Are you saying I should be happy he wants to kill me?"

"In a way, I suppose."

She shook her head. "Are all Italians so screwed up?"

He laughed. "The stereotypes are not entirely inaccurate. We are a passionate people."

"I hope you're not saying his behavior was justified."

"Not at all. Just… not unexpected. Southern Italian men in particular are rather possessive and mindful of slights to their honor."

"And you—do you consider yourself southern or northern?"

"Southern by blood, but northern by temperament. I was raised here. My father is disappointed I am not more like him."

Kate looked at him, her eyes soft. "I'm surprised he would feel that way."

Enrico shrugged. "He has his reasons." He stared out the window. "Perhaps I would not be in this situation if I were more like him."

"How do you mean?"

"If I had been more prudent, more careful about some of my choices…." He trailed off. That wasn't really true, except for the decision he'd made today about Kate. And it was his father who'd gotten him in trouble in the first place, his father who'd made the decisions that had bound Enrico to the Andretti family. But he couldn't fault his father. He'd probably have made the same choices.

"What are you thinking about?" Kate asked.

Enrico gave her a wan smile. "My father."

"You love him."

His throat tightened. "Very much." He rubbed at his eyes and swallowed hard. "He is a remarkable man. We do not always agree, but we both know family is the most important thing."

Kate smiled. "I get the sense you are more like him than you know."

Enrico looked at her carefully. "Was that a compliment?"

"I hope so."

He smiled. "I am glad you no longer seem to feel I have kidnapped you."

"Oh, I'm not happy about any of this. But… I'm grateful you offered to help me." She glanced at him, then her eyes darted away. "I feel I can trust you."

Warmth radiated in his chest, as if the sun had just come out. He touched her hand lightly, his fingers barely lingering over hers. "You can."

She didn't say anything for a moment, then she turned to him. "Does your father live near here?"

Enrico hesitated before forcing himself to admit what he didn't want anyone to know. "I do not know where he is, and he does not want me to know. I have not spoken to him in some time." He heard the wistful tone in his voice and tried to make it more neutral. "He had a heart attack when I was twenty-nine. I took over the family business then. It has been difficult for him since… the accident."

"What accident?"

He hated lying to her again, but what else could he do? "My mother and brothers were killed in a car crash when I was sixteen. It nearly killed my father. He has not been the same since."

"I suspect you haven't either." She gave him a concerned look and touched his hand. "I'm so sorry. I can't imagine how devastating that was."

Her somber tone, the slight quaver in her voice, took him back to that time-stopping moment of disbelief, when he'd first heard of their deaths. And then to the moment after that, when he'd first believed and the weight of the loss had threatened to crush him. He closed his eyes for a second, the ache in his chest nearly overwhelming. His family, Antonella... there'd been too many deaths. He cleared his throat and opened his eyes, but had to look at the ceiling of the car instead of her. "Thank you." He paused, then said, "I wish you could meet my father."

"You have no way of finding him?"

"He wants to be alone, and I am trying to respect that. He has earned his peace." *Dio* only knew if he had found any.

§⁃⁃⁃⁃⁃

They were silent as the car turned down a gravel drive, rounded a copse of trees, and Enrico's home suddenly appeared before them.

"You seriously live here?" Kate asked as they pulled up before a huge palazzo on the lake. He'd called it a villa, but that was far too modest a word for a structure that rose three stories and looked like it could house at least a hundred people. Stretching above them in the honeyed light of early sunset, the ivory edifice seemed clad in molten gold.

Enrico looked up at the many windows and balconies facing them and smiled. "Welcome to my home."

He escorted her inside the foyer, which opened into a soaring space that extended up two stories. She'd never been in a private home so grand, not even when she'd dated the doctor who had a place in the Hamptons. Two spiral staircases, which led to the separate wings of the house, curved upwards on each side. Marble was everywhere—on the floor, on the columns, even on the walls as decorative moldings. Her steps echoed as she turned around, trying to absorb what she was seeing. Old masters hung here and there, and sumptuous fabrics and finishes shone from various surfaces. The dark wood furniture was heavy and antique. Taken as a whole, Enrico's "villa" made her parents' home in upstate New York look like a shack.

Kate looked at Enrico. *Who is he, really?* "Looks like you crushed more than a few competitors to get all this."

Enrico shrugged. "It is mostly my father's doing."

"You can't maintain all this without a lot of cash."

Enrico surveyed her for a moment. After an uncomfortable silence, he spoke. "Would you care for a tour?" His tone was neutral, as if they both hadn't been less than polite.

"I would love it." She let his coolness slide by unremarked.

Kate followed him through a series of rooms on the first floor—a sitting room, a media room, a dining room, his study, a solarium, and so on—and then he took her up the stairs to her room on the second floor.

He opened a door midway down the hall, and they stepped inside an opulent suite. The room looked like something out of a museum. Steel-blue silk brocade covered the walls, and a king-size canopy bed stood at one end, yards of space around it. Heavy midnight-blue velvet curtains framed the two windows, which overlooked a garden and a large swimming pool. A delicate upholstered love seat and two chairs in silver damask curved around a fireplace opposite the bed. All the wood in the room was a dark, richly burnished mahogany that gleamed under the lights. She was afraid to touch anything.

A maid materialized out of nowhere and stepped inside, bowing her head to them. "This is Maddalena," Enrico said. "She will take care of your room and anything else you need. Just press this button on the wall." He tapped a finger beside a small round black button above the light switch. He pointed to his left at two doors. "The closet and a full bath are through there. Please make yourself at home. Shall we meet downstairs in my study in an hour?"

Maddalena bowed and left, and Enrico was about to follow her when Kate said, "I hate to bother you further, but I have only these clothes...." She gestured to herself.

His eyes swept up and down her body, and she blushed at the scrutiny. When he looked into her eyes, a smile crept across his face. "I believe there are some clothes here that may fit you."

"Will your wife mind?"

Enrico shook his head. "As I said earlier, she is dead."

"But didn't you remarry? You're wearing a ring."

He looked at the simple gold band. "I cannot take it off."

"Can't or don't want to?"

He froze, and she apologized, blushing deeply. *Idiot, idiot, idiot.* "I'm sorry, Enrico, that was uncalled for."

He stared at the carpet. "When you have lost a spouse you loved, then you will know how true that is." He looked at her then and gestured at her left hand. "And you? Do you still love your husband?"

Kate looked at the wedding and engagement bands on her ring finger. A mix of emotions closed up her throat. She'd entirely forgotten about the rings, but she'd be damned if she'd wear them for one second longer. Yanking at them, she found they wouldn't budge, and she cursed under her breath. By the time she finally wrenched the rings off and tossed them on the carpet, she was close to tears. One of the rings bounced up and hit the wall, landing near Enrico's shoe. He bent down to pick it up.

"Leave it," she said, her voice thick.

He looked at her questioningly. "It is an expensive ring."

"I don't want it." Her chest heaved with the effort not to cry. "I don't want anything that reminds me of him."

He bent down and retrieved both rings. "Would you like me to sell these for you? I know you could use the money."

She nodded, not trusting herself to speak over the lump in her throat. The softness of his tone only compounded it. How could he want to help her after what she'd said? *Can't or don't want to?* What a bitch she was.

He pocketed the rings, then turned and left. She followed him into the hall and stared after him, her face burning crimson. "Enrico." She raised her voice to just below a shout. He paused and half-turned. "I'm so sorry," she said, advancing toward him.

He nodded curtly, then turned and resumed walking. She faltered and stopped. *Damn it.* She hadn't handled that well at all.

ℴ)ℛ

Enrico burned as he continued down the hall. Maybe it had been a mistake to bring her here. Maybe she wasn't who he thought she was…. He took a deep breath. Actually, she was *exactly* who he thought she was. Intelligent, direct, and assertive. Her question had hurt because it was so on the mark. He'd been acting like Toni had an impossible to break hold on him when it was the other way around. He didn't want to let go of her. If she were still here, she'd have told him to quit wallowing and move on with his life. Hadn't she said as much at the end? That he had to let her go?

He reached the end of the hall and stepped inside his suite, closing the door behind him, shutting Kate out, shutting all of it out. He leaned against the heavy wood for a moment, absorbing the hush of his room. Then, before his nerve failed him, he crossed over to the double walk-in closets and opened the one that had been Antonella's.

All her clothes were still in their places. The dresses, the slacks, the satiny blouses she liked to wear. The rows of designer shoes and handbags. He inhaled deeply, picking up the scent of finely tanned leather, and underneath it, the freesia and jasmine of her perfume. The carefully sealed hole in his chest burst open, piercing him with an ache that reached up into his throat and threatened to strangle him. *Toni.* He closed his eyes, reaching out and burying his hand in the deep brown fur of her sable coat. When had she worn it last? Winter, two years ago, in the garden. Before they knew she was ill. She'd kissed him in that coat, her lush body pressed against his, buried under that softness, that warmth. How he'd wanted her.

He opened his eyes and let go of the coat, then released a shuddering breath. Clothes for Kate. He had to focus. He picked out a black flowing skirt, a pair of charcoal trousers, and a couple blouses. A swimsuit. Things he didn't particularly remember Antonella wearing. He added a red slip, one that still had a tag on it, to the pile. Something Kate could sleep in. He opened drawers, found an unopened package of lacy black underwear to add to the stack. That was enough for now. He'd get Kate her own clothes in a few days.

He closed the closet behind him, then marched back down the hall and knocked on her door. She opened it and looked at him bashfully. "Enrico, I didn't mean—"

"You did mean it." He stared at her for a second. "And you are right, it is time to let her go. Here," he said, thrusting the clothes at her. "We will get you something else soon."

She gathered the clothes from his arms. "I'm sorry."

"Do not be." He rubbed his chin, letting out his breath on a sigh. "I am not a child. I cannot keep doing this."

"Doing what?" she asked softly.

He took a steadying breath. "Acting like she is coming back."

"Oh." Kate looked down at the clothes, then up at him. "Do you need help going through her things?"

He wasn't ready for that. "No. I will take care of it myself."

"How long were you married?"

"Twenty-six years."

He could see the wheels spinning in her head as she calculated his age. He helped her. "I am forty-four."

"You don't look it. I thought you were about thirty-five."

He smiled. "I do not smoke. That helps."

After a brief silence, she said, "May I ask—how long has it been since your wife died?"

"A year ago today." Pain stabbed through him, but he forced himself not to let it show. He didn't want to break down in front of her. Or anyone.

Jesus! A year ago today? *She was the Queen Bitch of Bitchdom.* "Oh God, I was so awful to you—"

"You were right."

"But rude." She could barely look at him. He said nothing. "Forgive me?" She raised her eyebrows in a silent plea.

"I already have."

Relief flooded her body. "It's a good thing you don't hold a grudge."

"I have a long memory." His tone softened. "But only when I want to."

"I'll strive to remain on your good side then."

He leaned against the doorjamb and looked down at her. "I doubt you could ever fall out of my favor." When she met his eyes, he looked away, a rush of blood darkening his cheeks.

"Enrico, I don't want to seem… ungrateful, but…." She let her voice trail off.

"I expect nothing from you. Nothing at all." He paused. "I enjoy your company. There is no harm in showing my appreciation, yes?"

She smiled. "I enjoy yours as well."

"Then I hope this whole situation shall not be such an ordeal."

She sighed at the reminder. "What if you can't persuade Vince to leave me be? What am I going to do?"

He looked at her, his eyes heavy with meaning. "I *will* resolve this for you. If it is the last thing I do, I *will* see you safe."

The certainty on his face was heartening. "I believe you."

"Good. Now freshen up and we will meet for dinner in an hour, yes?"

She nodded, feeling better than she had all day. If Vince was the villain in disguise, maybe Enrico was the knight in shining armor. Even if that armor had a touch of tarnish.

Of course, that would make her the damsel in distress. Kate gritted her teeth. She hated being dependent. But she was in way over her head.

She was in so deep, she'd be lucky if she didn't drown.

CHAPTER 6

Enrico and Kate had just sat down to dinner when the house phone rang. Maddalena came in and told him it was urgent. "I will be back soon," he assured Kate.

He walked down to his study and picked up the phone. "What the hell are you thinking?" Dom shouted.

"*Ciao* to you, too."

"You know why I'm upset."

Enrico sighed. "I didn't have any choice."

"You always have a choice."

"He was going to cut her up, maybe even kill her. I repeat, I had no choice."

"*Basta!*" Dom took a breath. "It was just an excuse to have what you wanted."

Enrico flushed. *Where had he gotten that idea?* He couldn't let Dom's disrespect pass unchallenged. "You dare speak to me this way. Shall I replace you?"

"Shall *I* replace *you?* It is my right."

It was true. The *capo di società* could call for a special election at any time. "You wouldn't dare."

"Force me, and you'll see what I will dare to do."

Fuck. Why was the whole world coming down around his ears today? "We need to talk. Now."

"I'll be there shortly."

Enrico hung up and rested his hands on the desk, his head hanging down. He'd known Dom wouldn't like what he'd done. He hadn't expected a direct challenge to his authority, however. What had Ruggero told Dom about the fight? Had he implied that this was all about Enrico's libido?

56

Enrico stared at the phone, his anger rising. Dom had never spoken to him that way before. True, he'd always treated Dom as his equal, but Dom's behavior was verging on disrespect. Which Enrico could not tolerate and live long.

He walked back to the dining room, trying to wipe his face clean of worry. But Kate saw through him. "What happened?"

"Nothing. It is a business matter." He took a bite of his risotto, then said, "I am going to have to take a meeting soon with my cousin Dom. I am sorry, but it will interrupt our meal."

"It's about what happened today, isn't it?"

He was careful to keep his face neutral. "Kate, do not concern yourself."

She didn't say anything. No doubt that wasn't the end of it though. He'd have to think of something to tell her later.

₭ɒα

It didn't take long for Dom to arrive. Enrico heard his car pull up and excused himself from the table, going into the front hall and opening the door.

Dom stalked toward him, his face hard and set. Every muscle in Enrico's body tensed.

"Don Lucchesi," Dom said, inclining his head in a stiff bow. His sarcasm was not lost on Enrico.

"*Buona sera.*" He stepped aside to let Dom into the house.

They proceeded to the study in silence, Enrico closing the door behind them. He walked over to the liquor cabinet and poured two glasses of sambuca. He wanted a civilized discussion, if nothing else.

Dom took a seat on the sofa, and Enrico sat across from him in one of the chairs. He leaned forward and handed him a glass and clinked his own against it. "*Salute.*"

His cousin tossed back the drink and slammed the glass down on the wooden coffee table.

"So thirsty, Dom. Would you care for another?"

Dom crossed his arms. "What I would care for is an explanation. What the hell is going through your mind?"

Enrico studied his cousin. They had been through so much together, first as boys, then later as partners in the business of running the family. But Dom had never understood Enrico's decision to stick by Antonella. And he would not understand his decision to stick by Kate. Enrico took a sip from his glass. "What's going through my mind actually, is Toni."

"What?"

"I've never loved another woman the way I loved her." He looked at his glass, at how the cut crystal caught and reflected the light.

"I'm aware of that. Fool that you are."

Enrico cast him a sharp look. "I am your *capo*. Remember that when you talk to me." His eyes held Dom's.

Dom inclined his head the barest bit. "I apologize—for the insult. But not for the question."

"And you have every right to ask it." Enrico took another sip of the sweet liquor, then set his glass down and leaned forward, clasping his hands between his knees. "I've been miserable since Toni died. I'd begun to think I would never be happy again. That I would die alone. But I've felt more alive in the last few hours with Kate than I have in the last year. I finally want something again."

Dom raked a hand through his hair. "*Dio*, Rico. You've jeopardized everything for a woman. *A woman you cannot have.*"

"How could I stand by and let Andretti kill her?"

Dom sighed. "You must make this right. Carlo already wants your head. Now that you've insulted Vincenzo, I'm not sure there's any way out of a war with the Andrettis."

"Carlo cares about money more than he cares about Vincenzo's pride. We can fix this."

"At what cost?"

Enrico shrugged. "Perhaps we give him the meat-packing business in Milan."

"You will give him *millions* over this woman?"

"If I have to."

Dom went red, his voice taking on an ugly tone. "You say that like it's *nothing*. And maybe it's not to you. But that's taking food off *my* table."

Enrico snorted. "Your family is hardly starving."

"I have four children, and I'll soon have grandchildren. Not to mention my staff, my men. All of that costs money."

"You mean *my* staff, *my* men."

Dom uncrossed his arms, pointing a thumb at his own chest as he spoke. "*I* give them their orders, don't I? *I* run the business day to day, while you fritter away your time mooning over your dead wife. And now this American." He threw his hands up in the air. "You are out of control. Your father would never be so cavalier about chopping up the business. And all of this just to satisfy your lust."

Enrico's face flamed. "That's not true."

"It *is* true. And it's my job to make you see sense. Or take over." He held Enrico's eyes, his jaw set like a pit bull's.

A cool tingle of adrenaline ran down Enrico's back, cranking up his pulse. The threat was real. Although Enrico's father had been the *capo di famiglia* of the Lucchesi *cosca*, Dom was a Lucchesi too, and he had several sons to carry on, a clear line of succession. He had proven himself a strong and competent *capo di società*, and his management of daily operations was unquestioned.

Time to switch tacks. "Dom, do you love me, as your cousin, as your brother?"

"Of course."

"Then why deny me my happiness?"

Dom stared at him. "You can be happy with Delfina Andretti or some other girl of your choosing. Perhaps my Bianca. You haven't even tried to find another."

"And if I do try and I am not happy?"

Dom crossed his arms again. "This is foolishness. So much sentiment over a woman."

"I've never understood, cousin, how your heart can be so cold on the matter."

"Remember how you felt when Antonella died? Why go through that again?" A strained note ran through Dom's voice.

"Because I have no choice. *You* have no choice. You think you have hardened your heart. But it will break just the same." Dom's first wife had died in childbirth; the baby, a boy, had been stillborn.

Dom stared at the dark window that looked over the garden and the lake, even though he could see only his own reflection. "It won't."

"For your sake, I hope it does."

"You would wish that on me *again*?"

Enrico softened his voice. "I've learned life is not worth living without love."

Dom snorted. "You're being melodramatic."

"I'm being honest." He waited a moment, then continued. "Do you love your children any less because Angelo died?"

Dom avoided Enrico's gaze, then shook his head, his voice hoarse when he answered. "No. But I do not love Francesca the same as Vanda."

"That is your choice."

"I learned my lesson. When will you learn yours?"

"That is a lesson I don't care to learn."

"I can't allow you to continue to put our family at risk over this woman."

"I'll fix this."

"I wish I could believe you."

"So, what if I romanced Delfina? And what if I decided I still wanted Kate? What then?"

Kate pressed her ear against the door of Enrico's study. She could make out some of what Enrico and his cousin were saying, but most of it puzzled her. They were speaking in dialect—she supposed it was Calabrian—and most of the words were unfamiliar. But she picked out a number of names, Carlo's, Vince's, and Antonella's among them, and she was sure she'd been mentioned—she'd heard Enrico say her name and then she'd heard "*questa*

59

Americana" quite clearly, and Dom didn't sound the slightest bit happy when he'd said it either. But why were they talking about Carlo's granddaughter Delfina? There was a long silence, then she heard Dom's voice again.

"*If* your American would have you—*if* she would have the family—I would agree. But only if you try with Delfina first."

A worm of unease crawled through Enrico's gut. "You've already spoken to Dario."

"I have. And he agreed to consider it."

"I've made no promises. Carlo will never forgive me if he thinks I've broken a betrothal to his granddaughter on top of everything else."

"I'm perfectly aware of that." The pit bull was back, and now Enrico knew why.

"You already arranged it. It's done, yes?" He held his breath, hoping he was wrong.

"It's all but done. Or at least it *was*."

Anger frothed up in him, hot and thick. Enrico jumped up and paced away from Dom. "How could you do that without speaking to me?"

"We *had* spoken. You seemed amenable to it. Unless, of course, you were lying to me."

"You did this on purpose."

The challenge in Dom's gaze was clear. "Someone had to make you see sense. Someone had to save this family."

"How am I going to get out of this?"

Dom smiled without mirth. "So you *were* lying to me."

"It *is* a good idea. I just—I don't *want* to do it. Unless I can't have Kate."

"Make her your mistress if you have to."

"No." His tone was final. "You have overstepped your bounds."

"My job is to watch over you and advise you, and to take action if you do something unwise. That's what I'm doing. No one would disagree."

Blood thundered in Enrico's ears and a pressure rose in his chest. "Do you really want to be *capo*? Do you really want the weight of all this, the scrutiny, the target on your back?" He paused, eyeing his cousin. "Do you think *you* can steer this family better than I have? Do you think you have the long-term vision to strengthen us in the twenty-first century?"

"It's an enormous responsibility. I'm aware of that."

Enrico spoke slowly, enunciating every word to keep a leash on his fury. "Do you think you can do it better than me? Because if you do, I will *give* you the job."

Dom looked up at him. "You've always known what to do. You've led us well, I can't deny that. And I do lack your foresight. But I can't let you put this family at unnecessary risk."

"What are you saying? Do you want it?" He held his cousin's eyes, the rushing of blood in his ears the only sound he could hear.

"Not yet," Dom finally said, his eyes not leaving Enrico's. The pit bull would not back down so easily.

Enrico's stomach filled with acid. "I don't like your tone."

"And I don't like your recklessness. Are you trying to get us all killed?"

"Since you are not willing to call for an election, this conversation is over. You *will* respect my authority."

"And *you* will respect my position as your second. You must marry Delfina Andretti. It's the only way to resolve this." When Enrico started to speak, Dom held up a hand to silence him. "It's the only solution the *cosca* will accept. You've taken an enormous risk. I can't support you with any other solution." He paused. "Would you have us both lose our heads over this?"

Dom was right, damn it all. But Enrico, not Dom, was still the best choice as *capo*. The family needed him, more than it ever had. The entire world was changing, and the 'Ndrangheta had struggled to change with it. Enrico was one of the few *capi* among his colleagues who had the education and foresight to guide the clans in the right direction. Without him, the 'Ndrangheta would never return to the old codes. They would be men of honor no more.

"No." Enrico swallowed hard. His future with Kate, his hopes for revenge against Carlo were slipping away. He felt sick, his insides corroding, but he was damned if he'd let it show. "I will marry Delfina Andretti, if there is no other way."

Had she heard correctly? The words were different, but it sounded like Enrico was getting *married* to Delfina. Kate's brow wrinkled. Why would he marry the granddaughter of the man who hated him? And why didn't he act like a man in love? If he still couldn't take off his wedding ring, he was in no condition to marry someone else. And he seemed to be... interested in her. Had she entirely misread him? Did he really want to marry a girl half his age?

Unless... this was his solution, how he was going to solve his problem and hers. If he married into Carlo's family again, he'd have to give in to Carlo. And it would be to Carlo's advantage to go back to business as usual.

But the solution didn't make her happy. Enrico shouldn't marry someone he didn't love. Especially not to save her. She heard Dom speak again, but his voice was low, and she strained to hear it.

"There *is* no other way, Rico." Dom's tone was gentle.

There had to be another way. There had to. "I'll try talking to Carlo first. To see if there is a solution I can arrange with my personal assets. Agreed?"

Dom didn't immediately answer. He looked away from Enrico for a few moments. When he finally spoke again, his voice was hard. "Agreed. But do not endanger the family again over her."

"I won't. You have my word."

Enrico walked over to the liquor cabinet and picked up the bottle of sambuca. "Shall we drink to it?"

Dom nodded and held up his glass. As their tumblers met with a clink, he said, "You know I hate fighting with you."

Enrico grinned. "Especially since you never win."

"I beg to differ." But Dom was smiling.

Enrico hoped things were all right with them. And he hoped he could keep them that way.

"I hope she's worth it," Dom said.

The softness of his tone made Enrico look closely at him. "She is."

Kate pressed her ear harder to the door, but she couldn't hear what they were saying. Their voices had dropped, and all she heard was murmuring. Was Enrico getting married or not? It was tough to say. She wished her Italian were better, and she wished she knew their dialect. So many of the words were strange to her.

And there had been enough talk of "family" and enough mentions of *capo* earlier to make her wonder. She knew that Italian CEOs were also called *capo*. But so were Mafia dons. Had Enrico lied to her? Just what the hell had she gotten herself into?

She listened for more, but she heard only murmurs, then laughter. Then the sound of footsteps headed for the door. Her heart skittered in her chest. She sprinted down the hall, trying to land on the balls of her feet instead of the heels, hoping they couldn't hear her mad dash for the dining room. Enrico couldn't know she'd been spying.

CHAPTER 7

Damn him. Damn Enrico Lucchesi to hell.

Dom slammed his fist against the steering wheel, then turned the key and listened to the Lamborghini's engine roar to life. He slammed the wheel again. *Why did Rico have to be so damn stubborn?* Shaking his head, Dom settled back into the leather seat. Putting the car in drive, he tromped on the gas, spraying gravel behind him.

He drove the car through the hills, still burning from their discussion. It had taken everything he had to leave the house with a smile on his face.

So Rico thought he could get away with taking Andretti's wife, thought he could have his cake and eat it too, and not get killed for it. Why was he at all surprised? Rico was being his usual unrealistic self. And it would be up to Dom to get them out of this mess, since Rico didn't seem that interested in handling it.

Just like he no longer took any interest in the day-to-day operations. Dom had given Rico a break when Antonella fell ill, but that break had never ended. It had been over two years since Rico had given a damn about anything—other than his love life. First, there was the grieving over Antonella. Then the disaster with Fiammetta and her father.

Despite everything Franco Trucco knew, Rico had refused to get rid of him. Instead he'd tried to paper over the mess with money. If it had been up to Dom, Trucco would be buried alongside his daughter. Fortunately, Trucco had worked for the Lucchesis for too long to have lost his loyalty to the *cosca*. However, that didn't mean he wasn't still dangerous to Rico.

But this—this madness with the American, this threatened them all. Carlo would not stop until he'd crushed the Lucchesi *cosca* to dust.

Carlo was no Franco Trucco. Dom had his own future and that of his children to look out for. If Rico wouldn't fix things with Carlo, then Dom would. No matter what the cost.

He loved Rico, loved him like a brother. But he hated him too, as only a brother could. Rico had been made *capo* when he obviously hadn't wanted it, even though Dom had been ready and more than able. But Rinaldo had of course favored his own blood over his brother's.

In some ways, being number two was better—he had so much of the power and the rewards, without the scrutiny and the enmity that came with being the don. And when Antonella had proved barren and Rico had stubbornly refused to annul the marriage? So much the better. Dom and his sons would inherit the *cosca,* they would run it, after Rico died.

But not if Rico fathered an heir. Not if Carlo succeeded in destroying the Lucchesi *cosca.*

What would happen if Rico didn't see reason? What would happen if he raised a son—especially one with the same ridiculous principles—who would take over some day? What would happen to the *cosca,* to everything Dom had worked so diligently to build, to secure? Rico and his principles, Rico and his soft heart, would piss all that away, would get them all killed.

Dom had done his job as *capo di società,* and had done it well. No one could claim otherwise. He'd given Rico good counsel, had warned him of the consequences of his actions, had tried to make him see reason. He'd done what he could for Rico—he'd even offered up his own daughter to solve this madness. But it was time to cut Rico loose.

Tears threatened to unman him. Dom gulped down air and widened his eyes, blinking rapidly, swallowing down the rock in his throat. He loved Rico, he did. But he had no choice.

It was up to Dom to stop him, up to Dom to save the family and their future.

Up to Dom to make the tough choices, as usual.

CHAPTER 8

Kate had barely sat down again at the dining room table and caught her breath, when she heard the front door close and Enrico come into the room. He took his seat and glanced at her plate. It remained almost untouched.

"Are you not hungry?"

"I am." She took a hasty forkful of the now-cold risotto. "I was just waiting for you." She paused, then asked, "Is everything all right with your cousin? I heard raised voices."

"From here?"

She flushed. *Stupid!* She shouldn't have mentioned it. There was no way she could ask questions about what she'd heard.

"We must have been louder than I thought," he said. "It is nothing. Just a disagreement on a business matter." He studied her carefully. "Are you unwell? You look feverish."

Kate cursed her red cheeks. "I'm okay, really." Though she really wasn't. Could she trust this man? Had he lied about everything?

He rose from his seat and walked over to her. Placing one of his hands on his own forehead, he extended his other hand toward hers to check her temperature. "May I?"

She nodded, feeling foolish. Really, would a Mafia don give a crap if she had a fever? She felt his cool palm press against her forehead. He frowned. "You seem a little warm."

"I'm fine. No shivers, no stomachache. Just a little headache."

His hand dropped from her forehead to caress her cheek, his fingers skimming over the bruises Vince had left. Then his thumb traced over her swollen lip, his face darkening. "I could kill him for this."

Kate felt a jolt. *Did he mean that?* He looked so grave. She didn't want him to do something foolish; he'd already taken enough risks for her. "I'm okay.

Just a little beat up. I'll be fine in a few days."

He crouched down beside her and took her hands in his, resting them in her lap. "I am sorry I was not there earlier, to spare you this pain." His hands squeezed hers. "I will protect you from now on. I swear it. You will never be unsafe again."

Kate's throat constricted painfully and tears threatened to spill down her cheeks again. *Jesus, how did he know just what to say?* This man who looked at her with such tender eyes couldn't possibly be a mobster. Certainly her faulty Italian was to blame for what she thought she'd overheard.

Enrico leaned forward, one of his hands going to the back of her chair, the other releasing her hand and cupping her knee. He was now just inches from her, his eyes darkening with care, with… desire. Kate inhaled in surprise, her body suddenly on alert. He smelled sharply masculine, like citrus and pine trees mixed together, a hint of something that was all him underneath. He was too close, much too deliciously close. Her heart hammered out of control. She should stop this. She was still married, even if her husband had tried to kill her.

Enrico let go of her knee and placed his fingers under her chin, tilting her mouth to meet his. Kate stiffened, but after his lips touched hers, she relaxed. She did want this. After all that had happened today, she needed a distraction. And Enrico qualified as a big distraction. As well as a big "fuck you" to Vince. After all, why should she feel any loyalty to a man who wanted her dead? A man who'd called her a whore?

And so what if Enrico was thinking about marrying someone else? All the better. She had no intention of staying here, with him. She wanted out of Dodge, as soon as possible.

And, since Vince already thought she was fucking Enrico, why not do it for real? Enrico was certainly handsome enough. Drop dead, as her cousin Terri would say. But she wasn't planning to marry Enrico or have a future with him, or—

Enrico pulled back from the kiss. "Was it that bad?"

"No, no." She blushed.

"But you did not enjoy it." He sat back on his heels. "I promised I would not push you, and yet I have done so. I apologize."

She put a finger on his lips. "Stop." Placing her hands on his cheeks, she urged him toward her. "Let's try that again, shall we?"

This time she forced herself to stop thinking, forced herself only to feel, only to hear. The satiny brush of his lips across hers, the touch of his hands on her face, his fingers tracing her cheekbones. The groan low in his throat when she opened her mouth to his, when she let their tongues touch. He groaned again, the sound more urgent when she opened her mouth wider, her tongue swirling around his.

He pulled her up from the chair, his large hands gliding down to her ass, cupping the cheeks and crushing her to him greedily. When she felt the bulge of his erection against her belly, a warm tingle ran through her, zinging down between her legs. She rubbed against him.

My God, he was an amazing kisser. And if she wasn't mistaken, his body was going to be amazing too. He was all hard slabs of muscle and sinew, granite next to her softness. She ran her hands across his wide shoulders and down his back, unable to resist squeezing his ass. It was hard enough to bounce a quarter off. *Jesus. This was going to be out of this world—*

He broke the kiss, both of them breathing fast. She looked up at him, confused. Why was he stopping?

"Are you certain you want this?" he asked. "A lot has happened—"

"I'm sure. Very sure."

His lips curved into a slow smile. "Then we need some place more private, yes?"

She grinned up at him in answer, letting him lead her down the hall. When they reached the staircase, he swung her up in his arms, making her laugh. "Put me down! You'll kill yourself carrying me up there."

"I do not think so." He mounted the steps with ease. "I take good care of myself."

"So you do," she said when he put her down at the top. He was barely breathing harder. *Good God, what a man.* If only Vince could see her now. She wished she were taping this. Then he would see her with Enrico, then he would know how much she was enjoying herself. Then he would know she didn't love him anymore. Not one bit.

೫಄

Enrico shut the door to his room behind them, a hush falling over the enclosed space. He hadn't bothered with the lights; enough moonlight came in through the open curtains to bathe the room in a silvery glow. *Dio,* she was beautiful. And she was his. Finally his.

He could scarcely believe she'd agreed to this, that she was letting him have her. But she'd said she was sure. Very sure. And the way her mouth moved under his, the way she'd pulled him to her, the way she'd ground her hips against his, they all said she was sure too. He hoped she wouldn't regret this later. He knew he wouldn't.

He placed his hands on her shoulders, kissing her again. *Madonna,* he could kiss her all day. She had a wonderful mouth, her lips plump and inviting. He could feel the swelling in her lower lip from Andretti's slap. Andretti would pay for that. He slid his tongue over the lump, tasting her, soothing the hurt. She whimpered. Was she in pain? He hesitated, then she melted against him. No, not in pain, not at all.

He kissed down her neck, gratified by her soft exhales, her little moans, her sharp intake of breath when his lips touched the base of her throat next to her collarbone. She clutched him to her, her hips grinding against his, her high round breasts pressing into his chest. He had to touch her, had to get her out of these damn clothes. He started to unbutton her blouse, but she brushed his clumsy hands away and worked on the tiny little buttons herself. "Take your shirt off." Her voice was a husky whisper.

"Brilliant idea." He watched her face as he took off his shirt and gathered from her widened eyes that she liked what she saw.

Enrico was as magnificent as she'd guessed. Flat, firm pecs lightly dusted with dark hair, a tight six pack of abs that bunched as he moved, his obliques making a perfect V of his narrow waist. Damn. He definitely worked out. A lot.

Kate pulled her shirt off. He closed the distance between them, his big hands cupping her breasts, pressing against the peaks of her nipples through the lace of the black bra. He palmed her breasts for a while, then his fingers circled in until he was tweaking and pinching her stiff little nubs, sending shivers down her body. He undid the front clasp of her bra and hungrily mouthed her nipples, sucking on them, softly at first, then tugging on them with his teeth.

The combination of pleasure and pain turned her legs to rubber and made her moan. She sagged against him, but he didn't stop the torture until she pushed him away. She was so wet her panties must be soaked through. My God, Vince had never evoked such a reaction in her. He'd always been so rushed, so rough. How could she feel so damn good, just from a man's mouth on her breasts? A thrill ran through her as she thought about what Enrico's mouth could do lower on her body. That was something else Vince hurried through.

As if he read her mind, Enrico dropped to his knees in front of her and unzipped her skirt, letting it fall around her ankles. She stepped out of it, kicking off her pumps, and he ran his hands up her legs, his fingers skimming along the sensitive skin of her inner thighs, his touch teasing. He grabbed her buttocks, supporting her as his tongue and lips traced circles across her belly, his tongue darting occasionally under the top edge of her panties. *Lower, lower,* she thought, opening her legs a little. He laughed against her skin, and spread his large hands across her bottom, squeezing lightly, his fingers toying with the crack of her ass through the thin satiny cloth of her black panties.

"Oh for God's sake," she finally hissed. "Will you just—"

"Do this?" he asked, slipping a finger under the edge of her panties and stroking it up along her cleft, making her knees buckle at the touch.

"Yes." She breathed the word, spreading her legs wider.

He laughed again and pushed her toward the bed. When she reached it, she fell back, opening wide for him. He mouthed her pussy through the fabric for a few moments, then peeled her panties down, slipping them off her legs and kissing along her inner thighs as he did so.

He breathed in the scent of her arousal, his cock twitching. He loved the spicy musk of her. Blowing on the short curling hairs of her pussy, he enjoyed how she squirmed and panted, how she spread her legs wider for him, soundlessly begging for his mouth. He lowered his lips to her right leg, licking a path along her inner thigh that made her moan. When he came to her pussy, he parted the lips so he could reach her clit, sliding his tongue across the little nub, back and forth, delicately at first, then rougher when she pressed up to meet him. "Don't stop," she moaned. He loved her little pants, her helplessness, her greediness for the pleasure he wanted to give her.

He reached down between his legs and palmed himself, feeling how stiff he was through his trousers, trying to give himself a little relief. If only he had known he was going to end up with her tonight, he'd have taken the edge off that morning in the shower. It was taking all his control to go slow. He didn't want to rush this. Not at all.

He lazily ran his tongue up and down the length of her, dipping it inside her pussy, and when she moaned even louder at that, he slipped first one, then two fingers in her. "Yes, yes, fuck me with your fingers," she gasped, raising her hips, her hands clenching the sheets. There it was again, that wicked, sexy word he'd never heard her say before today. *Fuck.* The rawness of her language heightened his own need. He flicked his tongue across her clit, then settled in with firmer strokes as her breathing sped up. He slid his fingers in and out of her, faster now, deeper, harder, until her moans were practically sobs. He listened to her sounds, concentrating. He wanted her to come. Hard.

Kate bucked up with her climax, feeling like her whole body had seized with pleasure. She had never felt such delicious, prolonged, unmitigated bliss, had never had a release that shuddered through the whole core of her body. She caught her breath and collapsed back against the bed, breathing as if she'd been running. She heard a rustling of cloth, then Enrico climbed up onto the bed beside her. He was totally naked, pressed up against her side, the hard length of his cock making her curious. She sat up on her elbows and looked down. *Oh. My.* His cock matched the rest of him. *Magnificent.*

Biting her lower lip, she touched him. He moaned when her hand closed around him, and he thrust into the circle of her fingers. "I cannot take much of this," he panted. "It has been a long time."

She gave him a naughty smile. "Just a taste then," she said, and scooted down the bed so she could take him in her mouth. She loved the velvety skin covering his cock, the way it slid up and down over the steel beneath. She wanted to feel him inside her mouth, wanted to please him the way he'd pleased her. Wanted him at her mercy, as she'd just been at his.

Enrico hissed when she touched him with her mouth, a sound somewhere between surprise and pleasure. He could hardly believe this was happening; he'd never had a woman do that before. He'd seen it done in videos, of course, but Toni had felt the act was sinful; she couldn't bring herself to do it, and he'd felt bad for pressing her. When Fiammetta had learned of his interest, she'd tried to use it as a bargaining chip, promising him such a pleasure after they were married. As if that would have changed his mind.

But now that he was experiencing this wonder, maybe it would have, if Fiammetta had given him a preview. No, that wasn't true. The wonderful part wasn't the act itself; it was the idea that Kate cared about his enjoyment as much as he cared about hers. Perhaps even, she enjoyed it as well. Was it possible?

Letting go of such thoughts, he surrendered himself to pure sensation, wanting to remember every second. The feel of Kate's tongue was heavenly. She swirled it around the head of his cock, then flattened it and stroked it up and down the vein that ran in a ridge along the underside of the shaft. When she hit the sensitive spot just under the head, he nearly came. She pulled back for a second, then he felt her warm breath above the tip. He looked down, and the sight of his cock disappearing between her lips was entirely too much. He wanted her to keep going, wanted to savor the experience, but it was proving overwhelming in his current state. He had to have her. *Now.* If he waited, it would be too late. He pulled out of her mouth, and she gave him a puzzled look. "Did I do something wrong?"

"Not at all. But I am not going to last much longer." He reached down and tugged her up, flipping her under him with a quick movement. Using his knee, he parted her thighs, then he grabbed her left leg and pushed it up in the air so he could get in deep on the first thrust. His weeping cock had just touched her entrance, he was just about to push in, when he remembered. "Do we need anything?" he asked, looking up at her, hoping the answer was no. He didn't want to stop.

She hesitated at the question, abruptly thrust back into the real world by his concern. *Was this really such a good idea?* Maybe they should stop.

She stared at him for a second. There was such warmth, such tenderness on his face, she had to close her eyes. Had Vince ever looked at her that way? In the beginning maybe. They'd been happy once, hadn't they? Tears gathered behind her eyelids. Enrico must have seen what was happening to her, because he lowered her leg and eased off her. She opened her eyes and seized his arm. "No."

"Are you sure?"

She looked away for a moment. Memories of Vince intruded again. Their first date. The first time he kissed her. When he proposed. Then the menace on his face when he hit her in the office, when he pulled out the switchblade.

Her time with Vince was over. Done. There was no going back.

"Kate?"

Turning her head, she met his gaze. "Make me forget," she whispered.

He stroked the side of her face, his fingers lingering over her cheekbone, then sliding down to her lips. "We should stop."

Her throat closed up. His voice was so soft, so gentle, yet tinged with wistfulness. His tone told her that he wanted her but that doing right by her was more important to him.

Vince had never put her first. Ever.

She pulled Enrico close, kissing him. "No. I'm not letting him take over my life."

Enrico cupped her cheeks in his hands, searching her face. "You are angry. Perhaps you are not thinking clearly."

She put her hands over his, making her voice fierce. "I'm thinking more clearly than I have in a long time. I rationalized too much of his behavior. I let him make the decisions. I let him control my life. I'm not letting him ruin this too."

He raised his brows. "You are certain?"

"As death and taxes."

He smiled, then his lips descended on hers. The kiss was demanding, and she let out a low sound, which he echoed with a groan. He pushed her down on the bed, his mouth on her breasts, one hand between her legs, his stiff cock pressing into her thigh. He suckled her breasts for a few moments, then kissed up her neck. He stopped, breathing in her ear. "Do we need a condom?" he asked, his voice thick with urgency.

Since she'd managed to take her birth control pill that morning, she should be okay, at least until she could get more. His cock nudged at her thigh and she reached down between them to stroke it. "It's okay. Don't worry."

"*Grazie a Dio.*" He parted her legs, then surged forward, burying his cock inside her. Gasping, she moved underneath him, widening her legs, forcing herself to relax so she could accommodate him. He felt so damn good inside her, stretching her, filling her up. She clenched her internal muscles experimentally, flexing herself around him, and he let out a loud groan. "That feels wonderful," he panted. "But you must stop or I will not last."

"As you wish." She smiled, pleased that she could torture him a bit too.

He rose up on his knees, pushing her legs up toward her chest, almost bending her double as he started thrusting in and out, long vigorous strokes. *Good God, he was in even deeper, if that was possible.* His cock stroked something delightful inside her, again and again.

He did his best to hold off, listening to her breathing, trying to gauge how close she was. *Dio,* she felt good. So tight, so wet. So hot around him, clutching his cock like a fist. With a groan, he forced himself to concentrate. He wanted her to come again before he did.

After a time, her breathing turned more ragged, and soon she was keening, the noise getting higher and higher. When her cries peaked, a warm gush bathed his cock, and that throaty sound, that extra wetness, was all it took to send him over the edge right after her. He continued thrusting until his cock stopped pulsing, until she caught her breath and her quivers subsided.

Collapsing next to her on the bed, he inhaled deeply, trying to slow down his breathing. He rolled over to look at her. She nestled up against him, still breathing fast. "That was amazing," she said.

He kissed her lightly. "So were you." He lay back, putting his arm around her, pulling her close. Would it be mad to ask her to stay with him once this mess was settled?

Of course it would be. She was still married. And he was all but promised to Delfina.

On top of that, Kate didn't know who he actually was. And if she did, how would she ever accept him? And then there were the Andrettis, circling them like jackals.

If he hadn't already lost his head, he was about to.

CHAPTER 9

The morning after. Kate looked over her shoulder at Enrico. He was still asleep, one arm slung around her waist, his body snug against hers.

Even though they'd made love twice that night, he was ready again. She wriggled back against him, his erection a delightful hardness. She heard the change in his breathing as he woke, and then she felt the change in how he was touching her. His grip on her waist tightened and he pulled her to him possessively.

"Good morning," he murmured, kissing the side of her neck, his voice hoarse from sleep.

She turned her head to look at him again and he stretched to kiss her lips, the contact gentle and brief, but it stirred something in her. She rolled over in his arms and he pulled her flush to his chest.

God she loved kissing him. His early morning stubble rasped against her skin, a light scratching, but it felt good. He took her mouth slowly, his tongue exploring; he wasn't rough and demanding the way some men were. The way Vince was. Enrico didn't try to have it all with his kisses. They were just a prelude to the main course, a delightful tease.

His fingers caressed the hair from her face. "You don't know how long I've wanted to touch you like this," he said, running his fingers through the strands.

Kate smiled and reached up, brushing his hair back off his forehead. His black hair was thick and wavy, soft beneath her fingers. She remembered wanting to touch it, and now she was. He looked at her solemnly. "You're awfully serious about something," she said.

He was about to open his mouth when she stopped him, her fingers pressing into his lips. "Before you say anything, I want you to know I'm not going to stay for long. I don't expect anything from you. As soon as I can,

I'm going back to the States, and I'm going to stay as far away from men as possible."

His brow furrowed. "Then what are we doing here?"

"Having a good time?"

"Kate, this, you, mean something to me. I don't sleep with many women."

"I like you, Enrico. A lot. But I'm not sure it goes further than that. I barely know you." *And you still love your wife.*

He took her face in his hands. "I'd like to get to know you, to see if we can have a future together."

She couldn't meet his eyes. If he knew why she'd slept with him, he'd be hurt. The band of his wedding ring pressed into her cheek, and she reached up, tapping it with her fingernail. The ting of her nail against the metal seemed loud. "How can you say that when you're still wearing this?" She searched his face, seeing him wince.

He stroked her cheeks with his thumbs, his brown eyes turbulent. "Maybe you're right," he finally said, his voice thick.

She leaned forward and kissed him lightly. "Let's think of this as a fling, okay?"

"Can we leave it open?" he asked. "Just entertain the possibility there could be more?"

She sighed and dropped her head back onto the pillow. "Let's enjoy each other, and when the time comes, let's not make it difficult."

"Just consider it. *Per favore?*"

His eyes were unguarded, naked, vulnerable. Saying no would be a slap in the face. "Okay. But I'm not making promises. Do not misunderstand me."

He smiled broadly, his face relaxing. "I understand."

The joy on his face made her bury her worries in a smile. The last thing she wanted to do was hurt him. Not after what he'd done for her. But she'd been clear. When she decided to go, he'd have to accept it.

∾∾

They enjoyed a leisurely breakfast in the dining room, trading sections of the newspaper like an old married couple. Kate looked over at Enrico, his dark eyes roving over the business section as he sipped a cappuccino. Vince didn't like to read the paper, but they'd shared plenty of breakfasts together, many of them like this one, quietly companionable ones where little needed to be said. Some little part of her missed Vince and thought it strange she was here with this other man, a man who was definitely not her husband. "Excuse me," she said to Enrico, folding up her napkin and setting it beside her plate. "There's something I need to do."

Her voice must have betrayed her somehow. He looked at her for a moment, concern in his eyes. "Is there a problem?"

"No. I just need to check my voice mail."

"Ah." His face tightened, and she left before he could say anything. It really was none of his business.

Kate retrieved the phone from her purse. She'd been dreading hearing from Vince, but maybe he'd calmed down and seen how he'd overreacted. Maybe he'd agree to let her leave and get a quick divorce. Of course, if he knew what she'd done last night.... But there was no video after all.

She turned on the phone as she walked out to the terrace behind the house, trying to enjoy the view of the garden, the rolling lawns that led down to the lake. *What a gorgeous day,* she thought, with the sky clear and blue, the sun glittering on the water, the craggy peaks of the Alps rising high around her. But her stomach filled with butterflies as she waited for the phone to come to life.

A beep told her she had voice mail. No surprise. She pressed the button to check it, and sure enough, Vince's voice greeted her. "You fucking cunt," he said, his voice low and menacing. "I'm gonna slit your throat."

She deleted the message, her fingers trembling as she pressed the buttons. There was another from him; she deleted it too as soon as she heard the anger in his voice.

So much for the quick divorce. What the hell was she going to do? She couldn't stay with Enrico forever. She shouldn't be staying with Enrico at all. Not if she knew what was good for her.

She had to get the hell out of Dodge. This minute.

Ⅎℴ

Kate found Enrico typing on the laptop in his study. He was so absorbed she had to cough to get his attention. He started to smile but stopped. "Kate, what is wrong?"

She fidgeted for a second, not sure she wanted to ask him for help. "Vince called."

"What did he say?"

Her heart started pounding. "He threatened to kill me."

Enrico's eyes sharpened. "What exactly did he say?"

Her throat closed up, strangling her next words. "He said he was going to slit my throat." Her knees turned to jelly and she collapsed onto the chair in front of his desk.

Enrico jumped up and came around to her. He sank down on his heels, taking her hands in both of his. "Everything will be all right."

She shook her head, grateful for the warmth of his touch, the strength of his fingers around hers. She tried to keep herself calm, but a tide of worry overwhelmed her. "What am I going to do? Where am I going to go? How am I going to live?" She pulled a hand from his grasp, covering her mouth as tears spilled down her cheeks. Her eyes swam and blurred; she could barely breathe.

"Try not to jump ahead." Enrico's voice was low and soothing, and he rubbed his palms up and down her thighs. "There is no sense worrying."

"How can I not worry?"

His hands stilled and he looked at her closely. "I know it is difficult. But when did worry ever solve anything?" He paused, then squeezed her knees. "You need to keep your head, Kate. Panic never helps. I am here; I will help you. You can count on me."

She took a deep breath, then expelled it slowly. "Thanks. I needed to hear that."

He leaned forward and kissed her, one of his fingers tracing the line of her jaw. "Anytime you need me, I will be there." His voice was almost a whisper.

Such promise in those words, enough to send nervous flutters through her. Could he really live up to them? There was one way to find out. "I need to get away from here. Somewhere Vince can't find me. I don't want my parents to worry, so I can't tell them about Vince or ask them for money—"

"Say no more. I do not want you to go, but if that is your wish, I will help you."

"I don't want to owe you."

"You will not." After a moment, he added, "Your rings should yield more than enough to cover your expenses for quite some time." He cocked his head and looked at her. "You do not like depending on anyone."

"After Vince, do you blame me?"

"Not all men are bad."

She stared at him without comment, then said, "How soon can I leave?"

Enrico straightened, then sat on the edge of his desk, crossing his arms. "Your husband has someone watching the house."

Fear spiked through her, leaving her chilled. "He does? How do you know?"

"There is a man watching the front drive. No doubt there is another watching the dock to make sure you do not leave by boat either."

"Oh God." Kate rubbed her arms. "He sounded so horrible on the phone. He scared me, but I was hoping it was just posturing."

Enrico frowned. "We would be fools to dismiss him."

She looked up into his eyes. "I can't stay here forever."

"It would be best to wait a few days. Let them get bored. Then we leave at night by boat, no motor, travel up the shore a ways, meet a car." He paused, then continued. "I am not sure it is wise to take my private jet, in case your husband has staked out the airstrip, but there is no paper trail if we do. At least, not one that cannot easily be faked."

She looked at him, considering. "You've done this before."

"Not exactly. But it is best to think about these matters beforehand."

"You really are afraid of them, aren't you?"

"Not afraid. Cautious."

"I don't believe you. Who wouldn't be afraid of the Mob?"

Suspicion ruled Kate's gaze. Of course. The only people who wouldn't be afraid of the Mafia were people *in* the Mafia. "Okay. I am a little afraid," Enrico said.

"Only a little?" she teased.

He smiled, just a slight curving of the mouth. "Maybe more than a little."

"Good."

His brows shot up. "Good?"

"Now I know you're not crazy. Or one of them."

He was careful to hold her eyes. "If I was one of them, would we be having this conversation? Would I not have left you to your fate?"

She studied him for a second. "Perhaps. Still, you're way too good at this."

He grinned. "I am a businessman. I have to lie to people all the time. It is the way of things."

She leaned back in the chair and crossed her arms, not breaking eye contact. "You should know now I hate lying. More than anything."

Enrico felt a tremor in his gut. Her words implied a possible future for them at the same time that they damned one. "I will never lie to you about anything of consequence." He regretted the words as soon as he said them, wished he could take them back, could tell her there and then who he was. But she'd bolt.

"You'd better mean that."

"Every word." *Dio, please forgive me.*

"We do it your way then." He started to turn away from her, when her voice, a brutal punch to the ribs, stopped him. "If I ever find out you're lying to me, I will never forgive you."

He kept his face still, twisted half away from hers. When he thought he could keep his dismay inside, he turned to her. "I know."

"Then we understand each other."

He hoped to hell she could understand—and forgive—him when she found out the truth. If she rejected him, he wasn't sure what he'd do.

Or how he'd keep her alive.

CHAPTER 10

"You were supposed to get rid of Lucchesi. Not lose your wife to him!" Carlo exploded, his eyes narrowed on Vincenzo.

"Do you think that was the plan, Zio?" Vincenzo hissed.

Carlo stared at Vincenzo, a bit impressed by his anger. *So he has the balls to challenge me.* He looked over at Dario, who was watching the two of them with seemingly nothing more than mild interest. *How I wish my own son had a set like Vincenzo's.*

Carlo smoothed his hands down the front of his shirt while he considered his words. He wouldn't apologize of course, though he did soften his tone. "What then *is* the plan?" He knew full well his nephew had none. But a good *capo* always rose to a challenge. This would be a fine test.

Vincenzo rubbed a hand through his hair and paced across the room, stopping by the windows and looking out at Carlo's view of the lake. If his nephew looked far off to the west, he could see Lucchesi's villa. Where his fascinating red-haired *strega* was even now, with her lover. Vincenzo leaned against the sill, staring out. After a while he turned to face Carlo. "I got some ideas."

"Are you perhaps hoping Lucchesi will let down his guard? That will not happen, now that you let him know we are watching."

Vincenzo couldn't conceal his shock. "What about the box you sent him in Rome?"

"Ah, but Lucchesi did not take that seriously. He thought I was teasing." He chuckled.

"He might've thought that if Massimo hadn't shown up at his hotel."

Carlo shrugged. He rather preferred Lucchesi to know. He'd suffer from the anticipation of the blow almost more than the blow itself. "How many men did he have with him yesterday?"

"Four."

"Hardly an army."

"But more than he's usually got, if your guys are right."

Carlo patted his jacket pockets, looking for a cigar. "Still, you got around them."

Vincenzo smiled. "That was easy. His guys seemed more for show than anything else."

"And they say his man Ruggero is so good. His father Livio, he was good. He saved Rinaldo enough times."

"You had a guy inside Lucchesi's organization, right?" Vincenzo asked.

An interesting change of subject. Carlo lit a cigar and nodded. "Unfortunately, he was stupid. Lucchesi caught on to him. But a little too late." He studied Vincenzo through the smoke curling up from his cigar. "So that is your new plan? Get someone on the inside?"

"What about his accountant? What's Trucco told you?"

"Nothing much. He seems to think I will kill Lucchesi over his *puttana* of a daughter."

"I thought you was pissed about that."

Carlo stared at Vincenzo, his face growing hot. "I *am*. The insult to Toni... I will not stand for it. But I do not care to avenge Trucco's daughter. It was his fault for letting the *troia* run around."

"Trucco's got to know more. He's got to know a way into Lucchesi's house."

Carlo puffed on the cigar. It was a decent place to start, one he should have thought of himself. "Talk to Massimo. He knows how to contact Trucco."

Vincenzo nodded, a big smile on his face. His nephew was up to something. "You are not to do anything without my approval. *Capisci?*"

"*Sì, sì,*" Vincenzo said.

Carlo bristled at the dismissive tone. Time for a reminder. He stepped closer to Vincenzo, lowered his voice to a snake's hiss. "You remember when Giorgio and Giotto caught that squirrel in the garden?" The dogs had ripped it to pieces in front of them.

"Yeah." Vincenzo looked away from him.

"Imagine what they will do to your balls if I let them."

His nephew blanched, and Carlo smiled. Things always ran best if everyone remembered who was *capo*.

After Vincenzo left, Dario turned to Carlo. "Are you truly going to marry Delfina to Lucchesi?"

"I want them to *think* I agree. I will die before marrying that family to ours again."

"A war with the Lucchesis will be costly. Just like the last one."

Carlo looked at him, surprised he had an opinion. "What of it?"

"It would be cheaper to agree to the marriage as long as they lower the rate on the wash. And perhaps we can gain some territory too, to save Vincenzo's face."

On the surface, Dario was right. But he fundamentally didn't comprehend what it took to be *capo*. Carlo's hands itched to grab his son and shake him until his head rattled. "Where are your balls? Think about what Lucchesi did to your sister. To *us*. He spat in our faces. On our name."

Dario shrugged. "I thought you didn't like to waste money."

"I do not consider this a waste of money." He shook his head. "Will you never understand what it takes to run things? *Cristo*, if you're in charge, everything will be a shambles in weeks. Will you let all the other *capi* shit on you?"

"If we force Lucchesi to yield, to sacrifice his principles, is that not a victory?"

Carlo took a long drag on his cigar, studying his son. *Why hadn't Toni been the boy?* "Only for a coward. It is time to crush the Lucchesis for good. I will not see Enrico Lucchesi parading around an Andretti woman as his *puttana*, flaunting his cock in our faces."

No, he would see him dead. The woman too. And Vincenzo would be the sharp knife between the ribs.

CHAPTER 11

Enrico summoned Ruggero to his office. He'd put off disciplining him over the lapse at the orphanage for too long. When he thought about how close Kate had come to death or grievous injury, a nauseating dread pierced him, as if he'd run out of bullets during a firefight.

When Ruggero walked in, Enrico took a deep breath. He needed a clear head for this discussion. "You know why you're here."

Ruggero nodded and started disarming himself, removing a 9mm from a shoulder holster, another gun and a switchblade from his jacket pockets, a small snub-nosed revolver from an ankle holster, and two wicked looking knives from sheaths on each wrist, placing them all on the desk. Enrico silently watched the process, saying nothing. Ruggero stepped a couple feet away when he was done, clasping his hands at his back, settling onto his heels to wait for Enrico's pronouncement.

Enrico studied his bodyguard as if he'd never seen him before. Ruggero stood in front of his desk, his posture straight but relaxed. A hard slab of man, not overly large or tall, but a solid mass of muscle with a face hewn from granite. A scar that slashed across his left cheekbone spoke of a knife he took for Enrico's father. That was when Ruggero was shadowing his own father, Livio.

He'd known Ruggero for over twenty years, and the guard had been his constant companion for the last fifteen. They weren't friends and they never would be—Enrico was Ruggero's boss, first and foremost. Ruggero was a little too bloodthirsty for Enrico's taste, but until now, he'd always seemed stable, trustworthy. And most of all, loyal. If he couldn't rely on Ruggero, who could he trust?

"I'd like an explanation for what happened yesterday."

Ruggero met Enrico's eyes. "There is none."

"That's all you have to say?"

"*Sì.*"

Had he expected anything different? The answer was classic Ruggero. But the events of the last twenty-four hours were not. The incident at the hotel in Rome. What Ruggero must have said to Dom about Kate. What might have happened to her due to Ruggero's laxity. Most of all, the possibility that Ruggero was a traitor. The anger he'd been holding back filled his voice with venom. "You have failed me. Twice now. And poisoned Dom against me. Explain yourself."

One of Ruggero's eyebrows twitched, the only sign that he was rattled. "I'm disappointed in myself, *signore*. But how could I have turned Don Domenico against you?"

"Somehow, he got the impression that Kate and I… that my bringing her here was about sex. What did you say to Dom about what happened?"

"Nothing. Antonio's the one who called him. I was too angry with myself to make the call." He frowned, looking down at the floor. It was more expression than Ruggero normally showed.

"How am I to trust you again when you nearly got her killed?"

"You yourself were in danger. That's the part *I* can't forget."

Enrico sighed. "You're not going to defend yourself, are you?"

Ruggero didn't move.

The man was holding something back. "Look at me." When Ruggero met his gaze, he said, "What happened? Truly."

Something flickered through the guard's eyes. If Enrico hadn't been watching him so closely, he would have missed it. But what was it? He waited for an answer and got none. "Ruggero, speak to me."

"I allowed myself to be distracted. It won't happen again."

"Why were you distracted?"

Ruggero shrugged. "Does it matter?"

"What are you hiding from me?" He tried to inject the full force of his authority into the question.

The guard took a breath. "I swear it's nothing of importance to you or the *cosca*. Only to me."

Enrico felt like he was struggling to open a clam and losing the battle. "Are you working for the Andrettis?"

Ruggero blinked and his head jerked back. He spoke with fervor. "Never."

"You swear it?"

"Upon my father's grave."

Enrico tapped his fingers on the desk in a slow cascade from the pinky to the index finger, waiting for more. Everything Ruggero said felt like the truth. He'd never known the man to lie. "Will this ever happen again?"

"No."

"Your punishment is one month's wages."

Ruggero looked at him. "I expected much more."

"What do you think is appropriate?"

"I expected to be dismissed." Which was a nice way to say he expected a bullet to the head.

"Truly?"

"You could have been killed."

"So, you would fall upon your own sword?"

Ruggero nodded. "It is only fair."

Enrico took a breath and let it out. If all his men were like Ruggero, he would be a lucky man indeed. "Everyone makes mistakes. Even you."

"I can't afford to."

"The day will come when you will fail. There is no stopping it."

The guard let out a puff of breath. "If I do my job well, you'll live to be an old man."

"There are few old men in the *malavita*, and you know it."

Ruggero shrugged.

"You can go." He watched Ruggero re-arm himself. "Do not let this happen again."

"*Sì, capo.*"

Ruggero left. What could possibly be preoccupying the man? He'd always been a rock. Once the immediate crisis was resolved, he'd ask again, and he'd accept nothing less than a full disclosure. For now though, he was satisfied. Ruggero would do his job, as he always had. As he always would.

Or they both would die.

෨෬

Kate passed much of the afternoon roaming the grounds of the estate. At first she'd wandered about the house, but after encountering pictures of Antonella in nearly every room, exploring the gardens had held more appeal. Enrico had insisted that Antonio accompany her outside.

She hadn't known what to say to the young guard at first, but his English was serviceable, and he proved to be an enjoyable companion. She almost might have thought she was on vacation, but whenever she caught sight of the machine gun hanging from a strap across his back, reality confronted her.

They were strolling through the hedge maze when she decided to ask him about her host. "How long have you worked for Enrico?"

"Not long. A few months more than a... year, yes?"

"Yes, that's the right word." She looked at the sky for a moment. "Is he a good man?"

"Signor Lucchesi? No. He is not a good man." She looked at him in shock, and he smiled slyly. "Signor Lucchesi is a *great* man. My life would be nothing without him."

"Why do you say that?"

"My parents, they died when I have ten years. There was no one who could take me. After much struggle… I went to the Lucchesi Home." His voice grew hoarse. "Signor Lucchesi, he is like my own father."

"Is that why you work for him now?"

Antonio nodded vigorously. "*Signore* wants me to attend university, but I want to repay him for all he has done for me."

They walked out of the maze and into the rose garden, the heavy scent of flowers overwhelming everything else as the sun beat down around them. Kate stopped and sniffed a particularly large, lush rose, admiring the perfection of its deep pink petals. "So lovely, *signora*," Antonio said.

"Yes, these roses are gorgeous."

"I mean you, *signora*." She looked up at Antonio, saw the glint in his eye.

"Antonio!" She wagged a finger at him playfully. "You are too young for me."

He drew himself up and squared his shoulders. "I have twenty-one years."

"And I have twenty-nine."

"So?"

She stopped walking and gazed at him steadily. Antonio had blond hair, blue eyes, a face sculpted by Michelangelo, and the body to match. She supposed he was used to women falling all over him. "Signor Lucchesi would not like it."

He eyed her up and down. "*Bellisima*. Such a woman. It is hard to say no."

"You'd better say no. Because I am. Understand?" The last thing she wanted to do was stir up trouble between Enrico and Antonio. Especially since she'd be gone soon.

He let out a heavy sigh and placed a hand on his chest, exaggerating his heartbreak for her benefit. Then he smiled. "*Signore* makes a good choice in his woman."

Kate let that comment pass. She wasn't Enrico's woman, but why rub it in? She bit her lip, wondering if she should ask. "What was Signora Lucchesi like?"

A shadow passed over Antonio's young face, momentarily dimming his sunny features. "She is *bella, molta bella*. In here," he said, tapping his chest.

Kate's throat constricted. How could she possibly compete with the memory of a dead woman who had a beautiful heart?

But what did it matter? She wasn't going to stay. She wasn't ever going to be anything to Enrico other than a fling. End of story. Even though he'd said he wanted more, even though he'd practically begged her….

He wasn't free. Not really. Not yet. Maybe not ever. Could she risk her heart on a man who might not be able to love her?

She looked at the house and gave a start when she saw Enrico walking toward them. His lips curved up when he saw that she'd noticed him, and she couldn't help the grin that crossed her face in response. *Stop daydreaming.*

You're only here for a couple more days. Enjoy it. Enjoy him. Then forget everything.

He strolled up to her and slipped an arm across her shoulders, lightly kissing her cheek. "Has Antonio bored you yet?"

"Not at all."

Enrico raised an eyebrow. "Ah, then he has been flirting with you."

Her smile widened. "A bit."

Enrico glared at Antonio, but his smile undercut it. He said something in Italian she couldn't make sense of, but she was sure it amounted to a friendly "back off."

"He's also told me a bit about you. And Antonella." Her voice softened as she mentioned his wife's name.

He stiffened, then relaxed. "All good, I hope."

"According to Antonio, the two of you are virtual saints."

Enrico smiled. "Tonio remembers who pays his bills, I see."

The young guard laughed and bowed his head. "I am not stupid, *signore.*"

"You never were. Now leave us, please."

Antonio left with a nod to Kate, his blue eyes lingering on her for a second too long. What else might he have said if they'd had more time together?

"So what tales has he told you?"

"Antonio thinks the world of you. And he said Antonella had a beautiful heart."

Enrico's eyes misted and he looked away. He nodded and cleared his throat. "She did."

"I'm glad you had such a good marriage. It's rare to find that kind of love."

"I am glad too. Even though it aches to be without her."

She reached over and squeezed his hand. "I'm sorry."

"I am not. I was the luckiest man alive. How often does that happen?"

"Not often enough." She paused. "Probably not twice in a lifetime."

He looked at her. "That is where you are wrong."

"Am I?"

His eyes locked on hers. "I think so, yes." He flipped her hand over, his fingers feathering over her palm. He leaned forward and brushed his lips against hers. "Come to bed with me, Kate. Let me show you," he murmured against her cheek, his breath tickling her skin.

She hesitated. She shouldn't do this. "Well, it will make the time pass faster."

"You are concerned only with passing the time?" he asked mildly.

She gave him a naughty smile. "I suppose not."

ℰℭ

When she woke later that afternoon and thought back to what had happened between her and Enrico, Kate hardly remembered the trip into the house, up the staircase, into his room. But she did remember the feel of her palm against his, his large fingers clasped over hers, his pulse and hers throbbing in time.

The next thing she remembered was his eyes, the way they burned into hers, the way they devoured the sight of her breasts, her sex, as he undressed her. She had never felt so wanted, so desired.

And then she remembered his lips, his mouth taking hers, his tongue exploring, insistent, finally demanding. His mouth trailing down her neck, her skin tingling wherever his lips descended. The fire those kisses stoked between her legs.

His hands, stroking her shoulders, twining in her hair, cradling her waist, crushing her to him. His fingers plucking her nipples into points, his mouth taking over then, making her arch and moan, finally almost scream when he grazed her aching peaks with his teeth, when he bit down just this side of too hard.

Then his knee urging her legs apart, his mouth on her sex, his lips, his tongue, his fingers on her, in her, slipping in her wetness, making her scream and pant, and call his name, and beg him to take her, to fuck her.

And finally she remembered him sinking into her, making her open wide, his hips slapping against hers, harder and faster and deeper, until she came again.

But the thing she remembered most was the tender look in his eyes when he withdrew from her, when he rolled over and pulled her on top of him, when he brushed the hair out of her eyes and kissed her. When he said, "I believe it can happen again."

She almost believed it too.

₭)Cᴙ

Sunlight slanted golden and low across the bedroom as Kate slipped out of bed, not wanting to wake Enrico. Wincing at the soreness in her thighs and lower back, she smiled at the memory, almost a fever dream, of their sex. She corrected herself: their lovemaking. It was unlike anything she'd ever experienced before. She'd never lost herself entirely to sensation, to the moment. To the man. To the way he made her feel, inside and out. She felt cared for, wanted, protected, needed. Maybe even... loved. He'd implied it, there at the end. *I believe it can happen again.*

She stumbled into the shower, grateful for the warmth as the water ran over her hair, her arms, her back. This was all happening so fast. Too fast. It had to stop. *She* had to stop. But her mind kept racing down the one track she didn't want it to pursue.

Soaping up, she allowed herself to daydream for a moment. *If* she wanted to be with Enrico, how could that happen? Vince wasn't about to give her a divorce. The only way he intended to let her go was in a coffin.

Enrico opened the door to the shower and stepped inside. "Mmm," he murmured, putting his arms around her waist and pulling her close. His cock rubbed against her buttocks. He was hard again.

"Already?" Her voice came out sharp. Couldn't he leave her alone for one minute?

He stopped rubbing against her. "What's wrong?"

"Everything." She sighed. "We can't possibly be together." How raw her voice sounded. How could she care so much already?

"Kate, we will get through this." As he spoke, his lips moved against her neck. "We will. I promise you."

She turned around in his arms. "What about Vince? What about Carlo? How the hell can this *possibly* work?"

He regarded her somberly, his face beaded with water, his thick lashes heavy with it. "Let me worry about the Andrettis."

She pressed her hands flat against his broad chest. He wasn't seeing reality. "If you say so."

He hugged her tighter. "Trust me. If I did not think there was hope for us, I would not try for it." His voice went soft. "I do not want to get hurt either."

Her heart contracted. How did he know that was troubling her when she hadn't even known it? He stared at her, his eyes locked on hers, but he remained silent.

She took a deep breath. "Just remember I'm not making any promises." It was the best she could do.

"Good enough." He lowered his mouth to hers. His hips twitched, and she was again aware of his hard cock pressing into her belly. She slid her arms around his neck. Maybe they couldn't have forever, but they might as well have right now.

They were drying off from a second shower when she noticed the tattoo on his right bicep again. She'd been so caught up before, she hadn't taken more than a glance. It was all black, a small circle of roses with a design inside. She held his arm still to peer at the tattoo, conscious of his eyes locked on her face. The design turned out to be words done in a fancy swirling script. "*Quattro in tre*," she said aloud. "Four in three. What does it mean?"

"I do not want to talk about it."

"Why?"

His face darkened. "It has to do with the accident."

"When your mother and brothers were killed?" He nodded. "I still don't understand the reference."

"May we not talk about this now?"

His face was turned half away from hers, but his sorrow was still apparent. "All right," she whispered. "I'm sorry." Only a bitch would continue to press. And besides, the more she knew about him, the harder it would be to leave.

CHAPTER 12

Vince met with Franco Trucco in the public gardens of the Villa Carlotta. They spoke little until they turned off on a side path that led to a viewpoint for the lake. It was a good meeting place; they were far enough away from the crowds to speak freely, and the gravel on the path would warn them if someone approached.

Vince sized up Trucco. He was in his early sixties like Carlo, but Trucco seemed sick, as if he had a fever; his gray hair looked greasy and dark circles ringed his eyes. "What can you give me on Lucchesi?" Vince asked.

"Is there a death Carlo would like to distance himself from? I can testify I heard Enrico planning it." Trucco's words tumbled out, excited, unsteady.

"Carlo already tried to use one of Lucchesi's guys to tie him to the Judge Dinelli hit. But Grantini disappeared. We got to assume Lucchesi found him out. Grantini was the key. Without his testimony, we got nothing." He looked hard at Trucco. "You think you're smart enough not to end up like Grantini?"

Trucco swallowed. "I can prove tax evasion. That's why Dinelli was after Enrico and Carlo. And I could say I heard Enrico plan Dinelli's murder."

"Prison time ain't enough. Carlo wants him dead." Vince gazed across the lake, his hands crossed behind his back. "We want to know where we can get to him, either security-wise or family-wise."

"I might be able to locate Rinaldo."

Vince smiled. Now he was getting somewhere. "That's a start. Anything else?"

The accountant thought for a moment. "There is something I have always been curious about."

"What?"

Trucco shook his head. "I am not sure yet what it is. But he has gone to great pains to keep it concealed."

Vince didn't hide his interest. "Find out what it is, and bring it to us."

∾∾

After his meeting with Trucco, Vince hadn't expected to be able to move on Lucchesi for a while, even though he was dying to whack the guy. *But sometimes everything you needed just hopped in your lap and made itself at home.* He walked away from his second clandestine meeting of the day, a big grin on his face. He never in a million years would've expected to hear from someone else in Lucchesi's organization, especially not a guy so close to Lucchesi. A guy who knew everything necessary for a single man to take Lucchesi out.

Vince didn't doubt the truth of what he'd heard, once the man explained his reasons, once he made clear what kind of future he had in mind for himself. Yeah, it was a wrinkle to his plans, but no biggie. There'd be more than enough to go around after Lucchesi was on ice.

Now that he had what he needed, Vince was going to be a hero after all. He couldn't wait to see the look on Carlo's face when he pulled it off. Yeah, the old man would be pissed for a while. But he'd be happy in the end. And they'd both have their revenge.

∾∾

Vince circled the perimeter of the Lucchesi estate, keeping to the shadows even though it was the middle of the night. The moon was three-quarters full, the sky clear. If he wasn't fucking careful, he'd be spotted.

No one had ever broken into Lucchesi's home. The damn place was like a fortress—security alarms, armed guards, even dogs at night. Lucchesi had hired an expert to design a custom alarm system and kept him on the payroll to keep the man's mouth shut. If it had been an off-the-rack system, it could have been hacked. But no one had the specs for it. Which made breaking into the house undetected almost impossible.

But not if you knew the alarm codes. Not if you knew the guards' schedules. Not if you knew about the gate hidden in the hedges along the northern edge of the estate.

If you had all that, the job was a candy snatch from a baby. Except he intended to do far worse. Before the night was through, the bitch and that scum Lucchesi would be dead. And if all went as planned, he would take over a good part of the Lucchesi family's holdings in the aftermath. Vince grinned. He was going to enjoy this.

After a little fumbling, he found the gate in the hedge. He'd just entered the code and slipped through, twigs tearing at his clothes and hair, when he heard the low, rumbling growl of a Rottweiler padding toward him on his left. He'd come prepared. Reaching in his pocket, he withdrew the paper-wrapped lump of ground meat he'd laced with sedatives and tossed it to the dog. The Rottweiler stopped and sniffed the meat, eying him cautiously before bolting the treat. Vince didn't move, his heart doing a fucking workout routine in his chest. He'd never admitted it to anyone, especially not Carlo, but big dogs

89

scared the fuck out of him. He took a few breaths to calm himself as he watched the dog, careful not to stare at it too directly in case he pissed the fucker off.

After a few moments, the dog blinked heavily and whined, shaking its head, drool running from its powerful jowls. Vince tried to step past the dog, but it snapped at him, the whine turning back into a growl, and his whole body went subzero. *Don't fuck it up, asshole.* He looked around, wondering where the other one was. There were supposed to be two.

Peering into the darkness, he kept the big slobbering fuck in his peripheral vision. It wiped its face against the grass, then it finally flopped down with a heavy sigh.

Vince walked past the animal. He hadn't gotten far when he heard panting and paws rapidly striking the earth. It took everything he had not to jackrabbit. He already had the lump of meat in his hand. He chucked it at the noise, hoping to distract the dog. It wasn't long until he heard the clap of its jaws, the quick work it was making of the meat.

Fucking goddamn dogs. All they did was shed. And stink. And shit. He hoped the stupid fucks died from the sedatives. It was what they deserved. They hadn't even barked. And they'd gobbled down food from a stranger. So fucking dumb.

The second dog went down as quickly as the first, and Vince stepped around it, slinking through the shadows along the hedge, making his way toward the house.

He paused about a hundred feet from the back terrace and checked his watch. Two-fifteen. The guards would be less alert by now. Lucchesi and the whore would be fast asleep.

He settled against a tree to wait. A guard would pass by in a few minutes, then he could sneak up and punch the code into the panel next to the French doors.

He'd been so stupid about Kate. He'd married her too soon, had never bothered to look past her nice-girl face to make sure he knew the woman under it. His next wife would be a simple girl, probably a distant cousin of his. Someone beautiful and sweet, someone who knew about the family business. Someone who would only want to give him kids, who wouldn't need a career, who wouldn't ask questions. Or look at other guys. Yeah, his next wife would be *his*. And she wouldn't make a fool of him.

A guard walked by on schedule, light gleaming dully on the mini Uzi he carried. Vince waited until the guard stepped around the corner, then he sprinted across the open stretch of lawn up to the house. He flipped open the alarm panel, keyed in the code to disarm it, then picked the lock on the doors. Fucking child's play. He was inside in a few moments. Lucchesi was a lazy fucker. Vince shook his head, smiling. Everyone said Lucchesi was smart. What the fuck did they know?

He eased the door shut behind him, then crossed the foyer and started climbing the staircase on the left. Lucchesi's room was at the end of the north wing. He'd probably find the whore there as well. His gut twisted. *Katie.*

Maybe she wasn't a fucking slut. Maybe he'd gotten it wrong. Maybe there was hope.

His heart revved again as he crept up the stairs, quiet as a cat after a mouse.

Even if she wasn't with him, Lucchesi was going to suffer for taking his woman. And she'd learn her lesson too.

This was going to be fun. For him, anyway.

CHAPTER 13

Enrico didn't know what awakened him, but his hand was already halfway to the Glock in his nightstand drawer when he felt a sharp blow to his temple. He tried to shout a warning to Kate but managed only a stuttering gasp before everything went black.

When he came to, he was lying on his side. Someone had bound him hand and foot. The lights were on, and Vincenzo Andretti was straddling Kate's naked body on the floor.

Enrico's heart was a machine gun on full automatic. Andretti had a Beretta in his hand, and he was stroking the weapon down her body. He'd tied her hands together over her head. Kate whimpered low in her throat, her eyes glued to the gun, as Andretti spoke to her. "I hoped it wasn't true, but here you are, naked. You *fucking* whore. You jumped from my bed to his just like that."

"You tried to kill me!"

"I was just gonna rough you up a bit, keep you in line. But now that I seen this, I *am* gonna kill you."

Rage whipped through Enrico's body; his head buzzed, and his face grew hot. When he spoke, his voice sounded guttural, foreign to his ears. "Get the fuck off her. Now."

Andretti looked up at him, his lips twisted into an evil grin. "Welcome to the party."

"Get off her!" He wanted to strangle Andretti, but he could barely move his arms.

Andretti pointed the gun at him. "Lay back and watch with your mouth shut. I already told her I'd kill you if she screamed for help. The same applies to you, only I'll stick this gun up her cunt when I pull the trigger."

Enrico's stomach cramped. He should have had a panic button added to his room when Strasser suggested it. "How did you get in here?" He pitched his voice low so Andretti wouldn't try anything.

Andretti laughed. "There's a snake in your family."

Dom was right; there was a traitor. "Who?"

"Don't matter since you'll be dead soon."

Enrico struggled against the ropes. "*Vaffanculo!*"

Andretti raised his brows and shook his head. "Fuck you? No way. But the whore here"—he caressed Kate's cheek with the gun—"I'll certainly fuck her. You just get to watch."

Kate struggled against Andretti. "Vince, stop it. You're not a rapist. This isn't *you.*"

"Ain't it?" he asked. "I changed, you said it. And you made me this way."

"You're blaming *me?*"

"You act like a whore, you're gonna get treated like one."

As Andretti's hand moved toward Kate's breast, Enrico detected some give to the ropes binding his wrists. It wasn't much, but maybe it was enough. He went to work. The look on Andretti's face said he'd stop playing any minute. And then he and Kate would be dead.

℘〇℞

Vince squeezed Kate's breast hard, making her cry out in pain. He smiled, his eyes alight with cruelty. Adrenaline arced up her spine, and she couldn't control her breathing. It was the same look he'd had at the office, the day he'd attacked her. He'd kill her, then he'd kill Enrico. And this time Enrico couldn't help. She'd tried to leave some slack when Vince made her tie him up. Vince hadn't noticed anything when he double-checked her work; maybe she'd still tied Enrico too tightly to make a difference.

Vince squeezed her breast a second time, his fingers clawing into her, and she gasped again. "You like that?"

"I hate you."

"We got to work on your attitude." He lowered his mouth to her breast and bit down hard. The pain sliced deep; she couldn't stop the shriek that tore out of her. Vince clamped his hand over her mouth. When he raised his head, there was blood on his lips. Stomach acid raced up into her throat, and she had to suck in air through her nose to keep from vomiting. *Oh God, oh God, oh God. What am I going to do?*

His fist slammed into her head just above her ear. "Shut up!" He pointed his gun—the Beretta Storm, his favorite—in Enrico's direction. "Need a reminder?" She shook her head, and he removed his hand from her mouth. Licking the blood off his lips, he leaned closer. "Enjoying yourself?" When she said nothing, he laughed. "That's better, bitch." He raised himself up and pried her legs apart.

Hell no. Kate bucked wildly and clasped her tied hands together, bringing them down in a clenched fist on Vince's cheek. His head snapped up, and he struck her twice across the face, hard blows that made her head swim. "Knock it off or Lucchesi bites it."

Sobbing, Kate collapsed onto the rug. She couldn't risk him shooting Enrico. Vince set the gun down and yanked her legs farther apart, then unbuckled his belt. She closed her eyes, not wanting to see what was happening. When his cock touched her entrance, her whole body shuddered in rebellion. *This is not going to happen.* Raking her nails across Vince's face, she aimed for his eyes, her bitten breast throbbing. He needed to hurt.

"Christ!" Vince pressed a hand against the wound below his left eye and reared back. He raised his other hand to slap her, and Kate saw her death on his face. As soon as he was finished with her, the fatal blow would come. She had to stop him. But how?

A sound behind her attracted Vince's attention, and she tilted her head to look over her shoulder. Enrico had freed his hands and had his gun pointed at Vince. *Thank God.* Vince grabbed the Beretta from where he'd placed it beside her and sat back, yanking her up against him, using her body as a shield. *Fucking coward.* Kate kept her eyes on Enrico. He swung his bound legs over the edge of the bed and took aim again.

Vince raised his arm, pointing his gun at Enrico. *No!* Kate threw herself hard to the left, knocking Vince off-balance and pulling him forward. Both men fired at the same time, and she heard a heavy thud behind her. *Enrico!* "Kate!" Enrico yelled, his voice thick with worry.

"I'm okay!" Vince fell on top of her, blood pouring from his right shoulder. Pushing and twisting, Kate scrabbled out from under Vince and elbowed him hard in the chest, knocking the wind out of him. Though her tied hands were clumsy, she snatched the Beretta from his weakening hold. Scrambling to her feet, she pointed the gun down at him and flexed both hands around the Storm, trying to hold it steady. "Fuck you, Vince." Her voice trembled as much as her hands.

Vince leered up at her. "Aww Katie, you still want to be my pretty little whore?"

Her finger quivered on the trigger guard, and she adjusted her grip again, taking a shaky breath. Could she really pull the trigger? Or should she let the police deal with him? "Call me a whore all you want, but you're a gangster, Vince. You're scum."

He laughed, but it ended in a wince. "And Lucchesi ain't? He's one of the big bosses. Why you think my uncle hates him so much?"

"What?" Kate looked behind her at Enrico, who was untying his feet. When Vince's fingers wrapped around her ankle, her stomach lurched like a car on black ice. She'd done exactly what he wanted.

Vince jerked her leg out from under her. She fell to the other knee. "No!" she screamed and squeezed the trigger, firing two rounds into the base of

Vince's throat just as Ruggero burst through the door, gun drawn.

Kate swung around and aimed the Beretta square at Enrico, ignoring Ruggero, even though his gun was no doubt trained on her.

Enrico cried out for Ruggero to stop. Why was he so sure she wouldn't shoot him? Kate glanced at Ruggero. His gun was indeed pointed at her, but she didn't lower the Storm. Enrico was going to tell her the truth; a gun in the face would ensure it. "What was Vince talking about? Who *are* you?"

He left his Glock on the floor, then stood up. Skirting her and Vince, he crossed the room until he was between Ruggero and her, his eyes holding hers. When Ruggero moved to get an unobstructed sightline on her, Enrico turned to look at him, his voice angry. "Leave us."

"I can't. She has a gun on you."

Enrico stepped closer to her, blocking Ruggero's sightline again, but he was careful to keep his hands half-raised. "Kate, Vincenzo would say anything to drive a wedge between us."

Had Vince lied? He'd certainly meant to trick her. And he'd hated her. She looked down at his bleeding body and burst into sobs. Her hands started to shake, almost completely out of her control, and she put up the Beretta, letting it rest against her shoulder. Enrico slowly closed the distance between them.

She was sobbing full out now, scaring herself. She let Enrico take the Storm from her hands. He handed it to Ruggero as he folded her in his arms. The sudden heat of his body told her how cold she was. And naked. In front of Ruggero. She shivered. "What have I done? Oh God." Her voice sounded broken to her ears.

"Shh. It is all over, Kate. It is all over." Enrico cradled her close, stroking her hair. He looked at Ruggero over his shoulder. "Go. Now. Call the *polizia*."

The gun still kicked in her hands, Vince's blood still spattered her face, her arms, her chest. Her mind was still consumed by the coldness and determination that had filled her with one purpose—stopping Vince, one way or another.

She looked at his body again, the blood so red, so thick, a dark pool spreading across the carpet. Had she really done it? It seemed a dream, surreal, unreal. She never imagined she was capable of killing. But the way Vince had stared at her without seeing her—he wouldn't have stopped until she was dead. Until Enrico was dead.

She nestled closer to Enrico, then brought her shaking hands up to wipe her eyes. She jerked back when she saw the blood speckling her hands. Vince's blood.

Kate stared at the droplets for a few moments. Her tears dried up. She'd made the only logical choice. It was him or them. This was all Vince's doing, he'd set it all in motion. She was merely the instrument of his destiny.

"Are you okay?" Enrico pulled a blanket off the bed and wrapped it around her. Then he worked on untying her hands.

"No. But I think I'm a little better." She watched him work at the knots.

"This is all my fault, I should have taken extra precautions—"

"The one at fault is Vince." He finished untying her and she rubbed at her wrists, glad to be free.

"I feel responsible." He faltered, his voice thick. "I swore I would protect you."

Something inside her hardened. "Get over it." Enrico looked startled. She pushed away from him. "You can't protect me. No one can. I need to face that." She took a deep breath. "I'm still a dead woman. Now it's Carlo who'll want my head."

"He will need to take mine first." His eyes were dark with anger.

Kate gestured around them. "How are you going to protect me? What good are all the guards? Someone close to you wants you dead. Who the hell can we trust?"

That was the question, wasn't it? Enrico shook his head. "I do not know. But I will find out who is responsible."

"We're both *dead*, Enrico. We just don't know it yet." He reached for her shoulder and she pushed him away.

He tried again, not allowing her to shake him off. "We *will* survive this." He waited a beat, then said, "Vincenzo is dead. Just one more to deal with, yes?"

She shook her head. "Two. Carlo and whoever told Vince how to get in here."

He had a hard decision to make. He needed someone he could trust, someone in addition to Kate. But who?

Ruggero knocked on the door. "The *polizia* are on the way," he shouted.

Kate jumped at the knock. "I need a shower."

"Wait. The police will want evidence...." He trailed off. Had she been raped? An ache gripped his throat. "From your body," he finally said.

She hugged herself and tears filled her eyes. "I *need* a shower."

His chest tightened. There was no choice. "You must not. You killed him. They will need physical proof of what happened. That *he* did it. He was your husband, but you are here in my home, in my bed. His actions will need to justify yours."

"I want my clothes then." Her voice vibrated with anger.

He gathered them up and offered them to her before he dressed himself. He didn't know what to say.

The sing-song sirens of approaching emergency vehicles intruded on the silence between them. Within minutes, medics, police officers, and forensic investigators filled the bedroom. The medics checked Vince for vitals and pronounced him dead. Forensic techs took over, taking pictures and samples.

A police officer approached them, asked their names, took an initial statement from Enrico, then told them to wait.

₭₨ℂℓ

Kate watched the activity around them in a daze, Enrico's arms wrapped around her, his chest pressed against her back. As she looked at Vince's lifeless body, her anger abruptly gave way to sorrow. She placed her hands on Enrico's forearms.

An inspector in the black and red uniform of the *carabinieri* approached them. "Maresciallo Capo Silvio Fuente," he introduced himself. At Kate's look of confusion, he clarified his rank for her in lightly accented English. "Chief Marshal. May we talk elsewhere?" he asked Enrico, though it was clear from his voice that it wasn't a question.

They went downstairs to the study. Kate and Enrico sat side by side on the sofa and Fuente took one of the chairs, crossing his ankle over his knee. He removed his hat and perched it on his knee.

Enrico picked up the phone and called Maddalena. He asked for espresso for all of them.

Fuente looked at Enrico closely. "So, at last we meet, *signore*."

Something passed between Fuente and Enrico, and Kate picked up on it. "Why do you say that?" she asked.

Fuente raised an eyebrow at Enrico. "She doesn't know?"

"Know what?" Kate asked.

Enrico reached over and squeezed her hand. "Nothing." He turned to Fuente. "May we have a word in private?"

Fuente gave him a small, tight smile. "Of course."

They walked outside to the rear terrace. What did Enrico want to say to this man that he wouldn't say in front of her?

Enrico escorted Fuente out to the moonlit garden. He glanced at Kate through the window. One wrong word from Fuente in front of her.... He turned to the inspector. "You obviously know who I am reputed to be."

"Reputed? It is a fact."

Enrico smiled, the same tight smile Fuente had given him earlier. "But never proven in a court of law."

"The law has limits; the truth does not."

Enrico almost liked the man; he didn't mince words. "The *signora* does not know who I am alleged to be. For her own safety, I wish to keep it that way."

Fuente stroked his dark moustache with one finger. "You are friends with Maggiore Alfonso, yes?"

Enrico wanted to smile, but he held it in. Major Alfonso was the station chief in Milan. "I am. Very good friends."

"I have four children. They all wish to attend private universities, but I have only a *carabiniere*'s third-rank pay. It's hard to get a promotion to fourth rank."

"Practically impossible, as far as I know."

"*Sì.* It's almost unheard of for an inspector to be promoted to a commissioned officer's rank."

Enrico held in a smirk. "However, a man like you—a thorough, honest man—should be noticed and rewarded. I'll speak to Maggiore Alfonso."

Fuente inclined his head. "I am in your debt."

"And I am in yours." Enrico clapped the man on the back. "Do we have an understanding?"

Fuente smiled. "We do."

When they returned, Kate's eyes darted between them, questions on her face.

"I apologize for the interruption," Fuente said to her.

"It's nothing." She looked hard at Enrico. "What was that about?"

"My family was involved in a rather notorious case years ago."

"What happened?"

Time for the truth. Kate couldn't be frightened any more than she already was. "Carlo Andretti's men assassinated my mother and my two brothers."

She stared at him in shock. "You told me they died in an accident."

"I didn't want to alarm you. Carlo had intended to kill us all. But my father and I were both stricken with the flu and stayed home that day."

There was silence for a moment while she absorbed the information. Then Fuente spoke. "What Signor Lucchesi has failed to mention is that the alleged assassins were all found dead some years later."

Fuck. Enrico glared at Fuente. *What kind of game is he playing?* "I fail to see what that has to do with me."

"Their deaths came shortly after your return from England. Right before you married Andretti's daughter, I believe."

"Yes. A few days before. But again, I fail to see the connection."

"You're right," Fuente said. "Nothing was ever proven."

"I was never even questioned. And I resent being accused now."

"Am I accusing you?" Fuente asked, his voice mild.

Enrico took a deep breath. He'd taken the bait. *Stupido.*

"I was merely informing your..."—Fuente waved his hand at Kate—"houseguest of my interest in you."

"Are you finished?" Enrico kept his voice neutral. "We both are exhausted." To make his point, he took a sip of the steaming espresso Maddalena had brought in.

"My apologies." Fuente turned to Kate. "Signora Andretti, please tell me what happened here."

Kate recounted what had occurred and why. Enrico added details when she faltered or forgot them. Fuente nodded, asked questions, and took notes. "We'll need physical evidence from both of you," he said as he closed his notebook.

"We know. We haven't even washed our hands," Enrico said.

Fuente's eyes narrowed. "Nothing to hide, yes?"

"I know how important it is to preserve evidence."

"Of course you do, Signor Lucchesi. Of course you do."

"Anyone who watches television knows that much." His voice had more snap to it than he'd intended.

Fuente chuckled. "Touché, Signor Lucchesi."

Kate looked sidelong at Enrico. Had he murdered the men who'd assassinated his family? She recoiled a bit, but part of her understood. The Old Testament ruled here: an eye for an eye. If Vince had killed her parents... yes, she'd have wanted him dead. But wanting it was one thing, doing it was another. She knew that now, all too well. Even so, the part of her that was appalled, horrified, by what she'd done was already drawing its last breath.

This world certainly wasn't the one she'd grown up in. The rules were different; here the game had higher stakes than she could have ever imagined. And this was the only life Enrico had ever known. What would that do to a person? What part of him would wither and die, what part would blossom?

And yet—this man hadn't let all his love and compassion go. She'd seen it in the way he treated the children at the orphanage, in the obvious affection he felt for Antonio, and in how he was with her, loving and gentle.

Enrico was different from her, yes. More ruthless, more practical. Perhaps even more realistic, though she'd accused him of not being so. But he wasn't so alien that she couldn't accept him.

Unless he was who Vince said he was.

She couldn't love a man who killed for gain. That was a line she wouldn't cross.

"Signora Andretti." Fuente interrupted her thoughts. He motioned to a female officer standing in the doorway. "Brigadiere Clemente will take you to the hospital for examination."

"I'd like Enrico to go with me."

"Of course. We'll need to take evidence from him as well."

She got to her feet, grateful for Enrico's hand at her elbow, for the solidity of his presence beside her. She hated needing him like this, hated feeling weak. But she was so tired.

They walked out to a waiting police car. Enrico helped her inside. "I need a word with Fuente before we leave," he said, then he closed the door.

Turning to Fuente, Enrico laid a hand on the man's shoulder and steered him a few steps away from everyone else. "You are a clever man, *signore*," Enrico said.

Fuente grinned. "If I were a *truly* clever man, I would have recorded our conversation."

"What do you want?"

The smile left his face. "What I asked for. And no more trouble in the district. This is my warning to you."

Enrico stared at the man. "Understood. But hear me: you would much rather have me as a friend."

"As would you." Fuente placed his hat on his head and tipped the brim to Enrico. "This could be self-defense, it could be murder. You were lovers; he was her husband. It could go either way. Don't forget that." He smiled at Enrico. "*Buona sera*, Signor Lucchesi." He turned and walked away.

Enrico watched him for a moment, then he got in the car. He didn't want to alarm Kate, but Fuente was trouble. He could feel it in his bones.

CHAPTER 14

At the hospital, Kate refused to be separated from Enrico, insisting they be examined in the same room. Enrico tolerated the doctor's exam—the x-ray of his head, the photographing and cataloguing of his injuries—without protest. But his stomach churned during Kate's entire exam. Though she barely reacted when the doctor photographed the marks on her face and when he took samples from under her fingernails, she flinched when he asked if he could inspect the rest of her body. With tears in her eyes, she nodded, and Enrico gritted his teeth as the doctor scrutinized the bite mark on her breast, swabbing it for Vince's saliva, as he parted her legs and studied the bruising on her inner thighs. But the exam and collection of evidence was necessary to keep her out of prison. For anything less, he would have spared her the intrusion.

The doctor, a balding middle-aged man with a kind face, photographed the bite and the bruises, draping her with a sheet when possible to preserve her modesty. When he finished, he removed his glasses, closed his eyes, and rubbed the bridge of his nose while asking his next question. "*Signora*, were you violated?"

Enrico held his breath until she shook her head. "No. It was damn close though."

The doctor replaced his glasses and smiled, patting her arm. "Are there any other injuries?" When Kate said no, the doctor wrote her a prescription for Valium, then left them alone.

No matter how careful the doctor had been, how gentle, how respectful, the exam had continued Kate's violation. Enrico had never felt more helpless. He'd been able do nothing other than hold her hand and dry her tears with his fingertips. After he helped her dress, she leaned against him for a moment and whispered, "Thank you." Her gratitude made his eyes burn and his throat ache. He hadn't kept her safe. He'd broken his promise.

When they returned home, he helped her into a warm bath. Then he turned to go, to give her privacy at last, but she grabbed his wrist, her hand wet and slick on his skin. "I don't want to be alone right now."

He sat down on the closed lid of the toilet. "I'll stay." She soaped her arms while he watched. "Do you want help?"

She shook her head, not looking at him. After a moment, she said, "What was going on with you and Fuente?"

A tingle of adrenaline shivered through him. He'd thought she would shut down, but she'd kept her head. It was admirable, and a bit frightening. "Fuente wants help getting a promotion. I am friends with Major Alfonso, who heads the Milan branch."

"Will you help him?"

"I would be stupid not to." She studied him with steady eyes. What was she thinking?

"Were you bribing him?"

Enrico raised an eyebrow. He hadn't expected the question, but he should have. Kate was far from dumb. "A man can be bribed only if he wants to be."

"That's not an answer."

He smiled. She should have been a prosecutor. "The answer is no."

"The two of you were keeping something from me."

Enrico looked at the floor tiles. "Just the details of how my family was killed."

"Why? Was it really so horrific?"

Enrico fixed her with his stare, his anger hot and sudden. Words poured out of him. "Was it horrific? My mother, my brothers, they were slaughtered like animals. Mario was only eleven. It was his birthday. They shot him over and over as he tried to crawl away."

Kate gasped, tears glittering in her eyes. "I'm so sorry, Enrico." She reached for him, but he ignored her hand. After a moment, she let it fall to the edge of the tub.

He couldn't stop talking. "Andretti's men left them lying in the street. Carlo took advantage of my father's trust. He murdered them, women and children. He violated our codes—" He froze, his veins icing up.

"*Our* codes?" Kate asked.

"I mean as Calabrians. Women and children are not to be killed in disputes of any kind."

She lowered her arms and sank down in the water until just her head was visible. Her eyes never left him. "Vince wasn't lying, was he? And Fuente knows it too."

Panic roared through him. It took all he had to hide it from her. "Vincenzo *was* lying."

"Why would Fuente think you would help him get a promotion?"

"The police are underpaid. If you have money, they always try to get something from you."

"I thought you said you didn't bribe him."

"Which is the truth. He extorted a promise from me."

"Semantics."

"I beg to differ. I offered him nothing. He made a demand, and I agreed to it."

"Why?"

"I prefer to keep out of the papers. The less attention I attract, the better."

Kate crossed her arms. "I told you I hated lies."

He took a deep breath and let it out. "And I don't like telling them." He unbuttoned and rolled up one of his shirt cuffs. "But sometimes honesty is more trouble than it is worth."

Kate's mouth dropped open. "How can you say that?"

She was far more difficult to evade than he would have ever guessed. "It's been a long day and I need a drink. Would you like something?"

"Giving yourself time to think, I see. Are you trying to distract me?"

He smiled. *Ah, she was a hard one. What a woman.* "Yes, I am."

"I'm not a fool, Enrico."

"I never said you were."

"Treating me like one says it just the same." He felt her gaze on him as he fiddled with a button on his shirt.

He looked her square in the eye. "There are certain... realities of my situation that I would prefer to tell you about in my own time. When you are ready to hear them."

"You mean when I have such feelings for you that I can't overlook them? I already made that mistake once. I won't make it again."

"I am not like Vincenzo."

"No. You're worse." Her voice thickened.

A wave of heat tore through his body. "Why?"

"You're kind to me, and thoughtful, and... and if I can't accept what you're hiding from me...." She dissolved into tears. "It's just not *fair* of you."

The heat in him dissipated. "I promise I am nothing like him."

"How do I *know* that?"

He leaned forward and took her wrists, tugging her upwards in the bath, baring her chest. He traced his fingers over the bite mark on her left breast. "I would never do this to you." He touched her jaw, tracing the bruise there. "Or this." He looked pointedly at her belly beneath the water. "And I would never take something from you that you did not want to give." He cleared his throat, trying to keep the anger out of his voice. "I resent you comparing me to him."

She blinked away her tears and took a deep breath. "You're lying to me about something. Just like he did."

"Can you trust me, for a while longer?"

"I don't have much choice, do I? Fuente has my passport."

"I owe the man." Enrico smiled, hoping to coax one from her.

She sighed and sat back, looking down at the soap bubbles that covered her. "Even if I could go, Carlo is waiting to pounce on me."

"For once, I suppose I have something to thank Carlo for."

Kate studied him. "You do care about me."

"I do," he said, warmth welling up in his chest. Yes, she was difficult. But he liked it. He liked her. He liked sparring with her, he liked that she didn't take him at face value. He liked everything about her, even when she was impossible.

"I cannot imagine going back to the life I was leading before this happened. To the dead spot after Antonella. My life will lose all color again if you leave, Kate." He extended his hand and she took it. "I know it has been horrible for you, but it will get better. I promise you that."

She smiled at him. "It hasn't all been horrible." She squeezed his hand and yawned. "I desperately need some sleep. What time is it?"

He pulled his mobile phone from his pocket and looked at it. "Almost seven in the morning." He set the phone on the counter. "Here, let me help you." He reached for the washcloth in her hand.

She kept it from his grasp, her grin fading. "No. Not yet." She stared at the bathwater.

His throat constricted. It was a good thing Vincenzo Andretti was already dead. Because he wouldn't have been able to resist strangling him with his bare hands.

ෝᏙ

After Enrico got Kate bundled up in bed with the Valium the doctor had prescribed, he summoned Ruggero to his study. He wanted nothing more than to focus on Kate for the next few days to the exclusion of all else, but their safety was paramount. And that meant finding the traitor—and figuring out who they could trust—as soon as possible.

As much as he hated to do it, Enrico armed himself for the meeting, his Glock in hand under his desk. Just in case.

Dawn was approaching, a faint yellowy orange on the horizon, the plants of the garden slowly taking shape in the growing light. He felt so damn weary. It wasn't just the loss of sleep. It was the accumulation of all the years of his existence, of the constant struggle against enemies without and within the 'Ndrangheta. The never-ending vigilance of his life—guarding so many secrets, telling so many lies. And beyond that, making so many decisions that meant life and death, misery or happiness, for so many people. The weight of it all threatened to crush him.

But today, more than the responsibility wearied him. He'd been betrayed from within, by someone he trusted, maybe even someone he loved. If he had no one to rely on, no one to trust, how could he possibly go on? How could he survive? How could he ever keep Kate safe?

After a tap on the open door, Ruggero walked in.

"Close the door." He didn't invite Ruggero to sit. He said nothing, waiting for Ruggero to break the silence.

Finally the guard said, "I assume you want to know how this happened."

"And I'd like to know where Antonio was. Is." Enrico listened to Ruggero's explanation—the drugged dogs, the access by master code of the side gate and rear terrace, all timed to avoid the guards. "What about Antonio?"

"He met a girl. We were in for the night; it seemed safe to let him go."

"Are you sure that's what he was doing? Only four of us have the master code—you, me, Dom, and Antonio."

Ruggero frowned. "I'm certain of Antonio."

"Someone gave Andretti the master code. Is it possible it was anyone besides the four of us?"

Ruggero shrugged. "You pay him well, but someone could get to Strasser. And we haven't been meticulous about shielding when entering the code. Someone may have learned it."

"Do you think that likely?"

"I do not see an obvious suspect." Ruggero looked at him steadily.

"You don't?" Enrico asked, his voice sharp.

The guard's brow furrowed. "Don Lucchesi, I'm not sure what you're implying."

Enrico's heart was pumping fast; he could feel the pulse in his fingers where they gripped the gun. His hand tightened, and he angled the gun at Ruggero's knees. "Those lapses on your part. I'm not sure they were mistakes."

For the first time in their long acquaintance, Ruggero looked at Enrico with anger on his face.

"Don't I pay you enough?"

Ruggero reddened. "The Velas, we are an honorable family. I took a vow to you, to this *cosca*, and I am no oath breaker. Money does not motivate me."

"Then what does?"

Ruggero's already low voice deepened. "I am a man of honor. My reputation is all I have. I am not a man who will ever be don. I do not *want* to be don. I live to serve the don. That is my job, that is who I am. That is all I will ever be."

Enrico started to speak, but Ruggero held up a hand. "I have something more to say. My father and I followed your family from Calabria. We left everything behind. My father died protecting yours. When do you think I last saw my cousins, my sister?"

The switch of subjects baffled Enrico. "I don't know."

"Fifteen years ago, not since becoming your personal guard."

"You haven't asked for time off."

"My point is this: I've given my life over to yours. Perhaps I have already died for you."

"Is this what's been bothering you?"

Ruggero clasped his hands behind his back and looked at the carpet. "Indirectly."

Enrico felt himself relax, even as guilt overwhelmed him. It had never occurred to him that Ruggero might wish to visit his family. "Then you'll have a vacation as soon as this is over."

"The situation is more… dire than that."

Enrico raised a brow. "How so?"

"My sister's husband is dying, and she wants me to come visit."

Damn. Why did the bad times always multiply? "Who do you trust to take your place?"

"No one. That's why I didn't tell you."

"Be reasonable. What about Antonio?"

"Antonio is too green, and you are in severe danger. My sister is not."

"I don't want you to make a choice you can't live with."

Ruggero's voice was crisp, a rebuke. "I will keep my vows: the 'Ndrangheta and my don above all else."

Enrico studied his guard, seeing the resolve on his face. He would not be a fool to put his trust in this man. "I apologize for insulting you with my doubts." He brought the Glock out from under the desk and set it on top. Ruggero's eyes followed the gun, but he didn't look surprised to see it. "And I apologize for not treating you as a person with a life outside your job."

Ruggero nodded, the anger leaving his face. "It would be foolish not to question me. And I cannot expect the don to attend to my needs. That's my responsibility."

"It's mine. You aren't a machine, Ruggero." His voice softened on this last statement.

Ruggero took a chair in front of Enrico's desk. "I would like to think I am." He scrubbed his hand across his jaw, his fingers rasping against his early morning stubble. "I've failed to keep you safe. Again. The Andrettis are getting too close. It worries me."

Enrico's pulse sped up again. Ruggero, worried? Unprecedented. "Someone inside is working against me. Vincenzo admitted it. But who?"

"Between the falcon and now this, there are only three possibilities: me, Antonio, or your cousin. If you have eliminated Antonio and me as suspects, only Don Domenico is left."

His stomach flipped over. He didn't want to believe it. Dom. The person he loved and trusted most.

And then another possibility occurred to him. Who hated him more than anyone, aside from Carlo?

Franco Trucco. Fiammetta's father.

It wouldn't be hard for Trucco to learn what he needed to assist the Andrettis. Dom had warned him. He'd made a mistake showering Trucco with money, setting up scholarships for his remaining children, paying off the extensive renovations to his house. All the money in the world would never be enough. It would never bring Fiammetta back. It would never quiet the anger in Franco Trucco's heart. Or the guilt in Enrico's.

"What about Franco?"

"It's possible, though more difficult for him."

"But it *is* possible."

Ruggero nodded. "You want him watched?"

"I do."

"What about Don Domenico and Antonio?"

Enrico blew out a breath. "It's got to be Trucco."

Ruggero leaned forward. His voice was soft. "He has a most compelling motive, I agree. But he's not the only one."

"What do you mean?"

"If you die, childless, who stands to profit most?"

A chill washed through him. Dom. He'd inherit everything and his branch of the family would take over the *cosca*. "It cannot be. His blood is my blood."

"We must consider every possibility."

"And Antonio?"

Ruggero rubbed his chin with his fingertips. "He's smart. And ambitious. I think he'd like to be don someday. But he looks to you as a father. I don't think him likely. However, he is an outsider."

Enrico smiled. "Anyone who's not Calabrian is an outsider to you."

"That doesn't make it any less true. There's a reason we choose only our own." He paused. "There's another possibility."

Another? "Who?"

"Signora Andretti."

Waves of heat and cold flashed through him. "No."

"She held a gun on you several hours ago. If I hadn't been there...."

Enrico shook his head. "Her husband tried to kill her. She was upset."

"The whole thing could have been an act."

"But she killed him."

"She could have seen an opportunity."

"For what?"

Ruggero shrugged. "To be more than a mid-level man's wife. To be yours. Maybe even to bear you a child, then kill you and run the family in your stead."

"Few women have ever headed a family."

"But it's happened." Ruggero paused. "She certainly knows how to handle a gun."

That detail did bother him. It was highly unusual for the women of his acquaintance.

"And Americans are ambitious. The women are practically men. And just as ruthless."

"I don't think Kate is that kind of woman." *But she'd hardly missed a beat, had she?*

"She didn't have to kill her husband. She could've left that to us."

"It was too risky. Andretti almost got the gun back."

Ruggero shrugged. "Still, the timing's suspicious. She's here for less than two days, and we have a security breach. I don't want to overlook her."

"I think you're looking too hard."

"And I think you're in love." The words were gentle, but the message was clear. When it came to Kate, he was blind.

He'd be stupid to ignore Ruggero. The guard was a man of few words, but those he spoke were always worth heeding. "All right." He looked steadily at the man. "I want them all watched. I'm counting on you to solve this."

"I will not fail you."

"I trust that you won't." Enrico was about to say more when his mobile phone buzzed. He glanced at the display. "It's Dom. I need to take this."

Ruggero bowed and then left the study. Enrico waited for the door to close before answering. "What the hell happened?" Dom yelled when he heard Enrico's voice.

"Vincenzo Andretti broke into my house. He tried to kill me and Kate. But she shot him."

"Were you hurt?"

"Just some bruises, a mild concussion."

"You could have been killed. And all over a woman. I told you this would come to no good."

"At least he's dead."

Dom laughed without mirth. "You say that like it's a good thing."

"It is. He beat her and tried to rape her in front of me. He was not fit to live."

"He was also an Andretti. Or have you forgotten?"

Enrico sighed. "I'll figure something out."

"The hell you will. This is going to cost. Immensely. And you will have to marry Delfina, as soon as possible, supposing Carlo and Dario still agree to that."

"I will figure something else out."

"Are you unable to hear me? *There is no other solution.* It's marriage or it's war."

Enrico's pulse quickened. "Then it's war. I cannot marry her."

Silence hung thick between them for several moments, then Dom said, "You're forcing me to call for an election."

His adrenaline ratcheted up, sending Enrico's whole body into overdrive, his heart threatening to jump out of his chest. "Am I?"

"I have no other choice."

Ruggero's words came back with force. *If you die, childless, who stands to profit most?* Maybe this was Dom's way of forcing the issue without having to kill Enrico. It was clever. And he'd just played into Dom's hands if that was the case. "You don't want to do that."

"What else do you expect me to do? If I stand by and let you destroy this family, it's not just your head that's forfeit. Mine is too."

Damn it. Maybe this wasn't about Dom wanting to take over. Maybe this was about Dom protecting himself, protecting the family. Protecting Enrico. "There's got to be another way."

"I can't think of one." Dom paused. "Shall I speak to Carlo and Dario, to see if the offer is still on the table?"

Enrico damned himself as he nodded and hissed out the one word that meant the end to all his hopes. "Yes."

CHAPTER 15

Oblivion. She needed it. Craved it.

Aided by Valium, Kate slept through the day and the following night in the guest room. Enrico had checked on her that evening, but she'd asked him to leave her alone. Though the sedative helped, menace and anxiety laced her dreams.

However, the next morning's sun forced her to give up on sleep. Stripes of golden light streamed across the bed, and she stared at them in a haze.

She'd killed a man. Her husband.

Tears welled up in her eyes, but she blinked them away and swallowed the golf ball stuck in her throat. Vince hadn't deserved to live. And he didn't deserve to be mourned.

She hoped Enrico knew what he was doing. And she hoped she could trust him. That whole interaction with Fuente reeked of secrets.

Throwing the covers back, Kate rose. Time to find out what Enrico was hiding.

෨ଔ

Kate headed toward the rear terrace of the house. Enrico hadn't been at breakfast as she'd expected, and she'd found herself disappointed by his absence.

Not knowing what to do with herself, she'd decided to take a swim and soak up a little sun—as much as she could tolerate without burning.

She'd donned a black one-piece bathing suit and put on a white blouse over it. Just because Enrico wasn't around, that didn't mean she wouldn't run into one of the guards. She had to go shopping soon; she felt strange raiding Antonella's closet. Not that she'd ever step foot in that bedroom again. The carpet was undoubtedly still soaked with blood.

As she was crossing through the foyer to the French doors in the back, a loud thump came from down the hall. Then a moan, then a shout. "*Merda!*" It sounded like Enrico.

Kate poked her head in the door to his study. Enrico was cradling his head in his hands. "What's wrong?"

He looked up when she spoke. "I lost a whole morning's work. And now the bloody computer will not start up properly."

"I could take a look if you'd like."

He smiled. "I would be grateful."

She took his chair, and he sat down on the edge of the desk next to her. Kate rebooted the machine, trying to ignore the feel of his eyes on her. She asked Enrico to translate a few words in the messages on the screen. "Do you mind if I restore the system to see if I can get stable operating system files? It won't affect any data."

He shrugged. "Do what you think best."

As the computer went to work, Kate looked around his desk. "Do you have an external backup drive and restore discs?"

"I do not know."

"Who maintains this system for you?"

He rubbed his cheek and looked away. "It was Fiammetta's job."

"Was? Where is she?"

His face reddened and his eyes grew moist. "She died in a car accident about six months ago."

"You were close."

He nodded. "She was my personal assistant. The daughter of my accountant. I had known her from when she was a young girl."

Kate studied him. "You seem quite affected by her death still."

He gazed at the books over her shoulder. "The accident was my fault."

"How?"

"I was driving and I had been drinking. We were fighting."

"You and Fiammetta?" When he didn't say anything, she said, "She was more than just your assistant."

He nodded, still not looking at her. "Loneliness can be a powerful seductress."

Kate raised a brow. "It was *loneliness* that seduced you? It had nothing to do with her being a young woman?"

Enrico blushed, finally met her eyes again. "I missed Antonella. Fiammetta was concerned about me. When she suggested...." He trailed off. "I could not resist her."

"Couldn't or didn't want to?"

All trace of warmth left his face. "Why does this matter?"

"I wonder if you're not doing the same thing with me."

He leaned forward, putting his hand over hers where it rested beside the keyboard. "I am not with you for the same reasons I was with Fiammetta."

"Are you so sure? This house is a shrine to Antonella. There's at least one picture of her in every room. You still have all her things. It's like she just left for a brief trip and she'll be back in a few days."

His voice was hoarse when he replied. "I am moving past my grief."

Kate sighed. "I don't believe you." She held his gaze for a few moments, not looking away until the computer beeped. The system restore was complete.

"I think I've fixed it. But your virus protection is out of date, and you've got to address that today."

He looked chagrined, but happy to have the subject changed. "I think maybe I have been ignoring some things."

Kate rolled her eyes. "You really don't like to be bothered, do you?"

He smiled sheepishly, then met her eyes, his smile turning into something else. "I do when it is something I like, that I am interested in." She followed his eyes. *Yikes.* He was getting an eyeful where her blouse had gaped open. The swimsuit was relatively modest, but she was still showing a lot more skin than she'd intended.

Pulling the thin silk of the blouse closed, she leaned back in the chair, ignoring his comment. "You also need an uninterruptable power supply, a surge protector, and of course the external backup drive. And you need someone to make sure your home network is secure."

"Can you do all that?"

"I can. But could I get a little sun first?"

"No hurry." His face brightened. "Would you mind if I joined you?"

She grinned at his excitement. "Not at all."

He hopped off the desk, offering her a hand up from the chair. After she rose, he held her hand for a beat too long, looking at her closely, then slowly let go, his fingers brushing hers as they slid from his grasp. "I need to change clothes. And get something for you."

"What?" she asked, as he waited for her to precede him out of the room.

"You will see." He loped down the hall, then bounded up one of the staircases to the second floor. Kate continued out to the garden, the feel of his hand wrapped around hers lingering in her mind. *Stop thinking about him. He's still in love with his wife.*

Kate settled herself on a lounge chair by the pool. A few minutes later, Enrico strolled out, wearing flip flops, black swim trunks, and an unbuttoned white shirt that revealed his muscular chest and abdomen. Kate caught herself staring as he approached, hoping her sunglasses hid her gaze. It took her a few seconds to register that he had a large, all black, woman's sun hat in one hand and a bottle of sunscreen in the other. He held the hat out to her. "To protect your face."

She reached out and took it. "*Grazie.*" She started to place it on her head, then hesitated. "This was Antonella's too, wasn't it?"

He nodded. "Go ahead." He watched her don the hat, a flicker of something unrecognizable crossing his face. He tore his eyes away from her after a few seconds and busied himself with removing his shirt and pulling up another chair. He seemed to be avoiding her gaze, which gave her plenty of opportunity to admire his sleekly muscular body. She hadn't seen him so unclothed in broad daylight before, and the view was one she couldn't ignore.

Kate marveled at his beauty. There was no other word for it. He might be in his forties, but even in this light he seemed hardly a day over thirty-five. The way he looked, he could have posed for Michelangelo and made an even more striking David. Or he could do the modern-day version and pose in ads for underwear, cologne, or men's couture. She watched as he took the sunglasses perched on his thick black hair and put them on.

Enrico finally looked over at her then. *So the glasses aren't just for sun protection.* She wanted to ask him what was wrong, but it felt like prying.

Instead, she looked around the well-manicured garden surrounding them. "Your estate is lovely," she said. "You must be so happy living here. Well, at least when you're not afraid for your life."

"*Grazie.*" He looked around the garden for a moment. "Sometimes, yes, I am very happy living here."

"But not today?"

He froze, almost imperceptibly, but she caught the sudden hitch in his shoulders and neck. He sighed. "A house is not a home unless there is a woman in it."

"Will just *any* woman do?" she teased.

"You know what I meant." He looked at her. "Someone special."

There was too much want, too much need, filling his voice. She tried to brush it off with a lame attempt at a joke. "Well, you have me until Fuente says otherwise."

"Kate, I wish—" He broke off, then started again, looking at the pool instead of her. "I would like you to consider this your home. For as long as you want." His eyes sought hers.

It was her turn to look away. "That's a pretty open-ended invitation."

He sat up and swung his legs over the side of the chaise, turning until he was directly facing her. "I mean it. Now that your husband is gone, I see no reason why we could not... proceed."

Kate's belly clenched. She sat up and hugged her knees to her chest, clasping her hands around her shins. She needed to put more clothes on.

"Have I upset you?"

She rested her chin on her knees, then buried her face in them. She didn't want him to see the flush rising in her cheeks. "No. It's just—I can't have sex with you right now. Not anyone."

He chuckled. "I did not mean it like that. I want to get to know you. To court you. Anything else will be your decision. Always."

God, kill me now. She was an idiot. How could she look at him again?

Silence hung between them for a few moments. Then he picked up the cordless phone on the table between their chairs. "Would you care for something to drink?"

Perfect. "There's no need to bother anyone. I can get us something. What do you want?" She picked up her shirt to put it on.

"No, no." He waved his hand at her to sit down. "The servants are well-paid. Doing their jobs for them makes them upset. They think it is a comment on their work." When she gave him a skeptical look, he added, "Trust me. You do not want to upset Maddalena or Nonna Drina, or they will over-salt your meals."

She chuckled, then sat back down and let out a rush of air, feeling herself relax. He looked at her for a moment. "I am having a campari and soda. What would you like?"

"A dry martini would be heavenly. But all the martinis I've had in Italy have been dreadful. Half gin, half vermouth. They taste awful."

He laughed. "They are made the English way in my home. I did not spend my formative years in London for nothing."

"Then a martini it is."

He rang the house and placed their request.

She waited until he ended the call. "When were you in London?"

"From sixteen to eighteen. After my mother and my brothers were murdered, my father sent me to boarding school. He said I needed to improve my English."

"But?"

"Whenever I mentioned them, he changed the subject. I think he just wanted to be alone."

"Maybe he wanted to keep you safe from Carlo."

Enrico nodded. "Even though the engagement had been arranged by the time I left, I doubt he trusted Carlo much."

"Do you still miss them?" How would she handle such a loss?

"Every day. Especially Primo. Dom sometimes makes the same gestures, or his tone of voice will sound the same as Primo's, and I'll miss him all over again."

"I'd like to meet your cousin."

"You will. Though not for a while." His face darkened.

"Did the two of you fight?"

"He was upset about what happened." He paused, then added, "Dom knows all my business. He knows about Carlo. And Vincenzo."

"Oh." Everything that had happened the other night seemed like a surreal nightmare. Her feelings about Vince were a jumble—anger, relief, and yet a strange feeling of being adrift, alone.

"What is it?" Enrico looked at her closely.

"I don't know the woman who shot Vince. I didn't think I could."

He regarded her somberly. "We are all capable of killing, in the right circumstances."

"But—"

"You did the right thing. Accept it. You saved our lives. There is nothing wrong with wanting to live." He paused, as if to see what effect his words were having.

She took a deep breath. "I could have held the gun on him, I could have waited for the police."

"I would not have. You were too close to him. He could have taken the gun from you."

"I suppose you're right."

"I had to accept long ago that the Andrettis—or someone else—might force me to do the same thing one day."

Now was her chance to ask about Fuente's needling in the study. "Haven't you already done so?"

He looked down at his feet. "I cannot answer that truthfully."

So he *had* killed those men. She watched his face when he finally looked up at her. There was no remorse, no guilt on those features. Only defiance, and a touch of pride. "I have no right to judge you, Enrico."

Surprise flickered across his face, then he smiled. He pointed to the tattoo on his bicep, the one she'd asked about. "You wanted to know what this means."

He paused so long she said, "You don't have to tell me if you don't want to."

"I do, actually. Though it is unwise for me to be so frank."

"Can't we trust each other after all that's happened?" She caught his eyes with hers.

"What I am about to tell you, you cannot repeat. I could go to jail."

"I won't say anything."

He stroked the tattoo. "I avenged my family. I killed those men. All four of them. In three days. *Quattro in tre.*"

Kate couldn't suppress a gasp. "But weren't you just a boy then?"

"I was eighteen. And about to marry Carlo's daughter to save my family. I could not go after Carlo, but I could go after his men. I wanted him to know I would be no man's slave."

Kate sat back in her chair. Well, well. Enrico Lucchesi wasn't just a ruthless businessman; he was a street fighter too.

They were interrupted by Maddalena, with their drinks on a tray. She'd brought a pitcher of ice water as well. Enrico thanked her, then handed Kate her martini. He picked up his drink and touched it to hers. "*Salute.*"

The ringing chime of the crystal reminded her that they were supposed to be celebrating the day. She put on a smile for Enrico's benefit, and took a sip of the martini.

"How is it?"

"*Perfetto*." She took another swallow, feeling the gin burn her throat as it slid down. She had the urge to get spectacularly drunk, something she hadn't done in years. "I'm going to need another of these."

"You will get drunk."

"That's my intention."

He glanced at her. "I did not think you would miss him."

She took another swallow of the martini, then popped one of the olives in her mouth and chewed it, savoring its salty tang. "Neither did I."

"I think what I really meant is *why* would you miss him."

Kate turned to look at him. "He was my husband."

"But—"

She cut him off with a slash of her hand. "Do you think I was an idiot? Our marriage was good at first. He loved me. And I loved him. Yes, he had a temper, and sometimes he scared me. But maybe if I'd never talked to you, maybe none of this would have happened." To her mortification, her eyes blurred with tears.

"Kate." Enrico leaned forward and took the glass from her hand. He set it on the table, then touched her shoulder. "I have to say this." He waited until she looked at him. "You have nothing to feel bad about. Look at you." He gestured to her bruised arms and legs, his eyes lingering on her marked face and swollen lip. "He had no excuse for his behavior. None. Your only mistake was loving him. If it had not been me, someone else or something else would have turned him against you."

A wave of recognition passed through her and she looked away, her eyes finding a bruise on her left shin. He was right. And yet, it was all still her fault somehow. She could feel Enrico's eyes upon her, and as another truth hit her, a shiver ran down her back. He'd expected her to move on from Vince quickly. Hopefully on to him. Which gave him a motive for getting rid of Vince. And gave Fuente a reason to suspect Enrico, not just shake him down. She looked up. "Did you have *anything* to do with the security breach?"

CHAPTER 16

Enrico's eyebrows flew up at Kate's question. He stared at the pool for a moment before answering, not sure he'd heard her correctly. "Why would you think I would sabotage my own security?"

"Why are you stalling?"

She didn't miss anything. "I was taken off-guard."

"Well?"

"Of course not. I would never put you—or myself, or my people—in danger knowingly."

"How do I know that's true?" Her eyes seemed to penetrate into him.

"Where is this coming from?"

"Fuente wasn't just shaking you down. He knows something," she said.

"I have a lot of money. That is all he knows."

"There's something else."

Dio, she was impossible to throw off the scent. "What are you accusing me of?"

"What did Fuente say to you outside the car?"

Enrico sighed. He had to tell her. "He threatened me, us. He said the investigation could go either way, that because we were lovers, it could have been murder, not self-defense." He met her eyes. "I did not want you to worry."

"What are we going to do?"

Enrico took her hand. "Nothing. The physical evidence will clear us."

"But what if Fuente makes the evidence disappear?"

"There were witnesses. Ruggero. The doctors who examined us. He cannot make them disappear."

"Ruggero works for you; his testimony could be dismissed," she said.

"The doctors do not."

"But the test results could be lost. Or changed."

He shrugged. "I can only worry about what actually happens." He took her other hand in his. "Fuente will go away if I do the favors he has asked for."

"And if he doesn't?"

"I will handle it."

"I'm sorry for bringing this into your life." She looked down at their joined hands. Her voice was soft.

"I have been dealing with the Andrettis my entire life. I knew what could happen."

She looked up at him. "You could go to jail. Both of us could."

"Please stop fretting." He wanted to kiss her, but settled for pressing his lips to her cheek. "And stop arguing with me." He spoke lightly, hoping to break the mood.

She smiled. "Can I get drunk now?"

"Why not?" He handed her the martini and picked up the phone. "Two more," he said to Maddalena. Then he picked up his own glass and settled back in the chair.

A couple rounds later, they were both quite intoxicated. Kate looked down at her skin, starting to turn pink. "I'd better go in before I burn."

"No need." He fetched a large sun umbrella from where it stood next to the house and set it up over her. Then he picked up the bottle of sunscreen. "I thought you would eventually need this." He poured some onto his hand, adrenaline starting a flutter in his chest. *What if she says no?* "May I?"

Her wary eyes found his, the pulse jumping at her throat. But she didn't look away, so he waited, slicking the cream across his palms, trying to ignore the pounding of his heart, the silly flips his stomach was making. An eternity passed before she nodded and pulled off the blouse. He almost smiled, but held it in, as if it didn't matter to him one way or the other. Instead, he sat down on the edge of her lounge chair and smoothed the lotion over her left arm, massaging it into her skin with both hands. When he worked it up to her shoulders, she sat forward so he could apply it to her neck and upper back. She shivered beneath his hands.

He stopped, his mouth going dry. "Is this too much?" She shook her head, and he continued on to the other arm. Her skin felt heavenly to him, silky, warm. It had already been too long since he'd last touched her.

Hell, he shouldn't be touching her now. Not after he'd agreed to let Dom set up a betrothal to Delfina Andretti. His heart plummeted to his feet. How could he possibly give Kate up? How could he walk away from this wild and tender creature who trembled beneath his touch, whom he wanted nothing more than to soothe, to protect? How could he leave this fierce woman who had captured his heart?

He would have to, if he was going to keep his *cosca* safe.

But how?

He looked at the bruises on Kate's face and body. He had to leave her. It was the only way to keep her safe too. Unless....

Unless he made her his mistress, supposing she would accept that solution. He couldn't see Kate accepting second place in anything. But, here she was nevertheless, even though he hadn't removed his ring or packed away the pictures of Antonella.

Of course, maybe that was because Fuente still had her passport and Carlo had his eye on her. Somehow, he had to convince her to stay.

When he finished her right arm and her hand slipped from his grasp, he moved down to her feet, smoothing the cool lotion over them, between her toes, kneading the muscles of her arches, his fingers working over the delicate bones of her feet and ankles. Then the meat of her calves was between his hands. He slowly worked his way up to the tender skin behind her knees, one of his favorite parts of a woman. *Cristo,* they all were. She flinched when he touched that soft, soft skin, and he stopped and met her eyes. "Would you like to do the rest?"

She looked down at him, a bit unsteadily. His heart hammered like this was his very first time with a woman. "No. Go ahead," she finally said.

He gave her a slow smile, then coated her knees and thighs, his fingers working in concentric circles as he moved toward the juncture of her legs. *Slow down.* As his fingers neared her bikini line, she tensed and he stopped again. He took a shallow breath; it was the first one he'd taken in over a minute. Removing his hands from her, he sat back, his mouth parched. *This might be the last time you ever touch her; don't ruin it.*

She opened her eyes and stared at him for a few seconds. He couldn't read her. "You missed a spot." She motioned to her chest.

He let a lazy smile inch across his face. "So I did." Pouring more sunscreen onto his palms, he smoothed them across her upper chest, his fingers running over her collarbones, the little hollow at the base of her throat, the tops of her breasts. His heart thrashed in his chest. How he wanted to continue touching her. *Kiss her.* Looking into her eyes, he saw them filled with trust. He closed his own, forced himself to breathe, to ignore the demands of his cock. He was rock hard and ready. But now was not the time. He rose carefully, keeping his back to her, and waited for his erection to go down.

"Thank you," she said dreamily. He smiled to himself. *Mille grazie, Kate.* Even though it was agony to stop. He hoped she wouldn't think badly of what he'd done later, when she was sober. And he wasn't so completely besotted.

೮೨೦೮

Kate woke up in her lounge chair; from the position of the sun, it was

119

now late afternoon. She looked over at Enrico, reading in his chair. He'd obviously been moving the umbrella around to keep her shaded as the sun crossed the sky.

She could almost still feel his hands on her body. She'd nearly said no to the sunscreen, but the hopeful look on his face had made her change her mind.

Fortunately. Warmth filled her chest. When he'd stopped and asked if she wanted to do the rest—it was a small thing, but it was everything. Because he'd asked. Because he always would.

Though he had pushed her to accept his touch again. Once his hands were on her, they raised a hunger for him, for more. A hunger she wasn't ready for. She hadn't wanted the massage to turn to sex, but she hadn't wanted it to end either.

The cordless phone on the table between them rang. Enrico picked it up, spoke briefly, then seeing she was awake, handed it to her. "It is for you."

She took the phone. "Who is this?"

The man introduced himself, but she didn't register the name because of what he said next. "I am the director of the city morgue."

"Oh." Her stomach flipped, and she pressed a hand into her abdomen. She forced her voice to stay neutral. "I suppose you're calling about my husband."

"Yes. His uncle is here. He is insisting on taking the body."

"He can have it." She didn't suffer a second's debate.

She heard a hand slide over the receiver and a muffled discussion. Then a new voice came on the line. "I am glad you are seeing reason, *mia cara*."

As she recognized Carlo's cool, dry voice, her heart sped up. "I want nothing further to do with Vince. He's all yours."

"You *are* Lucchesi's whore then. I had wondered if my nephew was being hasty."

Every inch of her skin blazed white-hot. "He was. I was never unfaithful to him, until *after* he accused me of it. And I am no one's whore."

"That is between you and God."

"You have a lot of nerve, Carlo, invoking God with me. You of *all* people." Enrico motioned for the phone, his face angry, but she shook her head. The last thing she wanted was Carlo thinking he'd cowed her.

He chuckled. "Such fire, *signora*. Or should I say *signorina*, now that you are without a husband?"

His tone was almost flirtatious. "You don't seem all that angry with me. I thought you'd want me dead."

"Oh, I assure you, I do want that… and more. Beforehand of course. I have no interest in a cold body." An icy wash of fear coursed through her as his hints hit home. "However, I have read the police report and have seen the photos of what my nephew did to you, and I disapprove." Kate shuddered.

Carlo—*Carlo!*—had seen those pictures. "Such lovely… *flesh* should not be marked so." His voice lingered obscenely on "flesh," the sound conjuring disturbing images of Vince's attack, images she did not want to visit, but could not stop seeing.

Her hand went numb from gripping the phone too hard. "You son of a bitch," she finally whispered.

Carlo tsked at her. "Such language. You Americans can be so crude."

"You called me a whore."

Carlo laughed. "So I did." He paused for a second, and when he spoke again, his voice was harder. "But you earned that."

"Didn't you?" She fought to keep her voice from trembling with anger.

"What lies has Lucchesi been filling your head with?"

"You killed his mother, his brothers."

"Not that I am admitting anything, but did he tell you *why* I might have done such a thing?"

She frowned. "A business dispute."

Carlo barked with laughter. "He would put it that way." He paused. "His father kidnapped my son."

"What?" She laughed in surprise. "That's preposterous."

"Ask him."

"No. This conversation is over."

"If you say so. But do ask him, *signorina*. And watch him closely when you do."

The phone clicked in her ear, the line going dead. Kate stared at the phone for a few seconds, then absently placed it on the table.

"You are shaking," Enrico said. "Did he threaten you?"

"Sort of. Not really."

Enrico took her hands in both of his. "Then what has you so upset?"

"He saw…" Her voice trembled, broke. She took a deep breath. "He saw the police report. The photos of me."

He winced. "I am sorry."

She shook her head. "It's not that he saw them. It was his reaction."

"What do you mean?"

"He wants me." She looked away from Enrico. "I think he always has."

"I will not let him touch you."

She closed her eyes and shivered, picturing Carlo's avid eyes tracking her when she was with Vince. "He never said anything directly. But now I know for sure."

"You were his nephew's wife."

"And now I'm not." She was quiet for a moment. "I never realized being with Vince protected me from him."

"I will protect you."

She turned angry eyes on him. "Will you?"

121

Enrico swallowed down his natural response. He deserved her scorn. "I swear it."

"The only way you can protect me is if you know who's betrayed you."

He hoped he was right about Trucco. "Ruggero is working on it."

"Can you trust him?"

"With my life."

"I trust Antonio."

"So do I." Jealousy jabbed a knife in him, hard. So she trusted Antonio, but not him. And if she knew how he'd lied to her.... He squeezed her hand, looking into her eyes.

After a moment, she returned the squeeze, exhaling slowly. "I'm sorry."

"Why?"

"For blaming you. If it's anyone's fault, it's mine."

He shook his head. "This whole... mess has been going on for a long time. You just got caught in the middle."

"Carlo said something strange."

"What?" Her tone raised the hair on the back of his neck.

"He said your father kidnapped his son. That that was why he killed your mother and brothers."

Enrico sucked in a breath, trying not to show how rattled he was. What could he say?

When he didn't immediately answer, she continued. "I told him that was preposterous." She hesitated, studying his face. "Isn't it?"

He looked down at their feet for a second, then up at her. "I wish it was."

"How can this be? Unless—"

"Unless my father was in the Mafia? That is what you were going to say, yes?"

She nodded, holding his eyes.

Tell her. Tell her now. He searched her face, saw the dread in her eyes. *Not yet.* "He did arrange to have Dario kidnapped. My father had contacts—Carlo's enemies—and they helped. You know the saying, 'The enemy of my enemy is my friend'?" She nodded. "My father very much believed that. But it was a mistake."

"What happened?"

"They took him too seriously, or maybe they just hated Carlo too much. They cut off one of Dario's fingers and sent it to Carlo." Enrico damned himself for the lie. It had been his father who had done the cutting. If only he could tell her the truth about the situation. The whole truth.

Kate gasped. "That's horrible."

"Carlo thought Dario was dead. That is why he ordered the attack on my family." He hated making Carlo look reasonable, but saying anything else would make her suspicious.

"How do you live like this?"

He shrugged. "You get used to it."

"I never want to get used to this. I just want my life back." Kate withdrew her hand from his and hugged herself.

An ache started deep in his chest. How would she ever accept him, and the *malavita*?

He needed some advice, and there was only one person he wanted to consult. He leaned toward her. "We need to get away from all this for a few days."

"How?"

"We could go to Capri and get you a new wardrobe."

Her lips curved into a smile. "I've always wanted to go there. It looks so pretty in the pictures I've seen."

"It is." He hesitated. "And there is someone I want you to meet."

"Who?"

"My godfather, Vittorio Battista. Aside from Dom and my father, he is all the family I have left."

"But he's not related by blood?"

Enrico shook his head. "It does not matter. He is like my own father." He couldn't explain it, not yet. But Vittorio was more than just a godfather. He was Enrico's *compare*, his co-father. He'd taken the vow of *comparaggio* in front of the *cosca* when Enrico was born. He'd sworn that he would watch over Enrico, that he would never betray him. That he would regard him as a son. As his own blood.

She looked up at the house. "It's a shame you have no family living with you. You strike me as being rather lonely."

His throat constricted. How she cut right through him. "I am surrounded by people."

"Employees. Not family. Not friends." She paused. "Do you even have any friends?"

"Dom."

"Your cousin. Anyone you're not related to, that you're not in business with?"

He shook his head.

"That's not healthy."

His position, his business, made it impossible to have friends other than family. Family was all he had, and very little of that left now. His skin burned under the pity in her gaze. He'd never chosen this life. It had been forced upon him. It and all the consequences—no friends, a dead family, a target on his back, no respite, no rest, only constant vigilance. When was the last time he hadn't felt exhausted? He rubbed his hands over his face.

"I'm sorry. It's none of my business."

Anger flashed through him. He just wanted to be honest with her for once. But he couldn't. "I do not need your pity." He jumped from the chair and strode to the house, his feet carrying him without conscious thought. He'd wanted her, and even though he'd had her, he was no closer to what he really wanted. He was well past mere lust. He wanted her to be his. Maybe even, someday, his wife. He wanted her to understand, and accept, him. Him and the *malavita*. And that was never going to happen. Hell, he probably couldn't even make her his mistress, much less his wife. No, he had to marry Delfina fucking Andretti.

Her feet slapped on the flagstones as she ran up to him. She grabbed his arm outside the French doors that led inside. "Forgive me," she said. "I'm upset and frustrated and still more than a little drunk, and I'm taking everything out on you."

"That makes two of us."

"I really don't want to fight."

He smirked. "That seems to be all you have wanted to do since you came here."

She looked at the stones beneath their feet. "I'm scared. I don't handle it well."

He took a breath, then blew it out. He could be honest with her on this point. "I am scared too. I want so much from you, and I am afraid I cannot have it."

Kate's stomach filled with a hard lump of shame. She had no intention of staying. She had no intention of letting him break her heart when he realized she was no substitute for Antonella. "I'm sorry."

He put a finger on her lips. "Stop apologizing."

"I should say the same to you."

His expression was grave. "I am not sure how I can ever make amends for failing to protect you. But I want to try. Will you let me?"

She made her tone teasing when she answered. "As long as it involves a trip to Capri."

He smiled. "You will love it. It is one of my favorite places on earth."

Rising on tiptoe, she kissed his cheek. Going on this trip was probably not the best idea. But she was loath to leave his side. Not with Carlo out there, thinking about her. Making his plans. Dreaming his obscene dreams.

Better to choose the lesser of two evils. She looked at Enrico, the tenderness in his gaze squeezing her heart. She didn't want to think of him that way, but he had just as much potential to hurt her as Carlo. The difference was, Enrico wouldn't enjoy it.

But he would hurt her just the same.

CHAPTER 17

Ever since he'd massaged her by the pool the day before, Enrico hadn't been able to stop fantasizing about Kate. The memory of touching her hit him hard that evening as he was lathering up in the shower. He'd put himself through a grueling workout, but it hadn't helped.

He ran the bar of soap over his arms, unable to stop picturing her there with him. He wanted *her* hands touching him, not his own. When he'd rubbed the sunscreen on her, she was all softness, all curves, her body pliable, yielding. He closed his eyes. His hands kneaded her thighs, his eyes glued to the fleshy mound of her sex. He cupped it with his hand, then pushed the thin fabric aside, his fingers parting the lips of her slick little *figa*, his mouth on her high ripe breasts, her hard nipples rolling under his tongue. Her lush body beneath his, opening up to him.

He soaped up his cock, the length going rigid as he imagined her mouth on him, his cock moving in and out between her ripe lips, the little moans in her throat as she swallowed him down, her tongue swirling over the head, again and again, driving him mad.

Now he was taking her on her hands and knees, thrusting into her from behind. She was so tight, gripping him like a glove, and he was fucking her like it was the last thing he was going to do on this earth. His hand slid up and down in a desperate rhythm. *Cristo.* Her ass jiggled as she pressed back into him, as his hips slapped against hers, her moans deepening as he slammed his cock into her.

He came with a groan, his heart pounding, his breathing ragged, momentarily spent as he leaned against the creamy white marble wall of the shower. *Dio,* he'd fantasized about her before, but it had never been that good. Now that he knew what she felt like, what she tasted like.... He took a deep breath. He couldn't spend all day in the shower. And he couldn't make love to Kate right now. Maybe not for quite a while, maybe not ever again. His chest ached.

He turned off the shower and stepped out, scrubbing roughly at his skin with a towel. He was finger-combing his hair when the mobile phone on the bathroom counter vibrated. He picked it up and was greeted by a frantic voice on the other end.

Carlo had finally made his move.

As he hurriedly pulled on clothes, the mobile phone continued to buzz like an agitated bee. First Dom, then Antonio, then Ruggero, then several other reports came in, all bad. Carlo's men had struck three times that evening, in different parts of Milan, roughing up business owners under Enrico's protection, including the elderly and influential Giacomo Parini and his wife Marietta. Targeting the Parinis meant Carlo was serious; if they bolted from the Lucchesi family's protection, many others would follow their lead.

Dom called again, his voice urgent when Enrico picked up. "They shot Ottavio Bottura."

"Will he live?"

"The doctors aren't sure."

"Damn it!" Enrico's mind was churning. "Where did it happen?"

"Near the others. He was checking on the Morettis. Carlo's men were waiting."

"Have you alerted everyone?"

"I've got men on it." There was a pause, then Dom said, "You must accept Delfina."

He was puzzled. "I thought you'd already arranged it."

"I have spoken to Dario and Carlo."

"But?"

"Carlo doesn't trust you. He says you must give up the American."

"I can't." He should have guessed. Carlo wanted her too.

"He says he will not have his granddaughter insulted by a public mistress."

The anger he'd been holding at bay exploded. "Fuck him. Everyone knows he has a mistress. He takes her everywhere!"

"I'm not arguing with you. It's not fair, but it's what he wants." There was a long silence, then Dom said, "So, you're not changing your mind."

"Either I have Kate, or no Delfina."

"Carlo will not accept that."

"As I said—"

"Yes, yes. Fuck him. That might feel good to say, but it won't solve our problem. Carlo is trying to cut us off at the knees with this business today."

"I'm aware of that." Why couldn't he just do the right thing? Why couldn't he just walk away from Kate? Why was he selfishly holding on to her, keeping her in danger?

"Since you seem to be out of ideas," Dom said, "may I recommend hard measures later tonight in each district Carlo controls around Milan?"

Enrico ignored the jab. "No. We go with a two-pronged approach starting now. Send a few men out to trash Andretti's business clients—frighten the owners, but don't harm them. I want them grateful it wasn't worse. I want everyone else we've got hitting Andretti's bases throughout the city. Burn them out if you have to. I want him to hurt."

"We'll make him suffer."

"The families who've been affected—you've issued compensation and protection?"

"Yes. Enzo's at the hospital with the Parinis, and I'm en route to Ottavio and his wife."

"I'll be there shortly." Enrico flipped the phone shut and went in search of Kate. He found her working in the solarium. "I have to go to Milan."

She closed her laptop. "What's wrong?"

"Carlo attacked several of my businesses."

"Is anyone hurt?"

"Yes. I am going to check on things. Pino and Ruggero will go with me; Antonio, Santino, and Claudio will stay with you." He paused. "Please stay near the house."

"Do you think they'll come here?"

He hated the anxiety in her voice. "I do not think so."

"He did send Vince though." Kate took a deep breath. "This is really happening, isn't it?"

He nodded. Seeing the terror on her face, he made a decision. "If you wish to leave, have your bags packed and ready to go when I return."

"I don't have a passport."

"Do not worry about that."

"Do you *want* me to go?"

"Of course not. But if you are afraid—"

"I'm staying."

He couldn't have been more shocked. Or more pleased. He grinned at her, his chest going warm with pleasure. "I do not know how long this will take."

"I'll be here."

He turned to go. "Wait." Hearing the desperation in her voice, he spun back to her and found her suddenly in his arms. Her hands on the back of his head urged him to her for a tender kiss. The warmth in his chest expanded, grew, as her lips met his, as she sighed into his mouth. He pulled her close, crushing her to him for an instant. Then he let her go. He had to, or he'd never leave. "Come back to me," she whispered. It was the first passionate kiss they'd shared since Vincenzo had attacked them. Joy flooded through him. If he survived this, there was hope for them.

He stroked a few stray hairs off her cheek, then kissed her once more, letting his hunger loose for an instant. "I will return soon." Then he turned and left, jogging to the cars out front. He passed Antonio heading up to the house and stopped him. "Stay with her at all times." He pinned Antonio with a hard stare.

"*Sì, capo.* I will guard her with my life."

He clapped Antonio on the back, then hurried to the Mercedes, where Pino and Ruggero were waiting with the engine running. Both were heavily armed. As soon as Enrico slipped inside, they headed for Milan. Another car with three men followed them.

Ruggero was sitting in front with Pino. He pulled a 9mm Glock out of his jacket pocket and handed it to Enrico. The gun felt heavy and cool in Enrico's hands. He popped the clip and checked that it was full, then slapped it back in. Every gunman made sure of his weapon. It was one of the first rules his father had taught him.

He put the gun in his pocket and settled back against the seat. His heart raced. So it was finally upon them. He was almost glad to have the waiting over. He just wished it weren't happening now, not with Kate here. Not now, not while he wasn't sure of her. But that kiss…. He smiled to himself.

Ruggero must have been watching him in the rearview mirror. He half-turned to Enrico. "Feels good to be in the action again, yes?"

Enrico nodded. It did. Though the action he was thinking of didn't involve bullets. He shook off the memory of Kate's body pressed against his. He needed his wits about him.

En route, he pulled out his mobile phone and dialed his godfather. Vittorio answered on the first ring with "*Ciao*, Enrico, my son," as if he were expecting the call.

"*Ciao, mio padrino.* You know why I'm calling?"

"I've heard Carlo has stuck a thorn in you."

"I'm dealing with it as we speak."

"I wish you well. I have a meeting with Benedetto in the morning about this outrage."

"*Mille grazie*, Don Battista."

"Thanks are not required. You do us all a great service, my boy. Carlo is a rabid dog who would tear everything apart if left unchecked. It is difficult to be his keeper. Even Benedetto does not like to tangle with his brother."

"Thank you for your kind words."

Vittorio laughed again, ending with another rasping cough. "You are so much like your father. So modest. But without the temper."

Enrico smiled. "I have the temper. I'm just not as free with it."

"Perhaps you would do well to unleash it from time to time. Carlo needs a reminder of who you are."

"Wise advice, Don Battista."

There was a pause, then Vittorio said, "I wish you to come see me when this has calmed down. There is a matter we must discuss."

Enrico felt a little jolt. The old don was the liaison between La Provincia, the quasi-ruling body of the 'Ndrangheta, and the individual families. "Am I in trouble?" he asked, then regretted letting his anxiety show.

"Call it an old man's intuition."

Enrico wondered what was on Don Battista's mind, but since they were approaching the outskirts of Milan, he wanted to be on full alert. "I'll come see you. I'd already been thinking of it."

"I look forward to it. And bring this American of yours. I wish to meet her."

"Will do. *Ciao.*" He waited for the old don's reply, then snapped the phone shut. Why did he want to see Kate? How had he even heard about her? He thought for a moment. Dom, of course. So Dom had already been complaining to their *padrino.* An inquiry from La Provincia was the last thing Enrico needed.

They rolled up to the hospital. Pino put the car in park and left the engine running. He waited for the guards from the other car to surround them, then he got out and opened the door for Enrico. Ruggero joined them, and the four men flanked Enrico as they entered the hospital.

They were soon outside the ICU. Enrico checked on Ottavio Bottura and his wife. The man's condition was grave, but there was hope he'd recover. He prayed with Ottavio's wife, handed her a thick envelope of euros, then left. It was all he could do for them at the moment.

He headed down the hall to see the Parinis. Giacomo had been badly beaten; his wife Marietta, while bruised, was well enough to be sitting by her husband's bedside when Enrico walked in. Patches of gauze and tape covered most of Giacomo's exposed skin. His left eye was swollen shut and a dark purple bruise spread over most of the left side of his face. "*Madonna,*" Enrico murmured under his breath. "*Come stai?*" he asked when he reached Giacomo's bedside.

Giacomo rolled his head to look at Enrico out of his good eye. "Don Enrico," he said, his voice raspy. "I've been worse." Before his father had gone into seclusion, Giacomo and Rinaldo had been close friends. Giacomo refused to call Enrico Don Lucchesi as long as Rinaldo was still alive. Enrico didn't mind. Even after all these years, the title didn't quite fit. Don Lucchesi was his father. Not him.

Enrico took Giacomo's hand. The old man's skin felt like crepe paper, the thick veins beneath it creating hills and valleys on the back of his hand. He glanced at Marietta, shame burning his cheeks. Two more people he'd failed to protect. "I apologize deeply for what has happened."

"When I chose sides, I knew this could happen one day. But it would have been easier to bear a decade or two ago." Giacomo smiled, wincing when his split lower lip tore open.

"I am grateful for your support, and sorry it has cost you so much." Seeing Giacomo like this, feeling how frail he was, made his chest ache.

"I cannot in good conscience support Andretti. He's a snake."

"I will put two men in your shop at all times. Send me the bill for any extra help you have to hire while you're recovering." He pulled another envelope thick with euros from his jacket pocket and handed it to Marietta. "Let me know if this doesn't cover your expenses."

"*Grazie,* Don Lucchesi," she said.

Giacomo squeezed his hand. "We will remain loyal to you. You need not fear. However, you must seek peace with Andretti, you must settle this matter soon. Otherwise, there will be defections. I cannot long argue in your favor with the other merchants if they keep suffering."

"Carlo made an example of you to scare them."

"It's working. My mobile phone has been ringing all night. Most are terrified right now."

"I have men on the streets as we speak. Carlo will suffer for this."

"Make sure he does." Giacomo coughed, then let out a gasp of pain, squeezing Enrico's hand harder than he would have thought possible. "My ribs."

"*Signore,* please don't worry yourself. I have it under control."

"Do you?" Marietta whispered. When he turned his eyes toward her, she clapped a hand over her mouth and averted her gaze.

"Carlo will not trouble you further." His tone was firm, but he kept his voice soft.

She finally met his eyes. "We are counting on you, Don Lucchesi."

"As I am counting on you. I'll do my utmost to resolve this matter immediately." He gave the old man's hand another squeeze. Then he made the sign of the cross and said a quick prayer for Giacomo before he left.

But it was up to him, not God, to make things right. It was *his* selfishness, *his* stubbornness, that had gotten them to this point. But he wouldn't roll over for Carlo; that would be the worst move he could make. He had to play this carefully, or soon he wouldn't be playing at all.

He met Dom in the hallway. Their guards had split into three groups of two and were posted at the entrances to the ICU.

"Dom," Enrico said, inclining his head stiffly. He was still angry over what he'd heard from Don Battista. How dare Dom go to La Provincia?

Dom eyed him warily. "How are the Parinis?"

"Marietta is fine. Giacomo is badly hurt, but he will survive."

"We need to talk. Some place more private."

They walked outside, heavily flanked by guards, when a group of men on foot rushed at them from the shadows, shots blasting from their guns. Adrenaline flooded Enrico's body; he struggled to keep his breathing even and his mind clear as he and the guards raced toward the cars. Ruggero's gun was up and firing before Enrico had his in hand. He was about to pull the trigger when pain seared through his upper left arm. He grabbed at it with his right hand. His fingers and the gun stock came back bloody. He'd been hit.

His step slowed. *Keep going.* Crouching lower, he ran for the car, trying to make himself a smaller target. Ruggero glanced back at him a couple times, doing his best to keep his body in front of Enrico's. Another of the guards kept pace with them. Dom headed to his own car. He appeared to be unhurt, but it was hard to tell in the darkness.

They reached the Mercedes and found Pino slumped behind the wheel. Enrico dived into the back seat. "Fuck!" Ruggero exclaimed, wrenching the driver's door open and shoving Pino's body over to the passenger side. He motioned with his gun to the other guard, indicating that he should drive. Ruggero jumped in the back next to Enrico and they roared off, the cars with the other guards and Dom's men right behind them.

Ruggero looked at Enrico, seeing the blood on his jacket. "How bad?"

"I'll live." Enrico pulled his mobile phone out and called Dom. "Pino's gone. Did you lose anyone?"

"My driver, and one of my men is injured. I'm taking him to the field clinic."

"I'll meet you there."

"Perhaps you should return home."

"No." His talk with Dom couldn't wait.

He leaned forward and spoke to the guard behind the wheel. They changed direction and headed for one of their safe command posts in the city. Enrico settled back on the seat, closing his eyes, the wound on his arm throbbing. Dom was hiding something. They'd fought before, certainly. But never had Enrico doubted Dom's loyalty, his love. But now… Dom had gone over his head to La Provincia, which meant Dom was willing to risk Enrico's life. La Provincia wouldn't hesitate to eliminate a *capo* who wasn't acting in the best interests of his *cosca* or the 'Ndrangheta. And Dom would be ready to take Enrico's place if they did.

They pulled up to a building owned by the Lucchesi *cosca*. There were several soundproof, heavily armored apartments on the bottom floor with separate entrances that could be used for meetings or eluding the police. One of the apartments had been set up as a rudimentary clinic. The injured man was taken there so the doctor could attend to him.

Dom and Enrico entered the apartment next door and sat down at the simple wooden table in the kitchen, neither of them saying a word until Dom noticed the blood seeping from the hole in Enrico's jacket. "Shall I get the doctor?"

"No. It's nothing."

Dom frowned. "You're still bleeding. I'd better bandage it." He rose and fetched a first aid kit from the bathroom. When he returned, he pulled out bandages, gauze, and antibiotic ointment while Enrico removed his jacket and rolled up his left sleeve. The shallow tear oozed blood, but he'd been lucky.

While Dom was cleaning the wound, Enrico spoke. Business first, the things they couldn't discuss on the phone. "What's happened so far?"

"We've hit the Vigentino, Quinto Romano, and Crescenzago districts so far. I don't think they were expecting such an aggressive move. We took several command posts and many weapons."

"Casualties?"

"Three dead, five wounded on our side, at least a dozen dead on theirs. Carlo has let his men get sloppy. We have men fanning out to Carlo's other strongholds."

"*Bene.* Have you heard from Carlo?"

"Dario has asked to speak with you."

"When?"

"Tonight." Dom checked his watch. "In an hour."

"Where?" Enrico did not want to meet with the Andrettis. Not this soon.

"Any place of your choosing."

Interesting. Why would they be so conciliatory so quickly? He didn't like it. "Tell him no."

Dom looked startled. "He feels insulted. Refusing to see him will not help."

Enrico stared at him hard. "You made this mess. You clean it up."

"I was trying to help you."

"I don't need it." He watched Dom's face carefully, but hurt was all he saw. He leaned closer to his friend and lowered his voice. "I don't understand you. I've made my wishes clear, and yet you defy me. I spoke to Don Battista in the car on the way here. Why have you spoken to La Provincia about Kate?"

"I haven't. I mentioned her to Don Battista, but it was a personal question, not an official one."

"What was his advice?"

Dom lowered his eyes. "He said I should stay out of it, that he would speak to you."

"Are you going to listen to him?"

Dom looked up at Enrico. "He is my *padrino* too, so yes, I will let him handle it. But I would shake you until you saw sense if I could. You nearly got us all killed. Because of your selfishness!"

Enrico blanched. Dom was right. And wasn't he also right to involve La Provincia if he thought that necessary? "I'm sorry."

"Sorry won't save our lives." Dom smeared the antibiotic ointment over the wound, his touch rough.

"I know." Killing Vincenzo and turning down Delfina—both were grave insults. Vendettas had been waged over less, and there were many in La

Provincia who would sympathize with the Andrettis if the matter came before them for resolution. Giving Dario and Carlo fancy cars or a pile of cash wouldn't allow the Andrettis to save face. No, a deeper sacrifice was called for.

"I'm thinking about offering them the Bicocca district." It would strengthen the Andrettis' hold on the construction business in Milan, giving them more than half of it. "Kate is part of it—she walks away from all this and is let alone. And if she wants to stay with me, she stays."

Dom frowned as he taped gauze over the cut. "You're asking a lot."

"I'll marry Delfina as well, if necessary. But I keep Kate if she's willing."

"What if the Andrettis don't accept?"

Enrico blew out a breath. He didn't want to make the offer, but if he had to, to stop the bloodshed, to save Kate, he would. "We give them a discount on the wash."

Dom stared at him. "You're willing to sacrifice your precious principles?"

"I am. For her."

Dom sat back in his chair, his mouth open. "You really do care about her."

"What did you think? That I'd do all this on a whim?"

"I thought you'd give her up if you had to."

"That I will not do. Not unless she desires it."

"You would even marry her?"

"I would." His answer, so unhesitating, surprised even him. But it was true. He loved her; he could admit that now. It wasn't lust that drove him. It was love. It was her.

"You're a fool. She'll never accept you, she'll never accept this," Dom said, gesturing around them.

"That may be." Enrico returned Dom's stare. He was tired of all of this. Tired of waiting. Maybe Dario and Carlo were trying to set a trap, but this evening he was through being cautious. "Call them. Let's get this over with."

"You've changed your mind?" When Enrico nodded, Dom asked, "How deep will you go on the discount?"

"Up to five percent." It was a significant offer. If they didn't accept, he'd appeal to La Provincia. No one could fault his generosity.

"You know, this wouldn't have happened if we were stronger."

"I will not resort to drugs and prostitution to fill our coffers."

Dom sighed. "But think of what we could do then. We could hire more men. We could drive the Andrettis out of Milan. Don't you want that?"

Enrico's smile was bitter. "More than anything. But not at that cost."

"So you'll bend the rules to save her, but not to save the rest of us? You'll even weaken us over her." Dom smacked his fist onto his knee. "Don't you see what you're doing?"

Dom was right, and at the same time, he was wrong. It wasn't right to stoop so low to win. How could he look at himself in the mirror if he did? But he was risking them all, he couldn't debate that. And for a woman he wasn't even sure he could have. It was risky and foolish, and very unlike the Enrico Lucchesi he knew. But he couldn't help himself. He wanted her, and he would win her. If it was the last thing he did.

He looked at Dom. "I see everything very clearly. And I will be the victor."

ഇരു

They met the Andrettis on neutral ground, at a safe house owned by the d'Imperios. Dario and Carlo were already seated on one side of a highly polished mahogany dining table when Dom and Enrico arrived. After everyone had been searched for weapons, the guards retreated outside to wait. Dom and Enrico took seats across from the Andrettis.

Silence prevailed. Enrico ignored Carlo and looked at Dario first, his aquiline nose, generous mouth, and large dark eyes reminding him of Toni. His hair was even the same shade of blue black. *Cristo.* It hurt to look at him.

Dario flexed his right hand, and the missing little finger drew his gaze. He'd never spoken to Dario about that incident, all those years ago, when both of them had been caught up in the fight between their fathers. Dario was lucky he had a right hand at all, maimed though it was. He nodded in Enrico's direction, perhaps acknowledging the debt he owed him.

Enrico held his gaze for a moment, then he turned to Carlo. He hadn't seen him since Toni's funeral. He looked a bit thinner, but otherwise the same—his thick silver hair combed back off his face, his sharp nose jutting above thin lips, his cream suit finely cut, his attire expensive and ostentatious. The diamond ring on the little finger of his left hand and the gold Rolex at his wrist winked in the light from the chandelier overhead.

Carlo glared at Enrico, his eyes blazing. Enrico was sure his own were hardly more neutral. Dom shifted beside him, no doubt wanting to dispel the mounting tension. But Enrico knew the value of silence. Someone else—preferably Carlo—would be the one to break it.

Carlo pulled a cigar out of his breast pocket, his movements unhurried. He clipped the end off, then lit it, taking several slow puffs until it caught the flame. Smoke curled around his face as he sat back in his chair. He contemplated the burning cigar for a moment, dragging out the wait, then he raised his eyes to Enrico's. "So, you have the courage to meet my challenge face to face."

Enrico bristled, but that was what Carlo wanted. He took a breath, then let it out. "That was a challenge, was it? Beating old people, terrorizing my clients. How noble of you. If you wanted to meet with me, you could've just asked."

Dom nudged him, his eyes pleading with him to behave. Not bloody likely. He turned back to Carlo.

Carlo took a long drag on his cigar, then let the smoke out through his nose and mouth. "I could've just asked, he says." He looked at his son. "Do you think Lucchesi would have responded to a polite request?" Dario shrugged. Carlo turned away from him with a grimace.

Enrico looked at Dario, sizing him up as a possible ally. Dom had said Dario was angry, but he didn't seem upset. He turned his attention back to Carlo. "So what is it that you want—other than my head on a platter."

Carlo laughed. "Your head on a platter is just the start." He drew on the cigar, his cheeks hollowing out as he inhaled. Then he sent a stream of smoke across the table, into Enrico's face. "Aside from that, I want you and your"—he waved his hand to indicate Dom—"ilk out of Milan."

Enrico ignored the smoke. Carlo wouldn't bait him so easily. "Anything else?"

Carlo's mouth shifted into a leer. "Now that the American has shed her husband, she'll need a new man in her bed. I am willing to oblige her."

A surge of adrenaline sent Enrico's heart into overdrive. "I would think you'd rather avenge Vincenzo than cuckold his memory."

Carlo shrugged. "She already gave him the horns. What more damage could I do?" He sucked on the cigar again. "Though what you say has merit. He was my nephew." He met and held Enrico's gaze. "Of course, I blame you for what happened. She may have pulled the trigger, but his death was your doing. You couldn't resist an opportunity to hurt an Andretti by stealing his wife."

"You think I hate you that much?"

Carlo laughed, then started to cough. His voice rasped when he spoke. "Of course you do. Just as I hate you. That much." His eyes went flat and cold on the words.

Enrico leaned forward. "Enough with the pleasantries. Why are we *really* here?"

Carlo set the cigar in a crystal ashtray and clasped his hands together. "As I said, I want the Lucchesi stench out of Milan. Perhaps then I can forgive... certain transgressions."

"Vincenzo was not my fault. He brought that on himself."

Carlo's voice hoarsened. "And what of my Toni? Did she deserve your mistreatment?"

"What mistreatment? I *loved* her, I treated her like a queen."

"You know what you did. Your disrespect, taking that little slut into your bed when Toni was barely cold in her grave." He stared daggers at Enrico.

A flush rose up his neck. "She'd been dead six months."

"You couldn't wait to replace her. To get a child by some other woman." Carlo paused. "Of course, your own weakness thwarted those plans."

Enrico said nothing. His teeth ground together, the muscles bunching in his jaw as Carlo continued.

"You wanted to replace her all along, didn't you? You never loved her. All you wanted was an heir. And when she…" Carlo's voice broke. "When she failed—" He glared at Enrico, then gathered himself. "I wouldn't put it past you to have poisoned her."

His mouth dropped open. "You know as well as I do she had cancer. I would never harm her. *Never*." He took a deep breath, trying to calm his racing heart and churning stomach. The man was insane. Enrico was on the verge of becoming irrational himself. He stood and backed away from the table, pacing a few steps before turning back. "I was devastated when she died. You *know* that."

Carlo leaned back, his eyes not leaving Enrico's. "Your conduct afterward gives the lie to your grief."

"Fiammetta was a mistake. I admit that." He started to say more, then stopped. "I don't have to justify myself to you." He sat back down. "Stop this nonsense. Either ask for something reasonable or let's call off this charade."

"You want me to be *reasonable*, do you? So like your father." Carlo flattened his hands on the table and leaned toward Enrico. "Fine. I want the meatpacking and jewelry businesses in Milan." He paused. "And I want the whore. Tell me, Don Lucchesi, does the thatch between her legs match that glorious red mane of hers?"

Heat blasted through Enrico. He lunged across the table, grabbing Carlo by the lapels of his fine suit and pulling him half out of his chair. "Kate is no whore. And she is *mine*."

"Take your filthy hands off me." Carlo's voice was hard, but there was a smile on his face.

Dom put a restraining hand on Enrico's left arm. The wound throbbed in response to the pressure. "Rico, please."

Enrico let Carlo go with a shove that pushed him back into his chair. "You disgust me."

Carlo straightened his suit. "Likewise."

"This *discussion* is over," Enrico said. He turned to go.

"Wait," Dom said, putting a hand on his shoulder. "Let's be gentlemen, shall we?" He looked at all of them in turn.

Enrico crossed his arms. "What do you propose we do? Settle this with pistols at ten paces?"

"Carlo asked for something. The woman aside, do you think it fair compensation?"

Enrico breathed in deeply. He uncrossed his arms. "Both meatpacking and jewelry? Too much."

"My nephew's death is no small thing."

"You were willing to cuckold him just minutes ago. Your mourning is touching."

Carlo waved his cigar in the air as he chuckled. "You may have a point."

"So," Dom said, "what can we agree on?"

"I'm willing to part with half of each. No more."

Carlo considered it. "What of my justice regarding the woman?"

"She stays with me. And you agree her debt is paid."

"What about my Delfina?" Dario asked.

Enrico hated his answer, but they needed a marriage to cement things. "I'll marry her, if you still want that. But I keep Kate. Discreetly." *If she'll still have me.*

Dario looked at Carlo. Carlo puffed on his cigar, squinting against the smoke. "You can keep your whore. But Delfina must not be aware of it."

"Are we through here?" Enrico asked.

"Add the Fiat dealership, and we're done."

"Agreed."

They did not shake on the deal, settling it with curt nods.

But Enrico had the feeling nothing had been settled at all. Why hadn't Carlo asked for a discount on the wash? Carlo's demands had centered on territory. And Kate. That wasn't like the man he knew. Carlo was up to something.

He conferred briefly with Dom outside the house, telling him he was taking Kate to see Don Battista.

"I don't think our *padrino* is going to like the idea of you keeping her."

"I'll listen to what he says, but Kate stays with me, if she and I wish it."

"You would disobey him?"

"I'll make him understand."

His cousin shook his head. "What has gotten into you?"

Love. That was the only answer. "I won't be happy without her."

Dom sighed. "When will you be back?"

"Three or four days. It depends."

"On what?"

"On how it goes. And if my father is still there."

"You're flying down then?"

Enrico nodded. "I'll let you know when we're returning."

"Take your time. You look tired, Rico." Dom's eyes were heavy with concern.

Enrico sighed and rubbed his face. "I am. More than you know."

Dom clapped him on the back and saw him to the Mercedes. "*Ciao*, Rico." They embraced, Dom squeezing him much more tightly than Enrico expected.

"So we are friends again," Enrico said when they parted.

"We never weren't." Dom held his eyes. "Everything I've done, I've done because you're my brother." His voice quavered and he coughed, then shook his head. "You have that thick Lucchesi head, you know. If I didn't love you,

I wouldn't try to shake sense into you."

Enrico nodded, his throat so tight he could barely speak. "*Mille grazie,* brother." He turned and got in the car before his eyes filled with tears.

He let his head loll back against the seat as Ruggero drove them home. Hope warmed his chest. At least one good thing had come from this relentless day. He had his best friend back by his side.

He should be glad too that the fight with Carlo was over. Though the cost, the loss of Kate as his wife… it was far too much to pay. But she was safe. That was the important part.

Of course, there was no guarantee Carlo wouldn't find another excuse to go after them, sooner or later. Or no excuse at all.

CHAPTER 18

Soon after Enrico left, Antonio strolled into the solarium, a machine gun hanging from his shoulder. Kate looked up from the papers she was transcribing, her eyes zeroing in on the weapon. *Jesus, this was serious.* None of the guards had ever carried a large gun inside. When Antonio saw her alarm, he said, "Do not worry, *signora*. The house is safe. This is…." He patted the gun, apparently not knowing the word he wanted. "It is for caution," he finally said.

"You mean the gun is a precaution?" He nodded. She eyed the weapon, then looked out the window. In the fading light, she saw that Claudio and Santino, heavy guns slung over their shoulders, had taken positions in the garden on either side of the solarium. So much firepower, all for her.

"Is Enrico in a lot of danger?"

"Some." He paused. "He does not have to go, but he does."

"What do you mean?"

"He cares for his people. More than most men in his position." She heard pride in his voice.

"You feel great loyalty to him."

Antonio nodded. "He feels it to me, to all of us. I will do anything he asks of me."

"Including taking a bullet for me?"

"*Sì.*"

"Just because he asked?"

He nodded. Then his face changed and he looked uncomfortable. "*Signora,* I am deeply ashamed of my behavior earlier. I was not here when your husband—"

She cut him off. "You don't need to apologize. It wasn't your fault."

"I should have been here, *signora*. I will not neglect my duty again."

She was about to say something in response, but he turned away, taking a post outside the open door.

Kate set her laptop aside, mulling over what Antonio had said. It was clear he admired and loved Enrico. Her own feelings weren't so simple.

Stroking her thumb across her lower lip, she relived that last kiss. She'd surprised herself by initiating it, by saying she'd stay. She hadn't wanted Enrico to leave without knowing... what? That she wanted him? That she would be his? Well, maybe someday. If she thought Enrico could truly love her. If she thought he could put her first in his heart....

She let out a hiss. This was madness. He was keeping things from her. And he was a dangerous man to know. Or maybe *she* was the dangerous one and he ought to steer clear of her. She smiled. She'd certainly trailed her problems along with her when she'd come to his home. But he hadn't complained. And he hadn't shied away from the danger.

Even so, some piece of all this was missing, and she needed to know it before she could commit herself in any way. She could not be nearly as trusting as Antonio.

She picked up the papers and her laptop again, trying in vain to concentrate, but she kept losing her place. Was Enrico all right? How would she feel if he wasn't?

She didn't know how long she'd been lost in her thoughts when Antonio's cell phone rang. After exchanging a few clipped words with someone, he stepped back into the room. "Signor Lucchesi is returning. All is well."

She smiled. "Thank God he's all right." Her hand flew to her mouth, and Antonio returned the smile.

"*Sì, signora.*"

The papers slipped from her lap onto the floor, and she reached down for them, her belly doing a slow roll. Enrico was okay, and she was more happy about that than she'd expected.

And on top of that, her first instinct wasn't to run away. Far from it.

Every cell in her body was telling her to stay.

஻௸

When Enrico returned, Kate was waiting for him in the study with two glasses of sambuca already poured. As he walked in the door, she looked up at him, her eyes full of warmth, and something more. "All hail the conquering hero," she said, her voice teasing.

He smiled, his heavy heart suddenly feeling as light as her voice. He hadn't expected this. He'd been prepared for her to be worried, angry even. Something had changed, but he didn't know what. Lingering in the doorway, he stared as she rose from the sofa. What a sight, this woman he loved. Her auburn hair gleamed in the lamplight, her skin, white like cream. And those eyes....

Not to mention the rest of her. She'd changed into a dark green dress that clung to her in all the right places. The fullness of her hips and breasts made her look like ripe fruit.

Fruit he couldn't wait to taste.

If she'd let him. The kiss she'd given him before he'd left, the look in her eyes now, hinted that there was hope.

He watched as she carried the sambuca to him, mesmerized by the sway of her hips, the bounce of her breasts, the movements of her delicate wrists and ankles. She handed him the glass, lightly beaded with condensation. He heard the chink of ice, the ring of the crystal as their glasses came together. "*Salute*," she said, then raised her glass to her lips.

He did the same, tasting the liquor, inhaling its heady scent. So sweet, just like her. "Close the door," she said. He pushed it shut, a thrill coursing through him, then followed her to the sofa. He sat down, wondering where this was going, not really caring as long as it was going somewhere.

Kate was still standing. "Give me your jacket." He shrugged it off and handed it to her. She started to fold it to set it aside, when she noticed the blood on the sleeve. "You're hurt," she said, her voice rising as she looked at him, seeking the source of the injury.

He pointed to the bandaged wound on his left arm. "It's nothing."

"What happened?"

"I was visiting one of my men in the hospital. Carlo's men ambushed us when we left."

She raised a hand to her mouth, covering her gasp. "Was anyone hurt?"

He frowned, looking down at the carpet. "Pino's dead."

"Oh my God!"

He stood up and took her in his arms. "I have settled things with Carlo. We are safe."

"Are you sure?"

"I think so." He motioned toward the sofa and they sat down. "Do you mind if we do not talk about it right now? I would like to think about something else for a while." His heart ached anew. What would she say when he told her he'd accepted Delfina?

He took her hand, seeing that she was still shaken. For a moment, he almost gave in to the sorrow threatening to overwhelm him, but he fought against it. He'd had too much heartache for one day. Hoping to return to the lighter mood of just moments ago, he motioned to her dress, their drinks. "So what is all this, Kate? You were happy when I walked in."

She looked away from him. "I was thinking... oh, never mind."

"You were thinking about what?"

"You and me. Us." She shyly met his gaze.

He made his tone playful. "And what were you thinking about us?"

She blushed, color staining her cheeks. "It's not the right time, I know, but

I was thinking...." She took a breath before stumbling on. "We haven't, you know, since the attack."

"Ah." He smiled, his heart beating at a fast clip. He leaned toward her. "Were you thinking we should?"

She nodded, the red of her cheeks deepening, spreading to her throat. "I was."

"After you kissed me, you were all I could think about in the car."

She looked up at him then. He didn't hesitate. He took her face in both hands and brushed his lips against hers, feeling their plump softness. She gave a little whimper and threaded her fingers through his hair, her mouth opening under his. He licked the bottom edge of her top lip, pleased when her tongue finally reached out to his. Her touch was unsure, shy, but increasingly bold as they continued to kiss. This Kate, this demure creature, was new to him, and he wondered at the change in her. Once again, he wished he'd killed Vincenzo Andretti the first time they'd met.

They parted after some minutes, both breathing hard. Her hair had fallen into her face, and he pushed it back, so he could look at her. "What brought this on?" he murmured, amused and deeply happy.

She smiled and looked straight into his eyes. "I realized I don't want to go home." She said it lightly, softly, but he could see the depth of emotion behind it. It wasn't "I love you," but in a way, it was much, much more.

"I am glad to hear you say that, *cara*." Perhaps, at last, he'd whittled a hole in her armor.

§)(2

Kate's smile widened at the endearment. *Cara*. She liked the sound of it, his voice husky and sweet when he spoke.

His eyes moved down to her lips. She lay back against the cushions and he moved over her, pressing the length of his body against hers. He kissed her harder this time, his touch more urgent, and she could feel the bulge of his erection pushing into her hip. He was too close, too heavy, too large. Her breath caught, and an unfamiliar wave of anxiety crashed through her, making her heart thrash against her ribs like a bird trying to escape a cage. Panting, she pushed on his chest, needing space.

"Kate, what is wrong?" He shifted so he was sitting on the coffee table in front of the couch.

She sat up and shook her head. "I don't know. I just felt... crushed."

"We don't have to do this now. It's enough to know you want to. When you're ready."

Her eyes grew hot with tears. Vince wasn't going to win, he wasn't going to haunt her. "I *am* ready." She forced the words out, forced her voice to be steady.

"You don't look it." He leaned forward and took her hands in his.

"Just… go slow."

"*Cara.*" He turned one of her hands up, kissing the palm, sending a tingle across her skin. He took her face in his hands again, his thumbs stroking her cheeks, his eyes locked onto hers. His lips hovered over her mouth for a moment, then he feathered delicate kisses along its length, like a butterfly fluttering over a bloom. When she let out a sigh of pleasure, he put a few millimeters between them, his warm breath washing over her skin when he spoke. "You are certain?"

She nodded, not able to say it. It wasn't just the roiling in her gut that stole her voice. Her desire for him meant so much more to her now, and she was afraid he'd hear it if she spoke, that he'd know the power he had over her. That he would know how badly he could hurt her.

And yet, what had she been doing but trying to seduce him since he'd walked into the room? And then pushing him away. What a mess she was. But he was looking at her like she was the greatest thing in the world. More precious than gold. Warmth bubbled up in her chest and she took a deep breath. It was going to be okay. She was with Enrico, and he would never hurt her. That she knew with certainty, a certainty she rarely felt about anything. But she felt certain about this man.

Enrico waited until he saw the change in her, the tightness around her eyes and mouth receding, her shoulders coming down, her breathing slowing to normal. He wasn't surprised she was struggling, but he could go as slow as she needed to. He could spend hours just kissing her and doing nothing else. Now that he knew she wanted him, that she wanted to stay, they had all the time in the world.

Slowly, carefully, he kissed his way down her neck, licking the notch at the base of her throat, mouthing the end of her collarbone. She tasted like vanilla and honey. His fingers traced where his tongue had tasted her, and he remembered the last time he'd touched her, by the pool, the way he had ached then to kiss her, to hold her, to have her. He could hardly believe his good fortune now. She wanted him again. The way he wanted her.

He pulled down the neckline of her dress, kissing the top of one breast, then the other. He smiled at the light dusting of freckles; other than a few on her nose and cheeks, it was the only visible reminder of their afternoon at the pool. His hands looked so dark against her pale skin. He liked the contrast, so different from any other woman he'd ever known.

He returned to her lips for a moment, checking in. This time she kissed him back and moaned a little. Encouraged, he pushed the straps of her bra off her shoulders, freeing her breasts from the cups. They fit nicely in his hands, the areolas a delicate pink around the nipples. He massaged her breasts lightly, watching her face. The bite on her left breast was healing, but it wasn't gone entirely. Very carefully, he kissed the mark. When she smiled at him, he returned it, relieved.

He circled his fingers over her breasts, but avoided her nipples, watching as they stiffened, expectant. Finally he took one in his mouth, then the other, swirling his tongue around each one, sucking on it until she moaned and clutched his shoulders. The sound made his cock jump and his heart soar. He moved farther down her body, pushing the light fabric of her dress up her thighs to her waist, exposing pale pink panties that clung to her cleft like a second skin.

He peeled them off, tossing the nearly translucent cloth to the floor. He'd wanted to tear them off, but he didn't want to remind her of Vincenzo. He loved her, and he was going to show her how much. He ran his hands down the insides of her thighs in teasing strokes, inching toward his goal. Then he fanned one hand over her sex, massaging it lightly, his fingers caressing the lips of it, then slipping between them to the wetness inside. When he touched her, she drew in a breath, and he looked up into her eyes, waiting for her to smile again before he continued.

As his thumb slowly circled her clit, Kate closed her eyes and bit her lip to keep from crying out, to keep from telling him she wanted more, more, more. But he knew by now what she liked.

She felt him shift forward onto his knees and then his mouth was between her legs. She gasped at the contact and closed her legs a bit. It was too much, this pleasure. Enrico planted a hand on the inside of each thigh and pressed them open, giving him full access to her. As his tongue moved on her pussy, she flushed all over, heat rising in her face, her chest. This was madness. And heaven. What a shameless, wanton hussy she was, raising her hips to meet his mouth, then pulling his head closer to her. He slipped two fingers inside her, moving them in and out in rhythm with his tongue, his fingers sliding easily in her slick wetness. She came suddenly, the explosion of sensation surprising her into a throaty cry.

He planted a kiss just above the mound of her sex, then stood and pulled off his shirt, the muscles in his arms, chest, and stomach flexing in the most appealing way as he grinned at her. Then he kicked off his shoes and started removing his pants. She lay slumped against the back of the couch, her legs splayed open, a bit dazed, enjoying the tanned, well-muscled body he revealed to her, until he said, "You are wearing entirely too much."

Kate smiled and rose, skinning off the dress and unhooking the bra. As she stepped out of her heels, he sat down on the coffee table and pulled her to him, his face level with her breasts. He suckled them again, his hands cupping her ass as she ran her hands through his thick black hair. Then he sat her down on his knees. She reached between their legs, circling her fingers around him, giving his cock an experimental stroke. She loved the heft of it, a little longer and thicker than she could easily take, but she was ready for him. He groaned when her fingers traced the vein that ran along the underside of his cock, then he cupped his hands behind her buttocks and urged her forward. She held his eyes as she guided him into her. "*Madonna,*" he whispered as she opened to him.

"'Whore' is probably more appropriate," she teased.

He stopped moving and took hold of her chin so that she had to look at him. "*Never* say that again. I never want to hear that word applied to you, do you hear me?" His intensity surprised her. *What was* that *about?* He kissed her, then let go of her chin. His lips trailed down to her neck as he started thrusting inside her. "Not my woman, not my wife," he murmured, and her eyes popped open. *Wife?* She looked at him, wondering if he'd confused her with Antonella. His eyes were closed, and he seemed lost in the sensation of their lovemaking. Which, considering how good it felt, was no surprise.

She filed that comment away for later and wrapped her legs around his waist, letting him in deeper. He responded by moving faster, his hands tilting her pelvis up a bit more, his fingers pressing into her buttocks as he forced her to open wider. His breathing was ragged in her ear, and she bit down on his shoulder as she came again. He groaned and his strokes sped up, his hands moving to her hips so he could lift her up and down, so he could make his thrusts more forceful. Thank God he'd stopped treating her like a china doll.

Remembering the sweet torture she could inflict on him, she clamped her internal muscles around him hard several times in succession. He stiffened and cried out. After he caught his breath, he kissed her again. Then he pulled back so he could look at her, a grin on his face. "I cannot hold off when you do that."

His brown eyes seemed almost black as they scanned her face. She reached up and traced his brows, then his cheekbones. "Thank you for this," she whispered.

"I should be thanking *you.*" His grin widened. "At least we are not apologizing to each other anymore."

She looked at him for a moment more, wanting to ask about what he'd said earlier, but not sure how, or if she should. She stood up, but he pulled her back down onto his lap. "What's wrong?" he asked.

"What did you mean when you said, 'Not my wife'?"

Color rose to his cheeks. "That was… a mistake. I want you to be my wife, but…." His voice trailed off.

Did he just say he wanted to *marry* her? "But what?"

He pulled her closer. "I do not know how to say this."

Kate's heart sped up. She wasn't going to like this. "Just say it," she whispered, placing her head on his chest.

His voice was low and unsteady. "Part of the agreement with Carlo is that I have to marry his granddaughter, Delfina."

Her body went cold, then numb. *Oh God.* So that *was* what he and Dom had been discussing when she'd spied on them that first night. She wished she'd trusted in her Italian. She was a fool.

"Kate, look at me." He nudged her chin up, and when she opened her eyes, she was horrified to see her vision blurred with tears. "I am so sorry. I want to marry you, not her. But I have to keep you safe."

She sniffed hard, trying to hold back her tears. "It's okay." But it wasn't.

"No, it is not. Not now, not when I know you have feelings for me."

She shrugged. "It doesn't matter. You're still in love with your wife anyway. It's not like there's room for anyone else."

"That is not true."

"It is, Enrico. You still can't take off your ring, can you?"

※ ※

Enrico raised his left hand and looked at his wedding band. *Madonna.* Until he'd seen Dario, he hadn't thought much about Toni the last few days. He'd been so focused on Kate, on what had been happening with Carlo, that he'd almost forgotten his grief. "I can do it now." He pulled off the ring and set it on the table. His hand felt strange, lighter, without it. Strange, but all right. He looked at Kate. "I want to be with you. I want to be your husband."

Kate shoved back from him and retreated to the sofa. "You have a funny way of showing it. You're marrying someone else!"

"I will not marry her. I do not love her."

"You *should* marry her."

"What?" He could barely form the word, he was so confused.

Her eyes blazed. "You might as well. Marriage is just a business deal to you. How can you possibly make love to me right after getting engaged to another woman? You're using that poor girl like a bargaining chip. What is *wrong* with you?"

"I will not do it."

"So you're going to let Carlo kill us both then? Over what: your heart?"

Enrico stared at her openmouthed, appalled, his gut twisting. "Does this not matter to you?"

"Of course it does!" Her eyes filled with tears.

"I do not understand you. First you do not want me to marry her, then you do."

"I don't understand *you*. How can you be so cavalier about this? Who you marry should *matter* to you."

"It does. And I want it to be you." How could he make her understand? Delfina meant nothing; Kate meant everything.

Kate stared at him, her chest tight. "You don't know what love is." He may have removed the ring, but it didn't mean anything. He still loved Antonella. He had to. It was the only palatable explanation for how he was acting. There was no room for her in his heart as long as Antonella still filled it.

She looked away from him, wiping her eyes. "I want to go home."

"You cannot leave. You do not have a passport."

"You were going to figure that out earlier today. You said I could leave if I wanted to."

"I have changed my mind."

Kate clenched her hands into fists. *Bastard.* "You can't *do* that."

"I can and I will. You will wait until Fuente clears you. And in the meantime, we are going to Capri, as planned."

"No."

He leaned forward and put his hands on her shoulders. "I cannot let you go. Not just yet."

The rawness, the almost pleading note, in his voice made her soften. "Are you going to marry her?"

"No." He held her gaze. "I want you."

His behavior didn't add up. Unless…. She frowned, her stomach contracting into a ball. "So if you married her, you were planning what? To make me your mistress?"

His eyes slid away from hers. "Something like that. If you would agree to it."

A wave of heat blasted through her. Who did he think she was? "And have Carlo Andretti call me a whore at every opportunity? No thanks."

He touched her cheek, and she slapped his hand away. "Don't touch me."

"*Cara*—"

"Don't call me that either."

He took a deep breath. "I am *not* going to marry her. I made a mistake in ever agreeing to it. I thought it was the right thing to do, that it would bring peace." He paused. "And I was not sure of your heart." He took one of her hands in both of his. "Will you *please* allow me to make amends to you?"

There was a certain logic to what he said; she might be wrong about how he felt. There might be hope after all. "I'll go to Capri. But I'm not promising anything."

He smiled, his relief evident. "I will make it up to you. You will see how much I love you."

When she processed what he said, a barrage of emotions rocketed through her. "You *love* me?"

"Of *course* I love you, Kate. Why else would I want to marry you?" He seemed puzzled by her reaction.

She smirked, not wanting to let him know how shaken she was. "Well, it certainly isn't to save your neck, now is it?"

"That is unfair."

"It's the truth. It's the reason you married Antonella, and it's the reason you were going to marry Delfina." He said nothing. "Fair enough?"

He nodded. "Fair enough."

Enrico watched Kate dress. Her back was turned to him, and he wasn't sure where he stood with her. She'd whipsawed back and forth so many times in the space of a few minutes. He'd told her he loved her, and her reaction had been anger. Anger to cover her hurt. Hurt he had caused with his bumbling. Why hadn't he told her sooner? Why hadn't he told her about Delfina before they'd made love?

Had he ruined everything between them, just when it seemed he'd finally won her?

At least she was going to Capri with him. At least she was giving him a chance. Though the odds were more against him now than they'd ever been.

And he still hadn't told her who he was.

He desperately needed to talk to Don Battista.

For the first time in his life, he felt truly lost.

CHAPTER 19

After he returned home from the summit with Carlo and Dario, Dom called Carlo.

"Do you think he suspects?" Carlo asked.

"I don't think he trusts you, but I doubt he has any idea what we're planning."

"Your cousin doesn't have the head for this role. He never did."

Dom found himself automatically defending Rico. "Just because I think he's being a fool over this woman, that doesn't mean I think he hasn't done well for the *cosca*. I may have my quarrels with my *capo*, but he has more brains for business than either of us, Don Andretti."

"Are you worried about wearing the crown, Domenico?"

"I've been ready for this all my life."

Carlo laughed. "Wanting to be the alpha dog and actually being it are two very different things. Your cousin has balls, I'll give him that. You, I'm not so sure about."

"The nail that sticks out gets hammered back in."

"Said by men of no courage."

Dom bit back his irritation. "If I fight him openly, the *cosca* will plunge into chaos. But if he dies, I will be able to step in without spilling another drop of blood." He paused. "Of course, it would be to your benefit if that doesn't happen."

"You are learning, my boy. I am content to let you have his place, as long as you abide by our agreement."

Dom's skin erupted in flames. "I'll give you what you asked for: the discount and the American. But that does not make you my master."

"We will see about that."

Dom wondered. "Did your men forget it was me wearing the white shirt tonight? Some of those bullets were awfully close."

Carlo chuckled. "They did *exactly* as I asked."

"Play any more tricks like that, and I will have to rethink this."

"And do what? I have you by the balls. Don't think I haven't recorded every word you've said."

Ice slid down Dom's spine. There was no turning back.

He hung up. He'd known he was making a deal with the devil. Now he hoped the only price he'd pay for it was his soul.

It would all be over in three or four days. He was glad Rico was taking a vacation, glad Rico thought things were repaired between them. At least his cousin would die happy.

It was more than he expected for himself. He could only hope his children's lives would be better because of what he'd done. With any luck, he'd save the *cosca*, save their future.

But he couldn't save himself. That damage was already done.

He was killing his own blood; there'd be no mercy for him in the afterlife.

Tears pricked his eyes. No mercy was exactly what he deserved.

ℰℭ

Kate woke with a start, her heart a jackhammer in her chest. Her first instinct, which she didn't question, was to leap out of bed. Which is when she heard a voice that shouldn't have been there. "Kate?" Enrico mumbled.

She stood there panting, her eyes taking in as much of the room as she could in the dim light of early morning. She was in Enrico's room. Not with Vince. Never with Vince again. Yet why did he still haunt her dreams?

Maybe it had been a mistake to come back in here. The room had been cleaned up, and new carpeting covered the floor. But still she could smell the blood. Except this time it was Enrico's, not Vince's.

"*Cara?*" Enrico sat up in bed and scrubbed his eyes with his hand. "Did you hear something?" His eyes flicked up to the newly installed panic button. He opened the nightstand drawer and withdrew his Glock. "Kate?"

She inhaled deeply, trying to calm her breathing, then she walked over to him and put her hand out, directing the muzzle toward the floor. "It's nothing. You don't need that."

"What woke you? You leapt out of bed as if the hounds of hell were snapping at your heels."

She hugged herself, and he set the gun on the nightstand, then stood up and tried to take her in his arms. She flinched away from him. "Talk to me. *Per favore.*"

That Italian "please," along with the worry in Enrico's voice, grounded her. "I was dreaming. It was so real."

"Do you mind if we talk about this in bed, where it is warm?"

Kate nodded and let him steer her back to the bed. He got in beside her and pulled the covers over them where they lay face to face. She reached over and traced the high, broad bone of his cheek, double-checking that he was real. When she started to withdraw her hand, he trapped it in his, then pressed his lips to her palm before letting go. "Tell me about this dream."

"It was so real in every detail. Not like most dreams." She closed her eyes for a second, then opened them, shaking her head. "Vince had broken in and he was raping me. Carlo was there too, waiting for his turn. You were dead. They'd killed you." Tears slid down her cheeks and she wiped them away. "When is this going to stop?" Why couldn't she just be normal again?

Enrico's chest tightened. Her voice was so thick with tears he could hardly understand her. He reached out to her, his fingers skimming along her skin as he pushed her hair out of her face. "*Cara*," he whispered, "it will stop. But it will take time."

"As long as Carlo is out there, I'll never feel safe."

"He promised he would not harm you."

"That was when you were going to marry Delfina. Have you told him yet?"

"I will ask Dom to tell him after we leave. It will give him time to calm down before we return."

"He's going to want us both dead."

"I will think of something."

She sighed. "I hope so. I don't want to die over this."

Enrico didn't try to keep the bitterness out of his voice. "Over *me*, you mean."

"No. I don't want to die because I killed his nephew in self-defense. And because I'm the reason you don't want to marry his granddaughter."

Enrico relaxed, feeling sheepish. "Oh. I thought—"

She put a finger to his lips. "Don't think I've forgiven you just yet. I'm not sure how I feel. But I don't want you walking around with false ideas about me in your head."

It was not at all what he wanted to hear, but at least she wasn't furious with him anymore. After their argument in the study, he'd been surprised when she'd come to his bed in the middle of the night, but he hadn't asked for an explanation. He'd just been grateful, even though she'd stiffened when he'd reached for her, even though she'd said, "I don't want to be alone right now, that's all." He had hoped things would be different in the morning, but at least they weren't worse. He wished he'd understood then why she'd come to him. "Have you been having nightmares since the attack?"

She nodded. "It's gotten worse since I ran out of Valium."

"So that is why you came to me last night." She rolled over, hiding her face from him. He touched her shoulder, then pulled her close. "There is no shame in needing someone." Why did she always fight her need for him?

Kate took a deep breath. She was uncomfortably aware of his naked body pressed against hers, her lacy slip the only thing between them. She was still angry at him, still hurt he'd even consider marrying someone else. Still upset by her reaction when he'd told her he loved her. She hadn't been coolly neutral the way she'd wanted. Because her feelings about him were anything but neutral. But that didn't have to mean she loved him.

Despite her confusion, her body responded to his the way it always did, and she resisted the urge to wriggle against him when she felt his cock stiffen and press into her buttocks. She looked over her shoulder at him. "It's not going to happen."

He shrugged and moved away from her, propping himself up on his elbow. "As you wish. I cannot help it." His eyes lingered on hers, then slid down to trace the curves of her body. "*Bellisima,* so *bellisima.*"

She started to smile, then suppressed it. "Aren't you still intent on forcing me to go to Capri?"

He grinned. "I am."

"Then you'd better get in the shower." She lay back on the bed and watched him walk across the room, the hard, muscled beauty of his form making her breath catch and her sex go wet. She wanted him even now, damn her. When was she going to learn? Enrico Lucchesi was bad news in a sexy package. That was all. He was not the man of her dreams, he was not the man who was going to make her happy. She had to keep telling herself that until it sunk in.

Making love with him yesterday had been a mistake. A delicious mistake, but a mistake nevertheless. Whatever she did, she wasn't going down that road again. That road led somewhere she couldn't go.

೧೦෬

Humming to himself while Kate was in the shower, Enrico quickly shaved and brushed his teeth, then dressed in the clothes he'd pulled out the night before. He picked up the gun from the nightstand. Capri was generally safe, jet-set hotspot that it was, but you never knew. His father always said that the man who was prepared for anything had the advantage over the fool who trusted in luck.

He checked again that the clip was fully loaded, then put the gun in his jacket pocket. Was it fair of him to expose Kate to this life? Could he really continue to put her selfishly at risk? He scrubbed a hand across his face. *Madonna.* He didn't see how he could continue to endanger her—and yet, he couldn't see how he could let her go.

The shower shut off, then Kate stepped out and started drying herself. He walked over and leaned against the doorjamb, his eyes drinking her in. When she noticed him, roses bloomed in her cheeks. "Stop staring," she said, turning half away from him.

"I love the rear view too, you know."

Her cheeks bunched up with a smile, but her eyes stayed on her legs. He stepped closer to her and tugged at the towel. "Let me." She resisted for a second, then let go.

He rubbed the towel over her shoulders, tossing the dark red sheaf of her wet hair to one side. He dried her back, the planes of her shoulder blades, the curves of her buttocks, then turned her around and brushed the plush white cloth over her breasts and belly, his touch teasing, lingering. He loved this moment with her, the intimacy of it, her trust in him a welcome contrast to the wildness he'd woken up to. He hoped she'd let him in again. He hoped she could find it in her heart to forgive him. He hoped she'd someday tell him she loved him.

But if he was going to earn her trust, her forgiveness, her love, he was going to have to trust in her, wasn't he? He was going to have to tell her everything. And soon. Or he was going to have to let her go.

Kate looked at Enrico as he gazed upon her body. She felt an upwelling of warmth at his tenderness, the reverence with which he touched her.

"I'm sorry, Rico. For doubting you."

He looked away from his task, meeting her eyes. "You had every right." Wrapping the towel around her shoulders, he leaned forward and kissed her forehead. "I am asking a lot of you." He looked down at his feet. "Sometimes I think I *should* put you on a plane. Send you some place far from here. Some place safe."

Fear knifed through her gut. It must have shown on her face, because he said, "I will make sure you are safe, so if you want to go home, you can."

Kate wasn't sure what to say. She still didn't know what she wanted. Him, or home? She finally settled on "Thank you," trying to imbue the words with gratitude, hoping he could hear it, that he would understand what she was trying to say.

He looked at her, tension rising between them. He opened his mouth, looking like he was going to ask a question. Then his face changed and he said, "The plane is waiting for us."

Kate nodded and shooed him out of her way. She ran a comb through her hair, deciding to let it air dry, then pulled on some clothes and brushed her teeth.

Enrico started out the door with their bags, then he turned around and came back in. "What if we drove back? It will take a few extra days, but I would love to show you the coast. I can have someone bring the Maserati down to us."

She smiled. "I'd love it." Might as well see as much of Italy as she could. While she was still here. "But you have to bring that bag back over here then. I'll need some more clothes."

He shook his head. "I am buying you a new wardrobe, remember?" His eyes flickered up and down her body, a grin spreading across his face. "You

153

will love the stores in Capri."

She picked up her purse and walked over to him, her smile slow and teasing. "Will I now?"

"Oh yes." He leaned down to kiss her, his lips lingering on hers. "And I am going to love buying you everything."

"Everything, huh? Then I'm going to need more luggage too."

"As you wish, *mia cara*."

Kate tried not to feel guilty when she heard the endearment. She wasn't leading him on if she wasn't sure, was she?

CHAPTER 20

Franco Trucco had always prided himself on his discretion. It was what made him the ideal accountant. And being the *contabile* for the Lucchesi *cosca*, as his father had been before him, was a great honor. The *contabile* was a man of respect, third in charge after the *capo di società* and the don himself. In his role, Franco kept track of and dispersed the *cosca*'s funds to the men on the payroll. He also had the don's ear, so being friends with Franco had certain benefits. He never lacked for friends.

However, Franco prided himself on being a humble, modest man. Certainly, he was a man of means. But he was not king, and he didn't aspire to be so. Only a fool would want the crown, and the danger that came with it. It was so much better to be near the top than actually there. He had nearly as much influence with much less risk. And that was important. He'd seen what Carlo Andretti had done to Don Rinaldo's family.

So Franco had done his work quietly and with pride, enjoying his position and the fruits that came along with it. And he had loved Don Rinaldo and Don Enrico. Truly they were princes among men. When Don Rinaldo stepped down after his heart attack, Franco vowed to advise Don Enrico well and to serve him with all the discretion the Trucco family had always rendered. At the time, Franco had thought nothing could ever change how he felt.

But he'd been wrong.

As always, the end had come because of a woman. But not just any woman. Franco's daughter, Fiammetta. His youngest, and the smartest and most beautiful of his three daughters. Franco kept it to himself, but Fiammetta had been his favorite. He'd secretly delighted in her impertinence, her quick wit, her penchant for misbehaving. She'd done all the things Franco would have liked to have done, and had she been a son, he could have openly relished her behavior, instead of censuring it in public but winking at her in private and letting her off with a kiss. She'd kept the secret of his favor. It had been better for them both that way.

After Don Enrico's wife Antonella had died, an idea had come to Franco. The don needed a wife, and Fiammetta had needed a husband. Franco had seen how Don Enrico had rebuffed all the eligible girls presented to him; a direct approach would not work. Care—discretion—had been needed, as always. So when the don's assistant had moved into another position within the *cosca*, Franco had seen his opportunity. He'd had Fiammetta installed as Don Enrico's secretary within days. He'd whispered not a word of what he'd hoped for to Fiammetta. Despite their bond, she'd been headstrong enough to foil his plans. So he'd prayed to the Virgin and hoped.

The Virgin had answered his prayers. Franco had known it when one day Don Enrico's and Fiammetta's eyes had kept locking together, then sliding guiltily away during a meeting. The way Fiammetta had flipped her hair out of her eyes when she'd known the don was looking, the way she'd shifted in her seat and licked her lips when she had been taking notes, the way Don Enrico's eyes had tracked her movements like a cat eyeing its next meal—Franco had known what all these signs meant. He'd rejoiced in his heart. His status would increase; his family would be elevated further once they'd married into the Lucchesi family. His grandsons would be *capi*, would head the *cosca*.

But nothing had turned out as Franco had hoped. Instead, his daughter, the light of his heart, was dead. And the way Don Enrico could no longer meet his eyes meant he was responsible, even though his blood-alcohol test results had been lost, even though there was no proof, no admission of guilt from the don. Franco knew. Don Enrico was guilty. But how could he avenge his daughter?

Franco had long known about the unusual payments first Don Rinaldo, then Don Enrico had been making to Edmund Tyrell, their attorney in England. What he didn't know was why, as he'd told Vincenzo Andretti. Now it was time to investigate. Time to unearth the worms beneath the dirt.

Franco's arduous review of the books revealed that the payments had gone out to Tyrell every month at the same time for twenty-two years, before stopping five years ago. But these payments weren't the attorney's usual retainer. That was a separate payment. This one was marked Personal, meaning it was to be counted against the don's compensation.

Calling Tyrell and inquiring about the payments would of course be fruitless. The man was as tight-lipped as any man of honor. And making such a call would tip off Don Enrico to his inquiry. There had to be another way to find the truth.

Franco puzzled over this matter for days. The answer came while Franco was staring at another series of unusual payments to Tyrell. These payments started nine years ago and stopped after four years. They were also marked Personal, but with a second notation, "C.U.," and were for varying amounts. Since the amounts weren't round numbers, they must be payments for something specific.

What could "C.U." mean? Franco racked his mind for names of associates with those initials, names of businesses, names of places. But nothing came to mind. Because both series of payments stopped five years ago, the payments to the mysterious "C.U." in the spring and the others at the end of the same year, the timing suggested these payments were somehow linked.

Taking another tack, Franco dug into Don Enrico's trips to England. Perhaps something about his meetings with Tyrell would yield him a clue. At first, he saw nothing. Then he noticed a coincidence. About five years ago, Don Enrico had traveled to England, visited Tyrell, and then made a side trip to Cambridge in the summer, to attend the commencement ceremony for the son of a business contact in London. "C.U."—could that mean Cambridge University? Franco's spine tingled. Four years of payments could indicate that Don Enrico had financed someone's degree. But who? And why?

A phone call to the university, during which Franco posed as a government auditor looking into Edmund Tyrell's books, elicited the answer to the first question. The payment was for tuition, on behalf of Mr. Nicholas Reginald Clarkston.

Franco's heart stopped beating for a moment. Reginald. It was an alternate translation for Rinaldo. Could this man be Don Rinaldo's child?

An online search of Nicholas Clarkston's particulars made Franco's pulse race. The payments to Tyrell commenced the same month Clarkston was born. Judging by the date of Clarkston's birth, he was fathered while Don Enrico was at boarding school in London.

Franco was not one to believe in coincidences. Clarkston must be Don Enrico's illegitimate son, not Don Rinaldo's. Traditionally, at least one of the middle names given to a boy belonged to his grandfather. Thus, Reginald.

But he needed proof. He ordered a copy of Nicholas Clarkston's birth certificate. Since U.K. law dictated that only a paper version of the certificate could be ordered, it would take at least five days to arrive. Five long days, but then he'd have proof, assuming the father's name was listed. Proof Don Enrico couldn't refute or deny.

A further search for details about Nick Clarkston yielded another interesting tidbit: Clarkston had recently started to work at Interpol. Perhaps that too could work in Franco's favor. If he didn't get his justice the way he preferred, perhaps he could turn the son against the father.

Franco flushed with triumph. He would have his vengeance. An eye for an eye. A son for a daughter. And he knew just who would help him achieve his justice: Carlo Andretti.

∞

Kate and Enrico arrived at the private airstrip later than intended, but Enrico told her they could make up the time in the air. Soon they were aloft and winging south. A flight attendant brought them drinks and a light breakfast, then left them alone.

Enrico reached over and took her hand, saying nothing. What was he thinking about? Probably trying to figure out what to do about Carlo, now that he wasn't marrying Delfina.

Did she have any right to raise an objection to such a marriage, when she wasn't sure she wanted to stay with him? What if she decided to leave? What if he couldn't arrange something else with Carlo? What if she'd just doomed them both, and all for nothing?

They landed in Naples and took a car to Sorrento, where they shopped and had a late and very leisurely lunch before boarding a private boat for the trip to Capri. The sun was starting to set when they left Sorrento. As they motored away from the coast, Kate looked at the houses clinging to the gold-washed cliffs. She leaned against Enrico while they stood in the back of the boat, and he put his arms around her. Despite all the danger, despite their troubles, Italy was seducing her with its charms. Hadn't Enrico said that worry was a useless emotion? She sighed. "Italy is amazingly gorgeous."

He squeezed her tight and nuzzled her neck. "You would not love Naples in the middle of a garbage strike in August."

She laughed. "I suppose not." She turned in his arms. "Doesn't the Mafia control the garbage pickups?"

He nodded. "The Camorra control everything in Naples."

"Then why do they have strikes?"

"Money. They go on strike, people agree to pay more to end it."

A thought occurred to her. "Are we in danger here?"

"Not in Capri. The Camorra know the tourists butter their bread. We might be in some danger in Naples. But they would take offence if Carlo tried anything on their territory."

Kate nestled closer to Enrico as the wind whipped around them. "The idea of us being hurt is taking all the fun out of this trip."

"Forget Carlo. Forget all of it. Just be with me." He pulled her into the shelter of his body, squeezing her tight.

"With Antonio and Ruggero around, how can I possibly forget?"

He stepped back and looked at her. "Listen, *mia cara*. We will take some time for ourselves."

"Just you and me," she whispered, her voice husky with promise.

"When we get to the hotel..." he murmured, his voice trailing off, the hunger in his gaze speaking for him.

"When we get to the hotel... what?" she teased.

"You know." And to make sure she did, he started whispering in her ear all the things he would do as soon as they were alone.

Kate smiled at his imagination. She stretched up on tiptoe and kissed him, softly at first, then with heat. Damn it, just like all the New Year's resolutions she'd ever made, she was going to break the one not to have sex with him, wasn't she? And she wasn't going to feel that bad about it either.

As they pulled into the harbor, she looked up at the cliffs of Capri towering above them, encircling the bay. Houses of all sorts perched on those cliffs, nearly every square inch occupied, but somehow plenty of green survived and thrived, giving the island a tropical air.

They left the boat, luggage in hand, and headed for the funicular station. The little tram would take them up to the top, to Capri town proper, where no cars were allowed, not even for rich men like Enrico. Not even here, where money certainly talked, was Enrico any different from anyone else. Except that he was armed. And so were his guards.

Kate sighed, taking his hand as they boarded the funicular. They stood by the window, both holding the same pole as the tram started ascending. She watched greenery and homes pass by, caught the blue-purple of wisteria, the red and pink of bougainvillea, the creams and pastels of the houses, the bright colors starting to fade as twilight descended.

By the time they started walking to their hotel, it was full dark, the narrow winding stone streets romantically lit by the stores and restaurants that lined them. Enrico kept hold of her hand, his strong fingers locked around hers, giving them a light squeeze now and then when she remarked on something that delighted her. She felt a bit like a child with a father for whom none of this was new, except when she looked up at Enrico's face, she saw delight on his features as well. She was finally able to relax, to believe they were safe. Inhaling deeply, she breathed in the scent of jasmine and freesia. The lingering heat coming off the stone streets and buildings kept the air warm, and the humidity of the climate raised a sheen of perspiration on her skin, making her palm go damp in Enrico's hand.

He motioned with his chin to a large whitewashed building before them. "We are almost there."

Kate picked out the words "Grand Hotel Quisisana" set in gold letters on the building's face. Grand it certainly was. The naughty nothings Enrico had whispered to her on the boat echoed in her ears, and she quickened her pace, tugging on his hand, grinning up at him. Antonio jogged ahead of them, while Ruggero stayed behind.

Enrico handled their check-in. Antonio and Ruggero had the rooms flanking theirs. Kate nearly gagged at the cost of taking three ocean-view terrace rooms, then she forced it out of her head. Money was no object here. Fun and pleasure were the order of the day—or night, as it were.

She followed the men down the hall to the left of the lobby. A short set of stairs took them to their suites, which were spacious and high ceilinged with large marble baths. Kate barely set her purse down before Enrico shut and locked the door behind them. Then he was scooping her up and dropping her onto the king size bed.

He rolled atop her, his mouth and hands everywhere at once. Kate returned his fire for a few minutes, but when he started to unbutton her blouse, she stopped him. "Wait."

He looked up from kissing her neck, eyebrows raised. "Wait?"

She bit her lower lip teasingly. If she was going to break her vow, she was going to make it count. "We should have dinner first, maybe go for a walk."

Laughing, he questioned her. "Are you serious?"

"We just got here. Let's enjoy it a bit before we start enjoying each other."

Without a word, he pushed her skirt up and slipped a hand between her legs, his fingers shoving aside the thin fabric of her panties so he could touch her. When he encountered the moisture built up inside her, he said, "You seem to be of two minds about the subject."

When he starting stroking her, she gasped. Clamping her legs shut on his hand, she trapped it. Then she reached down and pulled his hand away. He wasn't going to distract her so easily. "Not yet." She sat up and kissed him. "Waiting will be good. You'll see."

Enrico groaned in frustration. He wanted to push harder. If it wasn't for Vincenzo, he could have. *Damn it.* He hated being on eggshells with her. He wanted to be more insistent, more demanding, more in control. But that could wait. He didn't have to have everything now, as much as his body argued otherwise.

He tried once more, giving her his best pleading puppy eyes, which she resisted, shaking her head. "Okay," he said on an exhale, rolling away from her. "Shall we eat here or go exploring?"

"Exploring."

He smiled. "I was hoping you would say that." He was in no mood for the three-hour plus dinner they'd get at the hotel's restaurant, as exquisite as the food was. He had only one thing on his mind, and he wanted it as soon as possible, Kate's wanderlust be damned.

She zipped into the bathroom, checking her hair and makeup and straightening her clothes as he waited for her on the bed, mulling over ways to short-circuit her plans. Perhaps a quick bite in a café he knew around the corner? Then a brief stroll around the hotel grounds?

Kate came back with her purse. "I'm ready."

Another possibility occurred to him. "The hotel has excellent room service."

"No room service today." She extended her hand to him. "Come on. The longer you pout, the longer it's going to be before we're back here."

He took her hand, rising with a long-suffering sigh. "True." He brought her hand up to his lips, brushing her knuckles with his mouth. "It is just that I have been thinking about you all day."

"Another hour or two won't hurt."

"For you, perhaps."

She skimmed her hand across the crotch of his trousers, making his half-hard cock tingle from her touch. "All good things to those who wait," she whispered. He chuckled at her audacity. The old Kate was back. Then she turned and tugged on his hand, urging them out of the room.

"Can we leave Antonio and Ruggero here?" she asked as he closed the door.

"Yes, it is safe." He'd told her a small lie earlier; Capri wasn't safe because of the Camorra; they didn't have even a toehold in Capri. Capri was safe because it was Don Battista's domain. Not even Carlo was rash enough to challenge him.

Enrico thought enviously of the night ahead for his guards. Room service and porn. Then again, he'd be coming back to the real thing. He hoped. He ducked his head in Ruggero's room and let him know they were going out, then they left the hotel.

As they walked the stone streets hand in hand, Enrico's head filled with images of him and Kate, what he wanted to do to her, with her. The sounds of it, the sights. The scent of her mingling with the scent of him. The way she'd feel in his arms, underneath him, above him, pressed between him and the walls of their room. He wanted her in all ways, in every way possible. And he wanted her now. Except they weren't alone.

They wandered for a while, Kate undeterred by Enrico's suggestions of where to eat. Realizing she wasn't going to be denied, he eventually gave up. He was just going to have to be good and hope she gave him what he wanted sooner rather than later.

Kate finally settled on a small, crowded café. Enrico slipped the waiter several bills to ensure expedited service. He was watching Kate read the menu, when he felt her hand just above his knee. *Madonna,* he thought, noting no change in her expression as her hand slid up his leg. It lingered at the juncture of his thighs, but her fingers didn't move. When he placed his hand over hers, she withdrew. Ah, so it was her way, or no way. Two could play that game.

He ordered a Caprese salad to start, eating it with his fingers when it arrived. He popped a mozzarella and basil covered tomato in his mouth, licking the sweet balsamic vinegar and olive oil off his fingers and thumb as he looked at Kate.

She smiled. "Trying to seduce me, are you?"

He said nothing and wiped a dot of oil from his chin with his index finger, then sucked the oil from his skin. He ran a thumb across his lower lip, then picked up another tomato, offering it to her. "You must try this."

She leaned forward and opened her mouth, accepting what he offered. Chewing slowly, she held his gaze, watching as he licked his fingers again. He reached out and wiped up a little vinegar from the corner of her mouth, then used his tongue to clean his finger. "Delicious, no?" he asked.

She nodded and watched him pick up another tomato, a smile playing with her lips. He was sure he had her thinking about what else his tongue could do.

Leaning forward, she placed her hand on his thigh again, but didn't move it. Shifting her weight slightly and giving his quad a squeeze, she brought her lips to his ear. "What if we didn't go back to the room?"

His cock twitched at the suggestion. "Do you have somewhere else in mind?"

"I'm sure we can find some quiet, secluded nook somewhere." Her hand slid higher. Almost, but not quite there.

Enrico felt a sheen of sweat building on his forehead and upper lip. This was definitely more fun than staying in the room. Definitely.

They finished their meal in rapid order, Enrico hardly remembering a word they exchanged. His whole focus was on her. On Kate's hand on his thigh, on the way her other hand occasionally toyed with the neck of her blouse or ran along the base of her throat. Or twisted the damp hair off the back of her neck. *Dio,* how he wanted to kiss her in all the places she touched. How he wanted her hand on his leg to move higher. But waiting had its benefits. He could see that now.

He paid the bill and took her hand, starting toward the darker end of the street, where it turned off into a residential area. Once they were in the shadows, he pressed her up against a wall, kissing her hard and deep, grinding his hips into her. She let out a moan and he smiled against her lips. "Who is eager now?" he teased.

She nipped at his lower lip playfully, then pushed him away and took off running, rounding a corner that led down to the beach. He loped after her, smiling when he heard her laughter, feeling both the urgency of sex and the excitement of being free and on his own in the dark. When was the last time he'd been like this? Years and years. Always it had been one worry after another. He hadn't taken a real vacation in far too long.

Kate dashed down a lane lined with trees, then popped through a gate that opened onto the beach. Enrico followed her, his shoes slipping in the sand. When she stopped to remove her sandals, he caught up to her. Wrapping her in his arms, he hoisted her off the ground and twirled her around as she shrieked with laughter.

Setting her down, Enrico smoothed the hair back from her face and kissed her, his tongue slipping into her mouth. When she sucked on it, he felt the sensation all over his body.

After they parted, both breathing fast, she said, "Let's find someplace."

He took her hand and headed for a thicket of trees. When they reached the low stone wall edging the beach, he helped her over it, then braced his arms on top and swung his legs over. "Not bad for an old man," she teased him.

"Old man," he growled, kissing her with force, cupping her buttocks in his hands and pressing her against his erection. "Does that feel like an old man?" He didn't wait for an answer. He took her hand again, tugging her up the hill, into the trees. Grass grew thick and long there, brushing against their legs.

Kate looked around and apparently decided it was secluded enough. "Here," she said, stopping and putting both her hands on his chest.

Enrico brought his lips to hers, cradling her face in his hands before sliding them along the sides of her neck. Kate's fingers wound into his hair as she deepened the kiss. When they parted for a second, Enrico stripped off his shirt and laid it on the grass, then drew Kate down with him. At last, he was where he wanted to be most. Alone with her, in the dark.

Moonlight filtered through the trees as Enrico bent over Kate. He kissed her cheek, then her mouth, then the side of her neck. Between kisses, he murmured, "It has already been too long." He rolled on top of her, his body almost fully over hers.

ℰℭ

The weight of him holding her down and something about the way the moonlight hit his face reminded Kate of Vince, of her nightmares. Of the attack. Fear ripped through her, making her shiver from a chill only she could feel. She shoved Enrico hard in a panic, and he quickly let her up. She sat up, panting for breath. *Damn it!*

Her eyes blurred, and she swiped at the tears leaking from them. "God, when am I going to be *normal* again?"

"Shh." He stroked the side of her face. "*Per favore*, do not cry, *cara*."

"I don't know what else to do." She looked at him. "I feel like I'm losing my mind."

"Much has happened these last few days. Too much," he said, leaning back on his elbows. "Maybe this—you and me—maybe it is moving too fast."

Kate lay back beside him, staring up at the stars through the branches. "I don't know. Maybe."

He was silent for a while, then he said, "Only recently have I stopped wishing I was dead."

She snapped her head toward him. "What?"

"Ever since Toni died, I have wished I did not have to go on without her." He put his arms behind his head, then he cleared his throat. "After she was gone, I carried on conversations with her all the time in my head. Sometimes all day."

The tightness in his voice moved her. Kate rolled over and placed a hand on his chest. "I can't decide if that's sad or romantic."

"I prefer to think of it as romantic." His words hung in the air for a moment, then he said, "I still love her, Kate. But I feel it fading the more time I spend with you."

She smiled. "Put a little pressure on me, why don't you."

"I do not mean to. Not exactly. I have felt like an impostor for a long time. I smiled and nodded in the right places, and I laughed when someone made a joke, but I was just pretending. With you, I feel alive again."

Her hand flexed against his chest. "You do?"

"Ever since I met you, I have hardly been able to think of anything *but* you. Having you. Making you mine." He picked up her hand and kissed it. "You have become my obsession."

"Now you're scaring me," she said, but kept her tone light.

"You should be scared," he joked. "I do not like to be denied anything I want."

"I'm sure that rarely happens."

He rolled up onto his side to look at her. "Somehow, you manage to deny me all the time."

"Only because you're under my thumb." She smiled and stroked his cheek.

Grabbing her hand, he planted a kiss on the palm. "Indeed, I am your slave."

She bit her lower lip. "That conjures up so many interesting possibilities."

He looked at her, her hand still upturned in his, his lips hovering over her skin. When he spoke, his breath tickled her palm. "Would one of those possibilities involve any sex?" he asked. He pressed his lips to her palm again, then his tongue followed the path of her lifeline.

Tingles traveled along her skin in the wake of his tongue. "You have been such a good slave, I suppose a little sex won't spoil you."

He kissed the inside of her wrist, the touches fleeting as his mouth moved up her arm. "I live to serve," he murmured, reaching her neck and the sensitive skin there. He parted her blouse, kissing along the hollow of her throat, then his lips moved down between her breasts. He made short work of the bra's front clasp, his hands and mouth seeking her nipples greedily. Kate lay back beneath him, winding her fingers in his thick hair, a bit amazed they were actually doing this. Somehow he'd managed to cope with her and change her mood for the better. Maybe he wasn't the only one who needed this connection between them.

One of his hands slipped down between them, pushing her skirt up to her waist, his fingers smoothing up her thighs, and Kate felt her anticipation rising as his hand drew near her sex. But he veered away from it, instead letting his fingers play along the outside of her hip, squeezing the flesh there.

Kate shifted restlessly beneath him, parting her legs slightly, though he didn't take the hint. Instead he slid his palm across her belly in slow circles, just feeling her skin. His eyes followed the progress of his hand, and she studied him, surprised at how mesmerized he was by what he was doing.

"You really like touching me, don't you?"

His eyes flicked up to hers. "Of course I do. You are so soft. So lovely."

She smiled and pulled him into a kiss. "My slave gives the best compliments," she said when they parted.

"So what would my mistress like?" His index finger circled her belly button.

"Anything."

"That is such a broad category." His hand stilled, lying flat and warm against her belly. "Tell me. Fingers or tongue?"

She turned her smile wicked. "Why stop at one?"

He laughed, soft and low, a sudden exhale at her neck that made her shiver. "Why indeed." He bent his head, mouthing the tips of her breasts again, then slowly kissed down her belly, lingering just below her navel, his breath hot on her flesh.

With the slowest of movements, he peeled her panties to just above the triangle of her sex, planting little kisses across her belly until she twisted her hips and let out a moan of frustration. She felt him smile against her skin. "This is for making me wait so long," he said.

"I knew I'd pay for it somehow. But it is better this way, isn't it?"

He nodded and finished taking her panties off. "Definitely." Parting her legs, he kissed the insides of her thighs, then blew on her curls, making her shiver. He ran a finger down the center of her pussy, finally slipping it between the lips. His finger went in easily; she was soaking wet.

Kate moaned when he pressed a second finger inside her. As he slid them in and out, he lowered his mouth to her, his tongue finding her clit and working around it in slow circles, a merciless tease.

She closed her eyes and heard the tide coming in, waves crashing against the beach in rapid succession, her own breathing the only sound she could hear above it. Clutching his hair, she raised her hips to meet his mouth, his wonderful, teasing, taunting mouth.

He brought her close to the peak several times, then backed off each time, making her groan with frustration. "Why are you torturing me?" she finally asked in a ragged voice.

He smiled up at her, then placed a hand below her breasts and urged her to lie back as he continued to skirt around her fulfillment.

At last he took her all the way. Her face flushed hot and she came in a belly-clenching, thigh-shaking rush, letting loose a cry that surprised her in its rawness.

Moving up her body, he caught her lips with his. "I want you, Kate," he whispered, his voice husky. "I want you so much."

"I want you too." She held his jaw and delivered a kiss fierce with her hunger. She felt him fumbling with his belt and unzipping his trousers. She let go of his face and dragged his trousers down, her hands seeking his hips to pull him over her. But he surprised her, grabbing her around the waist and flipping onto his back so that she straddled him. She placed her hands on his chest and leaned forward. Both of them moaned as she slowly lowered herself onto him.

She rocked over him, enjoying the freedom of the position. How had he known what she'd needed, when she hadn't? Moonlight striped his face as she looked down at him, but he didn't look like Vince now. He was so beautiful. Inside and out. Not perfect, not at all. But wonderful, nevertheless. Maybe she even....

She pushed the thought away. She couldn't be in love with him. She wasn't going to make the same mistake again, she wasn't going to allow herself to be swept away by a man she barely knew. Especially not by a man who was hiding something, a man who still loved someone else. A man who wasn't truly available, who could never be hers.

All he could give her was this, this ecstasy, this monumental pleasure. This bliss. And that was all she was going to take from him before she left.

CHAPTER 21

Enrico watched Kate sleeping. It was just after dawn, a little light filtering into their room. He thought back to those moments on the beach, what he'd said to her about Antonella.

It was all true. Even while he and Fiammetta were involved, Antonella's presence had hovered close to him. But now—well, more and more, especially the last few days—he'd stopped constantly thinking of Antonella. Which didn't mean he'd stopped loving her. He always would. Would Kate ever be first in his heart? He didn't dare hope for that.

All he wanted was to soothe the ache in his chest, to banish the loneliness that coiled around his heart. To stop wishing he was dead. And on those three counts, Kate was the answer he heard. He'd make her his wife—if she'd let him.

He watched the rise and fall of her breathing, the to and fro of her dreaming eyes. *Cristo,* he was a fool. Kate wasn't really his. She was in his bed, but that was all. If he demanded anything from her, she'd bolt. His stomach knotted. Could he suffer that loss, that emptiness, again?

No. He had to keep coping with Kate's indecision, her chaotic moods. Once she knew who he was, she'd come to see that she could trust him, that they could make each other happy. And if he had to hide the divided nature of his heart from her, he would.

When they were talking in the trees, a truth had risen unbidden in his heart: he wasn't yet fully in love with her, as much as he wished for it. He didn't love her the way he'd loved Antonella. If he truly loved Kate, he would put her needs first, not his. He would have sent her away, would have married Delfina to keep Kate safe from Carlo.

Instead, he'd followed the dictates of the selfish, greedy side of his heart. And that side said to keep her with him. And it whispered to him, as it was doing now: How could he ever be sure she was safe? How could he trust Carlo's word? Better to keep her close than to have her far away and in danger. That was the right thing to do, yes? The safest thing?

But if that was true, why did his conscience keep niggling at him?

He sighed. Maybe it was just nerves. Introducing her to Don Battista, that was monumental. His approval of Kate was necessary. Without it, there could be no wedding, no matter what Enrico wanted. And without Don Battista's approval, she couldn't leave either. At least not alive.

Under his breath, he cursed Dom for putting him in this position. If Dom had just kept his mouth shut, Enrico could have kept Kate under wraps for a while longer, could have given them both time to sort out how they felt about each other, could have given her the option to leave.

But now that Don Battista was aware of Kate, most likely so was La Provincia. Which meant Enrico's judgment would be called into question. He would have to account for his actions. He'd endangered the *cosca* and started a war with Carlo Andretti that probably wouldn't end until one of them was dead.

But he'd figure it out. He always did, didn't he?

Kate stirred, and Enrico had the pleasure of watching her awaken. Her eyelids fluttered before opening, and she took a deep breath, her nostrils flaring slightly. Then her green eyes took him in. A moment of anxiety flashed through them before she recovered and smiled. It was a definite improvement over yesterday morning. "Hi," she said, then bit her lip, her shy gesture seeming most fetching to him.

"*Ciao, bella.*" He leaned over and kissed the tip of her nose.

"How long have you been watching me?"

"Long enough to realize you are even more amazing than I thought."

"And all I was doing was sleeping. Imagine how much more impressive I'll be while awake."

He gave her a wolfish grin. "I was thinking about that. Debating whether to wake you."

"You're insatiable." She smiled.

"It is all your fault."

She arched a brow. "Blaming the woman for your lack of self-control, are you?"

How right she was. That was how they'd ended up in this mess. "If you were not constantly tempting me, I would be a model of restraint."

She chuckled. "I doubt it."

He growled and lunged at her, pinning her to the bed while he ravaged her with kisses. "I am such a beast, yes?" he asked when she dissolved into giggles.

"A very ferocious one." He rubbed his hard cock against her and she bit her lip again, this time holding his eyes suggestively. "Very ardent too."

"As I said, it is all your fault." He pressed a kiss to her lips. Then he pulled back and looked at her a moment, debating whether to tell her who he was. Was now the right time? Or should he wait?

"What has you so serious all of a sudden?" she asked.

He shook his head. He'd wait until he'd spoken to Don Battista. Much depended on his counsel. "Our meeting today with my godfather."

She looked up at him, questions in her eyes, then she said, "It means a lot to you, what he thinks of me, doesn't it?"

He nodded, his heart twisting as he wondered where his own father was, what he would think of Kate. Enrico wanted Rinaldo's approval too. But it was Don Battista's that mattered most.

She stiffened underneath him. "Enrico, I haven't promised you anything. I haven't decided to stay."

"I know. But I want you to keep an open mind." When she nodded, he kissed her quickly, then rolled off the bed, the easy mood between them broken. "We had better hurry. He expects us for breakfast."

&)(3

They took a small motorboat around the island, Enrico easily guiding it to a secluded inlet on the northern shore. He tied off at the dock and helped Kate out of the boat. They walked hand in hand toward a simple whitewashed house nestled among a grove of palm trees. Sun streamed down on them, and Kate was glad she'd chosen a light flowery dress that fluttered in the breeze. Near the end of the dock, Enrico stopped short. "Can you wait here a moment? There is something I want to discuss with him."

She frowned. "More secrets?"

"It is a business matter."

"Why can't I hear about it?"

"It is his business; he would not appreciate me disclosing it to a stranger." He gave her a pleading look. "It will take only a moment."

"All right." She sat on one of the pilings, watching him head toward the house. She didn't like all these damn secrets. She was going to force them out of him if she stayed. *If* she stayed.

Kate thought back to the sadness on his face when they'd talked about this meeting, about his father. She'd been afraid to say anything at that moment, afraid some quaver in her voice would give her away.

Damn him. The way he'd been looking at her then, he'd made her want to say yes, that she'd stay. That she'd risk him breaking her heart. That she'd stand by him, that she'd trust him to keep her safe from Carlo. But she was afraid to make those promises, afraid to let him have her heart. Afraid to break her resolution to leave.

&)(3

Enrico found Don Battista on the stone patio at the rear of the house. He was sipping espresso, and he put the cup down when he saw Enrico. "Rico, my son," he said, his wide smile revealing the small gap in his upper teeth. He rose and embraced Enrico, kissing him on the cheeks. "Where is this lovely American of yours?"

"She's on the dock. There's something I need to tell you."

"What is it?"

"She doesn't know who I am. What we are."

The old don's face turned stern. "Then why is she here?"

"I wanted you to meet her. To give me your opinion. I'm afraid...." He trailed off.

"Afraid of what?"

Enrico had trouble meeting his eyes. "I'm afraid I don't see her clearly."

"How do you mean?"

"I can't decide whether to tell her."

Don Battista picked up the cup and took another sip of the steaming liquid. "You know what it would mean if she can't accept it."

The knot in Enrico's stomach, the knot that had been there all morning, tightened. "I can't bear losing her."

"I'll give you my opinion after we speak. That is all I can do." He set down the cup and put his hands on Enrico's shoulders, giving them a squeeze.

Enrico finally looked up, meeting his gaze. "Thank you, *mio padrino*."

ⵠⵙ

Enrico seemed a little more relaxed when he returned for Kate. Taking her hand, he escorted her to the back of the house, where an older, somewhat heavyset man awaited them at a table laden with covered dishes. He rose as they approached.

"*Padrino*," Enrico said. "Allow me to present Kate Andretti. Kate, this is my godfather, Vittorio Battista."

Vittorio stepped around the table and extended his hands toward her. "At last we meet, Signora Andretti. I have heard tales of your beauty, but they did not do you justice." He took the hand she offered in both of his and kissed it.

Kate smiled and laughed. "If I didn't know you were Enrico's godfather, I would have supposed you were his father." When he gave her a questioning look, she said, "You're both so very gallant."

He looked at Enrico. "I do not know this word?"

"She means you are a flirt."

Vittorio grinned at her. "Ah yes, we share a weakness for beautiful women." He shrugged. "I hope you will forgive me."

"What is there to forgive?" she said, enjoying the way his face creased up when he smiled. She could see he'd been very handsome when he was young.

He was still handsome now, but in a distinguished way. He'd lost most of his hair, only a short grayish fringe remaining around the back and sides, but the look suited him. His thick salt and pepper moustache and intelligent eyes gave him an air of vitality. Though he was at least twice her age, he was far from dead.

Vittorio's eyes twinkled. "Ah, now who is the flirt?"

"I cannot help myself around a handsome man either," she said.

Enrico slipped his arm around her shoulders. "You will make me jealous."

She nudged him playfully with her hip. "I only have eyes for you." She surprised herself. It was true. When had that happened?

They sat down and removed the metal covers from the dishes. The meal was simple—cold cuts of various meats alongside olives, cheeses, fresh fruit, and a small pastry. And of course cups of rich, steaming espresso accompanied everything.

They chatted pleasantly while they ate, Vittorio inquiring about Kate's family and what she thought of Italy. She kept her remarks light and positive, not wanting to trouble the man. He accepted what she said without comment, then he surprised her. "*Signora*, I must extend you my regrets regarding what happened with your husband."

"Please, call me Kate. And there is no need to apologize."

"It was a terrible thing, and I have had some involvement in the matter."

"Oh?"

Enrico gave him a look she couldn't read, but Vittorio didn't seem to acknowledge it. "The conflict with the Andrettis dates back many years. It stems partly from my advice to Enrico's father."

Interesting. "What was your advice?"

"I thought he could do business with Andretti without getting hurt. I was wrong."

"You knew who Carlo Andretti is? That he's a mobster?"

Vittorio nodded. "I thought he was a reasonable man. He is not."

Kate let out a little sound of agreement. "Far from it."

"He will want you dead for killing his nephew."

She thought for a second, then started to laugh. The most ironic thing just occurred to her.

"What is it?" Vittorio asked.

"Vince is the one who taught me to shoot."

Vittorio smiled. He studied her for a moment. "You are at ease then, with killing him?"

The smile left Kate's face. "'At ease' is an overstatement. But I have come to terms with it. And I would do it again."

Vittorio nodded. "I can see it on your face. Most people, especially most women, I think, would not be so determined."

"There really was no decision to make. I was not going to die and neither was Enrico."

Vittorio took a sip of his espresso. "You are an unusual person."

"No, just very practical, in the end. I'm not happy I had to kill him, but I did learn something important about myself that day."

"What was that?"

"I learned what my limits are. What I will and will not tolerate. And it turns out, my limits are not what I thought."

"How so?" Enrico asked.

"You were there, Rico. I wouldn't let him rape me, and I wouldn't let someone else kill for me. I wanted my revenge on him, for hurting me." She smiled, but not pleasantly. "I'm more vindictive than I thought."

"I think killing him was more about survival than revenge," Enrico said.

She gave him a hard look. "Then why didn't I let you or Ruggero finish him?"

"I had not wondered about that."

"Yes, you have. Don't tell me it didn't cross your mind that I could be Andretti's spy."

Enrico looked at her in surprise. "It did. But I soon dismissed it."

"I would hope so. You'd be an idiot to keep me around if you thought I was a threat."

He held her gaze. "I would indeed. I have seen what you can do."

"Practice, practice, practice. There's no point doing something if you can't do it well," she said lightly, even though it seemed odd to be joking about shooting someone. She really had come to terms with it. Who was this person in her body?

Vittorio chuckled. "I like you very much, Kate. I hope you will make my Enrico happy and join the family."

Kate's heart stuttered. What had Enrico said to him about her? Was that the "business matter" Enrico had wanted to discuss with him? She smiled gamely. "*Mille grazie,* Vittorio. I like you very much as well. I know how much Enrico means to you, and I'm humbled you think I'm a worthy companion for him." Kate gave a mental sigh of relief. There, it was the truth, but it didn't signal her intentions.

"*Cara,* would you mind giving us a minute alone?" Enrico asked.

She nodded and hurried away from the table, heading back to the dock. She didn't want Enrico to see how unnerved she was. Was he planning to ask her to marry him? Was this all about getting his godfather's blessing? *Shit, shit, shit!*

₨₩

When Kate was out of hearing range, Enrico turned to Don Battista. "So, do you think she can bear the truth?"

His godfather nodded. "Of course, I could be wrong."

"And if you are…." Enrico inhaled deeply. "I can't kill her, Don Battista. I can't."

"I see that. Yet you can't marry her and not tell her who you are."

"I know." Enrico shook his head. "I hate this."

Don Battista leaned forward. "You are, as the English say, on the horns of a dilemma, my son. But remember this: the 'Ndrangheta comes first. You took the vows; you know the price you will pay if you don't honor them. I cannot save you. If you tell her and she doesn't accept you, you *must* kill her. And it would be a shame; she would make a lovely wife and mother of your children. Such spirit. She reminds me of Antonella."

"Me too." Enrico looked up at the old don. "And that worries me. Is that why I love Kate?"

Don Battista pursed his lips, considering. Then he shook his head. "She's like Antonella, yes. But different. She's her own person." He looked at Enrico for a moment before continuing, and Enrico wished he could read his godfather's mind. "She cares about you, but she doesn't love you the way Antonella did. She holds herself away from you."

"She knows I'm keeping something from her."

The old don sighed. "Either take the risk and tell her, or send her away now."

"I can't let her go. I don't trust Carlo not to hurt her."

"Then *you* must risk hurting her." He paused. "Better for her to die at your hands, than his, yes?"

Enrico recoiled at the idea, but he had to admit there was a perverse logic to it. At least he'd make sure she didn't suffer. "I'm not sure I could do it and not kill myself afterward."

His godfather studied him. "So this is what Domenico meant."

"What did he say to you?"

"You've changed."

Enrico snorted. "When haven't I been this way? I never should have been *capo*."

"Why did you take it then?"

"How could I disappoint my father after all he'd suffered? With Primo and Mario dead, I was all he had left."

"You did the honorable thing, my son. You always have. That's why I love you so much." The old man's voice roughened with emotion and he coughed to clear his throat. "But you must decide now what is most important to you: what the family needs, or what you want."

"I've already decided. I've already jeopardized so many lives for her."

Don Battista nodded. "There are some in La Provincia who think you need to be replaced."

"Benedetto, I assume."

"He's not alone."

"Who then?"

His godfather looked at him for a moment, then his eyes shifted toward the trees that sheltered his home. "I've defended you, but I must admit to having my own doubts. You will have to answer for this. Carlo has petitioned his brother for a hearing."

Enrico wasn't surprised to hear that. But he didn't like to hear that Don Battista doubted him. His pulse sped up. "You think I should step aside, and let Dom take over?" The knot in Enrico's gut doubled in size. If he lost his godfather's support, it was all over.

"No. I know what he wants to do to the *cosca*. The drugs, the girls—" Don Battista shook his head in disgust. "It would be against everything your father and I have stood for. I know it may be a losing battle, but I won't let the 'Ndrangheta turn into a cesspool without a fight."

"I don't want that either." *But I don't care about it as much as I care about her.*

The old man sighed. "You know what you must do, my son. What is best for everyone."

Enrico nodded, feeling defeated. "I know. And I will do it." He tried to keep the bitterness out of his voice, but he felt he didn't succeed. He rose to leave, but the don stopped him.

"There's one more thing."

"Yes?"

"This disagreement with your cousin needs to be resolved, very soon, or it will break the *cosca* apart."

"Which disagreement? The one about Kate or the one about the codes?"

"Both. He is hardening his heart against you. I didn't like what I heard in his voice."

Enrico bristled. "Dom is not the one in charge."

"Then make sure that you are." Don Battista's voice was firm, his tone final. "Your cousin needs to know that."

Enrico nodded. "Thank you for the advice, *mio padrino*." He quickly kissed Don Battista on both cheeks. He was turning to leave when the don stopped him again. *What now?*

"I have a surprise for you."

"You do?"

"Your father is here, in Capri. If you wish to see him, call this number." Don Battista handed him a slip of paper.

Enrico looked down at it, his stomach flipping over. "Did you arrange this?"

The old don shrugged. "Rinaldo has run from his problems long enough."

"But they're my problems now."

Don Battista shook his head. "Carlo has a long memory."

"So do I." Images of his brothers riddled with bullets and bathed in blood flashed through his mind.

"I will call you with the details for the meeting with La Provincia."

He thanked Don Battista, then left to find Kate, wishing his godfather had thought of some clever solution to his predicament. But of course there was nothing. There never had been. He was in this for life, or he was dead. And if he wanted to live, he had to protect the *cosca*. There was no other choice. Even if it meant cutting out his own heart. He could still run things without one.

CHAPTER 22

The entire boat ride back to the hotel, Enrico pondered when and how to tell Kate he was the Lucchesi family *capo*. The best time would be on the trip back to the lake. They'd be trapped in the car together; she wouldn't be able to run out on him. He'd have plenty of time to explain; she'd have plenty of time to think. And if it went wrong... well, at least he could control the situation. He'd need to talk to Ruggero in advance. He couldn't pull the trigger himself.

Damn it all, who did he think he was fooling? He couldn't kill her, and he couldn't ask Ruggero to do it either. No matter what Don Battista said. No matter if it cost him his own life. He simply could not do it.

He had to send Kate home, didn't he? But then, if Carlo went after her and killed her, everything he'd done—taking her under his protection, breaking the truce, violating his vows to the family—all of it would have been for nothing. And considering Dom had no doubt informed Carlo of his choice regarding Delfina, it was certain Carlo would want his revenge on Kate.

He had to take the risk, had to tell her, had to make her understand.

It was the only way.

Enrico hardly noticed what Kate said during the boat trip. He didn't recall when she stopped talking either. He only knew when they were back in the room that it was suddenly quiet. Too quiet. "What is wrong?"

"Nothing."

"Do not try to hide it from me. I know you by now."

She let out a skeptical sound. "Not as well as you think."

"What do you mean?" What had he missed?

"I know you were talking to Vittorio about our future together, but I can't stay."

His senses all jumped to high alert. "What is this about?"

She looked away. "You don't love me. You still love *her.*" Her voice was soft.

"That is not entirely true. I do love you. But there is room in my heart for her as well."

Kate turned eyes like ice chips on him. "That is hardly a ringing endorsement. Besides, if you loved me, you would trust me. And you would tell me your big secret."

Damn it—couldn't she wait a little longer? He couldn't tell her here; what if she got hysterical? "That has nothing to do with trusting you. There is a lot more at stake."

"So you say. If you loved me, you would tell me."

"I *will* tell you. Very soon. Please trust me."

She looked at the tiled floor. "There's no point to this anyway. I don't love you, Enrico."

A chill swept him up and down, and his ears filled with white noise. "What?"

"I told you from the start, this was just about fun." She crossed her arms.

"But it is more than that now." *At least it is for me.*

She closed her eyes. "I only slept with you to get revenge on Vince." He thought he detected a quaver to her voice.

She is lying. She has to be. "That is not true."

"I'm a vindictive person. You've seen how far I would go to hurt Vince. I shot him, for God's sake!"

What is wrong *with her?* "If that were true, if that were *all* of it, then why have you continued sleeping with me?" His voice was too loud; he was almost shouting.

She hunched her shoulders. In the smallest voice, she said, "I was terrified of Carlo."

"You thought I would not protect you if we were not sleeping together?"

When she nodded, it was a knife to the gut. "You think so very little of me?" His voice shook and he hated the sound of it, wishing he'd said nothing.

She started to nod again, then she shook her head. She looked up at him, her eyes full of tears. He wanted to go to her, but he was about to cry himself, and he didn't want her to see that. He headed for the bathroom, hearing her break into sobs, the sound piercing him.

Enrico shut the door and took a breath, pressing his palms into his eyes. He had to get control of himself. He couldn't fall apart the way he had when Toni died. The stakes were too high now; he couldn't afford to drink himself into oblivion for weeks on end. Yes, Kate had just cut his heart out. But no one else could know. He'd have to bury that sorrow; he'd have to dig its grave deep.

When he thought he could look at her again, he took a box of tissues to her. At the sight of her tears, his eyes grew hot. He wasn't as strong as he'd thought. "Here," he said, shoving the box at her in his haste to get away. Fumbling with the sliding door, he stepped onto the terrace. *Madonna.* How was he going to bear this?

He was staring at the sea when he heard her behind him. "I'm sorry," she said, her voice barely more than a whisper.

"I am sorry too. I wish you had been honest with me."

"I was. I told you from the beginning how I felt."

He started to object, but it was true. "Then I wish you had not kissed me the day of the attack. I wish you had not been waiting for me that night in the study." He couldn't stand how raw his voice sounded.

She touched him on the forearm. "I didn't mean to hurt you."

How dare she play stupid. He pinned her with his eyes. "You had to know what would happen. You had to know you were encouraging me." He stopped himself from saying more, wishing that he could be neutral, that he could somehow bear this without letting her know she'd lacerated him to the core.

"I thought…" She let her hand drop away. "I thought for a while maybe things could work between us."

The tentativeness in her voice gave him hope. He took her by the shoulders. "They still can. If you trust me."

"I can't. I just can't."

Anger frothed up in him, hot and dark, and he let go of her abruptly. How could she do this to him? How could she make him love her, how could she listen to him pour out his heart? How could she do all that, and then push him away?

She tried to touch him again and he jerked away. It took everything he had not to yell. "Leave me. I need a while to myself."

He heard her breath catch and then the scuffing of her shoes as she walked away. When the door to their room closed behind her, a strangled sound, halfway between a sob and a moan, forced its way out of his constricted throat. He pressed a fist to his mouth. He would not cry. He would not mourn.

He'd leaned on the edge of the terrace for countless minutes, maybe hours, his eyes staring at the water but not seeing it, the late afternoon sun hitting his face, when he saw Kate shuffle by below, wiping her eyes, the damn tissue box still clutched to her chest.

He looked away from the gleam of her auburn hair and the flutter of her flowered dress in the wind, but like a magnet, she drew his eyes back. He watched her for a while, his anger receding. If she didn't care, she wouldn't be suffering, would she? Hope flared in his chest, a sun in miniature, warming him from the inside out. She *did* love him.

He wanted to be angry with her, but this was his fault entirely. He'd told her he loved her, but he hadn't shown her that love. He'd helped her, yes, but he hadn't trusted her, not in the way that most mattered. Was it any wonder she was pulling away?

He needed to show her that he loved her more than he loved anyone else, including himself. That he trusted her. He'd have to tell her everything. Everything that could send him to prison.

And he'd have to introduce her to his father, so she'd understand how this life could be her death. If she was going to stay with him, he wanted her to do it with wide open eyes.

He pulled out his mobile phone and the number Don Battista had given him. His hand shook so much he had to punch in the numbers twice.

He hadn't seen his father in over ten years. Only God knew if he'd find anything other than a ruin.

CHAPTER 23

Kate left Enrico in the room and walked down to the lobby, still carrying the tissue box. She wandered around the hotel grounds, crying on and off, not caring who saw her. It was for the best. She couldn't let him plan a future with her when she had no intention of staying. That wouldn't be fair.

So why did she feel like such a bitch? *Really, Kate? Let's make a list: Because you lied when you said you didn't love him? Because you told him the real reason you first slept with him? Because you just had to imply he'd helped you only because you were in his bed?*

There were low blows, and then there were low blows. All Enrico had ever done was help her. And love her.

And this was how she repaid him.

He should throw her to the wolves. Hell, he should dump her on Carlo's doorstep.

But he'd do no such thing. Because Rico was a kind, decent man. Whatever he was keeping from her, could it be so bad? It must be a doozy, or he'd have told her just now, but he'd said nothing. And maybe *that* was for the best.

She'd been right to end their relationship before they got any more involved. Before she couldn't bear to leave him.

But if breaking up was the right thing do, why was she so torn? Why did she want to throw herself in his arms and take it all back, every single ugly word?

She swallowed a sob. Some things couldn't be unsaid. Some things couldn't be undone. Some things couldn't be forgiven.

And that's what she wanted, right? For him to leave her.

Then why had her chest turned into an empty gnawing pit? Why was her stomach threatening to turn inside out?

Why did she feel so damn horrible?

When Kate returned to the room, Enrico told her they were having dinner with his father.

What the hell was he thinking? "You don't seriously want to introduce me to him *now*, do you?"

"I need to see him. You need to eat."

She laughed. "I can call room service."

"Please humor me." He raked a hand through his hair, his face pained. "He will be better if you are there."

The look on his face tore something in her gut. "What do you mean?"

"You will see." He glanced at his watch. "We need to leave soon. Are you ready?"

"You're serious."

He stared at her for a moment before answering. "Yes. Can we go?"

"Let me wash my face. I've cried off all my makeup."

"You do not need it. You never have."

She almost rolled her eyes. "Do you never stop flirting?"

"I am not flirting with you." His eyes held hers, not a trace of mirth in them.

Ouch. "Give me a few minutes." She hurried into the bathroom, closing the door behind her. She washed her face, then stared at herself in the mirror. She looked like hell. And she didn't want to do this. She just wanted to go home. To leave.

To forget.

&ᙢᎦ

It took them about twenty minutes to walk to the address his father had given him. The house surprised Enrico. It was well-kept, but small and nondescript. Hardly the place one would expect a man of Rinaldo's fortune to live in. It was nothing like the grand house he'd bought on the shores of Lake Como. *How the mighty had fallen. Will this be me someday?*

His heart hammering, he knocked on the door and waited. They'd spoken only briefly on the phone; Rinaldo had shown little enthusiasm for seeing Enrico, but he hadn't said no either. "Fine," was all the answer he'd given.

The ghost who shambled to the door bore little resemblance to the hearty man of Enrico's youth, and he ached anew to see the change in his father. His thick hair was shot through with silver, his handsome face gaunt, his dark eyes nearly expressionless. *He looks like the walking dead.* It was a horrible thing to see.

After a moment of staring into his father's lifeless eyes, a hot, hard ball of anger started to burn in his chest. Rinaldo hadn't lost everyone that day. He still had Enrico. Why wasn't that worth living for? *Why am I not enough?*

Rinaldo stared at him for a moment, then he looked from Enrico to Kate.

"So you are the cause of all this trouble," he said to her.

Kate looked up at Rinaldo. Then she cast a doubtful look at Enrico. "Rico, maybe we should go," she whispered.

They stood there, the three of them frozen for a moment, then his father said, "I suppose we should get this over with." He motioned them inside and led them into a simple kitchen. Enrico and Kate took seats at a rough-hewn wooden table. A delicious aroma filled the tiny kitchen as Rinaldo opened the oven and pulled out a covered baking dish.

"Baked ziti," Enrico said.

A trace of a smile appeared on Rinaldo's face. "Just like Nonna Drina's." He set the pan down, then dished out generous portions onto plates. "How is she?"

"The same. She will outlive us all."

Rinaldo huffed with laughter. "Certainly she will outlive me."

"Do not say that," Enrico said, surprised by the catch in his voice. He took the plate Rinaldo handed him. His throat felt so tight he didn't think he could swallow a bite. Kate touched his hand, and he was grateful for it. Someone here cared about him. Even if she pretended not to.

Rinaldo took the seat at the head of the table, on Enrico's left. "Well, my son, it is true. My heart is no stronger, and I have had three bypasses. The doctors say I have another year or two. But that is all."

"Papà, I hate to hear you say that."

"You should never be afraid of the truth."

Enrico almost smiled. That was his whole problem, wasn't it? Not owning up to who he was, what he'd done. Hiding.

"So what brings you here?" Rinaldo glanced at Kate, then back at Enrico. "Certainly it is not merely to show off your latest acquisition."

He took a breath, steadying himself not to take the bait. "I am here because I wanted to see you. How you were."

"I'm alive. What more is there to say?"

Plenty. And we never say it. Enrico shoved away the plate in front of him and turned so he was fully facing his father. "Why did all the love in you die with them? Did I *never* occupy any space in your heart?"

Rinaldo looked startled for a moment, then his face closed up. "You have not lost what I have lost."

"I lost my mother, my brothers. And like you, I have lost a wife." He paused. "But my heart has not died like yours." He reached out blindly, finding Kate's hand and squeezing it, his eyes not leaving his father's face.

Rinaldo shook his head. "Maybe had I not suffered it all in one blow, maybe had I not buried two sons...." He looked down at the table, then back at Enrico. "I am sorry, *mio figlio*. I have nothing left for you. For anyone."

"Is it because I have disappointed you?" He had to know. "I know I am not Primo, I know I was not your first choice to take over."

"You avenged them, when I couldn't. How could I be disappointed in you?" Rinaldo's eyes watered. "If I had anything left, I would give it to you."

"You would?"

A tear rolled down his father's cheek. "How can you doubt it?" He wiped at his face.

Grief welled up in Enrico, and he couldn't hold back his own tears. "Papà," he said, choking on the word. Before he could stop himself, he threw his arms around his father, hugging him hard. He was starting to let go, when Rinaldo's arms encircled him, pulling him close. Warmth spread through his chest, overpowering his grief.

It was as close as his father had ever come to telling him he loved him. It wasn't much, but it was enough.

After a few moments, Rinaldo released him, patting him on the back. "We should eat. My ziti is getting cold."

Enrico glanced at Kate and saw the glitter of tears in her eyes. He should be embarrassed she'd seen this, but strangely he wasn't. He wanted her to know everything about him, including this.

They started to eat. "It's very good," Kate said.

Rinaldo chuckled. "It is all I know how to make. I should be good at it by now." He turned to Enrico. "When will you be married?"

Enrico heard Kate's fork hit her plate, but he didn't look at her. "Soon, I hope." She kicked him under the table. It was true. He wouldn't take it back.

Rinaldo addressed Kate. "I wish you good fortune. You will need it with my son." He gave her a half smile, his eyes taking on the barest glint.

"You are right about that." She smiled.

He gave Enrico a fond look. "We Lucchesis have always found trouble. Even in the stillest pond."

"That might be because you are the most stubborn, pigheaded, self-righteous men on the planet," Kate said.

Enrico snorted with laughter. His father grinned, then started to laugh. For a moment, he looked like the man Enrico remembered. For a moment, he looked happy. Enrico gave Kate a grateful smile, his heart full of love for her. If only she could wait, he'd make everything right.

🖂🖃

Enrico surprised Kate again by still wanting to drive back to the lake. She'd thought he'd want to return by plane, so he wouldn't have to spend so much time with her. But he'd seemed oddly cheerful when they returned to their room. When she asked him why, he said she would eventually understand.

Neither of them slept much that night. Enrico took the sofa, and Kate found herself feeling alone even though he was in the same room. Several times she stopped herself on the verge of asking him to join her. She'd already led him on once. She couldn't do it again. And he wasn't the only one she'd hurt. She hadn't ever ached like this over a man. Not even Vince.

Enrico only made the ache worse in the morning. He woke her early. She looked up to see him standing next to the bed, his hand still on her shoulder. There was a look on his face she couldn't read. "What is it?"

He sat down on the bed beside her and took her hand. "I want you to know," he started, then stopped. "Thank you," he said. "I did not thank you for last night, with my father."

"Rico, I didn't do anything—"

"Yes, you did."

She started to object again, then stopped. "I'm glad I could help."

"I love you, Kate. Even if you do leave me, I love you." He leaned over and kissed her forehead.

Kate caught herself before she said the words that rose up in her heart: *I love you too.* Instead she squeezed his hand. It was best to say nothing.

After breakfast, Enrico took her on a quick spree through several shops in Capri so she'd have enough clothes for the trip up the coast. Kate took little pleasure in the shopping, even though Enrico urged her to get whatever she liked. In the last two stores, Enrico was the one who picked out most of what she bought. When she remarked on it, saying, "I'm surprised you care about this," he smiled at her for the first time since their fight.

"It is genetic, I suppose. All Italians have it, the idea of *la bella figura*—always presenting your best face to the world. Looking the best you can afford, preferably better." He gave her a meaningful look. "But it is more than that. I want you to have the best. I want to give you that. Always."

She looked down at her feet, now clad in the softest, most buttery heels she'd ever worn. Heels that cost a fortune. "Bribing me won't change my mind."

His face darkened. "I speak from the heart, and you accuse me of bribing you." He took a deep breath, his hands on his hips. "I'm trying to love you, Kate, but you make it damn hard."

And I'm trying not *to love you,* she almost said. *But you make it damn hard.* She swallowed down the words. "I'm sorry. Thanks for everything. You're very generous."

"That is not the point. That is not why I am upset."

She looked up at him. "I can't give you what you want."

He shook his head, then waved a hand around them, taking in the whole store. "Are we done? Ready to go?"

She nodded, wishing that she could take it all back, that she could make him smile again. But she couldn't string either of them along any further. Getting through the next two days was already going to be murder.

෭෨ල

Enrico clearly enjoyed driving the silver Maserati convertible. He zoomed along the narrow switchbacks of the highway that wound along the Amalfi coast, a smile touching his lips, and seemed to have forgotten about her sitting next to him. Antonio and Ruggero followed in a black Mercedes.

They spoke little the first day of the trip, though after a time Enrico pointed out various spots and told her some of the history of the region. Kate could see why he'd wanted to make the drive. The rugged coastline and the towns they passed were all quite picturesque. The throaty purr of the car, the wind in her hair, and the salty tang of the Mediterranean almost made her forget why they were hardly speaking.

Still she wondered at his persistence in taking her with him. He could have sent her back on the jet or had her ride with Antonio and Ruggero. But, other than the extended silences between them, he seemed to be acting as if everything were normal.

When they stopped in Spoleto for the night, he'd even insisted on one room for the two of them, but he'd caved at her look and had gotten a suite instead. After dinner, Kate waited for him to knock on the door adjoining their rooms, but he never did until morning, and then it was only to make sure she was ready to leave.

His behavior unsettled her. She'd expected more anger, or more sadness. Not this curious cheerfulness among the silences. Twice she nearly demanded an explanation, but she didn't want to fight with him. She found herself missing his touch, missing his attentiveness. Missing him. Even though he was right beside her.

The second day, they left the coast in the early afternoon. Enrico soon fell silent, and she sensed a tension in him that grew as they climbed into the foothills of the Alps, drawing closer to the lake. Finally, he turned to her.

"There is something we need to discuss."

Here it comes. Something she was sure she wasn't going to want to hear. "Enrico, there's nothing to discuss. I'll go to Florence and wait until Fuente gives my passport back. Then I'll go somewhere else Carlo won't expect. My parents have money. I can lay low for a while."

"I do not think that will be necessary."

"Well, I can't stay with you forever. Not now."

"About that," he said, glancing at her. "I know why you do not trust me. Why you are afraid to admit you love me."

She stared at him, then recovered enough to say, "I don't know why you think I love you."

"I think so because it is true. You need something from me so you can admit it, and it is time I gave it to you."

"I don't need anything from you. I—" Kate cried out as a searing pain stabbed her below her right collarbone. She looked down, seeing a dark red blotch spreading over her blouse. She touched it, then looked at Enrico shouting her name as he wheeled to the side of the road. Holding her hand up to show him the blood on her fingers, she was unable to voice the questions in her mind: What was going on? Had she been shot?

CHAPTER 24

Antonio and Ruggero saw the Maserati swerve onto the shoulder, the *signora* holding up a hand stained red, their *capo* speaking to her urgently. Ruggero pulled over in front of them, doing his best to shield the convertible with the big black Mercedes. Antonio jumped out and Ruggero ran around the back of the car, then crouched down beside Antonio next to the front passenger fender with his gun drawn. Antonio saw a muzzle flash from the hills above, then heard the report of a rifle echoing around them. "Fucking Andrettis," Ruggero muttered.

Antonio turned to look at the Maserati, to see what was happening inside. Don Lucchesi was leaning over the *signora*, pressing a hand to her chest. A bullet sliced through the windshield, hitting him in the ribs below his left arm. Antonio watched in horror as his *capo* arched in pain, losing his hold on the *signora*.

Antonio bolted for the car, panic flooding him despite his training. "Don Lucchesi!" he shouted, opening the driver's side door. He threw his body over his *capo*'s, protecting him as he inspected the wound. "Can you breathe?"

"I'll be okay." Don Lucchesi turned to him, his face taut with pain, a sheen of sweat on his forehead. "Get us out of the car. Kate first."

Antonio pushed his *capo* down on the seat, flattening him over the *signora*, then he ran around the back of the car and opened her door. He dragged her out of the car and laid her on the ground beside it, sheltering her from the shooters. Don Lucchesi crawled out after them, kneeling on the ground next to her. He placed his hand over her wound again, pressing down. "What about you?" she asked, looking up at him.

"It is you I worry about."

"Why?" she asked.

But Antonio already knew. The patch of blood on her chest had expanded enormously in the short time it had taken to move her. The don tore off his shirt and wadded it up, pressing the ball of it into her chest. He looked at Antonio, who'd crouched down beside him. "Your jacket. She needs to stay warm."

"*Sì.*" Antonio ripped off his jacket and covered the *signora* with it. He pulled his mobile phone out, calling Don Domenico for help. Don Domenico said he'd send the *polizia*; it would take too long for enough of their own men to arrive.

Antonio ended the call and cursed. They were on their own, for God knew how long. Blood welled down his *capo*'s side, so he shrugged out of his shoulder holster and pulled off his shirt, urging Don Lucchesi to hold it against his own wound. Then he took a deep breath and rejoined Ruggero at the Mercedes. He needed to focus, needed to help Ruggero defend them.

There were two shooters above them, positioned on each side where the highway cut through the mountains, the perfect spot for an ambush. Bullets rained down around them, mostly hitting the Mercedes and the Maserati, but some whizzed into the dirt right beside them. Ruggero's shoulder was grazed when he popped up to get a better angle on the shooters, but their handguns were poor threats against the rifles. Ruggero nudged Antonio, and the two of them scrambled to the back of the Mercedes. The more serious hardware was in the boot. Ruggero pulled out two mini Uzis and a large black duffle bag. He tossed an Uzi to Antonio, just as he took a bullet in the left calf. Cursing, Ruggero looked at the wound, then tested out the leg as they scrambled back to better cover.

"How bad?" Antonio shouted at him.

Ruggero grinned and shook his head. "A scratch." He turned his attention back to the shooters above them, switching the Uzi to full automatic, and spraying the left hillside above. Antonio followed suit and took the right side, willing his bullets to find their targets. He wanted these men dead. *Per favore, Dio, let Don Lucchesi and the signora live.*

They kept up a steady barrage of gunfire, pausing only to slam in new clips. Antonio was thankful Ruggero had done the packing; there was enough ammunition in the bag for an army. He made a mental note to never under-pack when it came to firepower.

The sing-song wail of sirens finally reached their ears, and Antonio and Ruggero ceased their fire and waited. There were one or two more shots from above, then no more. The men in the hills apparently wanted to avoid the *polizia* more than they wanted to finish the job. Antonio cursed again; he wanted those cowards dead.

Ruggero jerked the gun out of his hand and stashed the Uzis in the boot right before the ambulance and police cars pulled up. Antonio kicked their sidearms under the Mercedes. Then the two of them held their hands up in the air, waiting for the officers and medics to approach. It wouldn't do to get killed now. Who would protect Don Lucchesi then?

℘℃

The eruption of gunfire from Antonio and Ruggero sounded like World War III to Kate. Enrico crouched down over her, molding his body to hers. She jerked at the roar of the guns, the noise thundering in her chest, then she wrapped her free arm around him, pressing her fingers against his wound. The pressure made him flinch, but he didn't cry out. He looked down at her. "We will survive this."

"I know." She fought to keep her voice steady. She looked up at him, her shock at learning his identity still in her mind. Don Lucchesi. That's what Antonio had called him. Vince hadn't been lying. But Enrico had, and yes, it was a doozy. Had he kept anything else from her?

The gunfire abruptly stopped, then she heard the sound of emergency sirens, then men approaching, their voices hard and demanding as they spoke to Antonio and Ruggero. Moments later, a confusing swirl of people descended on them, and Kate panicked, her heart rate surging when Enrico's weight was lifted from her. When the medics tried to separate them, she clutched at Enrico's hand, a weak protest leaving her mouth. She was shocked at how frail she sounded, at how difficult it was to close her fingers around his hand. He squeezed her fingers before turning to the medics and firing off a string of rapid Italian. She couldn't follow every word, but she knew he'd said she'd lost a lot of blood. And he insisted they treat her first.

As the medics labored over her, she found herself relaxing in the midst of the frenzy. It was going to be okay; the ambulance was here. She wasn't going to die in the dirt on this roadside. She looked at Enrico for confirmation, trying to give him a smile through the oxygen mask she wore. But when she saw him wince hard with pain and struggle to take a breath, a frightened bird beat its wings in her chest. She squeezed his hand, but he didn't return the pressure. He dropped hers instead, his hand flailing at his chest. He wheezed out some words to the medics, then two of them left her and started working on him.

"What's wrong with him?" she cried.

"*Puntura del polmone,*" the medic said. Lung puncture. He moved into her line of sight, cutting off her view of Enrico. "No worry, *signora.*"

The medics wheeled her away on a gurney, while the others were working on Enrico. She couldn't see what they were doing, if Enrico was all right. She got a glimpse of his face, his eyes closed, his skin gray. She didn't want to leave him, and when she struggled against it, one of the medics gave her an injection. Warmth shot through her veins, then she was drifting, her sight crumbling at the edges.

There was something she needed to do, something she needed to know, but the urgency and what it was quickly faded. The ambulance doors slammed, the siren wailed, and the gravel crunched beneath the tires. And then Kate's world fell silent.

℘℘

Enrico woke up in a hospital room, Antonio slumped asleep in the chair next to him. In place of the shirt and jacket he'd given up, Antonio wore a light blue surgical scrub top, the trousers of his dark blue suit dusty and bloody, the knees torn from scrambling about in the rocks next to the cars.

Enrico tried to talk, but his mouth was so dry he couldn't get much above a whisper. He coughed to get Antonio's attention, then wished he hadn't. It felt like someone was shoving an ice pick in his left side, and he barked out a curse. Antonio woke up then, his eyes wide. "*Signore?*"

"*Acqua, per favore.*"

Antonio poured him a glass and handed it to him. Enrico was surprised it took an effort to raise the plastic cup to his lips. The water was room temperature and flat, but it felt good and he downed the whole glass. And then he remembered.

"Kate, how is she?"

Antonio smiled. "She's going to be fine. They got the bullet and stopped the bleeding."

"*Grazie a Dio,*" Enrico said. Then he remembered something else. She knew. She knew who he was. Before he'd had a chance to tell her himself, to explain.

"I have to see her." When he tried to sit up, pain sliced through his torso. He cursed again, then lay back, panting, but even that hurt. Any movement involving his rib cage hurt. Horribly. He tried again, moving in the tiniest of increments, and found he could manage to get upright that way. Antonio restrained him with a hand to the chest.

"I'm sorry, *signore*, but you can't get out of bed. Your lung was punctured."

Enrico glared up at Antonio, but knew he was right. His next thought was his first practical one. "How many guards do we have here?"

"Ruggero's with the *signora*, and there are two other guards outside each room. We also have a man at each exit and entrance to the floor. You're safe."

"Not if they really want to finish the job."

"The *carabinieri* have their men here as well."

That earned a smirk from Enrico. "Maggiore Alfonso must want to keep my contributions to the policeman's fund."

"He's a smart man."

"What have they been told?"

"Only that someone was shooting at us. We didn't speculate about who it was, though of course Fuente asked if it was Andretti."

"And what did you say?"

"I shrugged. What else could I do?" He paused, then looked away from Enrico. "I'm not sure it *was* Andretti."

"What do you mean?"

"How would he know where we were at that exact moment? How could *anyone* know?"

"Maybe we were followed." Antonio shook his head. "Then what?"

Antonio rubbed his chin, his fingers rasping across blond stubble. "There are two possibilities. One, Ruggero or I somehow signaled the shooters. Of course, we'd have to do it without the other one knowing. You should check our phone calls and text messages to verify. Two, someone planted a GPS tracker on one or both of the cars."

"Have you searched the cars?"

"No. The *polizia* have them. And I didn't want to leave until I knew you were all right."

Enrico looked at the ceiling. Could this possibly be Franco Trucco's work? "Can you get Ruggero for me?"

Antonio was nearly to the door when Enrico stopped him. "Don't tell anyone about this. We don't want to alert the traitor."

"I understand, *signore*."

While Antonio was gone, Enrico struggled upright again. He had to get out of this damn bed and see Kate. He had to know whether she hated him.

He turned himself to one side, inching his legs off the mattress and over the edge of the hospital bed. He was clutching the metal frame, his lips pressed tight together, when Ruggero limped in. "What do you need, *signore?*" Ruggero asked, hurrying to his side. "Lay down," he added, when Enrico didn't answer.

"How's your leg?" He held himself upright with trembling arms.

"Fine. The bullet passed through." Ruggero grabbed hold of Enrico's arms. "You must lay down, *signore*."

He did his best to fight Ruggero, but it was like trying to move a mountain. He could barely stay up. "I need to see Kate."

Ruggero's mouth compressed into a thin line. "The *signora* is fine."

"She knows. She knows who I am."

Ruggero sighed, the breath gusting out of him wearily. "She's asked me twice why you lied to her."

"What did you say?"

"Nothing. She asked for Antonio, but I've kept them apart."

"*Mille grazie.*"

"It's your place to tell her, not ours." When he tried to stand up again, Ruggero frowned. "You must stay in bed."

Enrico ignored him and pressed forward. When he met resistance, he mustered up his sternest glare. "I am your *capo* still, am I not?" There was a pause, then Ruggero's grip shifted to one of assistance rather than restraint.

Enrico started to lower himself onto his feet when a sharp rap on the half-open door caught their attention.

A tall, thin, dark-haired man in a white coat and glasses stood there with Enrico's medical chart in his hand. It was Enrico's personal physician, Dottor Beltrami. He looked at Enrico and shook his head. "Where do you think you're going?"

"I need to see Kate."

"I must tell you something about her condition. She didn't want you to know. I think you should."

Panic sliced through Enrico. "Tell me."

"She's pregnant."

Enrico's brows shot up. Pregnant? Was the baby his? He remembered her hesitation that first time, the fact that they hadn't used condoms the first night. She said she'd been on birth control pills before then. The child had to be his.

Warmth spread through him. He was going to be a father in truth, not just in name, after all this time. He smiled at Ruggero and Beltrami. "I assume the child is all right?"

"We believe so. She doesn't show any signs of a miscarriage. The hospital is of course keeping a close watch on her."

"I have to see her." Enrico gingerly slid off the bed. He tried to take a step and wobbled. Ruggero grabbed his arm to steady him.

"You aren't supposed to be on your feet. You're still heavily medicated, and you could tear your stitches if you move around too much," Beltrami said.

Enrico growled in frustration. He wasn't sure he could cross the floor of his own room, much less make it to hers. "Wheelchair, then?"

Beltrami sighed. "You won't listen, will you?"

"No."

"I'll get a nurse. Sit down."

Ruggero helped him to the chair beside the bed. Enrico turned to him and whispered. "Antonio thinks a GPS tracker was used on the cars."

"It's possible."

"Find out if that's the case and who planted it. If it's Trucco, he needs to be dealt with, immediately."

The guard nodded. "I'll handle it."

A nurse came in with a wheelchair, followed by Beltrami. She frowned at Enrico and at the doctor, but helped him into the chair. They started down the hallway, IV stand in tow, and Enrico thought about Kate and the baby. She didn't want him to know about the pregnancy. Which could mean only one thing: she hated him, and she intended to leave him. Maybe she even meant to abort the child.

His gut cramped and a shudder racked his body. He couldn't let that happen. He had to persuade her to forgive him. Or at least to spare their child. If needed, he would raise it on his own. He would do whatever it took to keep his child safe.

℘ℂ

When he got the reports from his men, Carlo cursed God for denying him yet again. Enrico Lucchesi was like the proverbial cockroach: damned difficult to kill.

Carlo relished the image of stomping on Lucchesi. How he'd love to see him dead. But so far that had not come to pass, despite Domenico's assistance.

Even worse, Franco Trucco had come to see him the day before. And what he'd told Carlo made him burn even hotter.

Lucchesi had lied all along. He had sullied his marriage to Toni before it had even begun. Thank God his daughter had been spared the humiliation.

But her honor would be avenged. It was the least he could do to make up for marrying her to a Lucchesi, for consigning her to life as a housewife, when she should have been his heir, when she should have been running the Andretti *cosca* instead. If only he hadn't given in to her pleas to save her twin.... But what was done was done. All he had left to give her was vengeance.

What was the best way to draw out Lucchesi's suffering? Killing him was not enough anymore. He wanted to pummel Lucchesi, to strip him of everything before he died.

Before the last day of his life, Lucchesi would lose the ones he loved. Perhaps the bastard son first? The boy might be Lucchesi's blood, but the two must be estranged if the son worked for Interpol. Losing a son he wasn't close to? Not a good first blow.

No, the first blow would be Rinaldo's death, and Carlo would make it painful. Trucco had made clear that Rinaldo was aware of Enrico's bastard, that he'd started making the payments to keep Enrico's secret. Rinaldo had known the marriage and the truce were founded on a lie.

What if Rinaldo lost a finger or two before he died? That would be the perfect payback. Anger still gripped Carlo whenever he noted Dario's missing finger, the void a constant reminder of when Rinaldo thought he'd had the upper hand.

Oh yes. Carlo smiled to himself. He'd enjoy wrapping Rinaldo's fingers up in a box and sending them to Lucchesi.

And then... then it would be time to get more direct. To rob Lucchesi of what he loved most. The woman. She was the key to his suffering. Lucchesi would do anything for the American. She too would learn the meaning of pain. But not before they'd had some fun together. He'd earned a little indulgence.

The boy would be the final blow. The final nail in the coffin, the end of Rinaldo and Enrico Lucchesi's line. The ultimate grind of his heel before Carlo finished Enrico himself.

But before all that, Carlo would have his day in court. Benedetto had agreed to his petition to hear his case against Lucchesi before La Provincia. Lucchesi would squirm then, the little cockroach, and Carlo would enjoy making him crawl before all of La Provincia. Maybe he would even finally overcome his exile and earn a seat on the council.

Best of all, Lucchesi would have no idea that the pain was just starting. That all of this had merely been the appetizer before the main course.

Carlo picked up the phone and placed two calls. One to Domenico, the other to his favorite member of the *carabinieri*.

CHAPTER 25

Kate hadn't let Antonio leave her side since he'd come in her hospital room looking for Ruggero. She'd asked him two questions: How was Enrico? And why had he called him Don Lucchesi? He'd answered the first, and pretended he hadn't heard the second. So she'd asked again. Twice more. He'd looked increasingly uncomfortable with each repetition. So she asked a fourth time.

This time he got up and paced over to the open door, poking his head out and looking down the hall. Then he came back in. *This is it. He's going to tell me.*

Instead he sat down in the chair across from her bed and rubbed his hands over his face. He looked at the floor tiles and ignored her.

"Answer me, Antonio. Why did you call him Don Lucchesi?"

Two spots of color rose in his cheeks, but he continued to stare at the floor.

"Why, Antonio?"

Finally he met her eyes. "I cannot say."

"Yes, you can."

"I cannot."

She sighed, letting her eyes fill with tears. Maybe that would work on him. It was easy to summon the tears; she didn't have to think about anything in particular. She was so angry and frustrated. And worried. And happy about the baby. And terrified at the same time. It wasn't just her life in jeopardy anymore. Now she had two people to worry about. Two people to keep safe from Carlo Andretti. How the hell was she going to do that?

"*Signora, per favore,* do not cry." Antonio brought her a box of tissues, holding it out to her awkwardly, his face turned away from her.

"Look at me. Look me in the eyes and tell me why."

"*Signora,* I *cannot* say."

195

A knock on the door broke their gaze. A nurse wheeled Enrico in, followed by Dottor Beltrami and Ruggero. She looked Enrico over, glad his color had returned, though he was hunched uncomfortably in the chair. But she didn't want to see him. And she certainly didn't want to talk to him. Enrico looked at everyone around them. "Please leave us."

"That's not necessary," Kate said.

"It is." Enrico glared at the others. "*Per favore*, now. And close the door behind you." Antonio was the first to start edging toward the hall, then the rest followed suit. The room was clear a few seconds later.

Kate wiped her tears away with a tissue. She didn't want to appear weak for this conversation. "I wish you'd leave me alone."

"I had to see you."

"You've seen me. I'm fine. Now go."

He leaned forward in the chair, wincing. "Kate, Dottor Beltrami told me about the child."

She flushed with heat. "I asked him not to!"

"Why?"

She averted her eyes from his. "You know why."

"Because of who I am."

She looked at him then. "Yes." She held his eyes, waiting for more. When he didn't respond, she added, "You can't even say it, can you?"

He sighed and stared at his hands. "I am the *capo* of the Lucchesi *cosca*. There, I have said it." He raised his eyes and smirked after a moment. "You would not believe how many people in law enforcement have wanted to hear that."

She took a deep breath. "Why didn't you tell me?"

"Two reasons. One, you would not have trusted me if you had known. And two, that knowledge is dangerous. If I told you and you rejected me, I would have to silence you."

"What a nice way of putting it!" She waited a beat and then said, "So you're telling me now. Does that mean my choice is whether you or Carlo kills me?"

"Kate, I would never—"

"You just said you would 'silence' me."

"But I cannot. That is my dilemma. I cannot do it. And I do not want you with me because you have no choice. Nor do I want to leave you at Carlo's mercy." He bit his lip. "And I do not want our child to grow up without knowing me." He paused a moment, his voice hoarsening. "I already have one child I did not get to raise. I do not want that to happen again."

Kate's eyes widened. "You have a child?"

"A son. He is twenty-seven and lives in England. He was conceived while I was engaged to Antonella. I was seventeen. I was infatuated with an English girl, Veronica, and I did not want to marry a girl I had not chosen. I have regretted my behavior ever since." He looked at her. "I never told Toni. She already hurt so badly over not being able to have a child."

"Wow." Kate was silent for a moment. "You have a son only two years younger than me?"

"Does that bother you?"

"A bit. It's been easy to forget our age difference."

"I have a past, Kate."

She was silent for a moment, then she said, "So, do you see him?"

Enrico shook his head. "I have not seen him since he was eight. Well, I have not seen him up close. I have spied on him from afar a few times. He hates me."

"Why?"

"It is a long story."

"We don't have anywhere to be."

Enrico sighed. "He thinks it is my fault his mother killed herself."

"*Is* it your fault?"

He fiddled with the ties on his hospital robe. "Of course not. But sometimes I blame myself, for not seeing the signs. For not treating her better all those years ago. I should have told Veronica I was engaged. I should not have let her believe I was free."

Kate let out a sound of disgust and lay back against the pillows. "You are one fine piece of work, Enrico."

"What does that mean?"

She held his eyes with hers. "First this girl in England, and then your secretary. And now me. And your wife too. You lied to us all." Her anger rose, building into a flash of heat that burned her face and throat. She poured acid into her voice. "*Twice* I asked you, *twice* you denied it. You lied right to my face. That is *not* how you treat someone you love."

His eyes dropped to the tiles. "I cannot argue. I have no right to ask you to forgive me. But I will."

The gall of him. "How long have all of you been laughing behind my back?"

"No one has been laughing at you. It was necessary. All of us keep secrets all the time. It has become second nature." He ran a hand through his hair. "Frankly, I am weary of it."

"I'm 'weary' of all the lying too. How could you have so little respect for me?"

"I *do* respect you. I was trying to keep you safe. If I had told you earlier, you would have run, and Carlo would have found you."

It was true. But it didn't change the fact of who he was. "How many people have you killed?"

To his credit, he didn't hesitate. "Personally, a handful. I do not keep track of how many I have ordered to be killed."

She sucked in a breath. How casually he said this. "Don't you feel any remorse?"

He said nothing for a second, then he answered, his eyes on hers. "I kill only when it is deserved. Then there is nothing to feel guilty about."

"It's still murder."

"God kills every day. Is that murder?"

"So now you're God?" *The balls on this man!*

"No. But I do administer justice. I am sure that sometimes I am carrying out His will."

"But you kill innocent people! How can that be God's will?"

He leaned forward, his eyes intent on her, anger on his face. "Listen to me. I kill only those who deserve it. The innocent have nothing to fear from me."

"How can that be true?"

"Do you think the people of this area, do you think the Italian state, would tolerate me long if I killed the innocent? If I did not enforce, yes, law and order, upon my own people, and upon other 'Ndranghetisti? I serve a purpose here. I am their major defense against the likes of Carlo Andretti and Cosa Nostra and the Russian mob, and any other criminals who would like to infiltrate Milan and the lake."

If Enrico were gone, and Carlo Andretti were running the show.... Her stomach roiled.

"Can you forgive me?" he asked.

"I don't know." She looked down at her hands, twisting them in the light sheet covering her. What should she do? He was a Mafioso. And yet he was everything Carlo Andretti was not. Everything Vince had never been. Did that make him a good man?

"Then I am going to ask again. Do you forgive me? Everything I did, it was out of love. I wanted to give you a choice. I wanted you to come to me of your own free will. I wanted you with me because you love me. Not because you have to be."

"And the child, I suppose, is part of it?"

"I do not want our baby to grow up without me." He paused. "Or not to grow up at all."

It took her a second to grasp what he meant. "I'm keeping the baby."

He smiled, his body losing some of its tension. "I am glad of that at least." He rolled the chair closer to the bed, his face tightening with pain as he did so. "Kate, I want you to be my wife. Will you marry me?"

Adrenaline rushed through her at the words. She'd been afraid of them. And now that she knew who he was, she was afraid of him. Of what he'd do if she said no. "I can't answer that."

"Why not?" He looked at her, puzzled.

"Because I don't have a choice. It's yes, or that's it, isn't it?"

"If you want to say no, say it. I will figure out how to get you out of the country. And somehow I will keep you safe from Andretti."

"But won't you be in trouble for letting me go?"

"Most likely I will lose my head over it. But I will not force you to marry me."

Would he be saying that if she wasn't pregnant? "So were you ever planning to tell me? Perhaps not until after I was your wife, after I was pregnant with your child?"

"That would not be right. Remember when we were in the car? Just before you were shot, I said there was something I owed you, so you could admit you love me. And that something was the truth. I planned to tell you that minute, so you could decide. And then only you and I would know you knew, and if you wanted to leave, you could." He looked away from her. "I wish I had worked up the nerve to say it a few minutes earlier. I wish I had told you long ago. Then you would know you could trust me."

She thought for a moment. "Does anyone else know about your son?"

"No. I have kept him secret to keep him safe."

"So you trust me with this?"

He raised his eyes to hers. "I am trusting you with my *life*. You know who I am now." Then he added, "And with my heart too. I love you so much it tears me apart to think of never seeing you again. But I will let you go, if that is what you want, and I will face whatever I have to as a result." He reached out and took her hand, his warm fingers closing around hers. She kept her hand stiff at first, then finally relaxed it. She looked at him for a good long while, not saying anything. He trusted her; could she ever trust him?

"Kate?" he asked, his voice low, hushed. Waiting.

"If I wasn't pregnant, would you still let me go?"

"Of course. I would never harm you. Never. I would take a bullet for you."

She smiled. How many people could say that and literally mean it? "You did, actually, in the car. And with Vince, you almost did."

"Do not forget he tried to stab me, too, back in your office." He returned her smile.

He was always taking a risk for her; maybe it was time she did the same. "That's how this all started."

He shook his head. "Not exactly. I was in love with you for months before that. But I had to finish grieving for Toni first before I could see that."

He'd been through so much; he'd taken so many chances since that fight with Vince in her office, and all of them for her. Her throat tightened up. "You really do love me, don't you?" Kate fought to keep tears out of her eyes.

"God knows I do." He picked up her hand and kissed her knuckles. "I would do anything for you."

She blew out the breath she'd been holding. "Including lying, cheating, and stealing?" she teased.

"If you wish." He looked at her closely, his expression serious. "Will you forgive me?"

"Will you ever lie to me again?"

"Never."

"You swear it?"

"On the graves of those I loved, I swear it."

She looked into his eyes, so serious with his love for her. "Then I forgive you."

He kissed her hand again. "Will you do me the honor of being my wife?"

She searched his face. It was impossible to know how the baby was affecting things, impossible to know if he loved her as much as he loved Antonella. He'd broken the law, he'd killed. But he wasn't a cruel man. And he did love her. He had proven it in the most meaningful way possible. He had risked his life for hers. He had entrusted her with his two most important secrets.

And despite all the armor she thought she'd clad herself in, Enrico Lucchesi had touched her heart. She thought back to that day by the pool, how he'd brought her the hat and the sunscreen, how he'd moved the umbrella around to keep her shaded while she slept. They were little things, and yet they were everything true and decent about this man. He looked out for her, in all ways, large and small. If that wasn't true love, what was? Her eyes blurred with tears, and she let go of his hand.

₧₨

Enrico stared up at Kate, unable to read her expression. What were the tears about? Was it going to be a no after all? He was starting to look away from her, when her hand sought his. "You know, Enrico, there's something you haven't asked me."

"What?"

"You haven't asked me if I love you. I've never said it."

"I do not need to hear it." He wasn't going to press her for it; what did it matter? Someday perhaps, she would tell him what he already knew.

She let out a little huff of laughter. "I'd think your wife should be willing to tell you she loves you."

Hope kindled in him, that miniature sun glowing in his chest again. "She should."

"She does." She pulled her hand from his and stroked his cheek. "I love you, Rico."

Joy arced through him. He forgot his injuries, forgot the pain, forgot where they were. All his dreams had been answered at once. He'd told her who he was and she'd understood. She'd forgiven him. And best of all, she loved him. She truly did. What a comfort to hear those words, to have her confirm what he'd thought was true, but had known only in his heart. And had she just agreed to be his wife as well? It was too much at once. If he didn't do something, his heart would burst out of his chest.

He struggled out of the wheelchair and slid his arms around her, careful of their IVs, embracing her as gently as he could. Her eyes glistened with tears as she looked up at him. "I love you," she whispered again, and he murmured it back, a lightness, a warmth, he hadn't known for a long time filling his chest. He was whole again. Leaning down, he kissed her. Kate, *his* Kate, hugged him back until they both started to wince, and then he had to sit down, his legs ready to collapse.

He looked up at her. He had to be sure. "So you will marry me?"

She laughed this time, her face glowing. "Yes. That was a yes."

"You have made me the happiest man alive." He grinned at her, so wide it almost hurt.

"Likewise." She stroked his face again. "I'm glad you didn't let me get away."

He stared at her for a while, his heart pumping wildly with happiness. He was about to risk kissing her again when a hard rap at the door grabbed their attention. They both turned to the doorway.

It was Dom. Enrico saw Kate's eyes dart from Dom to him and back, comparing them, seeing how much they looked alike. He introduced them.

"A pleasure," Dom said to Kate, inclining his head slightly, then he addressed Enrico. "I sense I am interrupting something."

"Kate has just agreed to be my wife." Surprise appeared on Dom's face, followed by something else that flitted away before he could give it a name.

"Congratulations." He clapped Enrico lightly on the back. "And I hear there is a child on the way?"

Enrico shook his head in amusement. "Antonio, yes? That boy and his mouth. Yes, we will be having a child."

"I am very happy for you. Getting two things you have wanted for a long time."

"*Grazie.*" Enrico waited a beat. "So what brings you here?"

"I wanted to see how you were." He gave a significant glance at Kate. "And I wanted to discuss the ambush."

"It was Andretti."

"Of course. But the question is, how did he know where you were?"

"I have no idea."

"We need to speak in private."

"She knows."

Dom frowned. "We do not involve wives in the business."

With a laugh, Enrico said, "Next to you, Antonella was my closest advisor. She had a gift."

Dom switched to Italian, using a Calabrian dialect Kate wouldn't be able to follow. "It's one thing to tell her who you are. It's another to directly involve her. How do you know she doesn't work for Andretti?"

Enrico's gut burned, and he leaned back in the wheelchair. He answered Dom in dialect. "This *again*? Her husband nearly raped and killed her. She was just shot by Andretti's men. If she's on Carlo's payroll, he's trying damn hard not to pay her."

"It could be a trap."

"Hardly." Enrico switched back to English. "I have had enough of that subject. Do not mention it again."

"Fine. But someone close to you is behind this."

"I already know who it is."

Dom's brows shot up. "You do?"

"It must be Trucco."

"Perhaps. But how would he know exactly where you were today? This had to be arranged by someone very close to you. I hate to say it, but we cannot rule out Antonio. Or Ruggero."

"I trust Ruggero. He has men watching Trucco. And others."

Dom froze, his eyes narrowing. "Who is under surveillance? Why have you not told me?"

"It is my life that is in danger, and there is a traitor in my midst. Therefore, I have chosen to trust only one person with the details."

"I am your second in command." Hurt shadowed Dom's face.

"Surely you can see the necessity."

Dom looked at the floor for a second, then back at Enrico. "I am just... surprised not to know, that is all."

A cold hand gripped Enrico's heart. Dom should be yelling at him right now, asking why he didn't trust him. Dom should be cursing and pacing and throwing up his hands. Dom should be acting like Dom. But he wasn't. Don Battista's words came back to him: *He is hardening his heart against you.*

"We should know soon who it is. You will be the first to know after me."

Dom nodded absently. He seemed to be lost in thought. Then he said, "I must go." He stepped around to the other side of the bed and took Kate's hand. "*Signora*, please allow me to welcome you to the family. You will bring my cousin much joy. He has longed for an heir, and now he will have one, at last." He paused a moment. "He loved Antonella deeply, and you are lucky to be marrying such a devoted man. I do not think I love my wife half as much as Enrico loved his. I hope you will be happy becoming part of our family."

Enrico's jaw clenched. His devotion to Toni was the last thing Kate needed shoved in her face. Surely Dom knew that. He looked at Kate, but she seemed serene.

"*Mille grazie*, Domenico. I look forward to getting to know you and your family."

202

"As do I." He kissed her hand, then left without another word.

Once the door shut, Kate looked at Enrico. "He hates me, doesn't he?"

So she had noticed Dom's needling. "Why do you say that?"

"Whatever he said to you—I assume that was some dialect I don't know—it was about me, wasn't it?"

"Yes." Enrico sighed. "He thinks you are working for Carlo."

She laughed, then groaned and pressed a hand to her wound. "If I am, he's the worst boss ever."

"I know. I have pointed out the madness of what he is saying. He sees spies everywhere."

"Antonio, I assume?"

He nodded. "He even suggested Ruggero."

"Do you think he's trying to divert your attention?"

"From what?"

"From himself."

Enrico rubbed his chin. "The thought has crossed my mind." But he kept pushing it away. He knew Dom was angry, but this much?

"I know he's your cousin." She squeezed his hand. "But sometimes the people who are closest to you are the ones who hate you the most."

"I do not want to believe it." And he wouldn't. Not without proof.

Her voice was soft. "It takes a lot of love to breed strong hate."

"Are you trying to console me with that?"

She smiled. "That wasn't very good, was it?"

"Not at all." He laughed.

"I'll work on it." She caressed his cheek.

"Please do not. I always want the truth from you. As much as it hurts."

She stared at him, her gaze holding weight. "We're on the same page then."

"Always." He sat back in the chair, feeling abruptly exhausted. His left side ached, and there was no way he could manage the chair and the IV on his own. "Antonio!" he called. He turned to Kate. "I need to rest, *cara*."

"We've had a bit too much excitement these last few days, haven't we?"

"A bit. But some of it was good, yes?" He was so happy he barely cared that someone wanted them dead. Kate was his, finally his. He'd sort through the rest later.

"Very, very good," she said, smiling.

Kate watched Antonio come in and take Enrico away. When they were gone, her mind drifted back to what Domenico had said to her. It was a nice, pretty speech on the surface. But he was warning her, telling her that Enrico was marrying her for the baby, that he'd never love her the way he loved Antonella. And that last bit at the end, he was reminding her that she was part of all this now. Part of the family. Part of the Mafia.

And the only way out was in a pine box.

CHAPTER 26

Enrico wasn't surprised to see Fuente at his hospital room door the next day. He was surprised, however, by Fuente's high spirits. "By your grin, I take it my situation amuses you?" Enrico asked.

Fuente removed his cap and smoothed back his dark hair, shaking his head. "It's not that, *signore*. It's merely that you seem to be thrust into a dangerous game, one with little hope of escape. Luckily—"

"You're not in the middle of it." Fuente shrugged, and Enrico finally understood. "Ah, you're glad you're on the winning side."

The glance Fuente gave him was knowing. "You are beset on all sides, *signore*. No one to trust. Except perhaps me."

Enrico laughed hard, grabbing his left side when pain flared through him. He blew out for a second, waiting for it pass. Then he looked at Fuente. "You? Why would I ever trust you?"

"I can help." Fuente picked up the vase of flowers sent by Giacomo Parini and looked at it, then set it back down.

What was Fuente up to now? "How?"

"That evidence from the Dinelli case. The gun that mysteriously disappeared…."

"Yes, let's talk about that. Why did only one gun involved in that case have fingerprints on it? That was quite convenient for Carlo."

Fuente gave him a quizzical look. "And what would Signor Andretti have to do with that?"

"He stood to lose as much in front of Judge Dinelli as I did. He framed me."

"Not too well. He lost the witness and then most surprisingly the evidence. Do you expect me to believe that's what happened?"

Enrico flushed, hoping it looked like he was in pain. It was best to say nothing sometimes. This was one of those times.

"The cat has eaten your tongue, I see." Fuente sat down and stroked his moustache as he looked at Enrico.

"I'm innocent. I was not involved in the death of Judge Dinelli."

"Perhaps, perhaps not. But you are not innocent, *signore*. Never that."

Enrico couldn't find the words to argue. He hadn't ordered the murder, but he'd certainly exacted his revenge on the one who'd betrayed him, and he'd certainly tampered with the process of justice. "So what do you think you can do for me, Maresciallo Capo Fuente?"

Fuente pointed to the badge on his shoulder. "I'm a second lieutenant, now, thanks to you."

"Congratulations, Sottotenente. Again, I wonder what you think you can do for me."

"I have heard, perhaps, that this missing gun can be found. Avoiding a long prison sentence, that would be worth something, yes?"

Was he bluffing? "It would be. But someone wants me dead. I'm more concerned about that."

"And if I could help you with that matter?"

"That would indeed be worth something to me."

Fuente seemed to be deliberating some matter. Then he said, "My children's tuition has gone up again."

"Escalating costs are a certain path to ruin."

"Not if you know the right people." Fuente grinned and leaned forward. "I'll let you have this tidbit for free though. Franco Trucco is out for blood."

"That's not news to me."

"Ah, but I think there's a detail you do *not* know. Trucco has revealed something to Signor Andretti that has enraged him. A secret of yours. About a son in England?"

Enrico went cold to his core. "How did you hear this?"

"A friend."

His heart racing, Enrico grabbed his mobile phone. "I have calls to make, if you'll excuse me."

"Of course." Fuente stood up, placing his cap on his head.

A question occurred to Enrico. "Why did you tell me this?"

"I might find having a Lucchesi in Interpol useful someday. And I think I might find you doubly generous in the future."

He nodded. "Your children will have the best educations money can buy."

"You are a saint among sinners, Signor Lucchesi."

As the door was closing behind Fuente, Enrico punched in the number of his top man in London. There was much to arrange, and little time, if any, to do so.

When Tyrell answered, Enrico rapidly explained what was needed and why. "Use discretion, but keep him safe. Do not contact him directly or tell him anything unless you need to." Tyrell gave him his word, and Enrico told him he would call back later.

He snapped the phone shut, his stomach in a tight ball. *Please God, don't let Nico die.*

ଧୠଔ

Enrico and Kate were discharged from the hospital a couple days later, both of them sore from their wounds, but fully on the mend. Tyrell assured Enrico that his son was safe, that he'd made all the arrangements with Nico's supervisor to keep him away from London and out of reach for several weeks. It was the best they could do without telling Nico anything directly. If all went well, he'd never suspect a thing.

Sick of being cooped up in the hospital, Enrico had taken Kate out to the back terrace to get some sun and fresh air. They hadn't been home more than a few hours when Ruggero sought him out. "Antonio was right." He held up a small black device in a plastic bag. "This tracker was on the Maserati."

Enrico extended his hand for it. He turned the bag over, studying the device that had almost been their death. "Are there others?"

"I am checking all the cars myself. So far, no."

"How do we find out who planted this?"

"I will have it checked for fingerprints."

"Do the *polizia* know about it?"

Ruggero shook his head, and Enrico handed the tracker back to him. "Anything from the surveillance?"

"Nothing conclusive."

"I don't like not knowing." Enrico tapped his fingers against the armrest of his chair.

The grim lines of Ruggero's face hardened. "Neither do I. We will have an answer soon."

"I hope we have it in time." Enrico reached out and took Kate's hand. Then he looked back at Ruggero. "There are three of us counting on you now."

Ruggero nodded. "I will not fail you."

ଧୠଔ

Giacomo Parini arrived later that afternoon with a large black case. He met privately with Enrico in his study. "I have brought what you asked for, Don Enrico," he said, opening the case.

Enrico studied the rings before him. "Which would you give to the woman who owned your heart?"

"This one." Parini pointed to a ring in the middle row. "It's not the most expensive, nor the largest. But the diamonds have the most clarity, the most sparkle."

206

Enrico held the ring under the lamp on his desk. The diamonds refracted the light beautifully, sending out prisms of color. "I'll take it."

"*Bene.*" Parini smiled, then his face sobered. "I'm worried, Don Enrico. This attempt on your life, it was most serious. I'm not the only one who's concerned. Many merchants have come to me, questioning whether they should go over to the Andrettis. They fear what will happen if you die."

"So, to avoid the lava, they would jump into the mouth of Vesuvius?"

Parini shook his head. "I know. Your father told me the reason for Andretti's exile. About the boy in the barrel. Perhaps more people should know that story?"

Enrico shrugged. "Do what you think best." He gripped the old man by the shoulder. "If something happens to me, the *cosca* will protect you. It will go on without me." *It just won't be the same.*

"I hope it doesn't come to that."

He smiled at Parini, hoping it reached his eyes. "I have a wife to marry and a child on the way. I have everything to live for. I *will* see Carlo Andretti in the ground."

After Parini left, Enrico sat at his desk admiring the ring. Where and when should he give it to Kate? He wanted to make it a moment she'd always remember. He'd love to take her back to Capri, to propose in that lush little thicket where they'd made love. But there wasn't time right now. He needed something nearby.

What about the gardens at the Villa Carlotta, or maybe that elegant little bistro in Bellagio? Both were nice, but he wanted something more grand.

Then the perfect place came to him: the beautifully laid-out formal gardens of the Villa d'Este. Just the place for a marriage proposal, maybe even the wedding itself. And after he proposed, they could have dinner at the hotel. He called the maître d' and arranged dinner for the next evening. Any further delay and the wait would kill him.

𝕊𝕆ℚℝ

Fuente called on Enrico and Kate the following day. The three of them met in Enrico's study. Kate and Enrico took the sofa; Fuente took a chair opposite. The expression on Fuente's face flashed Enrico back to their meeting just after Kate shot Vincenzo. Fuente had looked then like a cat who'd just swallowed a very tasty canary. He looked even more full of himself today. Whatever it was, it couldn't be good.

"Are you here to update us on the investigation into Vincenzo Andretti's death or on the attack a few days ago?" Enrico said.

"We do have so many things to discuss, do we not?" Fuente paused for a moment, until he was sure of everyone's attention. "*Signore*, an interesting story has come my way."

"Interesting?"

"*Molto.* It seems your name has come up in yet another investigation. Another death."

"What are you talking about?" Kate asked. Enrico was wondering the same thing.

Fuente stroked his moustache. "Ah, *signora*, there is much you do not know about this man. I understand you are to be wed?"

"Where did you hear that?" Enrico asked.

Fuente shrugged. "You know how these small towns are. So hard to keep secrets."

"What's this story you mentioned?" Kate asked.

Fuente leaned forward, his face lighting up with a cold keenness. "A judge and his family were assassinated some years ago. This judge, Federico Dinelli, was well known for his anti-Mafia views. At the time of his death, a case had come before him. A tax-evasion case. Signor Lucchesi was the defendant." Kate turned to Enrico.

Where was Fuente going with this? And why? "Yes, there was a case," Enrico said. "It was dismissed for lack of evidence."

"But only after Judge Dinelli was killed."

Blood rose to Enrico's face. "That was not my doing."

"No one has been able to prove that it was."

"I had nothing to do with it."

"But you had everything to *gain* from it."

Enrico looked hard at Fuente. *Didn't they have an understanding?* "Mine was not the only case before him. Carlo Andretti was facing charges as well."

Fuente stroked his moustache again, looking at the ceiling, as if considering Enrico's words. "That is true." He played with the cap on his lap. "As you may recall, *signore*, some of the evidence in that case was lost. I was curious and did some digging. It took me days and days of searching, but I finally found that missing evidence. It had been misfiled, almost lost for good. Do you know what I found?"

Enrico could hardly breathe. "Please, enlighten me."

"One of the murder weapons—as it happens, the only one with fingerprints on it—was among the misfiled evidence. And the fingerprints on that gun belong to Sergio Grantini. He worked for you back then, yes?"

Adrenaline flooded Enrico's body. Someone had just put the first nail in his coffin. Someone who knew where that gun had been hidden. Was it Dom? He focused on keeping his expression neutral. "He did work for me."

"But Grantini disappeared soon after the murder."

Enrico nodded. "He abandoned his wife and son."

"Why would he do such a thing?"

"How am I to know? Sergio was young and not always faithful to his wife. Perhaps he ran off with a pretty girl." It could have been the truth. Only Enrico, Ruggero, and Dom knew that it wasn't.

"Perhaps." Fuente paused, his eyes boring into Enrico. "If we could find him, he could tell us why he shot the judge and his family."

"You do not actually know that he did. Someone else could have used the gun."

"Grantini's prints are the only ones on it."

Enrico shook his head. "Gloves. The killer could have worn them."

"Perhaps, Signor Lucchesi, you should have been one of us."

"A *carabiniere?*" Enrico snorted.

Fuente waved the notion away with his hands. "What was I thinking? No man as fine as Enrico Lucchesi would stoop so low."

"That is not what I meant."

Fuente's lips curved up. "Perhaps you meant no man as *corrupt* as you would think of it?"

There was no winning with this man. Enrico could feel the heat of Kate's stare. "If you have enough evidence to arrest me, I suggest you do so."

"Or what? You'll take care of me too?" Fuente grinned at him aggressively. "Perhaps I'll end up like the judge? Or perhaps I'll be 'misfiled' in some nondescript place like that gun?"

Enrico sat back, feigning indifference. "You have nothing."

Fuente leaned forward. "Ah, but I do." He pulled their passports out of the inner pocket of his uniform and tossed them on the table. "I assume you both would like these back."

"We would," Enrico said.

"You are fortunate, *signore.* I am in a generous mood."

"Are we cleared?" Kate asked.

Fuente looked at her, a tight smile on his face. "Patience, *signora.* Such matters take time."

They don't have to. He had to get Fuente out of the house so he could talk to Kate. So he could explain. "Is there some... assistance you need with the investigation?" Enrico asked.

"Not directly. But there is a matter that has proven most distracting to me personally, and it has hampered my ability to wrap up the investigation."

"Is it something I can help with?"

Fuente put on an embarrassed face. "I would not mention it, except it is the matter most pressing on my mind."

"What is it?"

"As you know, I have four children, and they all plan to attend university. But now three of them have decided they must go to America for that. Even with my recent promotion to third rank, I will be hard-pressed to fund their tuitions. I have heard, Signor Lucchesi, that you have sponsored some local children."

The audacity of this man. "If they have high marks."

"My children are exceptional scholars."

Enrico suppressed a sigh. "Well then, perhaps they would qualify for my scholarship program."

"I would be most grateful for any assistance you could provide."

Kate looked from one to the other of them, her disgust undisguised. "Are we done here?" she asked.

Fuente smiled again. "For now. *Signora*, my business with you is concluded." He turned and addressed Enrico. "I am still looking for Grantini. We will talk further when I find him."

"I hope you do. I am still paying his wages to his wife while we look for him ourselves."

Fuente bowed his head. "You are a *most* generous man, Signor Lucchesi." He rose and put on his hat. "*Arrivederci.*"

಄ఌ

As Enrico escorted Fuente to the front door, Kate sat on the sofa, stunned by what she'd just witnessed. How easily Enrico bought whatever he wanted—the outcome of a murder investigation, for example.

What a fool she was. How could she have accepted his proposal so quickly? He was a *mobster*, for God's sake. He'd admitted to her that he'd killed people. Killing a judge to stay out of jail? Obviously that wasn't out of the realm of possibility. He'd told her he didn't kill innocent people, but that was yet another lie. The discussion with Fuente had clearly rattled him.

How could she trust Enrico, now that she knew what he was capable of?

By the time he returned to the study, she could hardly contain herself. "How could you do such a thing?"

Enrico sat down beside her. "I did not do it, I swear. Carlo has framed me."

"Well, isn't that convenient. It's all Carlo's fault. Again."

"It is not convenient at all. He nearly landed me in prison, and I suppose he still will, if he does not kill me first."

"A judge *and his family*. How *could* you?"

"I did not, and I would not. Let me explain."

She held up her hand, palm facing him. "Stop. I don't want to hear it. It's just going to be more lies."

"Please calm down." He reached for her hands.

She slapped his fingers away. "I will *not* calm down. I will *not* let you sweet-talk me again. This is it. You heard the man. I'm free to go."

"*Per favore*, I can explain."

"No. I'm packing my things and leaving this country tomorrow. I don't ever want to see you again."

His voice deepened. "Carlo still wants you dead. And you are in no condition to fly. Even if you do not care about yourself, you have a child to think of."

She looked away from him, breathing hard, the stabbing pain from the wound in her chest confirming what he said. She had her passport, but she couldn't leave yet. "I can't stay under this roof. I can't bear to look at you."

"You must see a doctor before you get on a plane. You don't want to endanger yourself or the baby."

She threw up her hands. "Your precious, longed-for heir. That's the whole reason you're marrying me. Your cousin pretty much said so."

"I told you I loved you before I knew you were pregnant. Do you not remember?"

She did remember. The baby wasn't the real reason for the doubt that crept around her heart. After a few moments, she said, "You still can't tell me you love me more than Antonella."

His eyes shifted from hers. "Does that matter so much?" Then he looked at her. "I have risked my life for you." His voice grew hoarse. "What more proof of my love do you need?"

Her throat ached, and she willed herself not to cry. Not to show him how much he was getting to her. "You can show me you love me by letting me go instead of keeping me here against my will."

"I would never force you to stay here. I only want you to be careful."

"I can stay in a hotel until I'm better."

He shoved his hands in his pockets. "Hotels are hard to secure."

Cold washed over her from head to toe, as if she'd plunged into an icy pond. Enrico had lied to her for a long time. And not without a damn good reason: if he let her go, his life was forfeit. If he'd killed innocent people to avoid jail, what was he capable of when his life was on the line?

Enrico was still looking at her, as if he was waiting to say something. "What?" she asked.

"Do you hate me?"

"There are lines I can't cross. This is one of them."

"I will prove to you that I am innocent."

Enrico was about as innocent as a circus carny. She had to get away from him. "I need time, Enrico. Time to think. I got carried away when I accepted your proposal. Both of us had nearly died, we were both heavily medicated.... It was not the right time to be making such a decision."

He looked pained, but he nodded. "Must you leave? Can you not think about it here, where I can keep you safe?"

"I need to be away from you."

"I hate this."

I hate it too. Anger sank its teeth into her. "I hate everything about this situation!" she shouted. Clenching her fists, she lowered her voice. "I've told you what I want, what I need. And you're damn well going to give it to me if you ever want to see me again."

He held his hands up in surrender. "I apologize. I did not mean to push."

She softened her tone. "I don't know you well enough to marry you. I'm not sure what kind of man you are. I need time to think." She hated lying to him, but he'd let her leave more easily if he had hope.

"Whatever you need. I will always give you that."

Her throat constricted. He did love her. But how much? And was it enough? Did he love her more than his own life?

She was going to have to use his love against him. A cold hard stone formed in the center of her chest, and Kate hated herself, just a little. What she wanted, what Enrico wanted, none of that mattered, as long as the baby was safe.

"I'm counting on it, Enrico. You don't know how much."

Hope flared in his eyes, and she hated herself just a little bit more.

§)CR

Carlo listened to Fuente's report, a smile on his face for once. Things were proceeding as planned. He'd been worried when Domenico told him of the upcoming marriage. "The American was upset?"

"Most certainly. I do not think Don Lucchesi can talk his way out of this."

"You have done well, Silvio."

"And my children? They will benefit from your generosity?"

"Most certainly." Carlo ended the call, almost laughing at Fuente. The man was so predictable. Money was all he cared about. Carlo had plenty of that to go around.

Now all he had to do was wait for the woman to leave Lucchesi. And for Domenico to locate Rinaldo.

CHAPTER 27

Enrico insisted on putting Kate up at the Villa d'Este, despite her protestations about the cost. The choice was a bit ironic given his plan to propose to her there. His hand closed around the ring box in his pocket, his fingers sliding over its velvety surface. Would he ever get to put that ring on her finger?

Despite the ruined plans for his proposal, the Villa d'Este was the best choice for keeping Kate safe. It was close by, and because the hotel was a favorite of the jet set, it had better security than many others on the lake.

Kate and Antonio would check in under false names, as husband and wife. Enrico had booked them a suite with an adjoining door. The two guards he was sending with them, Paolo and Tommaso, were in the rooms on either side. Their job was to alternate guarding the suite. Enrico had threatened them with their family's lives if anything happened to Kate. But he was much more blunt with Antonio.

℘)(℘

Antonio was surprised by the summons to his *capo*'s study, and even more surprised by what his boss was telling him. And how he was telling him. "I love her. More than I know how to handle. If anything happens to her, it will destroy me."

Don Lucchesi pulled a small black ring box out of his trouser pocket. "I had planned to give her this tonight. Now… God knows if I ever will." The wounded look on his *capo*'s face was more than Antonio could bear. He studied the carpet, rather than look at that face.

Cristo. Antonio had never loved a woman like that. He was pretty sure he'd never been in love at all. Not if it was like this. He didn't know what to say.

"You must keep her safe, Tonio. I'm trusting you with the one who is most precious to me." Don Lucchesi paused. "With both of them. Look after her as if she were yours. Make sure she eats, that she takes the vitamins for the baby. Don't let her out of your sight."

"I will. I swear it." He meant it, but he'd say almost anything to get away from the intensity of that gaze, that pain. "I will guard her with my life."

"I'm counting on that. If something happens...." He didn't finish the thought.

Antonio wanted to comfort his boss, but he couldn't embrace him the way he would a father, not anymore. The days when Don Lucchesi would accept a hug from him were long in the past. They hadn't touched since Antonio was a boy at the Lucchesi Home for Children.

Something twisted in his gut. He wished he could do more for this tortured man in front of him, this man who meant so much to him, this man who had saved him from a life of ruin. But all he could do was take care of the *signora*.

Perhaps he could persuade her to forgive his *capo*. Don Lucchesi was the best of men; any woman who had his love would be lucky, and his child would be loved beyond measure. An ache spread throughout his chest. Don Lucchesi might never get to show that love to anyone. To his child, most of all. Antonio knew what it meant to lose everyone you loved.

"I will not fail you, *mio capo*. I swear it."

Don Lucchesi nodded and seemed like he was about to dismiss him, but Antonio couldn't go without knowing something. "*Scusa*, but what if you cannot convince the *signora* to stay? What will you do then?"

His *capo* met his gaze, his dark eyes flat. "I'll do what I must."

Alarm flashed through Antonio's body. Was he talking about silencing her? Then Don Lucchesi said, "I'll persuade her. If I can't...." He was silent for a moment, then he said, "I will keep her safe, and someday she will be mine again." He looked down at the carpet. "I must believe that."

"Will you silence her?"

Again, his eyes were flat. "How can I?" His voice when he continued was strangled. "I love her."

"But the vows—"

"I know my duty." His tone said there would be no further discussion.

Antonio didn't feel any closer to knowing his don's heart than he had a few moments ago.

Worse, he wasn't sure what he wanted to hear.

All he knew was that he must convince the *signora* to accept Don Lucchesi.

ഐᏜᏋ

Antonio took his charge very seriously, hovering over the *signora* at the hotel to the point where he risked irritating her. He swore to himself he'd make her see reason. At the least, he could remind her what her future would look like if Don Andretti got hold of her. He didn't want to frighten her, but he would if he had to. The stakes were too high to play nice.

In the meantime, he enjoyed playing her husband. Perhaps a little too much. Even with her current pallor, she was still a vision with that long auburn hair, those flashing green eyes, and that smooth, creamy skin he longed to touch. He took advantage of his role in public, touching her lightly at the small of her back, taking her arm in his, putting an arm around her chair when they sat down, playing with the dark red hair that hung down within reach of his fingers. She was intoxicating.

Not that she noticed any of his attentions. When she wasn't with him, he often heard her weeping. He had to remind her she was pregnant, that she needed to eat.

He also had to remind her to take the prenatal vitamins they'd given her in the hospital. He'd taken to doling one out to her each morning at breakfast. On the fourth day, she looked up at him when he gave her the pill and said, "Thank you. You've been very good about all this."

"It is my pleasure, *signora*."

She smiled at him. "Your English is improving."

He looked down, pleased she'd noticed his efforts. He'd spent all his free time since the break-in working on his English. It was time for him to grow up. If he ever wanted to be *capo di società*, his English had to be impeccable. Besides, it made it much easier to speak to the *signora*.

"Are you blushing?" she asked.

His face grew hotter, and he wished he wasn't so fair. He nodded, not trusting himself to speak.

She nudged his arm. "Stop that. I was just paying you a compliment. You don't need to be so modest."

He collected himself. "I'm sorry, *signora*. I'm not used to attention from someone...." He let that trail off. Flirting with her wasn't a good idea.

"Someone what?"

He shook his head. "It is nothing."

"I'd like to know."

He blushed again, unable to meet her eyes. "Someone so *bellissima*."

She slowly let out a breath as she looked at him. Finally she said, "That's nice to hear."

He recovered enough to look at her. "But not wise to say, yes?"

"If Enrico heard you—" She cut off that sentence.

"Yes, I know, *signora*. He would kill me."

ഇരു

Kate looked away from Antonio, a lump filling her throat. She toyed with the vitamin he'd handed her. She needed to take it, but swallowing the horse-sized pills was always a struggle. She set it next to her teacup. When was she going to get over Rico? It felt like an eternity since they'd last spoken. Why did she even care? He could very well be planning her death.

And yet she ached. Her baby would grow up never knowing its father. And she would never experience the joy of the marriage she'd looked forward to, however briefly. She'd thought she was marrying a good man, a different man from Vince. But she'd been wrong. Enrico was a mobster, just like Vince.

Except... he wasn't like Vince. He wasn't. He was... just in a terrible spot, wasn't he? His anguish at letting her go seemed genuine. But it didn't matter. She couldn't marry another man she couldn't trust. She had to be able to rely on her husband, and she had to be able to respect and admire him. Otherwise, it wouldn't be a marriage, not in any true sense.

She wished she could leave tomorrow, but the doctor had insisted on at least a full month of recovery time before she could fly, which meant she couldn't leave for another three weeks. At least it gave her time to think up a plan of sorts.

But who could she trust? Who would help her?

She didn't have many friends here in Italy. Mostly she and Vince had socialized with members of the Andretti family. Her co-workers at the orphanage all worked for Enrico, and the glowing tones with which they spoke of him meant they were unlikely to go against him. Besides, who among them had the resources or the know-how to get her out of the country without Enrico or Carlo being able to find her?

She looked at Antonio, returned the smile he gave her. He seemed to feel genuine affection for her. He would help her... except he would never cross Enrico. Ruggero she barely knew, and there was no point asking. He, too, would never turn on his boss. And no doubt they were under the same obligation as Enrico—to kill her to keep his secret.

Aside from her co-workers at the orphanage, there were only two other people she knew outside the Lucchesi and Andretti families: Dottor Beltrami and Silvio Fuente. But the doctor was clearly on Enrico's side—he'd told Enrico about the pregnancy with no hesitation. Besides, would he even know how to keep her safe? She was tempted to trust Fuente since he was in the *carabinieri*, but as much as Fuente taunted Enrico at times, Enrico had easily bought him at least once. Fuente would probably turn her in to Enrico for a handsome reward.

So who could she go to?

She remembered something Enrico had said. *The enemy of my enemy is my friend.* She thought back over what Dom had said at the hospital, why he'd said it. If he didn't want her and Enrico to marry, perhaps she could work with that. Of course, he was under the same obligation as Enrico and the rest of the Lucchesi *cosca*. But she'd run across something during the course of her work at the orphanage that might help. A secret she was sure Dom wouldn't want made public. Trusting him was risky, but what other alternative did she have? Between them, Enrico and Carlo had her trapped.

She needed to get hold of Antonio's cell phone. Once she contacted Dom, he could help her figure out how to leave without Enrico knowing. She had plenty of cash from the sale of her rings, enough to last her through the pregnancy.

The problem was where to go. She didn't want to be far from her parents now that she was pregnant. But she also didn't want to bring trouble to their doorstep. Perhaps New York City was big enough to hide her. Still, it might be risky being anywhere in New York state. Carlo would be sure to look hard for her there.

Kate sighed. How was she ever going to outwit Carlo? If Dom refused to help, she was going to have to crawl back to Enrico. Whether she liked it or not. Certainly he'd let her live until the baby was born, which gave her a little more than eight months to come up with an escape plan.

But first she had to try Dom. Unfortunately, Antonio kept his cell phone on him like it was a precious gem. How was she going to get to it?

She needed a distraction.

Maybe faking some morning sickness would work, though the thought of forcing herself to throw up wasn't high on her list. But it was much better than ending up dead.

She waited until they had lunch. She made herself eat a Caesar salad with anchovies. She'd never liked the salty little fish, and her pregnancy-enhanced sense of smell made them even more revolting. Halfway through the meal, she inhaled too deeply and gagged. Antonio put his hand on her back, leaning toward her. "*Signora*, are you unwell?"

Kate set down the fork, shaking her head. She wasn't going to have to fake anything. She looked at the salad again, seeing one of the little chopped up fish staring back at her, and her stomach churned. She pressed the napkin to her mouth, willing herself not to throw up here. That would wreck everything. "Please take me upstairs."

Antonio jumped out of his chair and offered her a hand. He waved to the waiter and asked him to send up the bill. Then he hurried Kate down the hall to the tiny elevator—little more than a glorified shoe box, she thought—and impatiently pressed the button. The door trundled open, and they stepped inside the heavily ornamented space, Antonio stabbing at the button for their floor. Kate concentrated on looking down. When the elevator jerked, she felt her gorge rise and she took a deep breath through her nose, swallowing convulsively. "*Signora*, what can I do?"

She clutched his hand, shaking her head. "Just get me to my room. Please."

He put an arm around her, and she leaned against him as the elevator crawled up to their floor. When it opened, Antonio motioned her outside, then scooped her up in his arms once she'd crossed the threshold. She should object, but she was afraid to open her mouth again. The image of that little fish head came back to her, and for a second she could smell it all over again.

Antonio raced down the hall with her, and she buried her face in his neck, focusing on inhaling and exhaling. He smelled great—a light, citrusy cologne mixed with his own scent. With her eyes closed, she could almost imagine it was Enrico holding her, Enrico carrying her upstairs to their room…. Her eyes snapped open. No good would come of thinking about Enrico. Especially about having sex with him.

When Antonio reached the door to their suite, he set her down and pulled out the key, unlocking the door in a flash. He followed her inside. She beelined for the bathroom and sank down on her knees in front of the toilet. Antonio hovered in the doorway. "*Signora*, should I call *il dottore?*"

"No." She actually wanted him to leave her alone with her roiling stomach, but her plan wouldn't work if he left. "Please just stay with me." She tried to give him a smile. "I'll be all right. It's just morning sickness."

He gave her a puzzled look. "It is afternoon."

She chuckled weakly. "It's called morning sickness in English because it's worst in the morning, but it can happen at any time."

He crouched down beside her, touching her arm. "You are ill from the baby, *si?*"

She nodded too emphatically, and her head felt woozy, her stomach roiling again. She forced herself to picture that chopped-up anchovy again, its dead glassy eye staring up at her, its companions swirling around in her stomach…. That was all it took. She lurched forward, heaving hard, the salad coming up in a flood of gastric acid and bile.

Antonio didn't flinch. He gathered her hair and held it back for her while she heaved until she felt empty and weak. She reached up and flushed the toilet, then sagged down beside it, Antonio letting go of her hair. He stepped over her and filled a glass with cold water and wet a washcloth to wipe her face. He brought the cloth and the glass over to her, crouching down next to her. She took both items gratefully, feeling herself flush with embarrassment. It had seemed like a good plan. Now, she wasn't so sure. She felt so exhausted, and after his initial uneasiness, Antonio seemed rather calm, not flustered. How was she going to get his phone?

Playing on her weakness seemed like a good ploy. He'd picked her up once, maybe he'd do it again. "I'd like to lie down, but I'm not sure I can walk to the bed…."

He smiled. "Not to worry, *signora*. I will take you." He scooped her up again, lifting her easily. While he was carrying her to the bed, she slipped a hand in his exterior jacket pocket, the one she'd seen him put the phone in that morning. *Got it,* she thought as her fingers closed over it. She shoved the phone under the pillow as he laid her down.

"More water?" he asked.

"No. *Mille grazie.*" She smiled up at him. "I'd like to sleep now."

"*Molto bene, signora.* I will be in my room."

As soon as he closed the door, Kate rolled over and grabbed the phone. She scrolled through the contacts, searching for Dom's number. She jotted it down on the hotel notepad on the nightstand, then ripped off the top sheet and stuffed it in the drawer. She'd just dropped the phone on the floor when she heard a tap on the door between their rooms. "*Signora?*"

She looked down at the phone and swore softly. The display was still lit up. How long would it take for it go dark?

"*Signora?*" he repeated, easing the door open a crack.

She looked at the phone. Damn it! Still lit up. She reached down to try to flip it over, but it was too far away. "Just a minute!" she said, raising her voice. She kicked off her shoes and hastily unbuttoned her blouse, staring at the phone the whole time. Finally it went black.

"*Signora*, are you well?"

"Just a second." She was rebuttoning the blouse when he poked his head in the door. He blushed and quickly withdrew. "What is it?" she asked, letting an edge into her voice.

"My phone. I cannot find it."

"Well, come in then." She sat up on the edge of the bed, her bare feet dangling above the phone.

He walked in, not meeting her eyes. "*Scusa,*" he said. "I must have it. Don Lucchesi will call soon to check on you."

She felt a surge of warmth, which was quickly dampened by the thought that Enrico could be checking to make sure she hadn't run off. Even so, she longed for information about him. "How is he?" she asked, while Antonio checked for the phone in the bathroom.

He walked out and immediately spotted the phone on the floor next to the bed. "There," he said, his face relaxing into a smile. When he bent down to get it, she swung her legs onto the bed and out of his way. He repocketed the phone, then rose and headed for the door as if he hadn't heard her question.

"Antonio." He turned toward her, holding the door half open. "Tell me how he is."

He faltered, looking away from her, then he closed the door and sat in the overstuffed chair next to the window. "Don Lucchesi is…" He groped for the words. "He is…" Antonio sighed and scrubbed a hand through his blond hair, leaving it sticking up in rooster tails. "He is not well," he finally said.

A little jolt zinged through her. "Does he have an infection? Is he in the hospital?"

He hastily shook his head. "He is not well *here*," he said, tapping his chest. "His heart aches for you."

"Oh." Kate sat back against the pillows piled in front of the headboard.

She crossed her arms over her stomach, imagining she could feel the barest little bump in her abdomen, even though it was far too early. She caressed the spot, feeling lonely all of a sudden. She missed Enrico, missed the way he smiled whenever he saw her, his face lighting up like the sun had just come out. She missed the feel of his arms around her. When she remembered his wild, infectious happiness after she'd accepted his proposal, her throat closed up until it ached. The last time she'd seen him, he'd been so distressed. Like all the joy had gone out of the world. "What does he ask about when he calls?"

Antonio shrugged. "How are you. Are you eating, is the baby well. If I know where you go when you leave."

She absently corrected him, feeling deflated that Enrico wanted to know her travel plans. "It's 'if I know where *you will go* when you leave.'"

"*Grazie.*"

"What do you tell him? About where I'm going, I mean."

He gave her a blank look and a shrug, his arms spreading apart. "Nothing. I do not know." He looked at her for a second, then he leaned forward, clasping his hands between his knees. "*Signora*, he loves you. And the baby too. He is a very good man. I do not understand this"—he waved a hand around in the air, as if searching for the right word—"this separation from him."

She leaned forward too. "He lied to me. About a lot of things. I cannot trust him."

"If he lied, it is to protect you."

Kate shook her head, holding his gaze. "Maybe about some things. But this lie was to protect himself."

"*Signora*, there must be a mistake."

"He killed a judge and his family. A judge who was trying to put him in jail."

Antonio sat back, his lips compressing together. He crossed his arms. "That is not true."

"How do you know?"

"I know."

"Are you sure?"

He paused. "I was not there, *signora*. But I know him. He is not that kind of man."

"He's a Mafioso. He does what he wants."

He huffed in amusement. "You think every man of honor is a criminal."

"Aren't they?"

Antonio uncrossed his arms and leaned toward her again. "Not all crime is bad."

"Next you're going to tell me black is white and the sky is red."

He took a second to process what she said, then he shook his head. "You do not understand me. Some crimes are necessary. For justice."

"You mean killing in revenge?"

"Yes, that is one. That is a law of God, so it is no crime. Not paying all of the taxes? Also not a crime. The Italian government"—he made a face like he smelled something bad—"is corrupt, greedy, wasteful. Don Lucchesi uses his tax money to build schools, homes for orphans like me, and other worthy causes. The government throws that money in the garbage."

"That may be true. But it *is* a crime to kill a judge for doing his job. It's a crime to kill that man's innocent family. You cannot tell me any different."

"I agree, *signora*. But Don Lucchesi will not kill a judge. He will never kill women and children."

"You don't *know* that."

He thumped his chest again. "I know in here. That is all that counts." He waited a beat, then said, "Don Lucchesi believes in the old ways, the old codes of the 'Ndrangheta. He does not sell drugs or women. He does not kill women and children. These things are forbidden."

Kate looked at him with interest, mulling over what he said. It reminded her of Enrico's slip about Carlo—"he violated our codes." But she couldn't be sure. Enrico could be a clever con artist. Like Vince.

She sighed. "I need to sleep."

He started for the door, then walked over to the bed instead. He sat on the edge, his blue eyes moving up her body. She was suddenly very aware of him, as she'd been when he'd carried her from the elevator. Her breathing quickened. He clasped his hands together in his lap, staring down at them. "I wish my English was perfect," he said. Then he looked at her. "I want you, *signora. Molto, molto*. But I love Don Lucchesi, so I will not touch you. I look, but I will not touch."

She stared up at him, her mouth dry. "What do you mean?"

"If Don Lucchesi was a bad man, I will not work for him. And I will do what I want." His eyes roamed the length of her body, but his hands stayed clasped together. Then he looked up at her, holding her eyes with his.

"I understand. Your English is good enough. But I do not agree with your opinion of him."

He frowned and stood up. He hesitated, then said, "*Signora*, you must go back to Don Lucchesi. If you do not, Don Andretti is waiting."

Antonio must have seen her shudder, for he said, "I am sorry. I do not mean to scare you, but if I must, I will. *Signora, per favore*. Consider what I say. *È molto importante.*"

"I will," she said, and meant it. She couldn't afford to forget about Carlo. But that didn't mean she was going to risk her baby's life on what she hoped and wanted to be true about Enrico. That Antonio shared her delusion didn't comfort her. The boy in Antonio longed for a father, and he thought he'd found one.

221

She hoped for his sake that Enrico was the right choice. But she couldn't take that risk herself. Not with the baby along for the ride. No, she had to be much more steely-eyed.

She waited for him to close the door, then she picked up her phone. Time to call Dom. Her stomach rolled over. Time to find out if she was on her own.

CHAPTER 28

Enrico paced his study again, certain he was wearing a hole in the Aubusson carpet. He hated this waiting. Waiting for the traitor to be caught. Waiting for Carlo to make a move. Waiting for Kate to leave.

Waiting for his world to crumble.

He threw himself into the chair, then leaned forward, propping his elbows on the desk and loosely clasping his hands in front of his face. He pressed his lips against his hands, stifling the urge to cry out, to let loose his misery at losing Kate. At losing everything. He didn't see how he could stand it if she didn't come back to him. If something happened to her or the child. If he lost her for good.

Losing Toni had been a horrible blow. He couldn't bear another one, ever. Certainly not this soon.

His chest felt empty, hollow, again. Dead inside. He passed a hand over his aching left side, feeling the bandage that still protected the stitches. He'd taken a bullet for Kate, and he'd do it again. He'd do whatever it took to have her back, to keep her safe. To get her to love him again.

He closed his eyes, tears welling up, his throat aching. He sagged in the chair, feeling like he'd lost every ounce of strength he'd ever possessed. He was drained, done, over with. He couldn't go on without her. He just could not.

He rubbed a hand over his eyes, willing himself not to cry. He hadn't given vent to his anguish over Kate. He couldn't allow himself to. Not even when Antonio reported her tears to him. If he let himself go, if he loosened the bonds holding him together, he might never stop weeping.

He had to keep going. He had to find the traitor and destroy him. He had to save the *cosca*. And he had to face Carlo Andretti tonight, before all of La Provincia.

He had to do these things for all the people depending on him. For all the people who looked to him for protection from Carlo.

So he held on to a glimmer of hope. But that glimmer grew fainter every day she didn't call, every day she didn't return to his home.

He should go see her, should plead his case. He wondered how she'd receive him. Butterflies in his stomach, he picked up the phone. Antonio could tell him how she was, whether she might see him.

Antonio picked up on the second ring. "Tonio, how is she?" He noticed a slight hesitation on Antonio's part, and his pulse quickened.

"She vomited from the baby."

"But she's all right?"

"*Sì.*"

He relaxed. He waited a second, then said, "I'm thinking of coming to see her."

Antonio hesitated again. "I spoke to her about you today."

"What did she say?"

Antonio let out a breath. "She thinks you killed the judge and his family."

Merda. Enrico felt queasy. "Did you tell her I didn't?"

"Of course. I told her you believe in the old codes. I think maybe she believed that."

"So there's some hope?"

Again, Antonio hesitated. "*Sì,* some."

It wasn't much, but he had to try. "I'll be there in an hour."

Enrico showered and shaved. He hadn't taken much care with his appearance since Kate had left. He took care with his clothes as well, choosing a dark blue suit he knew she liked, deliberately playing the peacock: diamond tie pin, platinum cufflinks, the signet ring with the Lucchesi crest, his best watch.

He looked at himself in the mirror. To the unobservant, he might be the same man he'd been before. But to anyone who looked closely, the wear of the days without her showed in the circles under his eyes, in the hollowness of his stare. He took a deep breath, willing himself to have hope.

A Lucchesi always got what he wanted. Enrico wasn't about to be the exception.

⊱⊰

Dom heard his mobile phone ring. He looked at the display, but since he didn't recognize the number, he let it go to voice mail. Then Dom picked up another phone, one he was certain wasn't tapped, and used it to check the mobile's voice mail. He listened to the message, unable to believe his good fortune. He scribbled down the number the caller left, then dialed it. When she answered, he said, "*Ciao,* Kate. It's Domenico. Where are you calling from? This isn't Enrico's number."

"He hasn't told you?"

"Told me what?"

"I've left him."

Most interesting. And alarming. Enrico should have told him. "Why?"

"He's lied to me too many times. He's done things I can't condone."

"What has upset you so much?"

"He killed a judge and his family. As I'm sure you know."

So Carlo's plan was in motion. "There is more to it than you know."

"I don't care about the details. He's guilty. You should have seen his face when Fuente told him they'd found the missing murder weapon." She paused. "And I'm sure I know how it ended up missing in the first place."

"Sometimes unfortunate choices have to be made in this business."

"Murdering innocent people isn't an unfortunate choice."

"Why have you called me?"

He heard her take a deep breath. "I have to leave the country. I need a fake passport, a fake American social security number, and transportation to the nearest train station."

"Enrico would gladly help you with that."

"I don't want him to know where I'll be."

"So it is final then?" he asked.

He heard a new firmness in her voice. "Yes."

"Why do you think I won't tell him where you are?"

"Because you don't want us together."

Dom held his breath for a second, debating. "That is true."

"I just want to disappear. After I'm safely away, I'll tell Enrico I've lost the baby. Then he'll marry Delfina Andretti, and everything can go back to the way it was supposed to be. I know how to keep my mouth shut, and I don't know anything of substance anyways. However, I'm not stupid; I know you're not supposed to let me go. So I have an incentive for you to help me."

"Which is?"

"I ran across something interesting while transcribing records at the orphanage. I know about the adoption you arranged. And I know the mother's name. I've written letters to several people that will be delivered if something happens to me. I'm sure you don't want this information to get out."

Dom clamped his jaw shut to keep from shouting and took a deep breath through his nose. Fucking nosy bitch. She was willing to ruin his family. And that couldn't happen. He didn't speak until he felt he could keep his voice even. "I would prefer that matter to remain private, as I was promised."

"Desperate times…." Her voice trailed off. "Do we have a deal?"

He smiled, then straightened his face to keep it out of his voice. She wouldn't like the reason he was smiling. "We do."

He could practically hear Kate sigh in relief. "So what happens next?"

"I need to make arrangements. Call me at this number in two days."

They said their goodbyes, then he snapped the phone shut.

This was an unexpected and welcome opportunity. He had something Carlo wanted very much. Despite the complications—which he was sure he could deal with—his heart filled with glee. Carlo wouldn't get Kate cheap. Far from it.

The cost of having her would be Andretti's downfall.

ℰℭ

The guards seemed startled to see Enrico outside the suite. Tommaso knocked on the door, and Antonio opened it a moment later and gestured him inside. Enrico glanced at the closed door that joined the rooms. "Is she still resting?"

"I assume so. She's been quiet."

He walked to the door and raised his hand to knock. He'd almost turned and said "May I?" to Antonio, but caught himself. Antonio had no claim to her. Enrico did. And he was going to exercise it. He tapped at the door, then heard her saying come in, the sound thrilling through him, like a shiver. How he'd missed the music of her voice.

He eased the door open, slipping inside. Kate lay on her back, propped up on some pillows, her eyes closed. They opened as he shut the door and approached. He studied her, looking for some clue to her feelings. Her eyes widened and her lips parted. A flush came into her cheeks. "What are you doing here?" she asked, her tone edged with steel.

He stopped where he was. "Antonio said you were ill."

She waved her hand in the air. "It's nothing. Some morning sickness. I made the mistake of having anchovies on my salad."

Enrico smiled. *What had she been thinking?* "I thought you hated them."

"I do. But I was craving the salt." She reddened.

"You could have put salt on the salad."

She looked up at him. "I know. I thought maybe some extra protein...." She trailed off. "Why are we talking about this?"

He lost his smile. "Because it is easier than talking about other things."

"There's nothing to discuss." She maneuvered herself to sit on the edge of the bed.

The careful slowness of her movements sent a spike of alarm into his gut. "Are you all right?"

She nodded. "Just a little dizzy."

"Have you eaten or drunk anything since you were sick?"

"A little water."

He walked past her and picked up the receiver for the bedside phone. "You need to eat something. How about penne with chicken and a little olive oil and parmesan?"

"That sounds good."

He called room service and ordered for her. Then he pulled up a chair so he could sit near the bed. "Kate, you need to take care of yourself."

She made a face. "Not you too. I already have one mother hen in Antonio."

"We just want you to be well." He sat back in the chair. He wanted to ask if she still loved him. But he couldn't do that. "Antonio tells me the doctor says you can leave in three weeks. Do you know where you will go?"

Her eyes iced over. That had been the wrong question to ask. "Where I go or what I do is no business of yours."

As her anger added bricks to the wall of tension building between them, he lowered his gaze to the carpet and made his voice soft. "I worry about what will happen once you are no longer in my care. Carlo has not forgotten about you."

"I'm well aware of that." Her shoulders hunched as she spoke.

He reached out, touching her knee. "I just want you safe. Even if you are no longer mine. Even if I never…" His throat tightened, and he had to pause for a few seconds before he could continue. "Even if I never see our baby. I want you both to be safe." He let his hand drop from her. *Stop it.* He'd get her back, he would. He couldn't lose another woman he loved. He couldn't let this child grow up without him.

Kate's eyes welled. "I'm working on a plan. I'll be safe."

He wiped his eyes, not looking at her, and sniffed hard. "I miss you," he ventured, his throat tight again, making his voice unsteady. *Dio*, he was losing control.

"I miss you, too." Her voice was soft, and he heard a quaver in it.

When he saw the sadness in her eyes, he wanted to wipe it away, to make her smile again. He had to try. He took her hand. "You must believe me. I can prove to you I am innocent."

Kate's hand went taut in his. "Stop there. You've told me so many lies, I can't take another."

"It is no lie. I swear to you." Why couldn't she see that?

She shook her head. "You're good at giving me pretty speeches, but not the truth."

"*Cara*, I am telling the truth. I have not lied to you since the hospital."

A tear rolled down her cheek. "This whole situation is so impossible. If I don't stay with you, you're supposed to kill me. How can we ever be honest with each other when that's the case?"

Sadness ripped through him. It *was* a horrible situation he'd gotten her into. "Forget that. I have told you I will not do it. I will let you leave if you must."

"Please stop. Just stop." She closed her eyes and pulled her hand from his. "It's over, Rico. Accept it. This is the end for us."

Pain seared through his chest and into his gut, as if he'd taken a bullet. Heart attack? He pressed a fist to his chest and took a deep breath. No. Just shock. He abruptly stood and turned away from her. *Do something. The door. Go to the door.* When he touched the handle, he paused. This might be the last time he ever saw her.

It can't end like this. But he couldn't bear to let her see his face. He took a deep breath, forcing his voice to be steady, though it was still thick. He spoke to the slab of dark wood in front of him. "You will always have money, protection, whatever you need. And if you ever change your mind, I will be waiting for you." His mouth dried up, the words he most wanted to say sticking in his throat. *I love you, Kate.*

"Rico." Her voice broke, and his eyes pricked with tears. "Be careful." Without thinking, he turned and strode to her, pulling her up into his arms and kissing her. For a moment she yielded and kissed him back, then she went rigid in his arms. *No.* He pulled back and studied her face, the tears streaming down her cheeks, the broken look in her eyes. A look *he'd* put there.

A great black hole opened in his chest, and he slipped into it, falling. He'd lost. With his thumbs, he swiped her tears away, his fingers tangling in the wet strands of hair that clung to her skin. This was the last time, the last time he'd ever touch her. Dropping his hands from her, he stumbled back towards the door. He opened his mouth to say something, but there were no words to put things right. "Take care, *cara.*"

He waited a moment for her to say something, to stop him, then he turned the knob, not wanting to hear more of the awful silence that was her answer.

Mute with anguish, Kate stared at Enrico's back as he walked out. She'd ended it. She could never unsay those words, those awful words. *This is the end for us.* And she could never take him back, or she'd never be able to leave him again.

Her chest ached, and once she heard the outer door close, once she knew he was gone, she gave full vent to her tears, not caring if Antonio heard her sobs. Not caring about anything else. She'd just about killed herself turning away the man she loved.

The man she loved, but could never trust.

CHAPTER 29

For the first time in his life, Enrico understood why people committed suicide. If he'd been the one behind the wheel on the drive home, he would have wrecked. And he probably wouldn't have cared.

His grief when Toni died was but half of this horrible ache, this gnawing despair. Toni's death had been something of a relief, her loss tempered by the fact that she was out of misery, that they'd had a long happy marriage together. But Kate—she'd rejected him. And she was taking their child with her. Another child he wouldn't get to love, another child who'd grow up hating him. Another child lost.

What more was Carlo Andretti going to cost him?

When they pulled up to the house, Enrico opened the car door himself, not wanting further contact with the driver or Santino, or any of the guards in the other car pulling up behind them. He hurried into the house, heading straight for the study. He poured himself a full glass of sambuca and took a large gulp, letting the sweet liqueur burn down his throat. He drained the glass and poured another. He paced around the room for a while, idly looking out the windows at the garden's fading splendor. Autumn crept in more every day. The leaves were turning, drying up, withering. He felt the same way.

A knock at the door startled him. It was Ruggero. Perhaps a distraction would help. "Come in."

The discomfort on Ruggero's face said that he knew. No doubt Antonio had told him. The boy meant well, but sometimes he went too far. "What?" Enrico snapped, his voice a blade.

Ruggero paused, obviously weighing his words. Enrico drilled his eyes into the guard, willing him not to mention it. Finally Ruggero said, "We've picked up Trucco. We confirmed he's had contact with Carlo."

Good man. He can read my mind now. He softened his voice. "Where is he?"

"Milan. At one of the safe houses."

"What has he told you?"

"Nothing. Yet. He says he'll speak only to you."

Cristo. Not now. Maybe he could let Ruggero handle it. But the don who couldn't deal with unpleasant though necessary realities had no business being in charge. He looked at his watch. The meeting with La Provincia was hours away, and dealing with Trucco meant he didn't have to think about Kate. "Let's go then."

In the car, Enrico tried to steel himself for what was coming. Death was the price for treason to one's don. Obedience and loyalty to one's *cosca* and to the 'Ndrangheta were paramount. Traitors could not be tolerated.

A lingering doubt niggled at Enrico. There was still Dom to consider. Dom, who'd done nothing but argue with him lately. Dom, who'd threatened his job. Dom, who'd tried to poison Don Battista against him. Dom's reasons were sound, his intentions focused on the good of the *cosca*, but still.... "Can you tie Trucco to the tracking device?" he asked Ruggero.

Ruggero kept his eyes on the road. "There were no fingerprints."

Fuck. It was too much to hope for. "Have you pulled the men watching Dom?" Ruggero looked at him. They had to be thinking the same thing. "You're not convinced it's Trucco," Enrico said.

"He's only part of it."

"You may be right."

"I'll keep the men in place until we're sure." Ruggero paused. "And I've decided to use the traitor's own tricks against Don Domenico."

Enrico stiffened. He almost defended Dom, then let it go. "A GPS tracker?"

Ruggero nodded. "If the men lose him, we'll still be able to see where he goes."

They pulled up to the safe house a short while later. It was a nondescript apartment building. The bottom floor, which had been heavily fortified against attack, contained a small soundproofed room. That was where they headed.

Trucco was handcuffed to a chair. Two guards sat opposite him, one smoking and playing solitaire at a small table pushed up against the wall, the other reading a newspaper. "Wait outside," Enrico said to them.

Franco's jacket had been removed, and he slumped in the chair, his shirt patched with sweat. His gray hair was tousled into greasy clumps, and there was a scratch on his chin, a large bruise on one cheek. "Why am I here, Don Lucchesi?"

Enrico took a seat a few feet from Trucco. He crossed his legs and leaned back. "You've been talking to Andretti."

Trucco swallowed. His eyes flicked to Ruggero, who stood by the wall, his hands loosely clasped in front of him. He'd donned a pair of black leather gloves, and Trucco couldn't seem to stop staring at them.

"Franco, we can do this hard, but I prefer easy. Out of respect for who you've been to my family, to me."

Trucco's eyes shifted back to Enrico. "You killed my Fiammetta," he hissed.

Enrico averted his eyes, shame and guilt washing through him. "I know I don't know your pain."

"You will."

Enrico looked up. "That's not going to happen."

"You don't know what I'm talking about."

"I do. You went digging. And you found something."

Something dark and nasty slid across Trucco's face. "Did you think you could hide it from me forever? I'm your accountant, Don Lucchesi. I see where *all* the money goes. It was a mistake making separate payments to Tyrell for Clarkston's education."

"Did Carlo tell you what he was going to do with this information?"

Triumph shined in Trucco's eyes. "He said you and yours would feel his wrath."

Enrico almost felt sorry for him. "I already knew all this. My son is safe." Ruggero's eyes snapped toward him, then darted away, the only sign he'd heard anything.

"That's not possible," Trucco said.

"I'm not the only one who's been betrayed." He looked to Ruggero and nodded. Ruggero pulled the bag with the tracking device out of his pocket and handed it to Enrico. Enrico held it up for Trucco to see. "What do you know about this?"

Trucco leaned forward, peering at the bag. "What is it?"

"A GPS tracking device."

"So?" Trucco shrugged.

"It was placed on my car and used to ambush me."

Trucco's face registered only surprise. "I know nothing about that."

Enrico stared at him. "You're lying."

"A son for a daughter. That was *my* revenge. It wouldn't work if you weren't alive to suffer through it."

True. Still, he needed to be sure. He nodded to Ruggero and took a breath. He wouldn't look away and he wouldn't flinch.

When Ruggero stepped forward, Trucco shrank back against the chair. "I swear, I had nothing to do with this. Just the boy."

A foot away from Trucco, Ruggero pulled a knife from his pocket. The switchblade opened with a click. Light gleamed on the sharp steel, drawing Enrico's and Trucco's eyes. Ruggero grabbed Trucco's head in an elbow lock and pressed the blade into the flesh below the accountant's right eye. "Shall I pluck out your eye with this, or with my fingers?" Ruggero asked, his voice low and menacing.

Trucco shivered. "I swear. I don't know anything."

Ruggero pushed the knife into the skin below the eye, drawing blood. Trucco whimpered. When Ruggero looked up at Enrico, Enrico nodded. Pressing the blade in deep, Ruggero drew it in a horizontal line below the eye. Blood welled up from the cut and dripped down Trucco's face. This time Trucco screamed. "Shall I take the eye now, or later, hmm?" Ruggero asked Trucco.

"I've told you what I've done. Why wouldn't I admit to this?" Trucco looked at Enrico, his eyes pleading. "I'm dead either way."

Enrico stared at him, then he looked at Ruggero, who gave the barest shake of his head. Trucco had told them all he knew. It was disappointing, but perhaps they could still make some use of his death.

He looked at Trucco, the man who had long been a friend to him and his family. "I'm sorry about Fiammetta. I tried to make amends to you." He stood up. "Dom was right; I shouldn't have shown such mercy when I knew the depths of your anger." He straightened his cuffs. "You've left me no choice."

Trucco's face reddened. "Someone lost the blood-alcohol test for you. Admit it."

"Going to prison for a mistake wouldn't have punished me more than my own guilt." He met Trucco's eyes. "I am sorry."

"I wish I could see your face when you hear your son is dead. Carlo will get to him someday."

Heat boiled up in him, but he forced himself into Trucco's hell. He forced himself to see the pain beneath the vengefulness. "I wish you to see your daughter again in heaven." Then he walked across the room to the door and nodded sharply to Ruggero. "Finish it." He turned away as the knife slashed across Trucco's throat. It was done. It should have been done many months ago.

He just hoped Nico wouldn't pay the price for his guilty conscience.

߆Ꮳ

After they returned home from dealing with Trucco, Ruggero needed to change. And Enrico needed another drink. Though he felt bad about Trucco, that wasn't the reason. He couldn't stop reliving those last moments with Kate. And he still had the meeting with La Provincia to get through.

Ruggero came for him a few hours later. Enrico had restrained himself to one drink. He needed his wits about him for this meeting. But it had been a fight to stay away from the bottle.

"We must leave now," Ruggero said. "Ready?"

"Yes," Enrico said, tightening up the tie he'd loosened earlier. *What a liar I am.* He was in no shape to appear before La Provincia. Seeing Kate today, of all days, had been a mistake. But he hadn't been able to stay away.

Enrico failed miserably in his attempts not to think about her during the drive to a house on the outskirts of Milan. Ordinarily, the meeting would have been in Calabria, in San Luca, home of Benedetto Andretti, and the seat of La Provincia. However, because Enrico wasn't able to fly yet, the meeting had been moved to a home owned by the d'Imperios. That was one thing Enrico had insisted upon. He would not meet in any location controlled by the Andrettis.

In addition to Ruggero, he had a driver and a second guard with him and two more cars of guards, one ahead and one behind. Ruggero sat in back with him instead of his usual seat up front. Enrico hated having to take such precautions, but he would not make himself an easy target.

As they drove, Ruggero was his usual tight-lipped self, probably figuring it was best to say nothing. As irritated as he was with Antonio, Enrico could have used his easy chatter now. Anything to keep his mind off Kate turning him away for good.

In a way, he was almost relieved the waiting was over. He'd been dreading hearing those words from Kate, and he'd been dreading this meeting. If La Provincia was going to punish him or kill him, he wanted it over. And the way he felt right now, he'd welcome whatever they wished to do. He was tired of fighting, he was tired of all of it.

Ruggero must have sensed his mood. As they neared their destination, he leaned toward Enrico. "May I say something?"

Enrico was curious. He nodded.

Ruggero pushed the button that raised a sheet of glass between them and the men up front. Despite the barrier, he kept his voice pitched low.

"*Signore*, you have two children to fight for. Regardless of the *signora*. You have them."

It was the right thing to say, and the wrong thing too. "I don't really *have* them. Nico hates me, and God knows if I'll ever even see the other."

"Much can happen in a lifetime."

"Too much has happened already." He leaned back against the seat.

"Your children need you. Carlo will come at you through them. Will you allow that?"

No. *No.* He was not going to bloody well allow that. He took a deep breath and sat up. Even if Kate didn't want him, he needed to look out for his children. And her. No matter how she felt about him, he still loved her. And he'd sworn to protect her.

And damn it, he needed to do something about Carlo. He'd just been sitting back, waiting for Carlo to make the next move, still unconsciously following his vow to Toni. That ended now. "Do you think we can make a move on Carlo here?"

Ruggero's brows flashed up. Then he smiled. "It'd be dangerous. We haven't planned it."

"But he won't be expecting it. Carlo will feel safe."

"True." Ruggero thought for a moment. "If I see an opportunity, I'll take it. But I won't throw away our lives on a whim. Do we agree?"

Enrico laughed, but it sounded forced, even to his own ears. "I'm not suicidal."

"I didn't think you were." But the look on Ruggero's face said the opposite.

ℰℭ

Enrico and Carlo were shown into a large dimly lit ballroom. Spotlights illuminated the center, where Benedetto and Don Battista sat side by side. Enrico and Carlo, and their respective guards, Ruggero and Massimo, had been thoroughly searched for weapons at the door.

Once his eyes had adjusted to the lighting, Enrico could see men seated in a circle two deep around them. He knew a few of the men well, but many were bosses who had flown in from Calabria. The strange, humorless faces staring back at him seemed ominous.

Benedetto broke the silence. "Enrico Lucchesi, you have been called here to answer charges brought by Carlo Andretti. How do you plead?"

Enrico felt a calm come over him. He thought of his father, of what would impress these men. A true Mafioso would keep his cool, would swagger his way through this meeting. Carlo would not get to him, no matter what was said. Enrico looked at Benedetto, letting a smirk take over his face. "I cannot say. I am not aware of the charges."

Benedetto's lips pursed, and a few of the men around them stifled their laughter. Benedetto coughed to get their attention. "The charges are violating the terms of the truce between your family and Carlo Andretti's."

"I plead not guilty."

Carlo shifted beside him. "You have balls, Lucchesi, I will give you that."

Enrico shrugged. "I have heard no proof against me."

"May I?" Carlo asked, nodding to his brother.

"You may."

Carlo turned to Enrico with relish. "You sired an illegitimate son while engaged to my daughter. You broke the betrothal. The marriage would never have taken place had I known."

Enrico struggled not to wince. He hadn't wanted his son to become public knowledge. But it was done. "What *actual* proof do you have of this, Don Andretti?"

Carlo produced a crisp piece of paper. "The boy's birth certificate." He handed it to Enrico.

Enrico took the paper, holding it rigidly to keep his hands from shaking. *Where had Carlo gotten it?* He scanned the paper, feeling faint. There it was,

234

under "Name and surname of father." His name. Except that he'd used his alias, *grazie a Dio*. "This says the father is Enrico Franchetti. Might I suggest you start wearing glasses, Don Andretti?"

Carlo reddened. "Enrico Franchetti *is* you."

"Prove it."

Carlo seemed taken aback for a second, then he said, "Franco Trucco, your *contabile*, can swear to it."

"Can he? Is he here?" Enrico made a show of looking around.

"No. But we can summon him."

"Please do." Enrico crossed his arms. "I can wait."

Carlo's eyes narrowed with sudden knowledge. "You've eliminated him."

"Why would you think that?" Enrico smiled, pleased by the look on Carlo's face.

"It's just like with Grantini." Carlo's hands clenched into fists. "You got rid of him too."

Enrico stifled a yawn. "Grantini, again? You're boring me."

"You can't deny you slept with Trucco's daughter before the year of mourning had ended."

"Can't I? Are there any pictures? Video, perhaps?" A slow ripple of laughter traveled around the room, and Enrico smiled again. He was actually enjoying this.

"Everyone knows you fucked that *puttana*. Everyone."

"Even if I did, the year of mourning is an outdated custom. Much like the one against having a mistress. Which everyone knows you do, Carlo. You take her everywhere."

There was a chorus of agreement surrounding them. Carlo's eyes drilled into him, and he took a step toward Enrico, breathing hard. "You will regret these lies. You will regret what you did to my daughter. You will regret you were ever born."

"Carlo, the secret to a life well-lived is to have no regrets."

"Have you no shame?"

"Have you no desire for peace? Must we fight this same fight forever? Will you never forgive my father for making you look like a fool?"

Carlo let out a roar and lunged for Enrico. Before anyone else could react, Ruggero had Carlo in a headlock. Ruggero's eyes flicked up to Enrico's, and Enrico could see it on Ruggero's face. One little twist, and it would all be over. But Enrico was not, after all, suicidal. He gave an almost imperceptible shake of his head, and Ruggero let Carlo go.

Enrico turned to Benedetto. "Are we done?"

"What about my nephew?" Carlo choked out. "You stole his wife, then helped her kill him."

A hush settled over the room. This was certainly a more serious charge. He had to tread carefully. "Vincenzo had beaten her and was threatening to

235

kill her when I took her under my protection. The night he died, he'd broken into my home and attempted to rape her and then murder us both. She killed him in self-defense." He paused. "If that is how the Andrettis treat their women, I will stop it every time." Enrico looked at the faces around them. "Protecting the women and children under our care is one of the oldest rules of the 'Ndrangheta. Keeping them out of disputes is another. And you have failed to do both."

"So you deny me my right to vendetta, to avenge my nephew?"

"He broke our laws. Not once, but twice. I had the right to help her." Enrico paused. "I take that back. I was *obligated* to help her."

"Did that include getting her pregnant with your child?"

Enrico heard a collective intake of air from the men surrounding them, along with a few whispered curses. "She is no longer married. She is free to choose the man in her bed."

"Do you deny you gave my nephew the horns?"

Enrico paused. Sleeping with another 'Ndranghetista's wife was strictly forbidden. "I don't deny it. But that happened only after he'd forsaken any claim to her. In fact, he told me I could have her." Enrico turned to Ruggero. "Isn't that what he said?"

Ruggero nodded. "He said that. But not so nicely."

Laughter broke out again.

"Silence." Benedetto's voice sliced through the air.

After some shifting in the chairs around them, the room grew quiet. "Is there anything else?" Enrico asked.

Benedetto turned to Don Battista, who cast Enrico a somber look. "There is one more thing," Don Battista said. "Some in your *cosca* have questioned your recent decisions. The involvement with this woman, for example."

"As I have explained, I was obligated to help her. If a relationship developed from it, well...." Enrico shrugged. "I am after all, a widower. Not a saint." He hated putting it that way, but it was the thing these men were most likely to understand.

"You have always acted in the best interests of your *cosca*?" Don Battista asked.

Enrico's mouth went dry. This was the toughest question put to him yet. "I have not. I should have remarried sooner. I have been without heirs this entire time. Yes, my cousin is prepared to take over should something happen to me. However, there is some risk because I have no direct heir. I am trying to correct that oversight."

Carlo's glare cut into him. "Are you saying you should have left my Toni?"

"I stayed with her for twenty-six years." He held Carlo's gaze. "There is your answer." He hated to make it sound like love didn't enter into it. But everyone understood their marriage was a business arrangement, more or less.

He turned to Don Battista. "Am I free to go, or must I continue to answer for every woman I have taken to bed?"

Don Battista started to talk, but Carlo cut him off, addressing the men around them. "Are all of you happy, *truly* happy, with how Lucchesi has run things? He controls your money. He decides how much each of us pays to wash it. If he doesn't like the business you're in, you pay more. And more. Tell me, are you satisfied with this arrangement?"

When a chorus of angry voices sounded around them, a frigid blast blew down Enrico's spine. *Merda.* He glanced at Don Battista, then gazed around him, trying to look into every face. "All of you have unfettered access to your money. I do not control it. You are free to put it wherever you like, to use any bank you wish. But only *I* guarantee that outsiders won't get hold of it, that the government won't steal it from you. Need I remind you what happened to Cosa Nostra when they used outside banks?" He looked around again. "Any of you are free to start your own banks, to launder your own funds. If you wish to do so, I can do nothing to stop you."

The men sitting in judgment were silent, but many were nodding. Enrico continued. "As for what I charge, that is also my right. Drugs, pornography, and prostitution are blights on our communities. Our ancestors recognized this; they forbade such dealings over a century ago. The drugs are worst of all; the money is for the taking, yes, but the price that comes with it is enormous. Who among you has not lost someone to drugs or to the violence that accompanies them? If my charges encourage you to pursue other avenues, isn't that in the best interests of us all?"

"You would make us weak," Carlo hissed. "We need the money we make from drugs to fight off the others who would take our territory."

"I'm not preventing you from pursuing many other highly lucrative avenues. And I'm not preventing you from pursuing the ones that are against our codes. Am I not free to determine my rates? Would you put price controls on all of our dealings? What's next, trade agreements and tariffs? Shall we charge each other VAT as well?"

The crowd broke out in laughter. Benedetto called again for silence. Enrico took a deep breath, then addressed the men surrounding him. "What say you? Am I free to go?"

A chorus of assent greeted him. Benedetto cut in. "We are agreed. You may go."

Enrico bowed his head to Benedetto and Don Battista, then took in the group. "I thank you for your support." He paused and looked at Carlo. "Perhaps you should listen to your betters."

He walked out, Ruggero at his back. Yet he still felt the daggers of Carlo's eyes piercing him. If they were at war before, it had just escalated to out-and-out nuclear annihilation.

They were in the car, heading back home, when Ruggero spoke. "I could've made it look like an accident."

Enrico laughed. "I doubt anyone would have been convinced."

"Shall I plan it then?"

"Yes." There would be no more waiting for Carlo's next bomb to come hurtling at them. He held Ruggero's gaze. "Thank you for earlier, in the car. It made all the difference."

"You reminded me of your father. How he was before."

Enrico leaned forward, unable to keep a smile off his face. "That's what I'd hoped for."

"They were in the palm of your hand."

Enrico felt energized, light, his body humming. Ready for a fight. It was so alien to how he'd felt an hour ago he could hardly believe it. He thought of Kate with a strange determination. He'd win her back, somehow. Certainty sizzled in the marrow of his bones.

But first he had to crush Carlo. It was past time to give up the high road. If Carlo wanted a street fight, he'd give him one hell of a rumble.

CHAPTER 30

Carlo and Benedetto were finally alone, heading to the villa for the night. Carlo could barely speak. Enrico had made him look like a fool, more so than Rinaldo ever had. He turned to his brother. "You did not support me."

Benedetto straightened his tie and shot his shirt cuffs. Even though he was balding and running to fat, he was, as always, immaculately dressed. He spent the GDP of a small third-world country on his wardrobe. "I'm supposed to be impartial."

"What a fucking farce! I was supposed to bring *proof*? Since when is my word not enough?"

"Lucchesi had the right to demand it. It was a trial, after all."

Carlo ground his teeth together. "You could've prepared me."

"I suspect Vittorio coached Lucchesi."

"And that excuses you? Why didn't I get the same help from you, my own brother?"

Benedetto smoothed his hair back. "You'll recall I advised you against such a course."

"You'd let the Andrettis be laughingstocks just to teach me a lesson?"

His brother looked him full in the face. "The only one who looks like a fool is you. As always, your breathtaking arrogance has gotten you into trouble."

"My arrogance is exceeded only by yours, dear brother."

Benedetto chuckled. "I've earned mine."

A great thundering roar invaded Carlo's head and chest. "*Vaffanculo!* You haven't earned a fucking thing. Everything was handed to you. I had to fight for everything I have. And never, not *once*, did any of you acknowledge what I've accomplished."

Benedetto studied his fingernails. "If this is about our father, you can stop now. Poor, poor, little Carlo. Always overlooked."

"You will get yours. You've raised a nest of vipers. Do you think your sons don't plot your death daily?" Carlo was gratified to see the tightening in his brother's shoulders. He'd scored a hit.

Benedetto lowered the glass that separated them from the driver. "I won't be staying the night. My jet, please." He raised the glass again. "I pity you."

"You *pity* me?"

"You are the smallest man I know."

His family. How Carlo hated them all. Toni had been the only exception. "I'll crush you, Benedetto. When I finish with Lucchesi, you'll be next."

"I'm trembling."

"I know how much you've lost at the gaming tables. I wonder, is it only *my* money you've borrowed?"

Benedetto's eyes snapped to his. He was right; Benedetto was in deep. He couldn't keep the smile off his face. "You've stolen from La Provincia, haven't you?"

Benedetto held Carlo's eyes. "Try to prove it."

Triumph flooded through him. "Don't think I can't get to you."

Benedetto shifted in his seat, leaning toward him. "Out of respect, Father and I have allowed you to operate without direction. That can change."

"Respect? Out of *fear*."

"Remember what happened to our dear brother."

Carlo's gut tightened. *Remo.* He could almost hear the echoes of Remo's screams, almost smell the burning of his brother's flesh, all these years later. He pushed the memory from his mind. "I remember."

"See that you do. Father would be happy to remind you about loyalty."

"No matter how big you think you are, Benedetto, you will always be under Father's thumb."

Silence fell between them as Benedetto turned away. *Good riddance.*

෴

Carlo had just left Benedetto at the airstrip and was headed back to the lake when he got a call from Domenico. "You'd better have good news. Where's Rinaldo?"

He could hear the smile in Domenico's voice. "I know where he is. And I'll soon have the American in my hands. Let me know where and when you want her, and she's yours."

Laughter bubbled up in Carlo's chest. He wanted to shout out loud. Lucchesi would regret every minute of the rest of his short miserable life. "You've gone up in my estimation."

"Will you renegotiate our terms?" Domenico asked.

"After I've dealt with Rinaldo and the woman, we'll see what you've earned."

He listened as Domenico told him where to find Rinaldo. After they hung up, Carlo sat back, considering. Perhaps *this* Lucchesi might be worth bringing into the organization. Domenico had several sons who needed wives, and there were certainly daughters in the Andretti family who needed husbands.

It would be nice to have someone to help with the dirty work.

Domenico smiled when he hung up with Carlo. As if he'd let the old man dictate everything. Carlo would never see him coming. Neither would Rico.

Fools, the both of them.

ℰℭ

A large package, unaddressed but beautifully wrapped in crisp silver paper with a large white bow, arrived at Enrico's villa three days after the meeting with La Provincia. Maddalena brought it inside and set it on the desk in Enrico's study.

Enrico looked at the box for a few moments, his heart thumping. The package looked eerily familiar. He called Ruggero, who advised him not to touch the box and to leave the room.

He couldn't stop staring at it, wondering at the contents. When he noticed a trace of red seeping through the wrapping at the bottom-right corner of the box, panic gripped him in its fist and squeezed. Had Carlo gotten to Nico? To Kate?

His stomach churning, Enrico went out to the front hall and called Antonio while he waited for Ruggero. Antonio assured him Kate was resting in her room. He hung up when Ruggero approached. Gesturing toward his study, he said, "It's from Andretti. I'm sure of it."

Ruggero looked through the doorway at the box. "It could be a bomb."

"It seems to be leaking blood. Besides, a bomb isn't Carlo's style. He likes his victims to suffer."

Ruggero rubbed his chin. "You say Maddalena carried it in?"

"Yes. So it's been jostled."

"That's not the same as opening it." Ruggero pulled out his switchblade and walked into the study. When Enrico followed him in, Ruggero stopped and looked at him. "The hallway, please, Don Lucchesi."

Enrico crossed his arms and stared at his guard. Ruggero didn't back down. "Let me do my job, *capo*," he finally said.

Throwing up his arms, Enrico walked out of the room. He waited, fingers tapping the seam of his trousers, his heart ratcheting up as he heard the long slit along the paper, a rustling, then silence. And more silence. Finally, Ruggero's voice. "Don Lucchesi."

He stepped into the room. The first thing he noticed was the concern in Ruggero's eyes. The look in them was soft, pitying. Not a look he'd ever seen from Ruggero. He raced to the box, seeing now that it was wood, and

241

ornately carved, reminiscent of the cigar box he'd received from Carlo in Rome. Breathless, he looked inside, and then wished he hadn't.

Fighting back tears, he looked up at Ruggero. "I want him dead."

"You shall have your wish."

Enrico looked into the box again, unable to hold back his tears. His father's head stared up at him. Surrounding it were bloody lumps Enrico couldn't identify at first. When he did, bile rushed up into his throat. The two biggest lumps were his father's hands; the strips of crimson-colored meat surrounding them were his fingers.

All ten.

The digits looked like they'd been crushed before being severed. He stepped away then, struggling not to vomit. Breathing hard, he stared at the floor for a long time, trying to burn the carpet's design onto his retinas.

When he trusted himself to look up, Ruggero and the box were gone.

Staring at the smear of blood left on his desk, his eyes flooded with tears anew. His father had endured so much heartache in the last three decades, only to meet a vicious, ugly end. *Papà, I hope you're with them again.* He crossed himself and whispered aloud, "I will see you avenged."

୫୦୯୨

Enrico was in the middle of his fourth glass of sambuca when it hit him: how had Carlo found his father? Don Battista certainly hadn't handed that information to him. So who *had* Don Battista told?

He'd reached a pleasantly blurry point when he picked up the phone; it was almost enough to allow him to forget what was in the box. Almost. He cleared his throat, willing himself to be steady while he waited for Don Battista to pick up. "*Ciao*, Rico. Why are you calling so late?"

"Carlo Andretti murdered my father. He sent me his head and his hands."

Enrico heard a wheezy intake of breath from the old man. "I'm sorry, my son." There was a pause. When Don Battista spoke again, his voice shook with anger. "It's your cousin who acts against you."

"How do you know?"

"Domenico called a few days ago and asked how he could reach Rinaldo. I knew he was angry with you, but I never dreamed he'd crawl in the gutter."

"It could be a coincidence."

"In my experience, there's no such thing."

Enrico took another sip of sambuca. "I know." Damn him, he did know, but he had to be certain. *Dom, how could you turn against your own blood?*

He ended the call with Don Battista, then summoned Ruggero. It was time to see what use they could make of Trucco's death. Time to prove there were no coincidences after all. Time for the traitor to suffer as his father had.

After all, as Dom had said about Trucco, now was not the time for mercy.

୫୦୯୨

Domenico paced his study, Kate on his mind. How best to get her away from Antonio and the guards. How best to get her to Carlo without being followed. He looked out the front window of his home, sure Ruggero's spy was still out there somewhere, and sighed in irritation. The men Ruggero had picked to watch him were very good. He hadn't ever tried to shake them. Best to lull them into complacency.

His mouth pursed. He was going to have to kill the man watching him before he went after Kate. If he eluded him, it would tip off Ruggero and Enrico. But if the man went missing, that was a problem too.

He tapped his fingers against his lips. He was going to have to eliminate them all, if Carlo wasn't able to. It was the only way. He couldn't hope to avoid detection. Enrico and Ruggero already suspected him, and Antonio wasn't dumb.

Dom was still looking out the window when he saw Ruggero's spy drive off. He looked up and down the street for a replacement, but didn't see anyone. Perhaps they'd decided to lull *him* into complacency. But he knew about the GPS tracker they'd placed on the car. It had been the first thing he'd searched for when he'd learned he was being watched.

He smiled. He'd use their own toy against them. Let the tracker lead them right into a trap. And double-cross Carlo in the process.

The phone rang. It was Enrico. "We got the traitor."

A jolt of adrenaline ran through Dom. That's why the spy had driven off. "Who was it?"

"Trucco. He gave the master codes for the house alarm to Andretti and he put a GPS tracker on the Maserati."

Dom's eyebrows shot up. "He confessed to all this?"

"More or less. He admitted he'd been helping Carlo, feeding him information. He wouldn't get specific. But there was no reason to press the point."

Was this a trap? There was something about Enrico's voice. "Have you been drinking?"

Enrico coughed and cleared his throat. "A bit. It's been hard."

"I'm sorry. I know you were close to him."

Dom heard only silence for a while, then Enrico's voice again, a bit sharper. "You'd warned me to take care of him, and I didn't listen." Enrico paused and cleared his throat again. "I'm sorry, too. I've ignored too much of your counsel lately."

Dom froze, a little hope seeping in. If he could avoid killing Enrico, he would. "You'll give up the woman and make peace with Carlo then?"

Enrico sighed. "I know it's the right thing to do. But I can't."

Dom exhaled slowly, unhappily. "Then it's still war with Carlo."

"Not necessarily. I plan to meet with him and Dario. Perhaps we can come to an agreement."

"Have you spoken to him?"

"Not yet. I wanted you to make the arrangements."

Dom's stomach clenched. This was it. No way out. "I'll see to it."

After hanging up with Enrico, Dom placed the call to Carlo, both of them knowing the meeting with Enrico would never take place, but playing the game for anyone who might be listening. Then he picked up another phone, one he was sure was clean, and called Kate and told her his plan to get her away from Antonio that evening.

He was glad he wouldn't have to kill the tail after all. He wasn't like Carlo; he didn't enjoy killing. And he wouldn't enjoy most of what was to come. But it had to be done.

He planned out the rest of what he had to do, including when he'd render Enrico blind to his whereabouts. It would be a simple matter to discard the tracker once he'd delivered Kate to Carlo. The tracker would lead Enrico straight to the Andrettis. If all went well, Enrico and Carlo would kill each other, and Dom would be free.

CHAPTER 31

Kate focused on her breathing, trying to settle her fluttering stomach as she got ready for dinner. She'd asked Antonio if they could dine at the hotel's restaurant instead of going out. She and Dom were counting on Antonio and the guards to be lax, since they were staying in the hotel. They had no reason to suspect Kate was going to run off, and she didn't want to give them one by acting at all out of the ordinary.

She made sure all her cash and her passport were tucked in the money belt she wore under her slacks. She wouldn't be using that passport for a while, but she'd need it someday, when she could go back to her normal life. Though she had no idea when that might be. Surely Carlo would give up eventually? If she hid for a year or two, that might be enough. Dom had promised her a loan, but money would eventually be a problem. Hopefully he'd be able to get her good enough documents that she could work.

Her parents would help. But if she could avoid involving them, she would. Her throat tightened; she couldn't see them, she couldn't even see her cousin Terri. She had to hold onto the thought that someday she would see them all again. And she'd figure out how to stay safely in touch from a distance.

She heard a tap on her door. "Come in." She'd chosen a loose, gauzy top in black with matching black pants and low-heeled shoes in case she needed to run.

Antonio was in a suit as usual. The dark blue of the fine cloth brought out his eyes. When he came into the room, he looked her up and down, a slight smile on his lips. "Ready, *signora?*"

She picked up her purse and crossed the room, leaning into the mirror to check her makeup. Perfect. She smiled at him. "That color suits you."

A flush poured into his cheeks. "*Grazie, signora.*"

She took his arm as he escorted her out of the room. The guards fell into step behind them. "You know," she said to him for probably the hundredth time, "you *can* call me Kate."

He shook his head. "No, I cannot."

"Why not?"

He glanced at her, his expression stern. "Do not tease me."

Kate bit her lip and looked away. Then she squeezed his arm. "I wasn't."

"Perhaps not. But you forget, and you should not."

She looked at the richly patterned carpet beneath their feet. "I apologize."

He made a little sound of amusement, and she looked up to see him holding back a smile. Realizing she'd been had, she nudged him with her shoulder and shook her head. "You're incorrigible, Antonio."

He raised an eyebrow. "I do not know this word."

"It means you're bad beyond reform."

He grinned. "That sounds like me."

She returned the grin, then looked away when she felt her smile start to falter. She was going to miss Antonio, and she hated deceiving him. But it was the only way. She tried to focus on her surroundings as they crossed through the lobby and down the hall past the drawing rooms that served as the central gathering places in the hotel.

The Villa d'Este was a former palace, and that lent it a different air than most hotels. Its design wasn't the result of some shiny corporate vision; rather it had been built to reflect the grandeur of the person who'd commissioned it. This particular history meant that some things had been retrofitted in later to make the hotel usable for guests. And one of those things, the thing she and Dom were counting on, was that the restrooms for restaurant guests were located below the ground floor, in a basement area that had been used by servants in the days when the hotel was a working palace. It was the perfect place for him to meet her, since there was a service exit just down the hall from the restrooms.

Kate and Antonio were seated at a table in the beautiful dining room, one whole wall nothing but windows so they could look out at the moonlit lake. Kate glanced at her watch. Still plenty of time to eat at least part of her meal, then meet Dom at eight thirty. She glanced around them, her foot tapping under the table.

Antonio touched her hand. "*Signora*, you seem... not easy."

Uh-oh. "I'm a little restless. We've been here over a week now."

"Perhaps a walk after dinner?"

She smiled. "I'd like that." Then she looked down at the menu. She wasn't going to take that walk. She wasn't going to see him ever again after this.

They ordered and ate leisurely, Kate struggling to keep up the usual small talk. Then Antonio introduced something of interest. "Ruggero discovered our problem."

She raised an eyebrow. "Problem?"

"The source of the break-in. And the trouble returning from Capri."

"Ah." The traitor. "Who was it?"

"Fiammetta's father."

Kate pressed her lips together. She could understand his reasons. Still, the man didn't care if anyone else got hurt while he got his revenge. "I'm sure Enrico is relieved."

"I think that is not all of it. None of us are convinced."

"Who else do you suspect?"

Antonio glanced at the guards, then looked at her. "I think you know."

She looked him full in the eye. "Yes, I think I do."

Antonio broke their gaze and looked down at his plate, using his fork to push around a few mouthfuls of risotto. "He is not to be trusted."

Kate's stomach dropped. *That's just what I'm doing. But helping me leave gives Dom what he wants. And he doesn't want anyone to know about the baby.*

"*Signora*, are you all right?" Antonio placed a hand on her wrist and leaned toward her.

"I'm just thinking."

He studied her. "You seem pale."

"Don't worry. My stomach is just fine." *Then why does it feel like I've swallowed a school of live anchovies?*

"Should I ask for the check?"

Kate shook her head and glanced at her watch. Eight twenty-five. "I'm going to the restroom. Please order me the panna cotta for dessert."

He rose and pulled out her seat. She walked away from him, Paolo following her. Kate glanced back at Antonio. He'd been so kind to her, so understanding. She had to blink furiously to hold back her tears.

She hurried past the lobby bar and the great rooms, then slowed when she started down the marble staircase that led to the restrooms. Her heels clicked on the marble, echoing in the space. Near the bottom, she stopped and turned back to the guard. "Paolo, I left my purse at the table. Could you get it for me?"

He hesitated. "*Signora*, I shouldn't leave you alone."

"What's going to happen?"

Paolo hesitated again, then nodded. "Do not move. I will return soon."

Kate waited until he reached the top of the staircase, then she rushed down the remaining stairs and rounded the corner to the left. The service exit was at the end of the hall. She didn't pause until she reached for the handle. Was she making a mistake? A sharp rap on the door made her jump and her heart gallop. She took a deep breath. She had to do this. When she opened the door, her hand slipped on the handle, her palm slick with sweat. Dom stood to the right of the door. "We must hurry." He motioned for her to precede him.

Her hesitation must have showed; he smiled, visibly relaxing. He looked so much like Enrico then that it was comforting. "Come, *signora*. The guards will soon miss you."

She glanced back over her shoulder, but the corridor was empty. There was nothing more for her here. She had to go, she had to be free of Enrico. And she had to save her baby. She touched her stomach, then stepped out the door.

Dom guided her to an unattended side lot, his car nearly hidden by a large spreading maple.

They got in and he started the Lamborghini, his movements quick and decisive. Kate looked behind them and saw Paolo burst through the service exit. Could he see her through the tinted windows? She ducked down as Dom pulled out.

Paolo rushed toward them, and she shouted "Go!" at Dom. He pressed down on the gas and the car leapt forward, its tires spewing gravel as they barreled through the open front gate.

They'd driven for some time, Kate checking the side mirror, looking for cars in pursuit. But no one was racing after them. "I'm surprised they aren't following."

Dom glanced up at the rear view mirror. "That is because they already know where we are."

"How?"

"Ruggero planted a GPS tracker on the car."

"Why?" Though she knew.

"He thinks I am the traitor."

"Are you?"

He laughed. "Who else would want both of you gone?"

"Why would you want *me* gone?"

His eyes flicked to her belly. "I will not lose the *cosca* to your child."

Kate's heart seized, and fear ripped through her, her stomach rolling in a way that made her nauseous. "You don't have to worry about that. Just help me disappear. Enrico will never see his child."

Dom shook his head. "He will never stop looking for you."

"I told you. I'll tell him I lost the baby. He'll give up on me then."

"What a fool you are. He has risked everything for you. He started a war over you." He shook his head. "He will never give you up, regardless of the child." When Dom spoke again, his voice was thick. "You do not deserve him."

Kate felt the truth of that with a bitter pang. "Neither do you."

"True. But I have to save my family's future. Rico is throwing it all away, over you. I have no choice."

"Yes, you do."

Dom let out a huff. "You do not understand. Rico has put the life of every man who works for him at risk. Carlo has already attacked us, and he will certainly do so again. Rico's refusal to deal in drugs has put us at a disadvantage against Andretti's deep pockets. The only way for us to survive is to make an alliance with Carlo. But Rico will not marry Delfina, even if you leave; he will not give you up. And so *I* have to make things right. *I* have to give Carlo what he wants."

"Which is?"

"You. And Rico. And a discount on certain services he receives from the family."

Kate shuddered and hugged herself. She couldn't let Carlo near her. She should open the car door and jump out. But Dom was driving so fast. What if she hurt the baby? What if she broke a leg? There had to be another way. She needed to remind him about the letters. "I thought you didn't want anyone to know about the adoption."

He laughed. "I don't. But it wasn't hard to figure out what you'd done. I did a favor once for the concierge at the hotel. It wasn't hard to intercept that package you were sending to your parents. The letters are ashes now."

Kate's stomach went hollow. She and her baby were going to die.

They drove higher into the mountains surrounding the lake. There were few homes, and the road was unlit. As they ascended, the road switched back and forth, making Kate queasy, the forest to their left an unbroken mass of darkness, the drop-off to their right an unending chasm. Finally Dom turned onto a gravel road that disappeared into a thick grove of trees. In the bouncing light from the car's headlamps, ghostly branches jutted into their path.

A little ways down, he stopped and pulled a gun. He held it on her while he opened his window. "Why are we stopping?" she asked, tensing herself to run.

"I need to get rid of this." He showed her the tracking device in his hand. "Ruggero is a fool to think I'd fall for my own idea."

Kate watched the tracker sail out the window and into the night. She grabbed the door handle and Dom shook his head. "Take your hand off that if you want to keep it. Carlo did not say I had to deliver you in one piece."

She looked into his eyes. He meant what he said. She'd have to hope for another opportunity. A better one.

The gravel road wound through a dense tunnel of trees. When branches scraped the doors on both sides, Dom muttered about Carlo being too cheap to keep the brush cut back.

Rage burned a hole in Kate's chest. "You're about to deliver me and my baby up to that horrible man, you're about to destroy your cousin's *life*, and you're worried about scratches on your car?" Her voice had become shrill. "What kind of monster *are* you?"

"A practical one. Better to suffer a few deaths than many. Better to save the *cosca* than have Rico destroy it." He drove around another bend, and she saw the glimmer of lights. "I want to save my children's future." He glanced down at her belly, then up at her face. "I am no different from you."

"Except I won't kill anyone to do that!" She yanked on the door handle.

He stopped the car and seized her wrist as the door popped open. "You are not listening. Your existence, your baby's existence, guarantees that many people will die before this is all over. But if I give you to Carlo, if Rico rushes over here to rescue you, that will be the end of it. Two deaths." He cocked his head. "Four deaths, actually. Ruggero and Antonio too. They will never trust me. But the rest of the men will."

Kate struggled against his hold. She tried to throw herself out the door, hoping her entire weight would loosen his hold. Gravel crunched as men approached. She screamed and tried to wrench her arm from his grip. Dom's fingers dug into her flesh. If she lived long enough, she'd be bruised to the bone. Lying almost flat over the seat, she brought up her legs and lashed out at him. One of her heels struck him hard in the face, and his head snapped back.

Dom lost his grip, and she scrambled out on her hands and knees. When Carlo's men started running toward her, she headed for the trees. She'd been so stupid, thinking she could manage Dom. And now she was on her own. Enrico would never find her in time. She should have taken her chances with a broken leg.

Her heart trying to beat its way out of her chest, Kate ducked through the trees, running blind in the dark, branches smacking into her, scratching her face and arms, snatching at her hair. She could hear the guards behind her, shouting to each other, though the noise loudest in her ears was her own breathing, a ragged panting as she sucked in oxygen.

A tree root snagged her right foot and she smashed into the ground, air whooshing out of her. Panicked, she gasped for breath, wheezing with the effort, struggling to stand. She'd just gained her feet when one of Carlo's men seized her around the waist. He lifted her in a bear hug from behind, his voice thunderous in her ear as he shouted for another guard.

Two men, followed by Dom, raced to them. "Don't let her get away," Dom shouted. The guard holding her laughed and said something in Italian. From the way the others laughed, he must have been insulting Dom.

The guard, a massive man in every way, scooped her up over his shoulder and carried her hanging down over his back. Kate kicked and screamed and beat at his head and shoulders with her fists, but she might as well have been punching a wall. After a while, the guard jostled her and barked at her to stop. When she didn't, he swung her down in front of him and pulled back his fist. Kate screamed and put up her hands. Too late. A blow to her temple rendered everything black.

CHAPTER 32

Enrico and Ruggero raced through the hills in the Maserati, followed by Claudio and Santino. Antonio, Paolo, and Tommaso were in another car, coming from the hotel.

"You're sure we won't lose them?" Enrico asked.

"I'm sure."

"Maybe we should call in more men."

"How many do you want to risk?" Ruggero looked at his boss.

"You're asking because she left me."

"And because we might all die."

Enrico looked at him. "If you want out of this, say so."

Ruggero shook his head. "I'll never abandon my don." He paused. "There are others at stake who perhaps should not be."

Enrico nodded. He'd persuade Antonio to leave. He closed his eyes and pressed his palms into them. "I'm well aware of what I'm doing. I shouldn't be asking any of you to help me. But I can't abandon her to that thug. I can't abandon my child." He looked at Ruggero. "Even if she never comes back to me, I couldn't live with myself."

Ruggero grunted in agreement. "I wouldn't wish Andretti on my worst enemy, much less on the woman I loved."

Enrico stared straight ahead. His throat was so tight he didn't trust himself to speak. Finally he said, "Love is the most wondrous thing and the most terrible thing. Because now you have everything to lose." He shook his head. "For the briefest time, I had everything I ever wanted." The lump in his throat felt like a *bocce* ball. He had to stop and take a deep breath. Finally the lump dissipated. "I will *not* lose it all again."

"I will not fail you, *mio capo*."

Enrico gripped the guard's shoulder. "You're a good man, Ruggero. And a great friend. I can't thank you enough for all these years you've stood beside me."

Ruggero nodded, keeping his eyes on the road. "Thanks are not needed. But I am honored you would call me friend."

Enrico squeezed his shoulder once more, then released it. There was nothing more to say.

Ruggero downshifted for the climb into the hills, the purr of the Maserati's engine taking on a deeper tone. "If we get out of this, I'm going to save up for one of these."

"You won't have to. I'll buy you one."

Ruggero smiled. "In that case, I'll make sure we survive."

Enrico returned the smile, surprised he could. "And just think what would've happened if a car wasn't on the line?"

They were interrupted by a beep from the phone Enrico was using to monitor the position of the GPS tracking devices. One of the trackers was now stationary, the other in motion. Dom must have found one. He probably thought he was clever, throwing them off the trail. But he hadn't counted on Ruggero, who tried never to leave anything to chance.

None of them knew where they were going. If Carlo had a house in this location, it was news to them. Enrico made a mental note to increase surveillance of the Andrettis. Clearly they had missed something crucial. He had expected this confrontation to take place somewhere in the industrial heart of Milan, not in the hills above the lake.

He picked up the phone and called the other two cars, updating them on what had happened. He hoped Dom knew about only the one tracker, that this wasn't some elaborate misdirection. If it was, they'd never find Dom. Or Kate.

Enrico tried to settle back against the leather seat, adrenaline creating a physical discomfort that plagued him. He itched to do *something*, anything, other than sit in this car and feel his heart race and his stomach churn. What was Carlo doing to Kate? The boy in the barrel sprang immediately to mind.

His father had told him that back in Calabria, in the early days, Carlo had tortured the thirteen-year-old son of a Camorra boss who'd tried to muscle in on Andretti territory. Carlo had killed the boy using acid and an acetylene torch, then left the boy's body in a barrel on his father's front step. That act had earned Carlo his exile from Calabria and had forced him up north.

Carlo was a monster.

When Enrico pictured what his father had endured before death, his stomach lurched and rolled, his last meal threatening to come back up.

Don Battista had called Carlo a rabid dog, but he'd gone well past that. He'd thought Rinaldo's murder through, he'd planned it, he'd savored it. And now...

Now he had Kate.

Dread gnawed at Enrico's belly. He had to save her, he had to reach her before it was too late. "Can we go any faster?"

Ruggero shook his head. "We run the risk with this"—he tapped Enrico's phone—"of overtaking him. It updates every ten seconds, but we're moving fast." He looked over at Enrico. "We'll get there in time."

Per favore, Dio, let Ruggero be right.

CHAPTER 33

Kate woke up in a bedroom. She assumed she was inside the large stone house she'd glimpsed when she and Dom had pulled up. Her head hurt and her chest ached where she'd been shot during the ambush. She took a deep breath and tested her limbs. Nothing seemed to be broken.

"At last, *mia cara*, you are awake." The voice was cool, dry, the accent a blend of British and Italian. And it made her skin crawl.

She rose up on her elbows. Carlo was standing at the other end of the room, next to the fireplace. The room had a rustic feel, all stone and exposed beams, as if it were part of a hunting lodge. Perhaps it was. And she was the prey.

Carlo started toward her. Her belly filled with writhing eels, the adrenaline that had fueled her earlier attempts at escape surging through her again. She trembled with it, unsure what to do. Her eyes flitted around the room, seeking the exits. There was a window to her right, a door to her left, another door to her far left, closest to Carlo.

Which one led out of the room? Would it be safe to jump out the window? How high up was she? She could see the tops of tree branches, which led her to believe she was at least on the second floor. Did the house have a third floor?

Scrambling up, she swung her legs over the edge of the bed, but the room spun around her before she could get to her feet. She groaned and swallowed hard, trying not to vomit. Carlo stopped at the foot of the bed and rested a hand on the iron bed frame. He puffed on a cigar, the heavy aromatic smoke rising in wisps around his head. "I would not move too quickly if I were you. Massimo was perhaps too enthusiastic when he subdued you."

Kate touched her temple, probing a large bump under the skin, making herself wince.

He motioned to a pitcher of water and a glass on the bedside table. "Are you thirsty?"

"Yes." She wondered at the rawness of her voice. It must be from the screaming. She poured herself a glass, taking a few sips, her eyes on him the whole time.

"Better? Perhaps you should have some more." Her stomach dropped. How could she have been so stupid? "You see I am not such a bad man, yes?" He advanced toward her, and she shrank away from him, setting down the glass. What was in the water? He frowned. "I see Lucchesi has filled your head with filthy stories about me."

"I'm sure they're true."

He waved the hand holding the cigar in the air, the smoke making half circles as he spoke. "Think, *mia cara*. How many times has he lied to you?" He watched her face. "More than he has told the truth, I suspect."

"He had to lie. At least some of the time."

"To *protect* you, yes? That is how he would like you to think. But he lies to protect himself." He took a long draw on the cigar, then let the smoke out through his nose and mouth. "Did you actually believe he would allow you to go, once you knew who he was? He will kill you to protect himself. That is the kind of man he is."

Kate avoided his eyes. She'd thought the same thing. Except that even Dom didn't believe Enrico would harm her. Dom believed Enrico was a fool, not a killer. "He would never hurt me."

"Perhaps not while you carry his child. But if you were to persist in this notion of leaving him...."

Kate shivered, then her face flushed and her skin burned with heat. Sweat broke out on her upper lip. She looked up at Carlo, going cold again when the head movement almost made her swoon. "Something's wrong." She couldn't keep her voice steady.

"Relax. I have given you something to make you more… cooperative."

Kate looked at the pitcher, then clutched her hands over her belly. "What?"

He smiled. "Remember when I said I did not care for my nephew's methods? I was not lying. I want you to be willing."

Kate's eyebrows shot up. "Why would I *ever* be willing for you?"

He pointed to her abdomen. "To save the child."

"You're going to kill me anyway."

"Perhaps all I want is to humiliate you. And to use you to get what I really want."

"Which is?"

"The death of Enrico Lucchesi."

She studied him. "Why wouldn't you kill me?"

He frowned. "Killing women and children is… distasteful. Weak."

"You killed Enrico's mother and her two sons."

Carlo's face stiffened. "Roaches have to be eradicated."

Keep him talking. "You married your daughter to a roach?"

He flicked the ash of his cigar on the stone floor. "Rinaldo was holding my son captive. He sent me his finger as proof. What else was I supposed to do? Wait for his head to arrive?"

Was that how Enrico would get her back? As a head in a box? She swallowed down the bile that rose in her throat. "You swear you won't kill me?"

Carlo smiled. "I am a man of my word."

"Then swear it."

"I will not kill you."

"Or my baby."

He tilted his head to the side, studying her. "I cannot swear the drug is safe for the child."

"What did you give me?" Her head felt strange, and a completely unwarranted sense of calm came over her. Warmth spread through her limbs.

He smiled. "It is called Rohypnol." He sat down on the bed next to her. "No more questions. Just do what I say, and you and the baby will be safe."

He'd given her the date-rape drug. She tried to focus on him, to focus on why she should get up, run away. Her limbs felt like lead. She fell back on the bed. *No! Get up!*

"Yes," he murmured. "Just lie back and be quiet."

Yes, that's what she should do. Enrico might never find her. It was best to earn Carlo's trust, to cooperate. She wouldn't be able to escape with this drug in her system anyway.

He pulled a cell phone from his jacket pocket. "First, we must call Lucchesi. To assure him you are still alive." He pressed a few buttons, then held the phone close to her mouth.

"Rico! It's a trap! I'm in the woods—"

Carlo cut her off by pressing a button. "That's enough."

She frowned. "You're not going to speak to him?"

He smiled. "I recorded you. For later. You might not be in a condition to talk then." She shuddered, her stomach clenching. He paused. "I mean from the drug, *mia cara.* I promised not to kill you."

Cold blasted through her body. He *was* going to kill her. And Enrico would be too late to save her. Somehow she had to stay awake, she had to fight the drug. And she had to fool Carlo into thinking she'd cooperate. How long before she was unconscious? Fifteen minutes? Twenty?

He set his cigar in the cut crystal ashtray next to the pitcher, then leaned over her. She smelled the smoke on his breath and hoped the drug would block her memory of what was coming. She didn't want to recall this. If she lived through it.

He kissed her cheek, then tried to kiss her lips. When she turned her head away, he grabbed her jaw, forcing her back. She ignored the kiss, just focused on breathing, staying still. Not fighting. The drug urged her to let go, to lie back and sleep. *Stay awake. Keep thinking.* There had to be a way. There had to be.

"*Mia cara*," he whispered. "I want this to be nice." She closed her eyes. That was what Rico called her. Tears hovered beneath her eyelids.

Carlo's hands slipped down to cup her breasts, and she stiffened in revulsion. "When I first saw you, you stole my breath. You were so *bellisima*, so exquisite." He kissed her lips again. "I dreamed of the day I could have you."

She kept her eyes shut. *This isn't happening. This isn't happening.*

He slid a hand underneath her blouse, his fingers playing across the lace of her bra. "So *bellisima*."

She opened her eyes and looked up at him, seeing the glaze of lust on his face, in his eyes. He was not paying as close attention to her now. That could be useful. "Remove your clothes," he said. He stood up to allow her to undress, and she scooted herself up to the pillows at the top of the bed. Now she was closer to the pitcher and the ashtray, both potential weapons.

Kate pulled off her top, revealing a black lacy bra. His eyes latched on to her breasts. "More," he said, his voice little more than a whisper.

She lay back down. "You do it. I'm too tired."

He stripped off his suit jacket and leaned over her. She moved her right arm up to the head of the bed, seemingly out of his way. But closer to the ashtray, closer to the burning cigar.

As he kissed the swells of her breasts, her fingers inched nearer to the ashtray. It was difficult to concentrate. She just wanted to close her eyes and go to sleep.

Her fingers touched the ashtray, the crystal cool and hard beneath her fingers. She looked down at Carlo. He was too absorbed in kissing her, touching her, to notice. She risked a glance at her target. Carefully, she closed her fingers around the cigar. *Got it.* With a triumphant surge, she shoved the cigar's burning coal into the side of Carlo's neck.

He roared in pain and jumped off her. She threw the lit cigar at his face. Clumsily, she dashed toward the far door, hoping it led out of the room. *Almost there.* The door slammed open and two men poured in, guns drawn. One of them was Dario, Carlo's son. The other was the man who'd hit her in the forest. Massimo, that's what Carlo had called the mountain of a man who stood before her. Both men stared at her chest, and she tried to dodge around them, but Dario caught her by the arm and yanked her close.

"Father, what are you doing?" he asked.

Carlo pressed a hand to the burn on his neck. "Get out and leave us alone."

Dario put himself between Kate and Carlo. "We did not come here so you could force yourself on Vincenzo's wife."

"She's not his wife any longer. She made sure of that."

"No doubt he deserved it." He stared at Carlo for a moment. "I know you were thinking of replacing me with him."

Carlo shook his head. "You are my son."

Dario laughed. "As if that counts. You have never respected me."

"That does not mean I do not want you to be *capo*."

"You do not trust me with it. Admit it. Vincenzo was much more like you. Much more... vicious. Like one of your precious dogs."

Carlo opened his mouth, about to say something, but was interrupted by the sweetest sound Kate had ever heard—a burst of automatic machine gun fire.

CHAPTER 34

Enrico's men regrouped at the turnoff indicated by the GPS tracking log. Dom was gone—Enrico's phone showed him headed back to the lake, presumably going home. They would have to catch up with him later. His main priority was saving Kate. And getting Antonio out of the line of fire.

They waited for Antonio, Paolo, and Tommaso to pull up. Claudio and Santino were already there, both conferring with Ruggero. Enrico and Ruggero had decided to split forces, three and three. They had no idea what they were walking into, how many men they faced. It was best not to go in as one team.

Should he have called in more men? He was being selfish as it was to have asked anyone to accompany him. And what if Dom had recruited others to help him? These men, these were the only ones he could definitely rely on. His personal staff.

A car pulled up, and Antonio, Paolo, and Tommaso piled out. Antonio looked stricken as he approached Enrico. "Don Lucchesi, I have failed you." He waited, head bowed, for his punishment.

Enrico put a hand on his shoulder. "Give me your phone."

Antonio pulled out the phone, questions on his face. "My gun too?"

"You're going to need that." He handed Antonio his own phone, which was still tracking Dom. "I need you to do something for me."

"Anything."

"Find Dom and bring him to the safe house. If I do not return, execute him, but make it look like it was the Andrettis. The *cosca* will need Dom's sons to run it—"

Antonio cut him off with a horizontal slash of his hand. "You will return, Don Lucchesi. I have no doubt."

Enrico smiled. "I wish I shared your certainty." He gave Antonio a light

259

push. "Now go." Antonio started to step away. What if this was the last time he saw him? "Wait." A pressure built up in his chest, his throat tightening. He placed his hands on Antonio's shoulders. "I want you to know, Tonio...." His voice trailed off, thickening. He squeezed the boy's shoulders. "You've never disappointed me." He paused, looking Antonio full in the face. "I never had the pleasure of raising my own son, but sometimes I've thought of you that way."

Antonio's eyes misted. "You honor me too much, Don Lucchesi."

Enrico embraced him, his heart contracting when Antonio returned it. Then he stepped back and gave him another little push. "Go now. And be careful. He is capable of anything."

Antonio nodded, not saying a word. He hurried back to the car and sped off. Enrico watched him for a moment, wishing he'd had more to offer the boy. More time, more love. There was never enough of the former, and the latter... the latter he'd held back out of respect for Nico. There was no replacing one son with another. But was there more room in his heart than he thought?

Enrico called Paolo and Tommaso to him and briefed them on what he and Ruggero had decided. Paolo could barely meet his eye. Enrico pulled him aside. "This is not your fault, understand? She made a mistake. Not you."

Paolo shook his head. "I know my training. I shouldn't have deviated from it."

"You can't protect someone who doesn't want it."

Paolo nodded, but still looked miserable. "I don't deserve your forgiveness."

"You'll earn it tonight, I promise you."

Enrico motioned for Tommaso and the others to rejoin them. "We'll leave the cars partway, blocking the road. No one leaves without killing us."

The men nodded.

"We have no idea what we'll encounter. Hopefully we have prepared well enough." Enrico gestured to Ruggero, who started handing out gloves, radios, knives, mini Uzis, and extra ammo clips in small backpacks.

"I'm leaving additional guns and ammunition in the boots of the cars," Ruggero said. "That's our fallback point, if necessary."

Enrico stepped forward again, as all the men checked their weapons. "Remember, Kate's in there, so be careful. This will all be for nothing if she's killed." He looked at each man in turn. "If any of you want to sit this out, I'll understand."

Each man held his gaze, giving a slight nod. Enrico smiled, his heart full. "Good. I knew you were the men I could count on."

They departed for the house, stopping after several hundred feet and creating a roadblock with the cars. The men continued on foot, careful to make no sound. As soon as they saw lights, they split into two teams and struck out through the trees. The plan was for the teams to circle the location and meet up to exchange intelligence.

Enrico chafed at not being able to charge up to the house and burst in. Anything could be happening to her. But it was quiet; that was a good sign. No screams, at least. Of course, Carlo could have her gagged. Or worse—she could already be dead.

Enrico and his men circled the building. It was large, three stories, made of stone. Thick vines had crawled up the walls; the structure appeared quite old. They counted the number of vehicles in back: only three, so the odds were good.

Creeping through the trees and underbrush that came up close to the house, Enrico wondered why Carlo had a place out here. It was inconvenient. But then it dawned on him—it wasn't inconvenient. It was secluded. No neighbors, no one to see or hear anything. And plenty of places to dump bodies where they'd be found only by animals. It was the perfect place for dark projects. And now Kate was one.

They met up with Ruggero's team. Together, the teams had spotted four guards outside, one near each corner of the house. They'd have to be dealt with first.

"Did you see anything inside?" Enrico asked.

"Two more guards. And Dario. They're playing cards by the fire," Ruggero said. "We have no idea how many are upstairs."

"Did you see her?"

He shook his head. "She must be upstairs. Carlo too."

The knot in Enrico's stomach pulled tighter. *If that bastard had laid one finger on her....* He took a deep breath, forcing himself to focus.

They could see front and rear exits, and part of the interior on the bottom floor, but that gave them little idea of the layout inside. Enrico looked up, studying the house. "How many lights are on upstairs?"

"I didn't see any on our side," Ruggero said, and Claudio and Santino nodded.

"I remember one," Enrico said. He looked at Paolo and Tommaso. "What did you see?"

"One, maybe two," Paulo ventured. Tommaso shrugged.

Enrico turned back to Ruggero. "I want your team and Tommaso to handle the guards outside. I'll take Paolo with me through the back door." He looked at his watch. "In two minutes, we head for our targets. Agreed?"

Ruggero nodded, sliding his knife out of its sheath. It was large, a hunting knife, the handle utilitarian black rubber. Claudio, Santino, and Tommaso slid theirs out as well. The four men faded away, sneaking through the brush toward their targets. As soon as Enrico and Paolo saw the others break cover, they were to run for the back door.

The plan went smoothly—Carlo's guards had little time to react, and none of them managed to raise an alarm. Soon all four men lay twitching on the ground, their throats gurgling as they choked on their own blood.

Enrico and Paolo were at the back door in a flash. It was locked. Enrico heard a dull roar inside the house, then the sound of feet pounding up the stairs. No time to pick the lock. He smashed a window panel with the butt of his knife, then reached through and opened the door from the inside.

Ducking into a low crouch, he scanned the darkened room. It was a kitchen. Paolo came in next and raised his gun, squatting next to Enrico. They heard shouts and cursing from above, and then Enrico heard Kate's voice. *Grazie a Dio*—she was alive.

Ruggero and the others slipped in behind them. They waited, but heard no one moving toward them. Had the broken window gone unnoticed?

They advanced toward the next room. When Paolo ducked his head out to see if all was clear, he was met by a machine gun burst. He slumped forward, his head a bloody mess. Enrico reached out to drag him back, but Ruggero tugged on his arm.

"Leave him. He's dead. And we're trapped," Ruggero said.

Enrico stared at Paolo. He shouldn't have brought him here. He shouldn't have brought any of them here. Then a scream from above—a woman's scream—focused him back on Kate. He couldn't wait. He turned to Ruggero. "Cover me."

Before Ruggero could stop him, he rolled out into the room, aiming for the back of a sofa he thought would provide cover. Ruggero crouched in the doorway behind him, spraying the room with bullets. The bright muzzle flashes and the roar of the gun were disorienting, especially when Carlo's man returned the fire. Enrico crawled around the side of the couch, looking for an angle to shoot his target.

He snaked under a coffee table, but heard the gunfire shift from Ruggero to himself, the bullets hitting the stone floor with sharp pings. Shards of broken rock flew up around Enrico's legs. He flattened himself until Ruggero's increased fire drew the man's attention.

Enrico rolled for the far sofa. Behind it, he could see it was a straight shot to the end of the wooden staircase that led to the rooms above, and to Kate.

Enrico crawled on his elbows and belly around the back of the couch. He drew his Glock, not trusting himself to fire the Uzi with any accuracy from such a position. He edged up to the end of the sofa. This was it.

He rolled out on his back, the gun up and sighted toward the guard, whose head flicked in Enrico's direction when he caught the sudden movement. The guard swung his gun around, but he was too slow. Enrico and Ruggero caught him in a crossfire of bullets. The man jerked a few times, dropped his gun and fell to the floor. Enrico didn't wait to see if he was dead. He was already on his feet and scrambling up the stairs. She'd just screamed. Again.

CHAPTER 35

At the sound of gunfire, Massimo ducked out the door, leaving Kate with Dario and Carlo.

"Give her to me. Now," Carlo said.

Dario glanced at the corridor behind him. He pushed Kate toward Carlo and pulled his gun.

Kate stumbled and screamed when Carlo grabbed her from behind. He wound his fist in her hair and jerked her head up under his chin, bringing tears to her eyes. "We will not have time for much fun, *mia cara*, so I shall make it memorable." He pulled a knife from his pocket, a switchblade that looked like the one Vince had tried to use on her. He pressed the point of it into the flesh below her right eye. "Such a shame," he said, then he pressed the knife harder, breaking the skin. Kate screamed. Enrico was here. He was here, but he was too late. Her only hope was herself.

She kicked back hard into Carlo's right shin, hearing a satisfying crack as the heel of her shoe connected with the bone.

Carlo howled in pain, and the knife moved away from her face, enough that she risked twisting to the left. He yanked viciously on her hair, and she was sure he'd pulled out a fistful. And maybe some scalp.

He slashed at her with the knife, the blade searing across her arm. Dario's voice cut across the room. "Stop that!"

Carlo looked at him, and Kate saw her chance. Blood dripped down her arm. She drove her elbow back into his belly, knocking the wind out of him, and he let go of her. She was free. She ran for the door and Dario. No one would stop her.

༄༅

Enrico was rounding the stairs, at the landing halfway up the first flight, when a burst of machine-gun fire whizzed by his head. Plaster chips hit him in the face, and he clamped his eyes shut and ducked down, retreating behind the wall.

When the firing stopped, Enrico peered around the corner. Massimo Veltroni, the huge man who'd threatened them in Rome, stood at the top, but this time his gun was real. He gripped a Steyr AUG in both hands. Behind him, light spilled into the half-lit hallway from an open door.

Enrico could see another man behind the guard, half in the doorway. Was that Dario? *Dio mio*, was he helping Carlo? What were they doing to her?

Kate screamed again, and all rational thought fled. He had to save her. He peered over the edge of the landing and saw Ruggero in the living room, taking cover to the left of the base of the stairs. "Cover me now!" he yelled at Ruggero as he darted forward.

Ruggero stood up and fired through the banister as Enrico crawled up the stairs, trying to duck low enough to evade Ruggero's fire.

Veltroni took a bullet in the leg, but he didn't stop firing. He fell down on one knee, and his shots canted lower. Bullets tore into the wood next to Enrico, who flattened himself against the stairs and the wall. He was pinned.

Enrico sighted the Glock at the man above him, but he didn't have a clean kill shot. Not unless he moved to the center of the stairs. He had only one chance.

He took a deep breath, loosened his grip on the gun, then tightened it. He looked up, memorizing where Veltroni was.

In one swift motion, he rolled sideways, snapping the gun to the point he'd memorized. He squeezed off two shots before he landed on his side against the banister. His partially healed rib cracked, the pain sharp and immediate. Veltroni choked and fell forward, tumbling down two steps. He'd done it. Scrambling to his feet, he charged up the stairs.

And straight toward the barrel of Dario's gun.

CHAPTER 36

Dario twisted toward the sound of Massimo's gunfire, taking his eyes off Kate and Carlo. Massimo groaned and slumped forward, then Enrico Lucchesi rushed up the stairs toward him. Dario retreated through the doorway, straight into Kate, who hurtled into him.

She nearly knocked him off his feet, but he grabbed onto the doorway with one hand and shoved her hard with his gun hand, sending her back into the room. He saw murder in Enrico's eyes. His only hope was to put Kate between them.

He spun and wrapped an arm around her chest, pulling her back against him, her arms pinned to her sides. Perhaps he could talk his way through this. Perhaps he'd survive, as long as he had the woman. And as long as Enrico didn't see him as a threat.

$\infty$$\alpha$

Enrico stalked toward Dario and Kate, holding his gun straight out in front of him, the muzzle leveled at Dario's head. "Let go of her. Now."

Dario shook his head and retreated farther inside the room. Enrico followed. His eyes flicked to Carlo, who was standing by the bed, close to the nightstand.

"Come away from there," Enrico said to him. "Into the center of the room."

"Shall I put my hands on my head?" Carlo said, his voice a lazy taunt.

Enrico risked a long glance at him. "Do it."

Carlo moved to comply. When Enrico returned his attention to Dario, he heard a noise coming from his left and turned back to see Carlo yank the nightstand drawer open. Reaching inside, Carlo tore out a gun taped underneath the top. Raising the gun, he pointed it at Enrico, who shifted his position so he was midway between Dario and Carlo. Ruggero came up on Enrico's right through the open door and trained his Beretta on Dario.

Enrico quickly shifted his full focus to Carlo. He barely met Kate's eyes—he couldn't chance being distracted by her. All he could risk was a glance that told him she was bleeding, but seemed largely unhurt. He had to trust that Ruggero could keep her safe.

Carlo smiled when Enrico met his eyes. "So here we are at last."

Enrico held his gaze. "It didn't have to be this way."

"This was... inevitable. Despite what my darling Toni wanted. You have never stopped wanting to kill me. Just as I have never stopped wanting to kill you."

"You murdered my family."

"And you and yours threatened everything I hold dear."

Enrico snorted. "A few percentage points was not going to make you weak."

"Obeying your family's pressure to go back to the old ways was going to do just that. I couldn't give in on the money *and* the drugs." He gestured with his gun up and down the length of Enrico's body. "Look where your precious principles have left you. Your *cosca* is too weak to challenge mine. It is only a matter of time before I own the entire lake and all of Milan. Soon, all of the north."

A hot coal of anger burned in Enrico's chest, but he tamped it down. He couldn't afford to lose control. "How petty you are. You want vengeance over *money*. I want mine for the wrongs done to my blood."

Carlo's composure wavered; his face darkened. "What about Toni! You spat all over her grave." He took a deep breath. "I should never have agreed to the marriage. You and Rinaldo *lied* to me and hid your bastard from me."

"I'm not proud of that."

"You lie. It's what you do best."

"What else could I do? You would have hunted all of us down like animals."

Carlo laughed. "Rinaldo finally paid his price."

The coal in Enrico's chest flamed hotter. He wanted to roar out his rage at Carlo, wanted to rip him limb from limb. But Kate was there; he couldn't act the savage in front of her, however much he wanted to.

Carlo cocked his head to the side. "Nothing to say? You were so full of yourself the last time we met. Did you use up your entire store of wit?" He waited for a reply; when none came, he continued. "I was quite disappointed I couldn't eliminate your bastard son as well. My men have been unable to locate him. Apparently he is somewhere remote and out of communication. An assignment, we were told. So, so lucky," Carlo said, shaking his head slowly. "So imagine my pleasure when I discovered that eliminating this troublesome... *puttana* here"—he gestured to Kate—"also eliminates your heir. Imagine how I felt." Enrico's stomach roiled, but still he said nothing, not trusting himself to speak. He concentrated on breathing, in and out.

Carlo smiled. "I felt happy. Finally at peace. Toni's honor would be avenged. And you would suffer to the end of your days, however short they would be."

Enrico found his voice at last. "You are talking about killing two innocents. Do you think Toni would feel honored by that?"

Carlo's brows shot up. "Innocent, our dear Kate? She murdered her own husband."

"He earned it," Kate spat. When she struggled against Dario's hold, he pressed his gun to her temple.

"Be quiet," he warned her.

Enrico's voice, cold and low, cut through the room. "If anyone here has a right to vendetta, it is me. You killed my mother and my brothers. You tortured and murdered my father." Enrico's voice shook when he continued. "You took pleasure in it." Enrico heard Kate's gasp at his words, but he couldn't look at her, couldn't risk her sympathy making him break down.

A slight smile curved Carlo's lips. "How could I not? Rinaldo earned his death long ago. He tried to make me look like a fool."

"And so this is *my* punishment, for making you the fool in front of La Provincia?"

Carlo's eyes went dead, his face still. "That is not what happened."

"Is that so? I heard laughter. Laughter at *you*."

So fast he almost didn't see it, Carlo's arm came up, the gun aimed directly at Enrico's chest. Kate screamed and Enrico fired. Carlo fell to the floor, blood pouring from his right shoulder, the gun falling from his hand.

Enrico stepped toward Carlo, coming to stand over him. "You killed everyone I loved. You pushed me into a life I never wanted for myself or my children." Enrico's throat tightened, his voice thickening. "You have taken everything from me, Carlo, but that stops today."

He smiled up at Enrico. "But it does not end here. You will owe my son a father."

"I think it a fair exchange for his hand."

Carlo's eyes widened. Enrico smiled. "He never told you that, did he? Yes, my father wanted to take the whole hand, to make you pay for what you did to my mother, to my brothers. But I stopped him." He glanced at Dario, then looked back at Carlo. "Dario is not the weak man you think he is. He never was. He knows when to fight, and he knows when to stop. It is a pity you never learned the difference."

Carlo looked at Dario; something Enrico didn't understand passed between them in that look. Then Carlo's eyes turned back to Enrico, and he smiled up at him and laughed, wincing with pain when his shoulder moved. "You are so blind, in so many ways, Lucchesi. You do not even know where you are weak. The day will soon arrive when you are overrun. A fine day it will be."

Enrico raised his gun. "I have owed you this bullet for twenty-eight years. It is well past time you received it." He squeezed the trigger, saw Carlo jerk once, then watched dark blood well out of a hole in his forehead.

It was finished, over at last. Something coiled tight inside Enrico let go. His eyes welled with tears, his throat closed up. Papà should have lived to see this day. If only he'd acted sooner....

Wiping his eyes on his sleeve, Enrico turned to Dario, who was still holding the gun to Kate's temple. He took a steadying breath. "Am I right about you, Dario? Will you return the mercy I showed you?"

Dario looked down at his father, his face contorted with a mix of emotions. Then he nodded and released Kate, putting up his gun. "It ends here," he said, his voice choked. He took a breath, then looked hard at Enrico. "But a price must be paid."

"Name it."

"Two million euros, plus your holdings in Rome."

Enrico blinked, staggered at what Dario was asking for. He countered. "Two million euros, plus the meatpacking business in Milan."

"I was not aware this would be a negotiation. I have named my blood price."

Enrico held his gaze. "And I have just made you the head of the Andretti *cosca*." He paused before his next words, treading gently. "Something we both know Carlo never intended."

Dario's mouth twisted. "Two million euros, half of what you hold in Milan, and half of the lake."

Enrico almost laughed. Dario was a cocky bastard. "You are outgunned, and it would be very much to my advantage to eliminate you. Must I?"

Dario shrugged, a glint coming into his eyes. "I had to try. I am my father's son after all." He chuckled, staring into the middle distance. "I never thought I would say that." Then he looked back at Enrico. "Two million euros, the meatpacking business, and the Turro district."

"Done." This would cost him dearly, and it would weaken the *cosca*. But if it brought peace, the price was worth it. He held out his hand. "Are we friends now?"

Dario took his hand, holding his gaze. "We are not friends. But neither are we enemies."

Enrico felt the missing finger in Dario's grip. "I shall have to settle for that."

With a nod, Dario let go of Enrico's hand. "My debt to you has been repaid."

Enrico watched him leave the room. Then he turned his eyes to Kate, free to look at her at last. She was only half dressed, blood clotted on her cheek, her hair wild about her face. A wicked cut spilled blood down her forearm. She started to tremble when he looked at her, then she ran into his arms. He pulled her close, squeezing her tight. Tears streamed down her face. "I love you, I love you, Rico," she said, choking out the words.

He looked at Ruggero over her shoulder, signaling him to leave. Once Ruggero was gone, Enrico let his own tears fall, for Kate, for his father, for Paolo. He pulled back from her, taking her face in his hands. She'd forgiven him. He hadn't dared hope for it. "I was so afraid I'd never see you again."

She stretched up on her toes to kiss him. "I knew you'd come for me."

"You did?"

Kate squinted up at him. She swayed in his arms, and he tightened them around her. "I'm not going to last much longer," she said, then she was dead weight in his arms. She'd collapsed.

CHAPTER 37

Fear spiked through Enrico's chest. Kate was breathing, but he couldn't seem to keep her awake for long, no matter what he did to rouse her.

Leaving Ruggero in charge of cleaning up the scene, Enrico grabbed Tommaso, who drove him and Kate to Dottor Beltrami's clinic. Enrico called Beltrami en route and explained Kate's condition.

The cut on her face was deep, but tiny. The one on her arm was more worrisome. Enrico applied considerable pressure to slow the bleeding, but it wouldn't quite stop.

Kate didn't seem to care. She was still dazed when they got to the clinic. He carried her inside, a pillowcase wrapped around her arm. Beltrami met him at the door.

"Something's wrong with her. She's been in and out."

"Was there a head injury?" Beltrami asked as Enrico laid her on the bed.

"Not that I know of."

The doctor motioned Enrico away. He took Kate's pulse, then pushed one of her eyelids up with his thumb and shined a penlight in it. He checked the other eye.

"I think she's been drugged," Beltrami said. "Her pupils are dilated." He examined her head, and found the bump at her temple. "Someone struck her, hard." He frowned. "I'll take an x-ray of this. If the *signora* has no skull fracture, we may be able to avoid the hospital."

Enrico bent over Kate and winced. Beltrami put a hand on his upper arm. "Are you hurt?"

"Cracked rib." He let out a little huff of amusement. "Same one I got shot in."

"I'll look at it later."

Enrico shook Kate gently. *"Mia cara.* Wake up, *per favore."*

Finally she opened her eyes and looked at him. "What?"

"We're at the clinic." Her eyes immediately started to close, and Enrico shook her again. "Kate, did they give you something?"

She looked at him, her brow creased. "What?"

"Did they drug you?"

Her face relaxed and she nodded. "Roofies."

"Roofies?" It was Enrico's turn to be confused.

Beltrami leaned in, shaking her again before her eyes closed completely. "Rohypnol?" he asked.

She mumbled yes. She was about to close her eyes again, but she fought to stay conscious. "The baby—will it be all right?"

Beltrami nodded. "I think so."

Enrico pulled him aside after Kate's eyes closed again. "Is that the truth?"

"Most likely the baby won't be affected by a one-time exposure." Then the doctor added, "She's strong, Don Lucchesi, and she's young. If something does go wrong...." Beltrami frowned and looked down at the tile beneath their feet. "She can have another."

Enrico nodded, but the doctor's words weren't much consolation. He'd suffered through enough miscarriages with Antonella to know that it was still a death. A death of hope, of possibility. The baby wasn't just a maybe, a could be. This child already existed for both of them. Kate had already been through so much. Would their relationship survive such a loss?

ℰℭ

Ruggero, Claudio, and Santino stayed behind to clean up—despite the gloves, they wiped down and threw all their weapons into the woods. Then they gathered up Paolo's body and wrapped it in a sheet. Ruggero did his best with some bleach he found in the kitchen to erase the traces of Paolo's and the *signora*'s blood, but it was a difficult task. Paolo's DNA wasn't on file with the *polizia*, but the *signora*'s was, so Ruggero took Carlo's clothes in case any of her blood had spilled on them. At the last minute, he thought to take the water glass, the pitcher, and the ashtray as well.

Dario Andretti sat on the stairs next to Massimo's body, waiting for them to leave. He pulled out his mobile phone at one point, but Ruggero gave him a hard look until he put it back in his pocket. Regardless of what Enrico had decided, Ruggero would put a bullet in Dario if need be. They both knew that.

When they were done, Ruggero walked to the foot of the stairs. "We're leaving."

Dario pulled out his phone. "May I?"

Ruggero nodded. "I haven't left anything for the *carabinieri*."

"Doesn't matter." Dario gave him a half smile. "I'm torching the place."

With a last glance around, Ruggero left the house, the scent of bleach and gunpowder burning in his nose.

They tossed the water pitcher, the glass, and the ashtray into the woods several miles away. Carlo's clothes they would burn. And Paolo they would leave in an alley in Milan. Ruggero regretted that, but it was Paolo's laxness that got them into this mess. In a few hours, he would place an anonymous call to tip off the *polizia* to Paolo's body. It was the best he could do for the boy.

ℰℭ

Enrico didn't relax until Beltrami had x-rayed Kate's head and hooked her up to machines to monitor her heart rate and her breathing.

"How is she?"

Beltrami looked at the readout. "Her oxygen level is a little low, but it's adequate." He turned away from Kate and placed the x-ray on the light box on the wall. "No fracture. She could have a concussion, so ideally she should be awake, but with the drug...." He shrugged helplessly. "At least it will make it easier for her when I put the stitches in."

The doctor worked quickly, using surgical glue to close the wound on her face, but he had to use many stitches on her arm. "I'm afraid she'll have a scar. I'm no plastic surgeon."

"Her face will be fine, though? I'm sure that'll be her major concern."

"The wound on her cheek was small, so there should be no noticeable scarring." Beltrami motioned Enrico up onto a table. "Now let's take a look at you."

Enrico shrugged out of his jacket and shirt. Beltrami prodded his ribs, listened to his lungs, then x-rayed him. "Will I live?" Enrico joked, as the doctor looked over the x-ray.

"*Sì*, but two ribs are cracked. I'll give you something for the pain."

Enrico watched Kate while Beltrami rummaged through a locked cabinet. She looked so pale, so still. If it weren't for the beeping of the monitor and the light rise and fall of her chest, he'd have thought she was dead. The thought pierced him—she'd come so close. So very close. It was all his fault for not acting more decisively. Was he being a fool all over again, trusting Dario to keep his word?

Passing up the opportunity to crush the Andretti *cosca*, to absorb all their territory—that certainly was foolishness of the highest degree. Don Battista would question his judgment. And many others would see his choice as weak.

And yet—Carlo was Benedetto's brother. Showing Dario mercy—surely that would be to Enrico's advantage somehow. Or at least he could use that as his excuse.

The simple truth was that he was still, after all this time, not a killer by choice, but only by necessity. For a Mafia don, that was a horrible liability.

His thoughts turned to Dom. Antonio had him under guard in Milan, in

272

one of the safe houses. Enrico closed his eyes, the knot in his stomach growing larger. How would he ever face Francesca and the children again? He was their godfather. Dom was the closest thing he had to a brother, he was almost all the blood family Enrico had left. Wasn't there a special place in Hell for those who committed fratricide?

But what other choice was there? Dom had plotted with Carlo. Dom had wanted all of them dead, and without dirtying his hands directly. All so he could "innocently" take over the *cosca*.

Enrico burned at the betrayal. Never would he have done the same to Dom. Never. Dom tried to justify what he'd done, he tried to claim he was doing it for everyone's good. Though Enrico would have liked to dismiss that notion outright, there was some truth to it. He hadn't been the best steward of the *cosca*'s interests. He'd let his heart rule instead of his head. In a way, he had forced Dom's hand.

But he couldn't live with any other course; he couldn't have walked away and abandoned Kate to the Andrettis. Somehow, he was going to have to make up for what he'd done. Though there'd be no bringing Paolo back. That price would always be with him. Just like the ghosts of Fiammetta, Veronica, and Franco. Soon Dom would join that list. The people he'd irrevocably wronged.

One of Kate's monitors began to beep frantically, catapulting him out of his thoughts. He jumped off the table and rushed to her bedside. Beltrami was already there.

"What's wrong? I thought everything was okay."

"Her heart is racing." Beltrami stared at the monitors, watching the readout. Kate started thrashing, then she came awake with a gasp and sat up. "Let go of me!" she yelled.

Enrico touched her arm. "It's okay, Kate. It's all over."

"It is?" She looked at him in disbelief.

He pulled up a chair and took her hand. "Tell me what happened."

Kate recounted what she could remember, including Dom's betrayal. "He said I was a fool to doubt you. And when the guy who wants you dead defends you, how could I not believe it?"

Enrico's chest grew tight. He asked Beltrami to leave the room before speaking. "*Cara*, I could never kill you." He smiled. "This is going to sound horrible, but that has been the problem all along. I could not tell you who I was, I could not let you go, and I could not kill you if you could not accept me. I have never been faced with so many bad choices."

Kate looked at his somber face and she cracked a smile. "I never imagined that *not* wanting to kill me would be a problem."

Enrico started to laugh. He shook his head. "I lead some life, yes?"

"And now, so do I." She squeezed his hand.

Enrico's heart sped up. "What are you saying?"

She held his gaze, her eyes tender. "Don Lucchesi, will you do me the great honor of being my husband?"

She wanted to be his wife after all, after all the lies he'd told, after everything that had happened. "I shall." He kissed her, making the touch of his lips soft, lingering. Then he kissed her cheek and stroked her injured temple, his fingers lightly passing over the lump beneath the skin. She nuzzled into his hand.

"What are you going to do about Dom?" she asked.

"I know what I *have* to do. I know what he tried to do to us, what he did to my father. And yet...." He looked down at their joined hands. "Since Primo and Mario were killed, Dom has been my brother."

Kate was silent for a moment, then she said, "Has *he* treated *you* like a brother?"

Enrico couldn't look at her. "Let's not talk about him anymore."

"I will support whatever decision you make." Her voice was soft. "But don't forget why I'm lying here."

He burned with shame at the reminder. "I won't." He had to call Antonio soon. He could just give the order, but he wasn't going to do that. He would let Dom say his piece first. It was the least he could do. He turned to her. "You do realize what you're urging me to do?"

She nodded, her face somber. "I never thought I'd feel like this, but I understand now. You don't live in the same world I grew up in. You never have."

Sadness overwhelmed him. "I regret that our child will grow up this way."

"At least our baby will have two devoted parents. That's more than many children have."

He smiled and kissed her cheek. "You've gotten much better at consoling me."

She laughed. "I had nowhere to go but up."

Enrico nodded. He should've been happy. But Dom was a weight hanging over him.

He got up and wandered around the room, stretching his back and belatedly remembering his ribs, physically unable to remain in one spot.

Kate must have guessed at his discomfort because she said, "*Mio caro*, you can go. I'm fine."

Enrico called Beltrami back in. "When can she leave?"

"I'm going to watch her until the drug wears off, then I'll send her home."

"See?" Kate said. "I'll be in good hands."

Enrico walked over to Kate's bedside. "You're sure?"

"Go on." She shooed him away. "You'll drive me crazy if you stay."

He kissed her on the forehead, then planted a quick kiss on her belly. He turned to Beltrami. "Call me if anything happens."

Enrico found Tommaso in the car out front. He instructed him to go inside and sit with Kate. "Guard her with your life. If anything happens to her, yours won't be worth living." His voice was sharp.

Tommaso nodded his grizzled head. "*Sì, capo.*"

Enrico took a breath, then patted the guard's shoulder. "*Scusa,* I'm—"

Tommaso cut him off with a smile. "We're all on edge, *signore.* It's been a hard night."

Enrico watched the guard walk inside, then he called Ruggero to pick him up. He snapped the phone shut and waited. He still didn't know if he could do it. He might have to ask Ruggero to step in. A good *capo* would never do such a thing. But he wasn't a good *capo.* He had just proven that in abundance.

೭൧ೞ

Ruggero pulled up shortly after Enrico placed the call. They drove in silence for a while, then Ruggero said, "I did my best to remove all traces of the *signora*'s blood. Dario says he will burn the house."

"*Bene.*" Enrico tapped a thumbnail against his lower lip, debating whether to make his request. He could feel Ruggero looking at him, waiting.

It was Ruggero who broke the silence. "This will be hard. There's been much love between you."

"And apparently much hate. Don Battista warned me."

"You've made your decision?"

Enrico looked out the window at the darkness surrounding them. "I am weak."

Ruggero huffed. "You are a man of principle. Like your father."

"I haven't been a good *capo* lately. I haven't been the *capo* this *cosca* needs." He looked at his hands in his lap. "I should have ceded to Dom when we first quarreled over Kate. All of this could have been avoided."

Ruggero snorted. "Carlo's been spoiling for your blood for years. And Don Domenico...." He trailed off. "Maybe that could've been avoided. But he made his choice."

"He has a point though. I was willing—*am* willing—to give up everything for this woman. The 'Ndrangheta is supposed to be first for me."

Ruggero said nothing for a while, then he sighed. "Don Lucchesi, you're good man. I'd rather follow you than many others. Outside my blood family, there's no one I trust more." He looked over and met Enrico's eyes. "There's a flaw in Don Domenico. He might have made a good *capo,* but he's a failure as a man. Money isn't everything in this life. Sometimes I think it's very little."

"You're quite philosophical tonight," Enrico said, rather astonished by this speech.

"I'm not finished." He grinned at Enrico. "A man's riches are this: his friends, his woman, his children, and any relatives who don't wish to stab him in the back. After that come his health and then his money. That is something

Don Domenico doesn't understand. But you do."

Enrico smiled. "When you put it like that, I don't feel like such a fool."

"If you've ever been a fool, Don Lucchesi, it was always for the right reasons."

"I never expected such a sentiment from you."

Ruggero shrugged. "The man who does my job is not always me."

So that's how he did it. There were two Ruggeros. Enrico sighed. He was going to need to follow suit, wasn't he? The man he needed to be in the future had better be a lot more ruthless. Or Kate and their children would suffer.

He had to rebuild the *cosca,* and he had to keep it strong by whatever means necessary. If he wanted to be a man of principle, he was going to have to pick his battles. If he could win the biggest one, the battle over the codes—that was the battle that mattered, the one that would do the most good in the world. Beyond his children, it would be his legacy.

They pulled up to the safe house where Franco Trucco had met his end. They got out of the car, the doors slamming behind them, fallen leaves and gravel crunching underfoot as they walked to the door. Enrico hunched his shoulders against the chilly edge in the air. Winter was coming.

Inside, Antonio was reading a book—one on economics that Enrico had recommended to him—and sitting in front of Dom, who was tied to a chair in the little kitchen. He looked sweaty and disheveled. Perspiration ringed his neck and under his arms. A large bruise blackened the skin below his right eye. The dread on his face made Enrico look away. "Rico, I beg you—"

"Stop." Enrico's hand chopped the air. He turned to Antonio and Ruggero. "Please give us some privacy."

They both nodded, then went into the other room where there was a threadbare sofa and a small TV. Ruggero put the TV on, and Antonio picked up his book. Enrico wasn't fooled. He was sure they'd hear everything he and Dom said. He just didn't want them to see the anguish on his face. He ought to be the other Enrico now, the impassive Mafia don, but killing his best friend, his cousin, his second in command—that should mean something. And he should feel it.

Enrico straddled the hardback chair Antonio had been using. He didn't look at Dom directly; instead he took a moment to compose himself. When he met Dom's eyes, he wasn't prepared for the remorse he saw there.

"Rico, you came. I wasn't sure you would."

"Do you think me such a coward?"

Dom shook his head hastily. "I know this must pain you. That's what I meant."

"You think this *pains* me?" His voice was a stiletto. "You have torn out my heart."

Dom broke Enrico's gaze. "I am sorry." He looked down at the cracked linoleum. "I don't know what came over me. How I could have betrayed you—"

"Greed is what came over you. Even though you have more than enough. Even though I would've given you whatever you asked of me."

Dom's face twisted with anguish. "I wish I could take it all back."

"You nearly got me killed. You allowed Carlo to torture and kill my father—your uncle. Do you know what Carlo did to him?" When Dom shook his head, Enrico continued, his voice falling as he struggled for control. "He crushed his fingers, then cut them off, every one. Then his hands." Dom moaned, and Enrico's face grew hot. *The nerve of him, acting like he cares.* "On top of that, you put Kate and my child in the hands of that monster. Thank God he was intent on having her instead of killing her."

"I'm so very sorry." Dom bowed his head, tears streaming down his face. "I beg you for mercy. I beg you for exile."

"What mercy was there for my father? Your uncle? Your *blood*?" Enrico slammed his fist on the table. "God *damn* you! How dare you ask me for mercy!"

"I beg you." Dom choked on the words. "Do you want to be the murderer of your godchildren's father?"

Enrico burned. Dom was using the one card left to him: guilt. And it was working. Francesca and the children trusted him to watch over them if anything happened to Dom. Dom's sons would someday run the *cosca*, if Enrico failed to have sons of his own. How could he ever look them in the eyes again?

"Please, I *beg* you. I was only looking out for the *cosca*. I was only thinking of the future."

Enrico heard a light step behind them and looked up. Antonio stood next to him, his gun held loosely at his side. "I'm tired of hearing this." He raised the gun and pointed it at Dom's face. "May I?"

Enrico touched Antonio's other arm and shook his head. "No."

Antonio's eyes turned to him but he didn't lower the gun. "Look at him, Don Lucchesi. The only thing he's sorry for is getting caught."

Enrico's eyes slipped from Antonio's to Dom's.

"Rico, please, you don't have to do this. Send me away. Strip me of my fortune. Just let me take Francesca and the children."

Enrico closed his eyes. Dom's suggestion appealed to the part of him that didn't want to believe Dom had betrayed him for greed. And yet—Antonio was right. Dom didn't understand what he'd done. He didn't feel the horror of it, the enormity of it. He didn't feel the loss of Enrico the way Enrico felt the loss of Dom. He didn't care the way Enrico did.

Had Dom always had this hole where his heart should've been? Had Dom always been able to hide this part himself? Or had Enrico just been blind?

Enrico remembered the difficult days in the wake of his mother's and brothers' deaths. The confrontation with his father over Dario. The hasty promise to his father, the confusing rush of taking his vows to the 'Ndrangheta. Dom had been at his side then, supporting him. Had he been blind to who Dom was then? No.

But shortly thereafter Dom's first wife and child died. He'd been heartbroken at the loss of his beloved bride and son during childbirth.

Enrico looked at Dom. "You weren't always this way. Losing Vanda and Angelo changed you." Dom evaded his eyes. "Is that when you hardened against everyone you loved? Is that when it happened?" Enrico's voice was soft, but the stiletto's tip danced along his words.

Dom's face crumpled and he looked down. When he spoke, his voice was thick with tears. "Love is a terrible thing. All it does is hurt you in the end."

A lump formed in Enrico's throat. Hadn't he said something similar to Ruggero just a few hours ago? He got up and walked into the other room, then went outside. He closed the door behind him, swallowing great lungfuls of the crisp night air.

He couldn't do it. He couldn't. Dom was already living in a horrible hell, and he, Dom's best friend, hadn't recognized it. All these years, Dom had been alone with his grief, his isolation. And Enrico, like everyone else, had assumed he'd recovered because he'd taken another wife and had other children. He'd assumed that Dom's grief was nothing but a buried memory. But grief, that most human of emotions, had warped him, had destroyed his very humanity. It had left him a shell of a man.

He heard the door open and recognized the sound of Antonio's step. He looked over his shoulder, saw the grim expression on Antonio's face. "What is it?"

"It has to be done, Don Lucchesi. Can't you see he's only sorry for himself?"

"I know that. But still... he is my brother."

"Would Primo or Mario have done this to you?"

The vehemence in Antonio's voice surprised him. "You seem more angered by this than I am."

"My feelings are not as mixed." Antonio's voice softened. "If you cannot be angry on your own behalf, think of the *signora* and your child. Think of your father."

"Enough." He didn't need Antonio's reminders.

"I've said my piece." Antonio went inside.

Enrico took a deep breath, then slowly let it out in a visible cloud on the night air. Antonio was right. But could he pull the trigger?

He had to. He was the *capo* of the Lucchesi family. It was his duty.

He spun around and strode inside. Ruggero was still on the couch watching TV. "I need a gun," Enrico said to him.

Ruggero pulled out a pair of gloves matching his own and handed them to

Enrico, who put them on. Then he took a snub-nosed revolver from his pocket. A cheap throwaway gun, perfect for a job like this.

Gun in hand, Enrico walked into the kitchen. Tears rolled down Dom's face. "I beg you. Please don't do this."

Enrico raised the revolver, his sight blurring at the edges from unshed tears. "You were my brother, as much as Primo, as much as Mario. I hate you for making me do this."

"Then don't. Let me leave. I will never bother you again." Dom paused, his eyes holding Enrico's. His voice hoarsened. "I swear it on Vanda and Angelo. I swear it."

Damn him. Damn Domenico Lucchesi to Hell. Tears threatened to stream down Enrico's face. He willed his voice to stay steady. "I've already learned my lesson about traitors. Mercy doesn't beget mercy." His finger tightened on the trigger.

"Before you do it, may I ask something of you?" Dom's voice was surprisingly steady.

Enrico nodded. Dom held his eyes. "I beg you to take the vow of *comparaggio* with my sons."

The lump in Enrico's throat nearly strangled him. Dom was asking him to be their father in his stead, to take them as his sons and never betray them. He didn't know what to say.

"Please Rico."

"Why?"

"Because you are the most honorable man I know. The only one I would entrust them to." He paused. "Will you do it?"

"I swear it." He couldn't stop a few tears from falling. *Damn you, Dom. Damn you.* Enrico took a steadying breath, then he squeezed the trigger.

Dom's body jerked, crimson blooming across his chest. Enrico took a step forward and put another bullet in him. He swallowed hard, looking at the body. Antonio stepped around him and felt for the pulse under Dom's jaw. Dom's open eyes stared at Enrico. "He's dead," Antonio said.

Enrico nodded dumbly, his throat too constricted to speak. He turned and breathed deeply. When Antonio touched him on the forearm, Enrico jerked away. "Leave me." He was damned. Would God ever forgive him for this?

He stood alone in the kitchen for a few moments, then set the gun on the table beside Dom. It was done, this most horrible thing, and there was no use grieving it. What other choice had he had? Dom knew the rules, he knew the price he'd pay for treason. They all did.

And still it cut Enrico to the bone to enforce that price.

He wiped his eyes, staring up at the ceiling, wondering why God had cursed him this way. "I must deserve it," he whispered to himself. He waited for an answer, some sign, but he heard nothing other than the inane laugh track from the show Ruggero was watching on TV. *Maybe that is a sign in itself.*

Quickly crossing himself, he swore to do penance. He'd look after Dom's family, he'd make sure they wanted for nothing. He'd take the vow of *comparaggio*. And he'd take Dom's sons into the *cosca*, if that's what they wanted.

Which reminded him—he had a job to do. He was the *capo*, and he needed to attend to business. He walked out to the living room. The men looked up at him. "Ruggero, please accompany me outside."

Ruggero followed him out the door. "What is it, Don Lucchesi?"

Enrico clasped his hands behind his back. He'd thought about this earlier, almost mentioned it in the car, but he'd decided to wait until it was official. But now it was time. "I need a new *capo di società*. One I can trust without reservation. You are such a man."

Ruggero smiled and inclined his head. "I'm pleased you think so. But my place is at your side, guarding you." He put his hands in his pockets. "Besides, you need a man with a head for business."

"Unfortunately, I can't wait to find such a person."

Ruggero raised an eyebrow. "With respect, *capo*, perhaps you can't see it." Ruggero motioned with his head toward the safe house. "The man you need is in there."

"Antonio?"

Ruggero nodded. "He's no longer a boy."

Enrico mulled it over. Yes, Antonio was a young man now. A smart loyal man with a generous heart. A man whose love he could never doubt. That was the most important thing in the end. Hadn't Dom just proven that?

He left Ruggero and found Antonio in the kitchen wiping the gun down, just in case. "We need to talk."

Antonio nodded. His eyes met and held Enrico's. "If you're angry with me, remember that my first duty is to protect you. And I've done so."

Ruggero was right. Nothing of the boy lingered in Antonio's face, in the hardness of his eyes, in the set of his jaw. "I need to replace Dom. Will you consider taking over?"

Antonio's brow furrowed. "You're offering me *capo di società*?"

Enrico nodded. It felt right, good, to be making this choice. To acknowledge how important Antonio was to him. "I would be honored to have you by my side."

Antonio grinned. "I accept." Then his face grew somber. "Did you mean what you said to Don Domenico? Mercy doesn't beget mercy?"

Enrico shook his head. "I don't know. I'm not sure I know anything anymore." He paused. "I never thought the day would come when I'd have to kill my own blood." He looked up, holding Antonio's eyes with his. "Are you certain you want this?"

"I am. I've seen the worst tonight. But it had to be done."

Enrico leaned forward, clasping Antonio in a loose embrace. He kissed both his cheeks. "Antonio Legato, you are now *capo di società* of the Lucchesi *cosca*. Do you swear fealty to me as your *capo* and to this *cosca*, above all others?"

"*Sì.*" Antonio returned the embrace and kissed Enrico on both cheeks, then he dropped to one knee and kissed the signet ring on Enrico's right hand, the ring emblazoned with the Lucchesi crest. "I swear it."

Enrico looked at Ruggero, noticing him in the doorway. "You're the witness." He looked back at Antonio. "Tomorrow we assemble the underbosses and spread the word." He clapped Antonio on the back. "There may be opposition, but I'll make clear my feelings on the matter." He looked down at Dom's lifeless body. "I don't want to be forced to kill my godsons. No one must know of Dom's betrayal or the price he paid for it. I'll swear Kate to secrecy. We four must be the only ones to ever know."

"What about Dario?" Antonio asked.

Enrico shrugged. "He's unlikely to speak of it."

Ruggero's lips tightened into a thin line. "I hate loose ends."

"As do I. But we must take the risk." He turned to Antonio. "You know what to do with the body. Leave it where it'll be found soon."

Ruggero coughed to get attention. "What about Tommaso? Certainly Paolo mentioned what he saw when Dom took Kate."

"I'll speak to him. If he knows, he'll swear to me."

Ruggero still looked troubled. "What?" Enrico asked.

"You're missing an opportunity to remind the men about loyalty. To remind them what happens to traitors."

"I'll tell them about Trucco. And that will provide a good reason for the choice of Antonio as Dom's replacement."

"Who'll replace Trucco?" Antonio asked.

Enrico shook his head. "I'll act as *contabile* until I find a suitable replacement."

"It is done then," Ruggero said, his voice soft.

A smile creased Enrico's face and he put a hand on each of their shoulders. "And we all survived. I wasn't sure we would."

Antonio looked at Enrico, his face shining with admiration. "I never doubted you, Don Lucchesi."

Enrico chuckled. "Then you are the only one." He caught sight of Dom again, slumped in the chair, his open eyes staring, blood dripping down his chest. Enrico's grin faded. He could have been in Dom's place, would have been if Dom's plan had succeeded. And yet....

Enrico stepped away from the two men and bent down. He reached out and closed Dom's eyelids. It was the decent thing to do. It was the last decent thing Enrico could ever do for him.

CHAPTER 38

After the monitors confirmed that Kate's breathing was normal, Dottor Beltrami released her, and Enrico and Ruggero took her home.

Kate and Enrico were finally in bed, freshly showered and curled around each other, when she said, her voice soft, "Tell me about the judge and his family."

"To prove my innocence, I have to confess to something else."

She raised her head, one hand pressed against her chest. She wasn't going to like this, was she? "What happened?"

He sighed. "It is a sad story. And I am not proud of it."

She held his eyes. "I need to know the truth, no matter how ugly."

"If you insist." He sat up and settled against the pillow behind his back. "One of my men, Sergio Grantini, thought he could play both sides. He started working for Carlo as well. When Carlo and I both came up for indictment before Judge Dinelli, Carlo saw his chance to escape the charges and put me in jail."

"How does Sergio fit in?"

"Sergio's gun—with his prints on it—would be used to kill the judge and planted at the scene. Sergio would ask for immunity in return for testifying against me. He would say I ordered the hit."

"How did you find out about this?"

"Sergio started driving a car he could not possibly afford, so Ruggero had him tailed. When he learned Sergio was meeting with Carlo, we questioned him. He confessed it all. In exchange, he asked for mercy for his family."

"What about Dom's family? You're not—"

"Of course not! They are my family too." He hissed in frustration. "I considered letting him go tonight. *That* is how much of a monster I am."

Kate stroked his bare shoulder. "I'm sorry. It's just..." She shook her head. "You live such a different life. I'm still getting used to it."

He crossed his arms. "I wish you had more faith in me. I am not Carlo."

Kate's eyes pricked with tears. "I know." She kissed his cheek. "I do know it."

He let out a breath, then put an arm around her, pulling her close. But her mind wouldn't shut off. "Where is Sergio buried?"

"He is at the bottom of the lake, weighted down. I am sure there is nothing but bones now."

She glared at him. "You say that so cavalierly."

"Was I supposed to go to jail for something I did not do? He *betrayed* me." He took a breath, then his voice lost all traces of anger. "Dom accused me of being softhearted when I spared Sergio's family. And perhaps I was. But they were innocents."

She held his gaze. He was still holding something back. "It occurs to me you benefit otherwise by keeping them alive."

"What?" he asked, startled.

"As long as they're alive, it looks like Sergio has run off. That he wasn't executed as a traitor."

"That was part of my thinking." He eyed her. "Maybe Dom was right. Maybe you *were* working for Carlo." The lightness in his voice told her he was joking.

"I'm not an idiot."

"Far from it. The way your mind works, it is as if you were born to do this."

Kate didn't want to agree, but she couldn't argue. "What if Sergio's boy discovers what you've done?"

Enrico shrugged. "He will have the right to vendetta. But only Ruggero, you, and I know what happened, now that Dom is dead."

"Surely, someone else knows. Who tailed Sergio? Your men aren't stupid."

"But they are well-paid."

"It wasn't enough for Sergio."

"It should have been."

Kate sighed and scrubbed her hands through her hair. "How can you stand it? You can never trust anyone."

When he didn't answer, she looked at him. He had the oddest expression on his face. "What?" she asked softly.

"That is why I need you, Kate. I need someone I can trust unequivocally."

She held his eyes. "So do I."

Neither one said anything for a while, then she said, "There's something I still don't understand. How does Sergio's death prove you didn't order the hit?"

"Because he was dead before it happened."

"So how did Carlo have the gun?"

"The plan was never for Sergio to participate. Carlo did not want to chance Sergio getting killed if the judge's guards got lucky. He needed Sergio to testify. But there was one thing wrong with Carlo's plan. My men and Carlo's always wear gloves, and they wipe the guns before dropping them. No one is so sloppy they leave fingerprints."

Kate nodded. "Yes, that's an obvious flaw."

"But not to a man like Fuente. Even though it is clearly a frame, he will never admit it."

Fuente. It still came back to him. Was there any way to get him to see Rico's side? "Tell me, what would you have done about the judge if Carlo hadn't intervened?"

"The judge was an inconvenient person," Enrico admitted. "Very inconvenient. Immune to bribes and other sorts of pressures."

"What pressures?"

Enrico pursed his lips. "Threats. He was not afraid to die."

"So what would you have done?"

"Kidnapping. His son. No man can resist once the threat to his family is real." He squeezed her shoulder. "The boy would not have been harmed."

Kate shook her head. "It's still a terrible thing to do."

"Not when there is no other reasonable alternative."

"How about leaving the 'Ndrangheta?"

She still didn't understand. After all this time… would she ever? He sighed. "It is unthinkable. And inescapable. As long as I live, I am a threat. Think of all I know. The 'Ndrangheta cannot—and will not—let me walk away. Ever. I can *never* leave this life. All I can do is live it according to my terms, my code. And try to impress that code upon my men and my successor. That is all I can hope for."

"You make it sound almost honorable."

"I am not afraid to face God. I've confessed my sins; I have atoned. My conscience is clear."

"The first commandment doesn't have an escape clause."

"I have never killed a civilian. I have never killed unnecessarily." He motioned around him, indicating the house and its furnishings. "And God has rewarded me for what I have done."

Kate was appalled. "You think *God* had a hand in this?"

"He punishes the wicked and rewards the just."

"Beware the righteous man," she whispered.

He touched her cheek. "I did not say I was innocent. I *have* sinned. Many times. I've broken the first commandment. But God knows why I have done so."

Kate smiled. Enrico was perhaps the first person of her acquaintance who used the phrase "God knows why" and meant it literally. His belief comforted her. It meant he had limits on his behavior, some complicated system of checks and balances she might never understand. But she trusted that the system existed, that his code existed.

"Do you trust me?" he asked. She nodded, and he tilted her chin up to look in her eyes. "Do you understand?" She felt he was asking for absolution.

Her mouth was so dry her voice cracked when she answered. "I think I do."

His face relaxed, and his gaze fell to her lips for a second, then he looked into her eyes again. "Do you still love me?"

Kate's chest constricted. "How could you ever doubt it?"

"Well, you did throw yourself into the clutches of a suspected traitor to get away from me."

She smiled. "Can I blame it on the pregnancy hormones?"

"I have heard they can make one a bit excitable."

She leaned forward and wrapped her arms around his neck. "Thanks for trusting me with this." Her lips brushed his in a feathery touch that sent a thrill of electricity through her.

"I don't know what I'd do if you didn't love me." He pulled her onto his lap. "I'd be lost." Then he kissed her, his tongue invading her mouth when she parted her lips.

"Rico," she murmured when he let her breathe. It was the only word she could think of.

He kissed down her throat. Then he paused. "Is it too soon?"

She shook her head and laughed. "Never for this. But are *you* up to it? I've at least had a nap."

He took her hand and placed it over the bulge at his crotch. She could feel his hardness through the layers of blankets and sheets, and she ran her fingers along its length. "Does that answer your question?" He kissed and nipped at her neck.

"More than adequately," she teased.

He flipped her on her back and started to push up her negligee, kissing her throat, when he suddenly stopped and looked her in the eyes. The expression on his face was strange, almost angry. "What is it?"

"I do not know if I should say this." He evaded her eyes.

"What's bothering you?"

He sighed. "This whole time, other than our first night together, I have been walking on eggshells with you, coaxing you."

"I hadn't realized." She stroked his hair. "Is there something I can do?"

He nodded, his face reddening. "I had not wanted to mention it, but I have felt a little... frustrated. I have not asked for what I want."

She'd been so selfish, so wrapped up in her own head. Pulling him down to her, she kissed him on the lips. "I'm sorry. I hadn't considered how you felt at all."

"It is all right. I just want us to be equals when we make love."

285

She smiled. "Is that *really* what you want? For us to be equals?"

He held her gaze, going utterly still, something about the look on his face making Kate hold her breath. She waited, but he only watched her, saying nothing. What was troubling him? Had she hit the truth with her wisecrack? She stroked his jaw. "You've been my slave more than once. Perhaps it's time I was yours?"

He grinned then and relaxed. "I did not know you could read minds."

"You have but to ask." She traced a hand from his shoulder down his back to his waist, feeling the cords of muscles beneath her hands. He was so strong, this man of hers, and yet he'd been so completely at her mercy. So afraid of losing her, he'd held himself back, even in this one place where there should be no secrets. That ended today. "So tell me, is there anything in particular you want?"

He hesitated. "I don't know the word for it in English."

"Describe it."

His face flushed with color again. "That first time, you put your mouth on me."

She laughed at his blush. He was such a good Catholic boy. "You want a blow job?"

He looked a little puzzled. "I do not recall you blowing on it."

"No. But that's what it's called. I'll show you."

"I'd like to stand while you do it." He rolled off her and met her eyes. Still looking for approval.

"Rico, I'm your slave. Tell me and I'll do it. I trust you."

A glint came into his eyes then. He stood up, pulled a pillow off the bed, and dropped it at his feet. "On your knees."

Kate grinned at the obvious delight on his face. She took her time getting up, enjoying the heat of his gaze upon her. Standing before him, she rose up on her toes and brushed her mouth against his, then she moved her lips to his jaw, kissing along the edge of it until she reached his ear. She breathed into it, a little moan that made him clutch her waist, his hard cock jutting into her belly. Smiling to herself, she continued lower, kissing down the side of his neck, her lips at last reaching the smooth skin below the stubble of his beard. There she kissed and licked him, nuzzling his tanned skin for a moment, breathing in his scent.

She stepped back, breaking his hold, and pulled the negligee off. He tweaked the nipple of her right breast, then leaned down to suckle it. Fire tore through her at his touch, and she had to close her eyes. She savored the feeling, enjoying it when he cupped her left breast in his other hand and gave it attention too. Then she pulled away. "This is about you, remember?"

He smiled. "Having your breasts in my mouth is one of my favorite things."

"You'll have plenty of time to enjoy them in the future." She kissed and licked his firm flat pecs, her tongue tracing around his nipples. He inhaled at the contact and she made a mental note to do that again next time.

Continuing her exploration, she sank to her knees and kissed his belly, her tongue tracing the ridges of his abs. She avoided the bruising on his left side. Had they ever made love when neither one was injured? She smiled against his skin, kissing him just above the swirl of his navel. Their course to true love certainly hadn't run smooth.

She brushed her hand over his cock, running her fingers up and down its length as he shuddered. Looking up at him, she took the root of it in her hand, her thumb teasing the underside of his hard flesh.

When he met her eyes, she took him in her mouth, just the tip, her tongue swirling around the head. Hearing him moan, she would have grinned if she could have. Widening her mouth, she eased down, swallowing more of his length. She couldn't take it all, but she'd make sure he enjoyed what she could do.

Popping him out of her mouth, she ignored his little sounds of protest, and instead ran the flat of her tongue up and down the vein along the underside of his cock. He moaned and thrust up a little. He certainly liked that. She made another mental note. There was much about Rico she had yet to learn.

Taking him in her mouth again, she lavished attention on the head, giving him all the gratification he'd given her so many times before. Then she began a slow descent, engulfing as much of him as she could, pleased by his groans and the feel of his fingers twining in her hair. How could she have neglected his pleasure for so long? She had a lot of catching up to do.

The feel of her mouth, her tongue, was pure heaven as she resumed working on him, speeding up her movements. After what had happened with Vincenzo, he'd feared asking Kate for anything, he'd feared making any demands on her at all. He'd feared reminding her that he had needs too. But if he trusted her, he had to be honest. Fear was not the heart of love; trust was. Honesty was. Faith was.

When he was getting close to the peak, he took her head in his hands, resisting the urge to thrust the way his cock urged him to. He didn't want to come in her mouth, not this time. "Enough." He was breathing hard, each inhale and exhale reminding him of the cracked ribs, though the pain was but a dull ache compared to the pleasure she was giving him. He'd endure it, he'd endure anything to have her. To be with her. To love her.

She sat back on her heels and stroked her fingers along his thighs. "What now?"

"I want to take you from behind."

"Like this?" She got down on her hands and knees.

"Yes, but on the bed."

She crawled up on the mattress and presented herself to him, feeling how wet she was from sucking him. She looked at him over her shoulder, her discomfort at being in this position making her seek eye contact, reassurance.

He stood behind her, his hands kneading her hips, then one slipped down between her legs and investigated her dripping pussy, two fingers sliding into her easily. "So wet," he murmured, leaning down and kissing her just above the crack of her buttocks.

She pushed back onto his hand, biting her lip to keep from groaning. "It's been too long."

"And whose fault is that?" he asked, his tone light. His hand moved up to her clit, and he massaged it between two fingers, making her groan.

"Mine, all mine. I admit it."

He laughed, then kissed her again at the base of her spine, his breath warm on her skin. His hand left her and his erection nudged at her opening. She pressed herself onto him, arching to give him the best angle. He sank into her, both of them catching their breath at the sensation.

He worked in and out of her, withdrawing to his tip before diving back in, but his movements were slow, frustratingly so. Kate soundlessly begged him to speed up, to satisfy the need deep within her for something raw and urgent, but his movements remained teasing, taunting. She clenched her muscles around him, even urging him out loud to fuck her, but his only answer was a sharp smack on her buttocks. He was going to kill her with this. Every plunge of his cock was a sweet torture.

Her climax was building, but she would need something faster to reach her release. They both would. Finally, it came to her. What he wanted, what he needed to hear. What she needed to say. "I love you, Rico."

Hearing those words unleashed something inside him. "*Ti amo, cara.*" The words tore out of him as he gave himself over to the silent pleading of her hips, to the contractions of her inner walls as she gripped and released him. He could feel she was lost like he was, utterly lost to this, to their pleasure, to the joy of being together.

He pulled her hips more firmly against him and delved deeper, abandoning himself to his desire to pound into her flat out, his breathing growing ragged with the effort to prolong their pleasure, to make the experience last. He never wanted to forget this moment. When she stopped fighting them both. When he started trusting her not to run.

She rocked beneath him, enjoying the searing pleasure of each thrust, each plunge he made into the very core of her. They were joined. They were one. And she would never leave him again.

CHAPTER 39

Enrico and Kate had been home for a week, and after burying his father, he'd somehow managed to put up a grief-stricken front through Dom's funeral. It wasn't as hard to do as he'd imagined; even though he'd pulled the trigger, the reality of what he'd done hadn't quite sunk in. He kept thinking of things he should talk to Dom about or that Dom would find funny, and he'd pick up the phone to call him and then abruptly remember all over again.

Enrico was looking through the *cosca*'s financial reports, although he wasn't in the mood to attend to business. His eyes fell on the picture of Toni by his computer, the reports completely losing his attention. He picked up the picture and went in search of Kate. He found her in the solarium, working on her laptop, transcribing records for the orphanage. She looked up when he approached. "What is it?"

He showed her the photo. "It is time I deal with this."

"Are you sure? I understand if it's not."

"I still love her. I always will. But she wanted me to carry on with my life, and I have." His voice thickened. "You own my heart now."

Kate set the laptop aside and popped up out of the chair. She was in his arms in an instant. "*Mio caro*, you don't have to say that. I know your heart is big enough for both of us." She took his hand and placed it on her belly. "For all three of us."

He smiled, tears pricking his eyes. "My heart is no longer divided. It belongs to you now. You and our baby. I hope you know that."

She slipped her hands into his hair and drew him down for a kiss. "I am so very lucky to be loved by you."

He couldn't speak, his throat was so tight. Instead he kissed her. How he loved her. More than he'd ever thought possible. More than he'd ever hoped for. When they parted, he wiped his eyes. He looked down at the picture in his hand. "I would like to leave one photo on display, if you do not mind."

"Not at all."

He took her hand. "Will you help me box up her things?"

She nodded and followed him down the hall toward the stairs.

৪০০৪

Enrico surprised himself by not shedding any tears while they worked. Instead he told Kate stories about Toni as they came to mind, mostly funny or romantic things. She'd had a good life with him. They'd had a good life together. It had been too short, but now he had Kate. "I feel like I have been given an incredible gift, *mia cara*. This chance with you." He touched his chest. "I used to have this horrible aching hole here. But now it is gone."

He stroked a few hairs out of her face. How he'd once longed to do such a simple thing. Now this precious creature was finally his. And she knew him, knew who he was. What he was. And still she loved him.

Kate smiled, her eyes blurring with tears. She took his hand and pulled him close, then leaned against him, listening to him breathe. For the first time in a long time, she felt at home.

He held her for quite a while. When he released her, he got down on one knee and produced a small black velvet box from his pants pocket. He opened it, revealing a ring inside, its diamonds sparkling. "I have been carrying this around with me since just after we got out of the hospital. I was going to do this someplace romantic, but now..." He gestured around the closet. "For some reason, this feels right. Marry me, Kate."

Her chest filled with warmth. "Of course I will." She held out her hand, watching as he slipped the ring on her finger. Then he stood and took her in his arms, kissing her. "You didn't have to ask me again," she said when they parted. "I already agreed. In fact, I believe I asked you."

He looked down at her, amusement on his face. "I know. But I wanted to do it right this time. With neither one of us bleeding or drugged. Or recovering from surgery."

She smiled. "Traditionalist."

He laughed. "Nothing about the two of us has ever been, or will ever be, entirely traditional."

"And isn't that what you like about us?"

He grinned and pulled her into a kiss. "That's what I love about us."

290

EPILOGUE

Dario Andretti leaned against the windowsill, looking at what was now his view of the lake. Turning his eyes to the west, he spotted the Lucchesi villa. How should he proceed?

His father had failed spectacularly and nearly gotten them both killed.

But Carlo had proved to be a father to him in the end. He could have revealed Dario's role in Rinaldo's death, could have condemned him and ruined everything. But he hadn't.

Dario's heart still ached. Lucchesi believed he'd given him the Andretti *cosca*, that he hadn't earned it with his father's consent. But better to live to see another day than to die over his pride. At least it was some consolation that Lucchesi hadn't seen what had happened right under his nose. Lucchesi was so sure he knew Dario, so sure he wasn't like his father.

But he was his father's son. He hadn't lied about that. And he'd put a plan in motion some time ago, a plan that would bear bitter fruit for Lucchesi. If it worked. The odds of success were slimmer now that Franco Trucco was dead.

Someday Lucchesi would learn who he truly was. Someday he'd see the truth.

But by then it would be too late.

AUTHOR'S NOTE

Due to the high level of secrecy maintained by the 'Ndrangheta (the Calabrian mafia) and the relative scarcity of former members turned state's witnesses, there are few resources detailing the inner workings of the society. Therefore, I have used artistic license in portraying certain aspects of the 'Ndrangheta, particularly as regards La Provincia.

Until July 2010, it was widely believed that there was no overarching body in charge of the 'Ndrangheta. However, with the arrest of several prominent 'Ndranghetisti, it is now believed that there is a *capi di tutti capi* (boss of all bosses) who oversees a commission (La Provincia) with direct power over the individual families. *Revenge* does not reflect this type of organization, though the formation of such an organization comes into play in later books.

Additionally, to make this series easier to read for American readers, I have used the term *cosca* rather than *'ndrine* to indicate an individual crime family. I have also greatly simplified the organization of individual crime families and have chosen to name crime families after their *capo*'s blood family; in real life, a *cosca*'s name may consist of a region or place, or a hyphenated combination of the names of the two or three primary blood families that control the *cosca*.

In Italy, women typically don't take their husband's last name; for simplicity's sake, I have chosen to reflect the traditional American practice of taking the husband's last name upon marriage.

Note that all persons mentioned in this series are fictional; no resemblance to actual people, living or dead, is intended. The family names used in this series were deliberately chosen not to reflect names of actual crime families.

MORE BY THIS AUTHOR

Revenge is the first book in the *Blood and Honor* four-part romantic suspense series, which is set in Italy among the underworld of the Calabrian Mafia. Each story features a hero and heroine forced to make difficult choices in a world where vendettas are quick to erupt and burn for generations; where family ties, both blood and criminal, drive every decision; and where passions flare up and threaten to blaze out of control.

The *Blood and Honor* series

Book 1: *Revenge* (available now)

Kate Andretti is married to the Mob—but doesn't know it. When her husband uproots them to Italy, Kate leaves everything she knows behind. Alone in a foreign land, she finds herself locked in a battle for her life against a husband and a family that will "silence" her if she will not do as they wish. When her husband tries to kill her, she accepts the protection offered by a wealthy businessman with Mafia ties. He's not a mobster, he claims. Or is he?

Enrico Lucchesi never wanted to be a Mafia don, and now he's caught in the middle of a blood feud with the Andretti family. His decision to help Kate brings the feud between the families to a boil. Attacks from without and within push them both to the breaking point, and soon Enrico is forced to choose between protecting the only world he knows and saving the woman he loves.

Book 2: *Retribution* (available early 2012)

Nick Clarkston, a young Interpol agent, threatens to undo the fragile peace between the Lucchesi and Andretti families when he tries to take down the Mafia don father who abandoned him. He allies with his father's sworn enemy, a mobster both devious and ruthless. The mobster's alluring daughter helps Nick negotiate the murky criminal underworld, but he soon learns she's using him. Trapped, and with nowhere to turn, Nick makes a tragic mistake that plunges him further into danger.

Delfina Andretti appears to be the typical Mafia princess—but this princess wants out. Delfina dreams of being a fashion designer, and hooking up with Nick is her ticket out of an arranged marriage. Her feelings for Nick are genuine, but he's leery of her. Even worse, his heedless drive for justice threatens to get them both killed and to put everyone Delfina loves behind bars—unless she and Nick can forge a new future for their warring families.

Book 3: *Redemption* (available late 2012)

Antonio Legato has always been an outsider, even though he's moved up in the Lucchesi mob organization. When he falls in love with Bianca Lucchesi, Antonio may at last become part of the family, but he's hiding an ugly secret about her father's death. Telling Bianca the truth will pit blood against blood and annihilate the family he loves.

Bianca Lucchesi is on a mission to help her brothers ruin Antonio so they can take their rightful place in the organization. As the don's assistant, Bianca seduces Antonio while pursuing her brothers' revenge. But her loyalty is divided—she and Antonio share a secret that he's unaware of. She longs to tell him, but fears he can never forgive what she's done.

When Bianca and Antonio learn that her brothers have rashly allied with a cunning enemy who is plotting against the Lucchesis, can they heal the family's wounds before everyone they love is destroyed?

Book 4: *Release* (available late 2013)

Ruggero Vela has long protected the don of the Lucchesi family. When his boss is framed, Ruggero is desperate to exonerate him. So desperate, he risks his life to protect the zealous anti-Mafia judge presiding over the case. She's incorruptible—and the only person they can trust to conduct a fair trial. Although Ruggero has always survived by keeping a cool head, he's blindsided by an irresistible attraction to the beautiful judge—an attraction that grows by the minute.

Loredana Montisi is renowned for her courageous struggle to prosecute Mafia thugs. But she doesn't know she's the pawn of much darker forces with a truly frightening agenda. When she unwittingly deviates from their plan and gets too close to the truth, they try to kill her. Information Loredana learns from her unlikely protector forces her to question everything she knows. Can she let go of her deep-seated beliefs and place her trust in a Mafioso?

Print and E-book
Available at Amazon, Barnes & Noble, and other retailers

www.danadelamar.com

294

Continue reading for a special preview of

Kristine Cayne's first Deadly Vices novel

Deadly Obsession

Available January 2012

When an Oscar-winning movie star meets a department-store photographer...

Movie star Nic Lamoureux appears to have a playboy's perfect life. But it's a part he plays, an act designed to conceal a dark secret he carries on his shoulders. His empty days and nights are a meaningless blur until he meets the woman who fulfills all his dreams. She and her son are the family he's always wanted—if she can forgive a horrible mistake from his past.

A Hollywood dream...

Lauren James, a widowed single mother, earns barely enough money to support herself and her son. When she wins a photography contest and meets Nic, the man who stars in all her fantasies, her dreams, both professional and personal, are on the verge of becoming real. The attraction between Lauren and Nic is instant—and mutual. Their chemistry burns out of control during a photo shoot that could put Lauren on the fast track to a lucrative career.

Becomes a Hollywood nightmare

But an ill-advised kiss makes front-page news, and the lurid headlines threaten everything Nic and Lauren have hoped for. Before they know what's happening, their relationship is further rocked by an obsessed and cunning stalker who'll stop at nothing—not even murder—to have Nic to herself. When Nic falls for Lauren, the stalker zeroes in on her as the competition.

And the competition must be eliminated.

Lauren rolled her eyes. "Fine. Do it."

Nic bent down and brushed his lips against hers. For the first few seconds, she didn't kiss him back, but she didn't push him away, either. Then, on a sigh, she leaned into him and her arms locked around his neck. His tongue darted out to taste her bottom lip. Mmm... cherry—his new favorite flavor. When her mouth opened, he didn't hesitate.

He dove in. And drowned.

He'd meant this to be a quick kiss, only now he just couldn't stop. His lips traced a path to her throat. Cupping her bottom with his hands, he lifted her up, grinding against her. She moaned. It was a beautiful sound, one he definitely wanted to hear again.

A loud noise pierced the fog of his lust. He raised his head from where he'd been nuzzling Lauren's apple-scented neck to tell whoever it was to fuck off, but as the sexual haze cleared, he swallowed the words. The paparazzi had gathered around, applauding and calling out crude encouragements. Some snapped photos while others rolled film. *Shit.* He'd pay for this fuck-up and so would she.

Print and E-book
Available at Amazon, Barnes & Noble, and other retailers

www.kristinecayne.com

14430725R00174

Made in the USA
Charleston, SC
10 September 2012